Mrs. Hudson in the Ring
(Mrs. Hudson of Baker Street Book 3)

Barry S Brown

Disclaimer

This story is a work of fiction and, although it makes use of real people and historic events, the situations described and the parts played by the story's characters are drawn entirely from the mind of the author whose grasp on reality remains tenuous at best.

Paperback ISBN 978-1-78705-361-8
ePub ISBN 978-1-78705-362-5
PDF ISBN 978-1-78705-363-2

Published in the UK by MX Publishing
335 Princess Park Manor, Royal Drive,
London, N11 3GX
www.mxpublishing.co.uk
Cover design by Brian Belanger

Dedication

To Rebecca, David and Mariam who have brightened and shortened my life

Acknowledgement

I am deeply indebted to Dr. Antje Almeida of the University of North Carolina at Wilmington who graciously shared her time and expertise in forensic chemistry without snickering even one time at the author's abject ignorance.
I am grateful as well to Joel and Bonnie Egertson for their comments and suggestions, and for consistently providing the support that makes criticism tolerable.

Chapter 1.
The National Sporting Club

Having completed the final passage of Mendelssohn's Violin Concerto, Holmes paused a reverent moment before pointing an accusatory bow at his colleague. "I tell you, Watson, our day is done. We are seen as no more relevant to modern criminal investigation than our poor dead friend lying there." Holmes transferred the bow's target from Watson to the bear rug lying between them, and resumed speaking without waiting for a response from either. "It's been months since we've been given a problem worthy of the name. The public is content to take its troubles to the police, and the police feel no need to consult us about the troubles they bring."

Watson pursed his lips, pulled a sheet of foolscap from a cubicle at his desk and placed it between the pages of Professor Murri's report of "A Cure of a Case of Hydrophobia" in the June 4 issue of *Lancet*, resigned to postponing indefinitely a discovery of the Professor's successful treatment. "Surely you exaggerate, Holmes, we've suffered through dry spells before and have always come on to cases that have demanded the best thinking of *all* of us."

Holmes ignored Watson's pointed reference to the leader of their team, preferring to draw attention to a member who was no longer with them. "As you know, Watson, I'm not a superstitious man, but I count our difficulties as starting from the time young Wiggins left us to become a printer's devil. He was, one might argue, our talisman. We never lacked for opportunity while he was here, and when we lost our page this 'dry spell,' as you call it, began."

Watson chose to let pass this line of discussion. Both men were well aware Wiggins had obtained his position through Watson's intercession and at Mrs. Hudson's urging. Watson had expressed his belief Wiggins was of an age to learn a trade, and Mrs. Hudson had expressed her concern that it was becoming increasingly difficult to hide from Wiggins the true nature of operations at 221B Baker Street.

"Holmes, this is simply intolerable. I'm going to call down for tea and the scones I'm certain Mrs. Hudson will have available. Over a pot of tea we can consider what's on in the city and see if there isn't something to tempt you." And before Holmes could offer objection, Watson rang for the housekeeper. His haste was unnecessary. Whatever resistance Holmes might have offered was overcome by thoughts of freshly baked scones and the likelihood of their being accompanied by a bowl of strawberry jam.

In fact, Mrs. Hudson's baking, and Watson's sudden inspiration were the result of careful planning. They had their origins in a meeting early that morning in Mrs. Hudson's kitchen in which Watson expressed the opinion that Holmes's melancholia was unhealthy, and Mrs. Hudson decreed they had "to get Mr. 'Olmes outside of 'imself." While they didn't speak of it, neither thought they could take another night of Mendelssohn, and both feared the needle could become Holmes's next source of diversion. Together, they devised a plan that would make use of Watson's gentle encouragement to undertake some sort of action, and Mrs. Hudson's firm insistence on a specific course of action. Both encouragement and insistence were to be leavened by a generous offering of scones and jam.

At the call from Watson, Mrs. Hudson mounted the stair with a tray laden with tea service, a quivering mound of strawberry jam nearly overlapping its bowl, and enough raisin-filled scones to satisfy the needs of a small contingent of the visitors wished for by Holmes. Mrs. Hudson had even fixed a frozen smile on her doughy face to suggest the good humor she did not feel. The smile was wasted on the figure now hunched over the violin on his lap, absently plucking its strings for their mournful vibrato.

She poured tea for each of the men and selected scones for Holmes and Watson, serving the larger one to Holmes. With seeming indifference, Holmes accepted the scone and took up the bowl of jam before turning his attention again to his colleague. "I don't mean to stand in your way, Watson. I'm afraid I'd be poor company and, in any event, I'm certain there's nothing in the City to attract me." With that, the corner of his scone, now heavily anointed with strawberry jam, disappeared into his mouth.

Watson shook his head in vigorous disbelief. "Good Lord, Holmes, this is 1892, and we are privileged to live in the most vibrant city in the world. There are attractions enough to interest any man."

Holmes gave his friend a tired smile. "I appreciate your concern, Watson, really I do, and I'm not saying there isn't something that might interest me on another night, but tonight there's nothing on any stage capable of luring me from these rooms."

"I'm afraid you'll 'ave to think otherwise, Mr. 'Olmes." Without waiting or needing an invitation, Mrs. Hudson seated herself in an easy chair after first pouring her own cup of tea and selecting a scone. She elected to forgo the strawberry jam in the interest of obtaining a fair test of the scone's quality.

"I beg your pardon, Mrs. Hudson; surely you're not turning me out into the streets."

"I'm doin' just exactly that, Mr. 'Olmes, both you and Dr. Watson. Lord Lonsdale 'as been after the two of you to visit 'is Sports Club ever since it opened last year. Just today 'e sent a boy around askin' you both to be 'is guests for dinner and a night of fisticuffs, and I told the boy you've been wantin' to join Lord Lonsdale and would be delighted to accept 'is invitation. You can expect the Earl's carriage at seven. We've been together more than ten years, Mr. 'Olmes, I know your ways better than you know them yourself, and I know that moonin' around 'ere night after night is not good for you, and it's no great shakes for the Doctor and me. Enjoyin' a fine meal with a gentleman as jolly as 'Is Lordship, and then watchin' two young men square off at each other could be just the ticket to get your spirits back up to where they ought to be."

What Mrs. Hudson did not tell Holmes was that while Hugh Lowther, the 5th Earl of Lonsdale, had indeed sent frequent invitations to Holmes and Watson to be his guests at the National Sporting Club, this latest invitation had come in response to an inquiry sent in Holmes's name to "my good friend Lord Lonsdale" asking if it would be convenient to join him at the Club for dinner and a night of boxing.

Watson, while not sharing Holmes's enthusiasm for what some described as "the manly art," nonetheless displayed the interest he had promised. "A superior suggestion, Mrs. Hudson. Holmes, it is past time to give Lonsdale's club a try. You know you've been wondering about the Marquess of Queensberry rules and how things have changed from your own bare knuckles days. This will be a fine chance to learn. You say the Earl will be sending for us at seven, Mrs. Hudson?"

Holmes took the last bite of his scone, washed it down with a generous swallow of tea and, after dabbing his mouth with a napkin, appeared to address his response to the cloth he replaced on his lap. "I see that my evening has been carefully planned. I know you believe me to be in a mood and mean to shake me out of it. It will not work of course. Only a new challenge can transform me, but as you say the Earl is good company, and you're quite right, Watson, I am curious about the Sporting Club and its Queensberry rules so I accept my fate as you've ordained it. For now, I will have another of your very passable scones, Mrs. Hudson, and I believe there is still time for Mendelssohn before dressing for the evening. Do please leave the strawberry jam, Mrs. Hudson."

Promptly at seven, the Earl's carriage, drawn by a team of perfectly matched chestnuts, pulled to a stop at 221B Baker Street. On the coach door, in a size meant to allow its recognition by all but the most near-sighted passer-by, was emblazoned the Earl's imaginative rendering of the Lowther family crest. At its center, a shield containing six rosettes was held in place by two spirited steeds standing on their hind quarters, and rotated just far enough to lavish a coquettish smile on their observer. The animals' gender was obscured by ribbons of dark cloth that appeared to have blown serendipitously across selected body parts. A five pointed crown with outsized fleur-de-lis flourishes on its either side stood atop an armor helmet and shield, while beneath shield, horses and crown, the family motto "magistratus indicat virum" somewhat obscurely declared the Lowthers' devotion to duty. But it wasn't the family's crest, the size of the coach or the splendor of the horses that occasioned second looks and long stares from passersby. It was instead the blaze of yellow in which coach, horses and servants were drenched. It was as though the Earl of Lonsdale was determined to bring sunlight in his wake regardless of the weather or time of day.

A footman, long accustomed to the curiosity of adults and the giggles of children, stood soberly at the coach's open door waiting to admit his passengers. Watson, feeling himself a minor character in an overstated farce, grumbled his way to the carriage as he sought to bury himself as quickly as possible inside the source of his embarrassment, while Holmes sauntered leisurely to the coach with smiles to a mystified but respectful public. Ordinarily, the sight of the slender figure in top hat and evening dress would be sufficient to draw knowing nudges between couples, and nods of recognition from those out for a solitary stroll. On this evening, Holmes found himself overshadowed by his transportation.

By Mrs. Hudson's reckoning this was the third time

Lord Lonsdale's coach had stopped outside their lodgings. The first had been two years before and the Earl had been in a frenzy. He declared his immediate need to see Mr. Holmes, refusing Mrs. Hudson's offer of a seat in her parlor, and waiting on the landing while Mrs. Hudson carried his card to Holmes's apartments. She recalled finding the Earl's appearance disappointing. From the newspaper accounts she had pictured a large and striking figure. Instead, the man was barely above middle height, with thinning hair imperfectly offset by long sideburns, a mouth that was slightly too large, a nose that was slightly too prominent, and eyes that were slightly too heavy-lidded. The Earl had himself long since relinquished any claim to striking in favor of a look of aristocratic disdain. On this evening neither disdain nor aristocratic bearing was in evidence.

Once admitted to Holmes's sitting room, the Earl explained he had recently made a count of the artifacts brought back from his Arctic Expedition, and found there were three less than were recorded when they were loaded for shipment. He could not identify which pieces they were, but considered all to be priceless. Holmes was delighted at the prospect of working with Lord Lonsdale, whose exploits were frequently detailed in the news columns or hinted at in the gossip columns.

His journey across the northwestern corner of the Americas had filled the dailies and weeklies, and fired the public imagination. All of London was aware of the sled dogs lost, the Indians fought, and his crossing the Arctic Circle to arrive finally at the tiny outpost of Kodiak—although not reaching the North Pole as the Earl had claimed in a moment of particular exuberance. He had returned with what was widely acknowledged to be the largest collection of Alaskan artifacts existing anywhere in the non-native world. Indeed, the success of his journey had largely obscured the reason it had been undertaken—the Earl's banishment by the Queen for his part in a very public brawl with Sir George Chetwynd to decide which of them was the more fit companion for Mrs. Lillie Langtry.

Mrs. Hudson, having arrived to pour tea, found her attention drawn to the Earl's twice-stated offer to retrieve his lost treasures at any price. She knew the Earl to have a castle of more than 300 rooms in North Cumbria, as well as three other homes, all of them of substantial, if somewhat more modest size. There was, in short, no question the Earl could, in fact, pay any price, and any lingering doubts on that score were offset by newspaper accounts of his having paid precisely that sum to acquire whatever fancies he found desirable, ladies of the London stage being one of his better known fancies. Within 15 minutes of their exchange Holmes agreed to take the Earl's case, promising return of the treasures and apprehension of their thief on the strength of his housekeeper's vigorous nod.

The mystery was, in fact, resolved with surprising ease. The Earl had returned from his expedition with three men expert in the area of native artifacts. They were charged with cataloguing the array of objects that filled the near endless procession of boxes and chests, or at least so it seemed to the footmen with responsibility for settling them safely inside Lowther Castle's library, ballroom, and music room, in each of which a different expert was settled. Their journals were brought to 221B Baker Street where Mrs. Hudson discovered the recordings of the three men were made in black ink over the first several pages of cataloguing, and were made in blue-black ink thereafter as the supply of black ink became depleted.

In one man's journal however, two items, topping well-separated pages, had been made in black ink while all those coming after were in the newly available blue-back. The two artifacts in dark ink were part of one tribe's religious ceremony. A third artifact, listed on an earlier page, related to the same ceremony. It was apparent to Mrs. Hudson, who made it apparent to Holmes, who made it apparent to Lord Lonsdale, that these were the three artifacts that had gone missing. The recorder had thought a second count of objects unlikely, at least until he was well on his way back to America, and so deemed it sufficient to have the number of items known to have been shipped accord with the number contained in the experts' lists. He had taken the single precaution of entering the three related items on widely scattered pages to prevent calling attention to them. He could not foresee the change in inks that would ultimately undue his subterfuge. He could, of course, have simply fabricated items or attributed them to differing ceremonies or tribes, but was undone, as was explained to the Earl, by being too good a scientist to stoop to such chicanery.

When confronted by Holmes, the man admitted his guilt with as much relief as shame. The three items he had taken were objects sacred to the Haida people. The guilt he felt for his part in removing them from the tribe had led the young man to scheme for their return.

On hearing the man's confession, Lonsdale refused to press charges, insisting that sending him back to America empty-handed was punishment enough. The Earl's argument was somewhat undone by the discovery he had provided the guilty party with fare for a first class cabin, and a supply of cigars sufficient to see him through his arduous journey and for several months thereafter.

On the Earl's second visit to Holmes, Mrs. Hudson saw the Lord Lonsdale better known to readers of the penny press. His dark eyes, no longer wide and darting, looked with amused tolerance to the world around him. He bestowed a bouquet of yellow roses on Mrs. Hudson, then bounded up the steps to Holmes's apartments to provide him with an equally concrete, if far more substantial expression of his appreciation. In so doing, the Earl made the same error regarding the proper recipient of his gratitude as all those who had come before. It mattered little to Mrs. Hudson. Before nightfall she would have the Earl's flowers in a vase and his check in the bank.

With the dramatically appointed coach of Lord Lonsdale having borne her lodgers to their evening's dinner and entertainment, Mrs. Hudson settled herself to her own meal of cold lamb, mash and vegetable marrow, to be washed down with a glass of cider, and followed by bread and butter pudding. She set beside her plate Sir Edmund du Cane's *The Punishment and Prevention of Crime*. Mrs. Hudson had decided it was her responsibility to learn something of the way the men—and occasional women—she was responsible for turning over to the authorities were treated while incarcerated. The success of the consulting detective agency she had established more than a decade earlier demanded such consideration, even as the memory of those early days coaxed a small smile from Mrs. Hudson.

Her newspaper advertisement had brought her the boarders she wanted and the figurehead she needed. No woman could be accepted as a consulting detective, not even one who had studied investigative strategies under the guidance of Tobias Hudson, her "uncommon common constable" husband and companion for 29 years. Sherlock Holmes looked and sounded the sharp-witted investigator he believed himself to be. His friend, Dr. Watson, provided an unexpected bonus, joining Holmes in the legwork of detection and meticulously recording findings from the investigations they conducted under Mrs. Hudson's direction.

Now, she would learn from Sir Edmund, the reform-minded past director of the prison service, the treatment accorded the people they had brought to justice over the years, and perhaps give her cause for optimism about the influence of prison on their lives. She opened the book, took a forkful of lamb, and began her study.

The coach Holmes considered curious and Watson found garish, carried the two men to 43 King Street, Covent Garden, a few streets and a world away from the Covent Garden Theater where Gustav Mahler was tuning the orchestra for its performance of *Tristan und Isolde*. The boxing exhibition to be offered at the National Sporting Club, and the performance to be staged at the Covent Garden Theater would each involve brutal conflict, although only Wagner's opera was scheduled to result in multiple deaths.

The building in which the Club was housed had begun life in the 17th century as the London residence of a succession of landed gentry, and spent most of the 18th century as home to several statesmen, a scientist and an admiral. The admiral, perhaps bemoaning his distance from the sea, had remodeled the second story frontage to resemble the forecastle of a ship jutting its way above the street, such that the building now appeared to be continuously seeking port among the hansoms, four-wheelers and omnibuses below.

After the admiral had himself put to port in the Great Harbor in the Sky, the building passed to a businessman whose fortune was to be made through its conversion to a "family hotel." When families failed to arrive, a second owner, sharing his predecessor's optimism about the building's use as a hotel, but differing with him about the choice of clientele, reconstituted it as an inn "with stabling for one hundred noblemen and horses." When patronage by noblemen with or without horses proved disappointing, the hotel became a theater and supper room, then a succession of theaters with restaurants attached. One of the several theater owners, even more hopeful than those who preceded him, extended and rebuilt the original theater to include the gardens that had been outside the house, and added three long balconies overhanging each side of the floor seating.

When the National Sporting Club assumed ownership, it placed a boxing ring at the center of the enlarged theater while installing other features designed to assure acceptance as a gentleman's club. A reading and writing room was created to accommodate Club members' pensive moments, while billiards rooms and a gymnasium were established for those of a more athletic bent. Two well-stocked bars were added as well to support recovery from whatever exertions Club members selected.

After transforming the building into a setting for boxing, the National Sporting Club set about transforming boxing into a sport that could find acceptance with a broad range of the public and, more significantly, with the narrow range who made and enforced public policy. The London Prize Ring rules that had long held sway as the code of behavior governing boxing were dropped, and the Marquis of Queensberry rules adopted. Holding, throwing, and wrestling were eliminated; rounds were no longer of indeterminate length ending only with one fighter being knocked down or pretending to have been, and the match itself was no longer to last until a fighter was unable to continue or both fighters agreed to a draw. Most significantly, fights were no longer bare-knuckled, but made use of "fair-sized boxing gloves," the exact size varying from contest to contest.

The changes were wrought, in very large measure, by one man—Lord Lonsdale—who supervised boxing through its metamorphosis in rules, and its relocation from Gerrard Street and the rakishly elegant Pelican Club to Covent Garden and the respectably elegant National Sporting Club. The Earl, as the newly installed President of the National Sporting Club, was determined to see boxing become a respected sport. That required change not only in the standards of behavior for those inside the ring, but in the standards of behavior for the sport's patrons as well. And in both instances there were signs of progress.

The winner of a contest was now far more likely to be determined by action during the match than by negotiation between interested parties well before the match began, and the evening's combat was increasingly contained within the boxing ring with club members and friends resigned to spectating during the bout and subdued reflection after. At the time of their earlier and only visit to the Pelican Club, Holmes and Watson had found it wise to occupy a comparatively quiet corner of the bar where, the dispute between fighters having been resolved, the guests entered into a hearty, if alcohol-tinged, rendition of *Knocked 'em in the Old Kent Road*, whose refrain they punctuated by throwing champagne bottles through the Club's windows as quickly and as often as the Club's staff could be coaxed into providing them. When the police arrived, Holmes and Watson exited by means of a backstairs, vowing not to return to the Pelican Club until either there was reason to believe its members would evidence proper behavior or hell froze over, it being Watson's opinion that the latter was the more likely.

Neither man was optimistic about witnessing substantial change in the club's activities on this night, but each believed the gamble necessary. Watson was certain Holmes's mood demanded radical action, and Holmes was certain Watson and Mrs. Hudson would make his life insufferable if he didn't agree to an evening at the National Sporting Club.

The doorman greeted Holmes and Watson with the warmth he had been instructed to display when they announced themselves as guests of Lord Lonsdale. He called to a nearby usher whose task it was to put them in contact with the Earl. The two men waited beside a marble nymph and a spray of ferns, maintaining their distance from the stream of men in top hats and evening dress nodding and smiling their way from cluster to cluster in an entry hall that teemed with good fellowship, and smelled of expensive cigars. Their messenger disappeared among the tuxedos and frock coats, and was never seen again. Nonetheless, the success of his mission became quickly evident.

The Earl of Lonsdale came into view, threading his way across the floor, sharing a thin smile of recognition with a stout dark-bearded man who called to him, clapping the shoulders or squeezing the arms of others he passed, waving to some beyond his reach, pausing long enough to hear a comment and share a laugh with yet another cluster of men until, breaking free of the many intent on acknowledging him and being acknowledged by him, he beamed a greeting to Holmes and Watson, shaking their hands vigorously while telling them how pleased he was to see them. He insisted they were to be his guests for the evening, then established it as fact by requesting their drink orders after first recommending the whiskey from Dublin and the Manzanilla just arrived from Spain. The Earl signaled to a waiter, who had been standing beside a stone nymph, his eyes darting frequently to the President of the National Sporting Club as he otherwise matched the statue movement for movement. He now sprang to the Earl's elbow and, taking the empty glass handed him, nodded his intention to return with a whiskey and soda for Watson and His Lordship, and a Manzanilla for Holmes.

While waiting for their drinks, Holmes expressed more gratitude than he felt for the Earl's invitation, and Watson expressed more gratitude than he felt for the Earl's transportation. Lonsdale expressed the pleasure he sincerely felt for their company. When the drinks arrived, Holmes and Watson commented on their excellence, declined the offer of cigars and spent the next twenty minutes, glasses in hand, in pleasant, if disjointed conversation as each new arrival sought to pay his respects to Lonsdale. For his part, the Earl greeted each man warmly, while giving none of them the smallest encouragement to linger. He introduced Holmes and Watson to a select few who made phantom bows in the direction of the lean brooding figure. The Earl recounted the theft and recovery of his native carvings to those receiving introduction, Holmes's ingenuity reaching new heights with each retelling. Privately, the Earl revealed he had made the artifacts available to the British Museum, waving off the men's praise for his action. At last, the Earl, taking note of the thinning crowd and the smoky aroma of meat cooking on an open fire, suggested they make their way to the Club's grill.

The Sporting Club's grill was larger, but otherwise much the same as that of the Pelican Club. Thirty white-clothed round tables stood in five perfect columns. There were chairs for ten at each table although few were occupied as the Club members who had stood bantering with each other in the entrance hall now stood bantering with each other in the dining hall. Most were in their middle years or older, nearly all wore black or white tie, a few were in dark frock coats and trousers, and a smaller number in military uniforms bearing ribbons won in the Afghan and Zulu campaigns. Every two tables were attended by a waiter in white half apron, a tray under his arm that would, in a short time, be laden with steaks, chops and jacketed potatoes.

At one end of the room, beside a furled Union Jack, there stood portraits of Victoria and the Prince of Wales. Beneath the portraits there was a long rectangular table positioned to allow those seated behind it to have a commanding view of the room and the sea of Club members. Its eight chairs were reserved for Lord Lonsdale as Club President, Peggy Bettinson and John Fleming, the Club's founders and its Co-Directors, and such guests or Club members as had been honored with seats beside them. On this evening, there would be three such honorees. The Earl escorted Holmes and Watson to places at the head table and introduced them to Fleming and Bettinson, who were engaged in earnest conversation at one end of the table. Each man rose to greet their guests without fully relinquishing the scowls they brought from the discussion they were forced to break off.

Neither the gravity of their conversation, nor the long faces of the two men conducting it would have surprised any Club member. The two Directors were known to share a passion for the sport of boxing and for the Club they had jointly founded, while sharing little else. John Fleming was described by friends as tenacious and by all others as forbidding, and John Fleming had few friends. He was a burly man, well into his 40s, with black hair parted at the center, and a small forest of moustache that left unclear whether he possessed a mouth until a gruff voice gave his audience assurance of its existence, and second thoughts about the wisdom of having made its discovery. He had been the landlord of several public houses that catered to a clientele less interested in the quality of their drink than its quantity and the speed with which it reached them. Quite by accident he had graduated to boxing management and then to promotion, eking out an existence, many believed, by scheduling not only the onsets but also the outcomes of bouts, thereby satisfying the needs of those who found it more desirable to wager on life's certainties than its possibilities.

A. F. (Peggy) Bettinson was, by contrast, above any such suspicions. Like himself, his friends, of whom there were many, were successful men of business. He had come to an interest in boxing by way of his own athletic background, having laid claim to England's amateur lightweight championship ten years earlier. Traces of the athlete survived in his still wiry body even as his light brown hair had begun a steady retreat, and harsh lines were forming at the edges of piercing blue eyes.

The two Club founders shook hands with Holmes and Watson, Bettinson noting that the name Holmes was often in the news without offering further elaboration. With the amenities concluded, the two men again took their seats and, with furrowed brows still in place, they returned to their private discussion. Holmes and Watson each looked to a sixth place setting at their table, then to their host, who smiled his understanding and called to a thickset man who was leaning into the task of shaking hands with everyone around the table nearest to where the Earl and his guests waited.

"Arthur, there'll be ample time for conversation with your friends, for now there's a dinner to be had."

Several of Arthur's friends waved their apologies to Lonsdale, who grinned and brushed aside their concern with his own rather more elaborate wave. Arthur removed his hand from that of the last of his well-wishers and came quickly to the long table, a broken smile and mumbled apology his twin concessions to the Earl's gentle rebuke. He gave the same chagrined smile to Fleming and Bettinson, and mumbled the same apology. To the surprise of Holmes and Watson, the expressions of the Club founders unclouded to the extent of smiling broadly to the newcomer. Lonsdale pumped his hand wordlessly and at length. He then put one hand on Arthur's shoulder, and the other on Holmes's.

"Mr. Holmes, I want you to meet my dear friend, Arthur Trent. Arthur, I give you Sherlock Holmes, the renowned detective who did me a great turn not very long ago and who is honoring us with his presence tonight."

There was a small pause as Holmes cleared his throat and turned his head the least bit toward his friend and colleague, after which the Earl continued, "Indeed, we are doubly honored in having with us Dr. John Watson, his fellow detective, if I may call you that, Dr. Watson."

As Watson harrumphed his way to a response, Holmes replied, "You may indeed."

Arthur Trent looked to both men with wide shining eyes and an easy, open smile. He was well into his 50s, below middle size in height, and still possessing a more prominent chest than stomach. His long, curly hair was grizzled and his thick moustache a matching salt and pepper. He had a weather-beaten face and heavy brows, one of which was split by a thin white line. He struck Watson as having a toughness about him that contrasted oddly with his easy manner. "I am truly honored to meet you both. Lord Lonsdale speaks of you often, and of course your accomplishments are well and widely known. But I had no idea you had an interest in boxing. I trust you will be staying to see the fight tonight?"

Lonsdale spoke for Holmes. "Of course he will. I really want the two of you to know each other. Holmes not only shares our interest in the manly art, he has himself had several amateur bouts. I believe you made rather a study of boxing at Cambridge, Holmes, and I know you went three rounds with McMurdo and showed yourself to good advantage in the exchange."

Holmes inclined his head toward the Earl and gave him a sly grin. "Now, who is the detective? I'm impressed, Lord Lonsdale, although I feel it only fair to point out I may well have caught McMurdo by surprise."

"If I might interrupt, gentlemen," Bettinson looked to the four men who were now the only ones in the room still standing. "I believe it would be well to order before it gets much later and we risk delaying the match."

Murmuring acknowledgement of his concern, the four men took their chairs. Watson sat at one end of the table with Arthur Trent placed between Holmes and himself, and Lonsdale, Fleming, and Bettinson filled out the rest of the places. Their waiter traded his studied nonchalance for an energetic concern with serving the six men at the table that was his sole assignment. He nodded understanding as each man placed an order he committed to memory—at least until he was out of sight and could record the selections on the pad beneath his apron. He then hurried to the kitchen lest he bear the blame for delaying dinner and the start of the evening's spectacle.

17

With their waiter properly dispatched, Lord Lonsdale explained Arthur Trent's presence. "Mr. Trent has been gracious enough to make McLellan Manor, his estate in Yorkshire, available for training by one of the participants in tonight's exhibition, and it's the Club's custom to seat any member contributing to the evening's events at the head table with Peggy, John and myself. It's intended to be an honor, but I'm not certain it's always seen as such by those who have to endure our company."

Arthur Trent protested amidst muffled laughter.

Peggy Bettinson called from his place at the end of the table. "And we want to thank you again, Trent, for this past weekend and the wonderful time you and Mrs. Trent organized for us. Fleming and I had hoped to thank your lady again before leaving, but as you know we had to get away early to attend to some Club business. Your wife was a wonderful hostess under any conditions, but especially so after her accident. That's what we hoped to tell her, as well as wishing her a rapid recovery." An endorsement for Bettinson's comments rumbled from his Co-Director colleague.

"Thank you for that—thank you both—and let me assure you we both knew of your need to get away early," Trent said, then recognized a need to respond to the blank looks of the two men who had not shared the weekend with him at McLellan Manor. "Mrs. Trent had a very bad accident when she went for her morning ride yesterday. Her horse stepped in a hole throwing her in a ditch. Fortunately, Lonsdale was with her and helped her get back to the Manor. It turned out there were no broken bones, although she does have a rather severe ankle sprain. And I appreciate your concern on that score, Bettinson, but she's really doing quite well as long as she remembers to use her cane and keeps off the stairs as the doctor ordered. I'm certain you observed that Mrs. Trent is a strong woman; she takes the attitude she's having it a good deal easier now than the last time she suffered a sprain. She was a girl of twelve then, and sprain or no she was up with the sun to light the ovens for her father's baking."

"Well, if that's her outlook I'm sure she'll be back riding before very long," Lonsdale spoke breezily in hopes of setting the conversation on a happier course. "And, Arthur, I can only hope you will prove a greater help to your wife than you did last night. What exactly was the problem that called you away in the middle of dinner? I know there was something about a cow and some vegetables and a vicar, but I never did get an understanding of it all."

After allowing the Club's Co-Directors to admit their own confusion about the evening's activities, Trent undertook to clarify things, again directing his explanation largely to Holmes and Watson. "Lord Lonsdale is referring to a dispute between two of my tenants who have been neighbors and adversaries for a good many years. On this occasion, it appears one man's cow wandered into his neighbor's garden, and the man whose garden was trampled decided to keep the cow to teach the other a lesson. Oxley's Chief Constable— Oxley is the town I live in—came to fetch me after neither he nor the vicar were able to calm the situation. The Chief Constable had hoped to leave me out of it knowing I had company, but felt he had no choice, not wanting to put the two of them together in the one cell of our tiny jail where he'd have to break up the fight they'd inevitably get into."

"Which is exactly what he should have done, and simply declare in favor of whoever won the fight," volunteered Fleming.

"I suspect he was tempted, but, after all, the two men are fundamentally harmless. They'd had a little too much to drink, and it sort of combined with cows and gardens and a long history. I really quite sympathize with the Chief Constable's position."

"You would," was Fleming's response, but it came

without the speaker's customary growl.

Trent grinned his way past Fleming's interruption. "After our work with the tenants was done, I discovered in my haste I had come away without a key to get back in. Not wanting to wake the household when everyone would be well asleep, I agreed to spend the night at the vicar's, and that good soul brought me back home the next morning. I'm only sorry for the inconvenience I caused, inadvertent as it was."

Peggy Bettinson shook his head in protest. "Not at all. It couldn't have been more pleasant for us. I'd never been to your part of Yorkshire before, and I must say I found the moor as dramatic as any in Scotland. Besides which, the shooting was excellent, and my wife insists your plant collection rivals the Kew Gardens. She hasn't stopped talking about it, and I'll blame you if I find myself having to bring on a gardener."

Tiring of reports of his hosts' Yorkshire idyll, Holmes sought to turn the conversation again to boxing. "And who is the fighter who's been staying with you, Mr. Trent? Would it be someone I might know?"

"I rather doubt it, Mr. Holmes," Trent replied. "He's a middleweight who goes by the name of Sailor Mackenzie, although you shouldn't let the name fool you. It's the creation of an earlier manager who thought it might suggest a certain toughness that would be helpful with more impressionable opponents. I believe we are now about as close to the sea as the Sailor has ever been."

"How good a fighter is he?" Holmes directed his question to Lord Lonsdale.

"I guess that's what we'll find out. He's had his day, and is getting a little long in the tooth for our sport. He's cagey about his age like a lot of boxers, but his wife, who's staying with us as well, let the cat out of the bag and told us he'd just had his thirty-fourth birthday. I'm afraid the Sailor was not at all happy with her sharing that information. As you'll see, he's not the fanciest of fighters and, truth to tell, his style was probably better suited to the old London rules. He's a mauler who likes to push his opponent around and wrestle him down, which I'm told is exactly what he would do in the days when that was allowed. The high point of his career was probably when he went up in class to go twenty-one rounds with Charlie Mitchell, who you'll remember was the one-time British heavyweight champion. He had him down once before Mitchell caught up with him and the Sailor's manager decided he was unable to continue. That knockdown gave him a wee bit of a reputation and got him some handsome purses for a while. But from what Mr. Caplehorn, his current manager told me, if it was the making of him, it was also his undoing.

"He stepped up his drinking about then, what with all his new friends wanting to buy a round for the man who knocked down Charlie Mitchell, and the Sailor never had been what you would call a teetotaler. It's gotten to the point where he's never without his flask of Scotch whiskey. I'm sure he's got the flask hidden away someplace even now. All in all, he's probably getting to the end of the string at this point, but it's my understanding he's still got a punch, will keep on the offensive, and now and again can surprise an opponent who's not ready for him."

"And what of his opponent tonight?" Watson called his question over the clatter of dishes as waiters settled platters overlapped by steaks and chops before diners in the great hall.

"That will be my coachman's son, young Rochester Cochrane," Lonsdale replied. "He's had some amateur bouts and done quite well, and for the last two and a half weeks we've had him sparring with Jem Mace, the great former champion who was my own mentor years ago. You'll see that Rochester is what they call a scientific boxer. That should make him well suited to the Queensberry rules and its three-minute rounds. It's a very different style from anything you've seen, Holmes. The boy has the reach over Mackenzie and he'll jab, jab again and dance away until he sees an opening where he can attack. The Sailor, being a brawler first and last, will stalk my young man, hoping to take him out with one big punch. The problem for the Sailor, apart from having a referee to cut down on his roughhouse ways, is that he'll be wearing gloves for the first time in his boxing life.

"I was up to McLellan Manor a little over a fortnight ago to observe Mackenzie in his sparring sessions and gauge my boy's chances. He didn't look at all comfortable using gloves, and it's my bet they'll take just enough out of his punch to keep him from knocking out young Rochester. You see, Holmes, the gloves have to hold four ounces of horsehair and our Mr. Corri will make certain they do. All in all, it should make for a very entertaining contest, likely not the most artful, but entertaining nonetheless." Lonsdale lightly fingered the fork at his place. "Perhaps I could interest you, Holmes, or maybe you, Dr. Watson, in a small wager on the evening's outcome. Just for fun of course."

The Earl's offer to increase his guests' evening pleasure was ignored for the moment as the waiter, having arrived with their orders, began setting plates in front of each man, his face clenched with a determination to put them down quickly and get to the ale he knew they'd be wanting the moment their food arrived. After putting a last plate at Watson's place, he hurried for the pitcher even as John Fleming pointed to his empty glass.

Holmes kept his focus on the well marbled thick steak he was cutting into while he addressed Lonsdale in as offhand a manner as he could manage. "I think I'll pass on placing a wager, not knowing the fighters at all. But tell me have you introduced changes to the rules for spectators as well?"

Lonsdale winced as he recalled the events to which Holmes referred. "I know you and Dr. Watson were present at a very unfortunate performance by Pelican Club members. I assure you there will be no repetition of the events you witnessed."

Concerned that pursuing this line of discussion risked turning a difficult evening into an unpleasant one, Watson steered the conversation back to the competition at hand. "Well, that change will of course be most welcome. Tell me more about your young fighter. Are you grooming a new champion at Lowther Castle?"

"Probably not a champion, Doctor, although I think he can be a good boy if only he'll concentrate a little more on what he's about. He loses focus at points and that can be dangerous inside the ring. Still, he's only nineteen and has time to learn. He's got speed and enough of a punch that in a few years he could be quite something if he decides to stay with the sport."

"You know I'd quite forgotten he's Parker Cochrane's son. How is old Cochrane doing? I'd hoped to visit with him for a moment during the weekend, but never got the chance." Trent spoke a quick aside to Holmes, "Parker was my groom before becoming Lonsdale's coachman."

The Earl nodded an accompaniment to his words. "He's doing very well. You were absolutely spot on to recommend Parker to my attention. He knows his horses and there's been no return to his earlier difficulties. Frankly, he's as good a man with my stable of chestnuts as I've ever had."

"You and your bloody horses. They'll be the death of you yet if you don't bore the rest of us to tears first." John Fleming's grumpy baritone sounded nearly jolly as the conversation turned to a topic of frequent bantering between the men.

Peggy Bettinson followed Fleming's lead. "Are you still buying horses, Lonsdale?"

"Not horses, Peggy," the Earl corrected with a broad smile, "Chestnuts, hunters and whatever ponies catch Lady Lonsdale's eye."

"And is it true your chestnuts must stand no more than fifteen hands?" Bettinson asked with an exaggerated note of sarcasm in his voice.

"Not true at all; the chestnuts can go to fully fifteen hands two inches." The three Club officials roared while Trent, Holmes and Watson smiled politely.

As the laughter died down and the smiles relaxed, Peggy Bettinson, taking note of the dwindling number in the dining hall, tugged a watch from his waistcoat pocket and frowned at what he saw. "I'm afraid it's getting close to time. We have a little more than five minutes and it wouldn't be right to keep everyone waiting."

The Earl nodded, made one final swipe with his napkin before placing it next to his empty plate, and rising, made clear to those still in the room that dinner was at an end. Fleming led the way from the dining room, leaving it in the care of the detachment of half-aproned men who would attend first to the pitchers of ale, hastily emptying those before clearing the room of the remainder of its residue, and returning the hall to the pristine state in which the Club members had found it and would expect it to reappear.

Chapter 2.
Holmes Answers a Challenge

The building's theater had been converted to a boxing arena with a speed that left part of its earlier life still clearly visible. A roped-off square had been inserted into the middle of the theater's orchestra section with chairs set out on three of its sides. On one of those sides the stage of the music hall remained intact, complete to a drawn curtain exposing a peaceful forest glen backdrop. Between the curtain and ring 100 chairs stood where JW Rowley had once performed graceful somersaults while singing *Up with the Lark in the Morning*, doubtless to some of the same patrons who were now seeking a somewhat more raucous display of athleticism. In all, 800 spectators could be seated on the ground floor and in the six balconies, while another 500 standees could be accommodated behind those seated around the ring.

Fleming shot ahead while Lonsdale strolled to his place in the front row. The Earl pointed to five empty chairs at ringside and Holmes and Watson took seats, avoiding those labeled with the names Bettinson and Fleming. Arthur Trent had left their company shortly after entering the arena to take his own assigned chair.

Fleming's reason for bolting ahead became quickly evident. He stood in the center of the ring, megaphone in hand, glowering his impatience at spectators standing in the aisles, most of whom carefully avoided eye contact with the would-be announcer. The arena was now filled with the sound of last minute wagers being loudly negotiated by elegantly attired men.

In the conduct of the agency's investigations it fell to Watson not only to record exchanges with clients, witnesses, informants, and suspects, but to detail the characteristics of individuals significant to each case. It was a practice that had become so routine over the years, he often found himself slipping into it even where there was no investigation ongoing. Such was the case tonight. Over dinner, he had catalogued key features of the men at his table and now he began the same process with the men inside the ring. They faced each other from opposite corners, apparently oblivious to the controversy raging throughout the arena over which of them would be carried from the ring at evening's end. Both were bare-chested, wearing tights ending just below the knee, and lapping dark stockings leading to high-topped leather shoes. While their outfits were identical, the men themselves bore no resemblance to each other.

The older man, whom Watson judged to be Sailor Mackenzie, glared across the ring at his opponent, not even appearing to blink as he tried unsuccessfully to lock eyes with him, all the while pounding the fist of one thinly gloved hand into the open palm of the other. A tuft of black hair at the front of his scalp lay separate from the thinning hair at its back, the incipient baldness making him appear older than his 34 years. He was thickset, his stomach having long since caught up to and surpassed a still powerful upper body. More than once, while staring at the other fighter, he put a fist to his stomach, grimacing slightly each time in what Watson took to be an effort to make clear the punishment he meant to inflict on the young man opposite. His face was puffy, either from his profession or the drinking Trent had described, or maybe both, and his eyes seemed lost in caverns of scar tissue forged over a decade and a half of scheduled fights and spontaneous barroom brawls. Sweat glistened across his face and chest, and hung in the two day growth of beard he had acquired either as a further effort to intimidate his opponent or from unconcern with his appearance.

Standing in his corner, some steps from the boxer, was a man in his early 60s, smaller and trimmer than the fighter, his many scars and inexpertly repaired broken nose attesting to a history inside the ring; his age and a suggestion of weary command indicating he was the Sailor's manager. A tall muscular black man, 35 or maybe a little older, in shirt-sleeves and light colored pants was positioning a water bottle, bucket and sponge, and a brandy bottle on the strip of apron outside the ropes in preparation for their use between rounds. The Sailor's second ignored the opponent across the ring and turned his attention to the crowd, making brief eye contact with Lonsdale, taking note of Holmes, and exchanging glances with Watson before looking beyond him to whatever or whomever had captured his interest.

In the opposite corner, Rochester Cochrane jogged a few times in place, stopped to shake his head sending straight sandy hair flying in all directions, and resumed his jogging. He repeated the sequence several times, looking neither right nor left, the task of bouncing up and down absorbing his full attention. He was a good deal taller than his opponent, and his body was leaner and more finely sculpted. His slightly pink face was unmarked, and he looked very much the boy of 19 that he was. Behind him, a sandy-haired man, an older, heavier version of the boy, massaged his neck and shoulders whenever the boy lit in one place long enough for him to do so. He returned the Sailor's glare on behalf of his son, but while Mackenzie's look held a small sneer intended to cow his opponent, the father looked to his son's opponent with jaw set and eyes narrowed. The boxer's second stood beside him, a boy even younger than the fighter, who searched the arena in wide-eyed and terrified wonder. On another day, indeed on nearly any other day, he would have been the stable boy to the coachman who now acted as his son's manager.

Fleming's voice sounded through the megaphone in his best imitation of amiability. "My Lord President, my Lords, Gentlemen, good evening and welcome to the National Sporting Club. Tonight we have a match pitting youth against experience. This will be a contest of eight rounds, conducted under Marquis of Queensberry rules, between Mr. Sailor

27

Mackenzie from Glasgow, Scotland and Mr. Rochester Cochrane of North Cumbria. The referee for tonight's proceedings will be Mr. Corri and the timekeeper Mr. Zerega."

The two men thus acknowledged were seated together at a rostrum to the left of Lonsdale, their chairs set on a low platform lifting them a little more than a foot above the spectators. Each man waved to the small smattering of applause that greeted the announcement of his name. Eugene Corri was jowly and stocky, the image of the successful stockbroker that he, in fact, was. E. Zerega (what the E stood for was a matter of much speculation at the Club), although no less successful, had sunken cheeks and was slender to the point of appearing gaunt. Both wore top hats and evening dress, both chewed on small unlit cigars, and both focused wholly on events in the ring with a no-nonsense air about them.

Fleming allowed the small show of appreciation for the officials to subside before putting the megaphone again to his moustache and the lips that were somewhere beneath it. "We ask all who are in attendance to obey the rules of the Club. I particularly want to make certain those rules are known to any guests joining us for the first time. We maintain silence throughout each round of the match. Conversation and a show of appreciation for our fighters' efforts are permitted during the minute between rounds, but we ask you to conduct yourselves respectfully at those times as well." After pausing to allow his message to be absorbed, he looked to each boxer with the same solemnity he had shown their spectators. "Gentlemen, I remind you we make use of Marquis of Queensberry rules. I know these have been explained to you and we ask you to observe them faithfully throughout this match." He paused to stare at Mackenzie whose own eyes never left his opponent. "Mr. Corri, Mr. Zerega, I turn the proceedings over to you."

John Fleming exited the ring, exhibiting as much dignity as he was able while climbing over one strand of rope and ducking beneath another. He took his assigned chair between Lord Lonsdale and Bettinson, while the referee, Eugene Corri, minus only the top hat he had laid on the seat he vacated, replaced him as the official inside the ring. The men who had accompanied the boxers into the ring now left as well, crouching on the arena floor behind the corners of their respective fighters.

The room, that moments before had echoed to the sound of challenges being offered and accepted, now grew silent as if suddenly emptied of its noisy humanity. Here and there, catching the flicker of gaslight, a silver flask appeared, sometimes to be shared with a neighbor, more often to provide its owner momentary relief or stimulation, and then disappear if only briefly. The boxers continued their pre-fight routines, waiting on the timekeeper's signal to begin the contest. The Sailor again pounded one gloved fist into the open palm of his other hand, with greater force now, but still rhythmically, mechanically; Cochrane shuffled from one foot to the other, danced a small distance from his corner jabbing the air with his left hand, then danced back, still jabbing the defenseless air.

And then, Mr. Zerega, cigar in one hand, chronograph in the other, pressed the short stem of his timepiece, called, "Time," and the match was on. The men came to the ring's center, exchanged the obligatory handshake, then confronted each other without further pretense of goodwill.

The fight followed the pattern Lonsdale had predicted. Rochester Cochrane hunched low to his task, jabbing with his left hand, looking for an opening to cross with his right, bobbing his head down, back up, sometimes jerking it left or right, all the while dancing backwards, then side to side in no set pattern. The Sailor plodded forward, not dancing, not bobbing, not jabbing, simply stalking his ever active target.

From his son's corner, the senior Cochrane risked antagonizing the Club's directors with soft cries of encouragement. The Sailor's corner observed the request for silence.

Neither man seemed able to gain an advantage. Cochrane's jabs landed infrequently and weakly on the Sailor's gloves, and the opening he sought never seemed to materialize. The Sailor was achieving even less success as he lumbered after his opponent across the ring, then up its one side and down the other. He seemed confused by his young adversary's strategy, panting loudly as he gave chase and staggering at times, even catching himself on the ropes at one point. The crowd grew restless, although none expressed their unease with words in accord with the vow of silence they had agreed to observe. Instead, chairs creaked and coughing, that might otherwise have been an insignificant background noise, now seemed to echo through the arena.

Perhaps his sense of the crowd's displeasure, perhaps his own discomfort led the young man to deviate from the plan crafted by his father. His dancing now took him nearer the Sailor. At first, the strategy seemed to work. His jabs found the top of the Sailor's balding head then grazed his temple. He pulled back his right hand to follow a left jab with a right cross, leaving himself momentarily unprotected. It was the opportunity Mackenzie had been seeking. He looped a left hand catching Rochester solidly on his right cheek. As the young man's knees buckled, the Sailor, although off balance and lurching, managed a right uppercut that sent the coachman's son backwards in a sprawl across the floor of the ring. The Sailor, reeling himself and breathing heavily, caught hold of the top strand of rope before moving away from his opponent in accord with the direction he received from Mr. Corri. The referee began a count while Mr. Zerega stared fixedly at the watch he held, the contest was now between Mr. Corri's ability to count ten and the ticking of Mr. Zerega's timepiece to the end of round one. Rochester Cochrane, oblivious to the contest between timekeeper and referee, raised himself to a knee before slipping down again. Seeing that, his father ended the contests between both the fighters and the officials. Entering the ring between the strands of rope to minister to his son, he declared the fight to be over.

As he knelt beside him, the young man turned to his father, and in the still silent arena his words were clear. "I'm sorry, dad, I'm sorry. I didn't get it done. I'm sorry." His father rejected his statement with a vigorous shake of his head as he stroked the boy's forehead. "You done your best, son. There's no shame in that. His Lordship will be proud of you and so am I. There's no use talkin' more, you need to get your strength."

Together with his stable boy, the coachman lifted his son to his chair a few feet from Lonsdale. The Earl came quickly forward to assure him he was indeed proud of the young man and urge him not to concern himself on that score, although Watson thought Lonsdale too had been shaken by events in the ring. Dr. Lang, the Club physician, appeared from the crowd of spectators, looked hard into Rochester's eyes, had him follow the index finger he moved side to side, asked him his name and to identify where he was, and then turned away declaring him fit to be moved.

Lonsdale, who had remained with the group while the doctor conducted his examination, asked the coachman to take his son to the upstairs dormitory where the two of them and the stable boy should plan on spending the night. Applause showered down on the young man as he retreated from the arena, and a second wave of applause greeted John Fleming's return to the ring to raise the arm of Sailor Mackenzie, declaring him the winner of the evening's contest. The spectators, now freed of their requirement to sit mute, took to making claims on each other for the payment of wagers won, and to argue the merits and shortcomings of the fighters they had just observed.

The Sailor was not, however, content to leave the ring just yet. He grabbed the megaphone from Fleming, and began an unsteady circle to face all parts of the arena with the same contemptuous glare he had shown Rochester Cochrane. "Ye put me up agin a wee boy, and no doubt ye made a packet doin' it. Now, I'm askin' if there be one among ye what's man enough to climb inside o' this ring wi' me. I'll wager every bit o' me purse agin any man what's got the heart to do it."

Without looking at him, he snapped the megaphone back to Fleming who held the instrument far from his body as if the Sailor's brief possession had ruined it for any further use. He stared wide-eyed at the boxer, so taken aback that the lower lip of his open mouth had become clearly visible. A silence consumed the arena so profound that Watson would later swear Mackenzie's grunts were the only sound in the crowd of nearly a thousand men. Then, the person seated next to him stood, and leveling his cold gaze at the man inside the ring, responded to the challenge.

"You may keep your purse, sir. If someone will only fit me out with tights and shoes, and if I may have Dr. Watson for my second, I'll take you on." The arena erupted in applause and shouts of encouragement, and this time John Fleming made no effort to interrupt the pandemonium that swept the National Sporting Club. Instead, he smiled his approval as Sherlock Holmes moved down the aisle to be quickly joined by the Earl of Lonsdale who would have the honor of showing him the way to the changing room.

At 221B Baker Street Mrs. Hudson had completed dinner, washed up her few dishes, and placed Sir Edmund du Cane on top of two other books to be returned to the British Library. She had come to the conclusion that if she read anything further of the reforms imposed by Sir Edmund during his term as Chairman of the Prison Commission, she might feel obliged to give up the investigation of crime, or at least the delivery of criminals to the judicial system. Sir Edmund, she had discovered, believed that apart from those few first offenders he described as "wayward and impulsive," all lawbreakers were to spend their time contemplating the error of their ways and suffering the consequences of their actions. Contemplation was obtained through a nine-month period of solitary confinement at the beginning of each sentence, affording each prisoner opportunity to examine fully the nature of his transgression. Suffering the consequences of one's actions was achieved through use of a plank bed, a diet designed to sustain life while promoting its monotony, and assignment either to the treadmill, or the crank; the former to be trod upon, ten minutes on and five minutes off, for ten hours, the latter to be turned by the prisoner a thousand times each day after first being tightened to the warder's satisfaction.

Mrs. Hudson was a firm believer in the punishment fitting the crime, but found herself wondering what crimes could fit the punishment Sir Edmund viewed as appropriate for anyone not meeting his definition of "wayward and impulsive." In their lifetime together, Constable Tobias Hudson had recounted stories of men and women who had stolen out of desperation to feed themselves and their families when honest work could not be found. She failed to see how practice walking the treadmill or turning the crank would prepare them to care for themselves or their families. She resolved to discuss the subject further with Mr. Holmes and Dr. Watson. For now, however, it was well past her bedtime and she couldn't wait any longer for her boarders to return. She extinguished the lamps in her kitchen and parlor, and took a last hopeful look from her parlor window. Finding only an empty Baker Street, Mrs. Hudson padded off to bed.

Lonsdale led his guests to a long narrow room below

33

the arena that had been an oversized pantry in an earlier incarnation, and now served as the Club's undersized changing room. It accommodated the evening's two combatants simultaneously, demanding each man demonstrate some reasonable tolerance for the other before mounting the stairs to clobber him. One wardrobe served to hold both men's clothing and such other possessions as they were willing to store in an unlocked, unguarded room. Two long tables covered with thin blankets were set up as far apart as the limited space permitted. Three sets of shelves extending the length of one side wall held boxing gloves, a medicine ball, Indian clubs, towels, boxing tights—some rolled up, some neatly folded—stockings and shoes of various sizes and evidence of wear, as well as empty bottles, bottles filled with mysterious looking liquids, liniments, and the cotton, gauze, and plasters needed to dress the wounds of battle.

Holmes located a pair of tights he said would suit him. They were the longest of the folded pairs and, although they ended at his knee rather than below it, Holmes indicated satisfaction with them before the Earl had opportunity to sort through the rolled up clothing. Stockings and shoes provided less challenge regarding size, although Holmes tried not to think about when—or if—the stockings had been washed, or what might be the history of the scuffed and battered shoes he chose. He was unaccustomed to the gloves Lonsdale pressed over his hands, and opened and closed his fist several times by way of becoming as comfortable with them as he could manage. Before leaving the changing room, Watson packed his cheeks with cotton and put additional small wads over his upper and lower front teeth. As a result, Holmes bore resemblance to a tall slender squirrel, but happily traded his usual elegance for the added protection.

Holmes pronounced himself ready, and the small procession returned to the arena to a rippling of applause that grew to a tidal wave as Holmes climbed between the strands of rope held apart by the Earl and Watson. Holmes did his best to ignore both the ovation that greeted him and the softer, but clearly audible calls for better odds against the certainty of his defeat. Across the ring Sailor Mackenzie glared his contempt. He shook a fist at Holmes, a promise of things to come, then pressed a glove to his midsection, grimacing as he had done with his earlier opponent. Fleming again took his place at ring center, arms crossed and silent. When the last wagers had been negotiated, and shouts had quieted to conversations, Fleming's gruff voice sounded again. "My Lord President, my Lords, Gentlemen, we will now have an unscheduled bout which will be set at a maximum of eight rounds and will pit Mr. Sailor Mackenzie against Mr. Sherlock Holmes. As before, spectators are asked to remain silent while the contestants are engaged. Mr. Corri and Mr. Zerega will again officiate and I now turn the proceedings back to them." For a second time Fleming exited the ring and Mr. Corri entered. For a second time Mr. Zerega studied his chronograph, called, "Time," and the second fight of the evening was on.

Watson and Lonsdale had given Holmes identical advice as he went to meet his opponent: "Stay away from Mackenzie's right hand." It was the strategy Holmes had decided to adopt before receiving their instruction, and he now put it into practice in association with Rochester Cochrane's scientific boxing style. He believed the basic strategy sound and its earlier failure due to a lapse in its application. To that end, Holmes danced right, then left, then backward in differing sequences, while Sailor Mackenzie reprised the strategy that had worked for him earlier and, bending himself nearly double, lurched forward trying to catch up to his ever active opponent. Whether he was more tired, or Holmes was more artful, the Sailor seemed to be having greater difficulty with Holmes than he'd had with the younger fighter. He appeared to become more quickly out of breath, and the staggering seen earlier became near stumbles as he made effort to follow Holmes's footwork, snarling his contempt for the dancer before him.

Nearly two minutes passed and neither man threw a punch as they circled the ring. Holmes stayed focused on the Sailor's right hand and found it to be making a steady descent from his jaw, to his chest, and still lower, drifting to his middle from time to time and finally catching there. It seemed to Holmes the right time to become the aggressor. He moved forward, threw a left jab to the Sailor's temple, and followed it with a right hook that caught his opponent high on the forehead as he dipped below the full thrust of Holmes's punch. While the Sailor thought to duck, Holmes remained upright, intent on admiring the effect of the blow he confidently expected to result in the Sailor lying spread-eagled before him. Instead, he felt an explosion in his left cheek and saw a wad of cotton fly to the ring's surface, a path he followed a split second later.

Holmes found himself imprisoned in a silence more intense than any John Fleming could have hoped for. A man stood over him, elaborately mouthing words he couldn't hear. Beyond the man, he recognized a deeply distressed Watson standing amidst a crowd of elegantly dressed men outside the roped enclosure in which he lay. And then, as suddenly as it had disappeared, sound returned. The man was mouthing numbers not words, and calling them out at a measured pace. He had reached five when Holmes took note of a second figure leaning a gloved hand on the top rope of their enclosure. And then he remembered the second man was Sailor Mackenzie and he was in the fight of his life. He was up at nine, as Mackenzie yelled to the referee that he should have reached ten long ago. The Sailor lumbered after Holmes, who found, as he backpedaled his retreat, that the bounce in his stride, which moments before had easily taken him beyond the Sailor's awkward reach, had now mysteriously deserted him. The Sailor made small circles in the air with his left hand, but

Holmes only had eyes for the right, and his objective had again become its avoidance in a renewed application of the strategy he, Watson, and the Earl had embraced a short time earlier.

He got trapped in the Sailor's corner and, unable to escape, fell against the fighter's sweaty body, absorbing an uppercut in the process, but at such close range the Sailor was unable to bring any force behind the blow. Holmes held tight until the voice that had been counting earlier called for the men to break. The brief pause helped. Holmes found his head was clearer and he had gotten back some of his former strength. He held his adversary another few seconds in spite of Mr. Corri's admonition, then whirled him around and danced back toward the ring's center. The Sailor let out a groan of disappointment, and renewed his plodding attack until a second voice sounded, "Time," from ringside and the first round was over.

In the Sailor's corner, his manager and second had set out a chair, pail and bottles of both water and brandy. While his second used the towel to fan his fighter, the manager offered him the water bottle which was rejected in favor of the brandy.

In the opposite corner Watson examined the inside of Holmes's mouth, shook his head at what he found, removed the remaining wads of cotton, and gave Holmes two swallows of water before withdrawing the bottle. Holmes took note that the cottons were bright red, and in spite of Watson's care, the lip he sponged was painful to the touch and likely on its way to increasing significantly in size. Watson inserted new wads of cotton, taking especial care in replacing the one that had been ejected by the Sailor's punch. The Earl meanwhile sponged down Holmes's shoulders and back, predicting Holmes's certain success in the next round in a voice that did not match the confidence of his words. Watson did not speak until the minute of rest was very nearly over. "Holmes, you had the right idea until you got careless. He's tired and leaves himself terribly open. Take it to him with your left, but keep your right hand high and be ready to duck and dodge. And for God's sake, keep moving."

Holmes grunted his understanding and pushed off his chair as Mr. Zerega called, "Time." His energy was back, and he began again to dance to his right and away from the Sailor's right hand. As the Sailor's right dropped lower and lower, he came quickly forward, blocking the Sailor's left hook with his right forearm and sending a stiff left jab above the Sailor's heart, then a right to his midsection, and as both hands lowered to protect his body, Holmes sent a looping right cross that caught the Sailor's chin as he was pulling away. Mackenzie fell to the ring's surface with his hands still at his stomach and his body contorted into a fetal position. A thin trail of vomit trickled from his open mouth.

Mr. Corri counted to ten a hair more quickly than he had counted over the fallen Holmes, and loudly enough to be heard above the crowd's fidgeting as they prepared for the celebration they hadn't dared to believe would be theirs. As the cheers began, and with all eyes focused on the crowd's champion, the Sailor's body twitched and then grew still. Fleming raised the hand of a weary Holmes in triumph, while both Lang and Watson, who alone in the crowd had been studying the prone fighter, climbed into the ring and jointly began a somber examination of Sailor Mackenzie.

First Lang, then Watson felt for a pulse, Lang next turned the Sailor on his back and put an ear to the center of his chest. He looked to Watson with narrowed eyes and pursed lips, shaking his head slowly from side to side. He tried without success to get the attention of Lonsdale, who stood beside Holmes beaming with pride at the accomplishment of his adopted champion. With a nod to Watson, Lang interrupted the Earl's effort to lead the Club members in awarding three cheers to Holmes, and delivered a terse message to the President of the National Sporting Club. "Lord Lonsdale, I regret to inform you this man is dead."

The Sailor's second and manager had joined the others in the ring, remaining at a respectful distance from the medical men and the Club officials. They had set out a chair on which their fighter would never sit, and now stood beside it waiting for instruction. They looked to Dr. Lang, and to Lord Lonsdale, before turning their attention finally to the boxer whose lifeless eyes held their gaze longest of all. The jubilation the spectators felt at the defeat of the man who had dared their courage now subsided in waves, as those nearest the action communicated their knowledge of the tragedy to their neighbors behind. Peggy Bettinson had come into the ring and taken the megaphone to confirm what was already known, and then to report the Club's need to contact the police, leading several men to leave as quickly as a proper regard for the amenities, and the need to collect sticks and hats permitted.

The ring too emptied out in a matter of minutes. Lonsdale declared it his responsibility to alert the authorities, and left to go in search of a potboy to send for a constable. Fleming and Bettinson excused themselves, and left for the office they shared to get things in order for the visit from the Yard they saw as likely. Arthur Trent exited the ring without apology or explanation. Sailor Mackenzie's manager and second nodded their respects to the departing Lord Lonsdale and Arthur Trent, and then joined them in melting into the thinning crowd and disappearing. In short order, only Holmes and Watson, Dr. Lang and Sailor Mackenzie remained in place.

Dr. Lang reported he would remain with "the deceased" if Holmes wished to change his clothes. He suggested, as well, that Watson might want to attend to Holmes's wounds with the plasters and liniments in the changing room. The two men accepted the wisdom of both of Lang's suggestions, and made their way back down the stairs leading to the changing room. As they neared the room, they caught sight of someone bolting out its door and turning the corner at the far end of the corridor. Whoever it was never turned to face the two men. It wouldn't have mattered if the person had. With the instant available for observation, and the twilight condition of the underground walkways, all they could say for certain was that the person they saw was below medium height, thickset and wearing a workman's jacket and cap. The two men proceeded in silence to the changing room, a silence interrupted only by Holmes's groans as Watson applied what dressings and liniments he could find to Holmes's cuts and bruises.

By the time Holmes and Watson reappeared in the arena, the police had arrived. Sailor Mackenzie's manager and second had returned, and stood behind the corner of their fallen fighter appearing more uneasy than grief-stricken. Lonsdale and Trent had joined Dr. Lang, and all three were answering questions being posed by a fourth figure whose presence embarrassed Holmes, pleased Watson and surprised them both. The prominence of the National Sporting Club's membership led to the unexpected appearance of the lean stooped figure of Inspector Lestrade who had been summoned from home to take charge of the inquiry. He held a briar pipe firmly in his teeth although no smoke came from its bowl. When he saw Holmes, he removed the pipe and let his eyes grow wide before his face creased into a bemused grin. This was not the Holmes of calm reserve and dignified bearing to whom he was accustomed. A black tie hung loosely around his neck, his shirt front was not fully buttoned, and dark strands of hair went their separate ways across his long forehead. Any question about the cause for Holmes's dishevelment was answered by the plaster he wore over a badly swollen lower lip and the bruise over his left eye.

"Goodness me, Mr. Holmes, if I'd of known you were on the evening's card, I would have told the missus I was on a case and come directly here to see your bout." He chuckled at his own joke before becoming aware he was alone in finding humor in the situation. He cleared his throat noisily from behind a fist, arranged his face in a show of studied concern, and began again. "Mr. Holmes, don't tell me you're in any way responsible for my being here this evening."

Holmes had recovered his faculties, but not yet his composure, and allowed Watson and Lonsdale to bring the Inspector up to speed. Watson provided a chronology of the evening's events; Dr. Lang offered his opinion that deaths in the ring were always unfortunate, but far from unknown. Lestrade nodded his way through both reports, cleared his throat a second time, and turned his attention back to Holmes.

"And what is your opinion, Mr. Holmes? With what sort of a blow did you strike the man?"

Holmes hadn't thought about the sequence of punches thrown, and now found himself working to remember the individual blows in a series of events that had never been more than a blur to him. "In truth, Lestrade, it's difficult to recall all that happened. I know I hit him a solid blow to the area of his heart and another to the stomach, and I believe I hit him on the jaw, but I can't say how solid that blow was. I do remember I thought at the time his going down was likely a delayed reaction to my blow to his heart."

Lonsdale interrupted Holmes to correct any hint of false modesty on his part. "I think you underestimate yourself, Holmes. It was, as you say, a solid punch to the heart that clearly staggered Mackenzie, and your right hand to his head was enough to take him down. Doubtless the man's habits played a role here, Inspector. His vulnerability was almost certainly increased by his problem with drink. As Dr. Lang says, it's a tragedy regardless of the circumstances, but the truth is, what with his drinking and the little care he took of

41

himself, the man had likely been courting death for years."

Lestrade grunted. He was a deliberate man who had gotten where he was by following established procedure with no steps left out. Smarter men than he had found established procedure too slow or simply unnecessary, and had cut corners and drawn conclusions that later turned out to be unfounded. Those men failed to get the pay rises and promotions he'd gotten. Lestrade was thorough not brilliant. More importantly, he knew his shortcomings as well as his strengths, and he never let his strengths blind him to his shortcomings.

"I appreciate all you're telling me, but I'll feel a good deal more comfortable if the coroner has a look at the body to be sure there's nothing been missed. Are those belonging to the dead man as well?" Lestrade gestured to the pail, water bottle and brandy bottle where they had been left beside Sailor Mackenzie's chair together with a towel draped over the top rope. He received a nod from Trent and a grunt from Lonsdale. He turned to address a young constable standing at near attention outside the ring. "If you'd just organize those and bring them along, Hawkins. And see about having the body loaded into our hearse."

This last produced a spluttered dissent from Dr. Lang who had been scowling more deeply with each statement by Lestrade. "Really, Inspector, is all this necessary? I don't wish to interfere in police business, but this seems a dreadful waste. I count myself a capable physician. I've seen this kind of thing … it's in the nature of the sport … never desirable of course, but it happens."

Lord Lonsdale picked up the thread of Lang's argument as the physician fumbled for words that could break through the policeman's irrational obstinacy. "I have to agree with Dr. Lang, Inspector. This does happen I'm afraid. We do all we can to prevent a tragedy from occurring, but it remains a dangerous sport even with the many precautions we've added. What I'm saying, Inspector, is it's an unhappy event to be sure, but I'd hate to give the penny press cause to drag the Club's name through the mire after all we've done to assure the Club's respectability. I know there's the need to cross every t and dot every i, and I do respect that, Inspector ... Lestrade is it, but I wonder if it might be possible for me to speak to some of my friends in the Home Office to help you see how unnecessary an investigation would be, and perhaps have them suggest an alternative way to handle this situation."

Lestrade listened patiently to the one man's objections and the other man's threats, but his narrowed eyes and the tight line of his mouth made clear that, in one thing at least, Dr. Lang was right. As Holmes and Watson could attest, Lestrade could be obstinate, although neither of them had ever known his obstinacy to be without cause.

"I'm afraid, gentlemen, there is a need to dot every i and cross every t as you put it, Lord Lonsdale. I mean no disrespect for your judgment, Doctor, and I appreciate there could be some little dust-up for the Club, but an autopsy's what's called for in this situation. I see no reason it can't get done as expeditiously as possible, and if you think your friends in the Home Office can hurry things along you're certainly at liberty to get in touch with them." Lestrade looked meaningfully to the Earl who met his gaze in a contest that ended finally with Lestrade's pronouncement, "I will be making my report in the morning."

Watson sought to mediate a dispute he found unnecessary. "Surely, there can be no harm in gathering as much information as we can about this sad affair. I feel certain that Mr. Mackenzie's family, for one, will want as full an accounting as possible, and while the professional judgment of my colleague provides the most likely explanation," Watson gave a peremptory nod to Lang who sniffed acceptance of Watson's qualified support, "there is, after all, just enough question to suggest we do what's necessary to rule out the possibility of anything more sinister."

The only response to Watson came in a shuffling of feet and a tightening of the grimaces on the faces of both Lonsdale and Lang. Watson's comments were welcomed by Lestrade alone. They also reminded the Inspector of a further duty. He turned to face Trent whose silence he hoped signaled a more respectful view of police work. "Can you tell me if the dead man had a family?"

Arthur Trent spoke in the measured tone appropriate to the occasion. "A wife, Inspector. Mrs. Mackenzie has been staying at my home in Yorkshire together with Mr. Mackenzie while he was preparing for his match."

Lestrade groaned. Like all policemen, dealing with the next of kin was the part of the job he found most distasteful.

Arthur Trent recognized the source of Lestrade's discomfort. "If you like, I'll send Mrs. Trent a telegram explaining the situation and ask her to speak to Mrs. Mackenzie."

Lestrade looked to Trent as if he'd found a brother long given up for dead. "That would be most appreciated, sir."

Assuming Holmes and Watson had arrived by hansom, Lestrade offered to share his carriage with the two men for their return to Baker Street. They looked to Lonsdale who expressed regret he couldn't see them home given all that needed to be done at the Club, and Watson quickly agreed to exchange the Earl's yellow spectacle for the black coach of Scotland Yard. Trent nodded soberly to the three men, expressed his regrets to Holmes and Watson that they had met under such unfortunate circumstances, and handed his card to the Inspector with an assurance of cooperation in whatever tasks needed to be undertaken.

They rode to 221B in near silence, each man feeling the need to organize his own thinking before sharing it with the others. Lestrade pondered what might be the upshot of his call for an autopsy. He felt certain it was the right thing to do; it was certainly the prudent thing to do even if it riled Lord Lonsdale and the Club's doctor. What they said was of course perfectly true—fighters' deaths were not uncommon—and the doctor had been ready to put his name to a certificate of accidental death. If Doctor Watson had supported the Club's doctor he would have wondered about his demand, but Watson had not and that made him confident in his decision.

For his part, Watson was glad Lestrade had stood his ground, and glad he had defended Lestrade's position. He still thought Lang was likely correct, and that Holmes's body blows had led to internal hemorrhaging and death. But the signs were there for poisoning as well—the fetal position of the body, the small trail of vomit, the face contorted in pain, and as he now thought about it, the staggering, panting and feverish look of Mackenzie during his fights. It was good police work for Lestrade to commandeer all the drinking materials for analysis. He concluded it was concern about the reputation of the National Sporting Club that had led Lonsdale to discourage an autopsy to the extent of threatening Lestrade, and to characterize Holmes's blows as more powerful than only the most partisan observer would have claimed.

One such observer did wonder if the punch to Mackenzie's head could have been lethal. He hadn't believed it at first, but now thought his judgment about blows struck in the heat of battle was suspect, and the judgment of a knowledgeable observer, as for example, Lord Lonsdale, was likely more reliable. Having accepted responsibility for possessing a lethal combination, he now struggled to accept responsibility for its consequences. There was some comfort in knowing each man willingly accepted a risk when he entered the ring. There was even greater comfort in remembering that Mackenzie was a professional whereas he was the amateur, and that Mackenzie was a bully who had done his best to shame his audience after defeating young

Cochrane. But there was as well the fact that Mackenzie had a wife, perhaps a family. It was the dreadful outcome for which no one was ever prepared. The risk was supposed to be one of defeat with the likelihood of cuts and bruises, perhaps even temporary unconsciousness, but nothing more—never anything more. All in all, Holmes was now even more convinced his first inclination to spend the evening with Mendelssohn had been the right one.

When they stopped at the familiar sandstone lodgings, Lestrade took leave of his fellow passengers with the same gray look he had worn throughout the short ride. He did not bid them goodnight as that seemed an impossible wish, instead he advised them he would be by the following day to tell them the Yard's determination and plans. He called to the driver to go on before either man could respond. They watched the carriage rattle its way up Baker Street; both of them aware that Holmes's earlier concern about their irrelevancy was no longer warranted. The Inspector meant them to be a part of whatever investigation was undertaken of Sailor Mackenzie's death. Reentering 221B, they took pains to open and close doors as silently as they could so as not to wake their housekeeper. There was no need of caution. After setting aside Sir Edmund du Cane, Mrs. Hudson had fallen into a deep and restful sleep. It would stand her in good stead for the days ahead.

Chapter 3.
Lestrade's Dilemma

Watson slept uncharacteristically late the following morning. He dressed and again took up his medical journal, planning to revisit Professor Murri in hope of discovering his cure for hydrophobia, but found his attention drawn to the pungent aroma of bacon that had worked its way from Mrs. Hudson's kitchen to the sitting room he shared with Holmes. From long and pleasant experience, he knew where bacon sizzled, eggs would be frying, bread would be toasting, and sausage—perhaps even kippers—would be grilling. He had intended to wait on Holmes before going to breakfast, as much to check on his friend's condition as to share his company, but found himself feeling famished as well as burdened with a sudden responsibility to prepare Mrs. Hudson for Holmes's appearance.

Entering Mrs. Hudson's kitchen, he found his hopes for a hearty breakfast fulfilled up to and including a platter heaped with kippers, and his plans for preparing the housekeeper for Holmes's appearance unnecessary. Holmes sat at his accustomed place at the table, his state as apparent as Mrs. Hudson's intent to ignore it. His mouth and one eye were quite swollen, with the area around that eye now a perfect complement to his purple dressing gown. Watson decided to steer a middle ground between polite disregard for the obvious and the responsibility he felt for the medical well-being of his friend.

"Good morning, Holmes, Mrs. Hudson. I trust everyone slept well." Watson received a mumbled attempt at good cheer before continuing. "Mrs. Hudson, I believe you have outdone yourself this morning." Without taking his eyes from the substantial portion of fried eggs he was in the process of spooning onto his plate, he spoke as though inquiring about the day's weather. "I assume you've informed Mrs. Hudson of the events of the evening, Holmes?"

"I'd only gotten as far as explaining how I felt called upon to do battle with Sailor Mackenzie, and hadn't yet described the fight or its unfortunate outcome. I'd be pleased to have you report the rest, Watson. You have a way of adding color to stories in ways that seem to me unnecessary, but others appear to find appealing." With that, Holmes took a forkful of the piece of kipper he had cut in two, sliding it as inconspicuously as he was able into his unmarked right cheek.

"I can tell you, Mrs. Hudson, that Holmes gets full marks for his actions last night although it did lead to a terribly regrettable outcome." With that, Watson told of Holmes's response to the challenge thrown out by Sailor Mackenzie, of Holmes being knocked down, and of his rising from the floor to win the day, suggesting in the course of his narrative that it might be well for Watson to look him over after breakfast—"just as a precaution." He went on to describe the appearance of Lestrade, his confiscation of all drinking materials, and his intent to request an autopsy. He informed Mrs. Hudson that the Inspector planned to visit them later in the day, and would likely be requesting their assistance if there was reason to believe the boxer's death was other than accidental.

Mrs. Hudson raised her teacup and lowered it without drinking. "And you and the Inspector think there could be reason. Perhaps I should 'ear more about Mr. Mackenzie and all that went on last night. Let's start from when you first got to the Club, and leave nothin' out right to the time you started for 'ome."

For the next hour, both Holmes and Watson gave their views of the evening's events. Throughout, they were subjected to the probing questions and scowl of concentration they had long since come to expect from Mrs. Hudson. In the end, a picture emerged that left all of them anxious to hear Lestrade's report.

Unknown to the residents of 221B, Lestrade was every bit as anxious to share his findings as they were to receive them. After enduring the icy response his report drew from his superiors, Lestrade was convinced he would need Holmes's assistance if a proper course of action was to be taken. There was nothing unusual about his contacting Holmes for help in an investigation. He'd never said otherwise inside or outside the Yard. Holmes had a way of seeing things in ways Lestrade hadn't seen them before, and if he was honest about it—and he was—might never see them. But this was the first time he would need his help to make certain there was an investigation.

Within an hour of his meeting at the Yard, the Inspector was occupying an easy chair in the sitting room at 221B Baker Street, holding an armful of afternoon newspapers he now set on the table next to Holmes. The papers, he thought, might help persuade Holmes to provide the assistance Lestrade needed.

"Mr. Holmes, I thought you should know what's being reported about Mackenzie's death." The cause for Lestrade's caution was readily apparent. Each paper placed the fighter's death on its front page, and all of them detailed Holmes's role in his death. The *Globe* cried out: "Boxer Dies after Pounding from Famed Detective"; the *Evening News* chose alliteration: "Sleuth Slays Slugger at Sports Site"; while the *Evening Standard*, showing comparative restraint, announced: "Fighter Killed in Grudge Match at Gentlemen's Playground," and took fully three lines before naming Holmes as "the inflamed battler responsible for Mr. Mackenzie's death."

Lestrade fidgeted in respectful silence while Holmes grunted acknowledgement of each account. He spent little time reviewing the articles before passing the stack of papers to Watson, turning his head away as he did so as if avoiding a disagreeable odor. Watson devoted considerably more attention to the articles, his fierce squint suggesting he felt more strongly about their contents than his colleague. Both remained silent and it was left to Lestrade to comment about the materials he had shared.

"I'd keep an eye out for the scribblers, Mr. Holmes. I'm afraid, like it or not, you've become news, and you're likely to have some of those fellows tagging after you, wanting to pepper you with questions or maybe snap you with the cameras some of them have got."

Holmes fingered the swelling at his lip at the mention of cameras. Lestrade nodded an acknowledgement of Holmes's sensitivity. "Your Constable Chase is a good man. I'll ask him to shoo the reporters away from your doorstep, but it's likely they'll stay on the lookout for you, leastways until they come up with some new horror they think will sell papers."

Holmes shrugged his indifference. "I appreciate your concern, Lestrade, but I don't mean to let those fellows interfere with my life." Holmes accepted a cup of tea from Mrs. Hudson, who had entered noiselessly while the men were examining the newspapers. Lestrade looked to the diminutive housekeeper, nodded his gratitude for the cup of tea she offered, then beamed an appreciation for the raisin-filled scones and strawberry jam he sighted on the nearby table.

Then Lestrade did something he had never done before. He looked to the housekeeper and then to the door of the sitting room, took a sip of tea, looked back to the housekeeper and waited. However novel the action, Mrs. Hudson understood Lestrade's request. She picked up the empty tray, looked around to make certain the room was in order, and left mumbling something about a need to return to the kitchen.

As the door closed behind the housekeeper, Watson asked for the information he assumed Lestrade had come to share. "Tell me, Inspector, what is the word from the coroner?"

Lestrade growled his response. "There is no word, Doctor. And there'll be none—at least none beyond what I'm telling you now. There was an investigation of the water bucket and the bottles we took away from the National Sporting Club. Nothing suspicious was found in any of them. For that reason the decision was made *not* to do an autopsy." With that the Inspector took a sip of tea, bit off the corner of his scone, and waited for the expressions of astonishment he felt certain would be forthcoming. He did not have long to wait.

"I don't understand, Inspector," Watson began. "The condition of the man's body was enough to justify an autopsy regardless of what was found from the bottles and pail. And I know the Yard. They've put bodies across the medical examiner's table that were a lot less suspicious than Mackenzie's. What reason was given for this decision, Inspector?"

Lestrade looked to the door through which Mrs. Hudson had passed before speaking. When he did speak, it seemed as though the words were being torn from him. "What I've got to say is going to sound like I'm being critical of the Yard. I'm not. There's politics in every job and it's no different at the Yard. In fact, it's probably a lot better at the Yard. But when you've got a club with important people for members, some of them officers of the Crown, and some of them able to call on the Royal Family—well, that's where things can get complicated."

Lestrade leaned in toward Holmes as if he was about to share a confidence that could destroy his career—as indeed he was.

"Man to man, Mr. Holmes, I'd appreciate your help. Which is to say the Yard needs your help, but there's no one to ask for it except me. Mr. Mackenzie's death might be an accident like everyone wants to believe, but I've seen them as were poisoned looking too much like Mr. Mackenzie not to wonder about it, no matter what was in his bottles and pail. I had the impression you had the same thought, Doctor." Watson looked up from the writing he had begun to give the Inspector a small nod of agreement. Small though it was, it was enough to strengthen the Inspector's resolve.

"There's an investigation that needs doing. If you were to see your way clear on this, Mr. Holmes, there'd be no one to stop you, what with your having a personal interest in knowing exactly what happened to Sailor Mackenzie. As far as anybody was to know, you'd be asking questions to satisfy your own curiosity. And I'm wanting you to ask those questions."

Having made his plea, the Inspector sank back against the couch's cushion, his lips a tight line as he waited on his host's answer. He had never before expressed such traitorous thoughts to anyone and doubtless never would again. Holmes and Watson exchanged a look that made clear their awareness of the conspiracy they now shared with Lestrade. It was a glance, nothing more, but it allowed a common understanding of Lestrade's plight, and of the response they believed was owed their frequent colleague.

"Of course, Lestrade, I'll do whatever I can to be of assistance to you—and to the Yard."

Lestrade looked to Holmes for a long moment, then to the bear rug between them, finally engaging in a brief period of throat clearing before he looked again to Holmes. When he spoke, his voice sounded the relief he felt.

"Thank you, Mr. Holmes. And I know the Yard will thank you in its own good time. I'll explain things so it's understood you've got your own reasons for looking into Mackenzie's death. You might want to know I've asked Mr. Trent and his people to stay in London one more day so I can finish getting statements from all of them. Mr. Trent will be at Lord Lonsdale's home in London and all the others, meaning the Cochrane boy, his father and the two men who were with Mr. Mackenzie at the fight, are all staying at the Sporting Club—should you find reason for wanting to talk to them." Lestrade stopped to light the pipe he had filled with the tobacco Holmes offered, and took a long draw before continuing. "I'll leave the rest to you, Mr. Holmes. I'll stay in touch of course, and you can tell me if there's anything you need." He took the hat and stick he had placed next to him and rose to leave. "And I won't forget to talk to Constable Chase about shooing the reporters away."

With that, the Inspector shook hands with Watson as solemnly as their secret agreement seemed to demand, then turned to Holmes, opened his mouth to say something further, appeared to think better of it, and settled instead for a prolonged handshake before making his way to the stairs. He smiled broadly to Mrs. Hudson as he passed her on the landing below. Holmes and Watson meanwhile looked to each other, wordlessly sharing a single thought—what would be Mrs. Hudson's reaction to their decision to investigate Sailor Mackenzie's death with no client other than an unappreciative Scotland Yard, and without even the certainty of a crime having been committed.

For a second time, the three members of the consulting detective agency gathered in Mrs. Hudson's kitchen. Watson read from the detailed notes he had taken during Lestrade's visit, making clear his own disappointment with the Yard's decision to forego an autopsy, then beginning a justification for the action he and Holmes had taken without seeking consultation. "There is something more you should know," he said, but got no further.

"You've told the Inspector you'll do what you can to learn what really 'appened to Mr. Mackenzie."

Watson's eyes widened and words failed him before a knowing smile stole across his face. He had traveled this road before. "That is correct, Mrs. Hudson."

She shrugged her acceptance of the situation. "That's fine. It was the right thing to do."

Holmes groaned softly, and Watson raised the question Holmes would have gone to his grave without asking. "But how did you know that, Mrs. Hudson?"

There was a second shrug. "A combination of things, Doctor. There was 'is comin' 'ere fresh from a meetin' with 'is people at the Yard lookin' like 'is dog and 'is best friend just died together. Somethin' terrible 'appened at that meetin' to get the Inspector that much out of sorts, and what could that be except 'e didn't get the answers 'e was lookin' for. When 'e wanted me to leave so only the two of you would know what 'e 'ad to say, it could only mean 'e wanted to talk about goin' against whatever was decided at 'is meetin', which is to say 'e wanted to talk about goin' against 'is superiors. And then, when 'e left just now, 'e was the Inspector we're used to seein' only a little more so. That could only be because you promised you'd 'elp 'im with whatever was causin' 'is troubles. And when you told me there's to be no autopsy of Mr. Mackenzie, which means of course there's to be no investigation of 'is death by the Yard, it was clear what was causin' 'is troubles and what you agreed to do." With that, the housekeeper pushed back from the table. "I believe the tea is ready. Will you be wantin' the rest of the scones?" The two men mumbled assent as Mrs. Hudson made her way to the stove.

With cups refilled, the raisin-filled scones set between them, and Mrs. Hudson again seated across from the two men, it was time to begin the investigation promised Lestrade. Watson withdrew his accounts book and pencil from his waistcoat, while Holmes relit the pipe he had allowed to lose fire and screwed his face into a stare of fierce concentration.

"Let's begin with what we know and see what it is we need to know." Mrs. Hudson took a long sip of tea and set the cup firmly back in place on its saucer. "Mr. Mackenzie died after 'is fight with Mr. 'Olmes in what's bein' called an accident by the doctor at the boxin' club and by Scotland Yard. Why should we think it's anythin' different?"

Mrs. Hudson answered her own question as her audience knew she would. "There's first of all the question of whether one or even two solid blows could kill an experienced fighter like Mr. Mackenzie." Holmes's unsoiled eye widened and his purpled eye struggled to follow suit. Mrs. Hudson responded to his unspoken dissent. "With respect, Mr. 'Olmes, this was a man who made a livin' takin' and givin' punches and was doin' it for a great many years. No, Mr. 'Olmes, even knowin' your boxin' skills, there could be a problem thinkin' it was the blows alone that did in Mr. Mackenzie. And then we've got the other things you reported.

"There's the look of Mr. Mackenzie when 'e went down. Dr. Watson, I believe you reported 'e looked to be in pain, was curled up with both 'is fists to 'is stomach. I wouldn't be surprised if you saw a little bit of throw-up as well." She got a look from Watson that made clear her surmise was justified. "I don't want to get ahead of ourselves, but I wonder if we might be lookin' at the effects of a poison that didn't cause Mr. Mackenzie to die right away, and whose action was maybe 'elped along by the battlin' with you, Mr. 'Olmes, and with the other young man. Of course, any such poison would 'ave 'ad to be given to Mr. Mackenzie some way outside of the bottles the Yard 'as analyzed."

Watson responded to the housekeeper with a wary eye to Holmes, "I believe poison is a distinct possibility, Mrs. Hudson. As I look back at it, Mackenzie showed several of the signs. He was sweating heavily before the first fight even started, and he showed what I would now call labored breathing throughout the evening. Then there's the staggering during both of his fights. I thought at the time it was due to his clumsy style or perhaps he'd been drinking before the fight.

55

Taken together with how he lay after being hit by Holmes, it's a very real possibility something more is involved even if nothing was found in the bottles."

"And now we know there's somethin' besides the bottles that bears lookin' into," Mrs. Hudson added. "As I remember it, Dr. Watson, you said that according to Mr. Trent, Mr. Mackenzie was never without 'is flask of Scotch whiskey. But there's been nothin' said about a flask. Now I find that a whole lot more than curious. If 'e was always carryin' a flask, and if 'e was known for 'avin' a problem with drink, it only stands to reason it's the flask that could be the way to get poison into 'im if someone 'ad a mind to. And then there's the two of you seein' somebody leavin' the changin' room just when you were gettin' to it. Was that someone comin' to get the flask before anybody could find it? And since we also know from Mr. Trent that Mr. Mackenzie tried to keep the flask 'idden from folk, there's question whether that someone succeeded in findin' the flask or might 'ave gotten scared off by you, meanin' the flask is still there."

Watson paused in his writing. "You have a plan in mind, Mrs. Hudson." It was not a question; it was a statement of what he knew to be fact.

"I do, Dr. Watson. We'll be wantin' to be in two places tomorrow, and we'll need to organize ourselves to get it done." Mrs. Hudson looked to her colleagues' puzzled expressions and elaborated on her thinking. "We've only got tomorrow to get to the people the Inspector is keepin' in town, and we'll also want to get up to where Mr. Mackenzie was stayin' in Yorkshire and 'ave ourselves a look around there. We can talk about all that later. Just for now, I believe I'll take a trip over to the National Sportin' Club to make a search of the changin' room on behalf of Mr. 'Olmes, who thinks 'e may 'ave left a pocket watch behind what with all the excitement of last evenin'."

Chapter 4.
Mrs. Hudson Investigates

Mrs. Hudson did not reveal to her colleagues her intention to take the Underground to the National Sporting Club. She would travel from Baker Street station to Charing Cross. It would leave her with a half mile walk to Covent Garden, but would save the firm nearly four shillings over the cost of a hansom. Besides which, after a passing shower, it had turned into a fine summer's day, and a brisk walk would get the blood circulating and clear her mind. She placed coins and a handkerchief in her reticule, and after first patting her hair in place, she set over it the blue-ribboned hat that had been Tobias's favorite.

At Charing Cross, a small crowd of exiting passengers breezed past her as she made her way up Villers Street. Somber young men in somber dark dress led the charge as they made their way with grim purpose to the Charing Cross Hospital, where they would study medicine under the watchful eye of older men whose private carriages had earlier deposited them at the hospital's front door. Some few nurses trailed more slowly behind, distinctive in their milk white aprons with matching cuffs and collars worn over blue dresses with great puffy sleeves, and small triangular hats perched in the very center of their upswept hair. They were joined by a smattering of businessmen in soft homburgs and frock coats, and a larger number of workmen in great floppy caps, muslin shirts and rumpled trousers that had seen a great many, but no better days.

Approaching the Strand, Mrs. Hudson could hear the clacking and snorting of horses, and the angry shouts of coachmen even before she could see the traffic clogging one of London's major thoroughfares. Turning onto the Strand, the sounds attached themselves to hansoms, four-wheelers, and horse-cars noisily competing for space and riders. The men in soft homburgs grew in number, and there now appeared women in long flounced dresses with short jackets and a rich variety of millinery. There were wide- and narrow-brimmed hats, most of them high-crowned, some appearing to contain an entire bird and nest, some limited to the bird's feathers, all of them in colors designed to simultaneously complement and brighten the rest of each woman's outfit. None of them took notice of the woman they hurried past, nor did she pay attention to them.

There being no sweepers interested in an older woman of apparently modest means, Mrs. Hudson picked her way across the Strand carefully avoiding evidence of the street's horse traffic. She continued her travels down Bedford Street past the tea-dealers, drapers, lace-men and upholsterers whose shops lined the way to King Street where she turned east past St. Paul's Church, ending her journey finally at 43 King Street and the National Sporting Club. With no liveried doorman to challenge her entry, Mrs. Hudson strode to the front door and leaned her weight against its bell.

The porter who answered her ring looked to Mrs. Hudson, then beyond her as if finding it inconceivable the short stub of a woman was the sole cause of interruption to his day. He pushed back the shock of dark hair that had fallen across his forehead when her ring wakened him to his watchman duties, and spoke without moving from the threshold he blocked with his slender frame.

"Do you have some business here, ma'am?" The porter's tone made clear the impossibility of an affirmative response.

Mrs. Hudson straightened to her full, if unimpressive height. "Good day to you. I'm Mrs. 'Udson, 'ousekeeper to Mr. Sherlock 'Olmes and I am 'ere at 'is express request. Mr. 'Olmes, as you may know, was 'ere last evenin' as a guest of Lord Lonsdale, and was a participant in the fisticuffs your people seem to enjoy. Mr. 'Olmes believes 'e may 'ave left a pocket watch in the room where the men get into their fightin' clothes, and 'as asked me to learn if it's been found and, if not, to look for it myself."

The doorman grunted his recognition of the names carefully inserted by Mrs. Hudson. "Well, I suppose that's all right then. If you'll come with me, I'll look to see if there's a watch what's been turned in." He opened the door wide enough to admit the housekeeper and led her across the center hall, their footsteps echoing throughout the empty lobby. He stopped at a door half hidden by ferns and a life-sized statue of one of the several nymphs keeping watch over the entry area. The statue's barely obscured and generously sculpted charms were sufficient to cause Mrs. Hudson to develop an intense interest in the room's marble columns and extensive plant life.

The porter fumbled through his keys, coming at last to the one he found appropriate. He waved for her to follow as he entered a small windowless room containing a roll-top desk that appeared to have come to its final resting place after passing through a downward spiral of users, and an armless chair that did not match in style, but was otherwise well suited to the much abused desk. He selected a box from one drawer of the desk and rummaged through it in search of the non-existent watch. Achieving the inevitable failure, he scowled his disappointment, and began the process all over again, this time with painstaking care. Mrs. Hudson made a show of patient hopefulness, aware that naming both his employer and her lodger had stimulated his pointlessly thorough search. Finishing his second rifling of the box's contents, the porter's scowl deepened and he hunched still lower over the unyielding box. Fearing a third or even fourth search could be in the offing, Mrs. Hudson offered an alternative plan of action.

"I believe you've given it a fine look as I will certainly make clear to Mr. 'Olmes. I'm just now thinkin' it's so recent that 'e lost the watch, it could still be in the room where 'e changed 'is clothes."

The porter grunted, but didn't relax the scowl he directed at the box. When he was satisfied the box had been sufficiently chastised, he turned to face her. "You could be right, but the changing room is off limits on account of Sailor Mackenzie's dying." For a moment he remained committed to protecting the sanctity of the vacant corridor, and Mrs. Hudson thought she might need yet another ploy if she was to see the inside of the changing room. But then the porter took a deep breath, made his face into a fierce squint of resolve, and declared his opinion that since it was Mr. Holmes, he was certain he could make an exception. He led Mrs. Hudson from the room and proceeded down the narrow hallway, turned a corner at its end and continued on, leaving Mrs. Hudson the task of keeping pace with his rapid strides. He stopped at a flight of stairs leading to the floor below, looked back to make certain the housekeeper could see where he was headed, then disappeared from her sight.

The next time Mrs. Hudson caught sight of him, the porter was standing outside the room to which Lord Lonsdale had proudly led Holmes and Watson less than 24 hours earlier. The porter's scowl had deepened, its object now someone or something inside the changing room. When he spoke, it was apparent the object of his displeasure was someone.

"May I ask what you're doing here, Mr. Cochrane. You know full well this here is off limits to everybody that ain't the police. It was Lord Lonsdale's express wish you was to remain upstairs, excepting to take your meals or if you was called for."

Mrs. Hudson arrived at the doorway in time to see the large sandy-haired man who had been Rochester Cochrane's manager the night before, and was now, as he began to explain, fulfilling his more familiar role as Rochester Cochrane's father. "I beg your pardon, Mr. Overby. I beg your pardon I'm sure. But I only come for my boy. I was remembering there was medicines down here, and he's needing liniment something awful. If you can direct me to it, I'll be happy to get back upstairs to him. In fact, I'm wanting to get back if I can only take him something to ease the pain he's feeling." Mr. Cochrane screwed his own face into a semblance of the pain he reported his son to be having, while he waited for the porter to relieve both their afflictions. He seemed to take no notice of the diminutive woman next to Mr. Overby, nor did Mr. Overby feel any greater need to introduce Mr. Cochrane to the housekeeper than he had felt to introduce himself to her.

"All of the medicines are on the shelf right next to where you're standing. You'll find the liniments there. Take a bottle for now, but make sure you return what you don't use. You can leave it with me or Mr. Beschner if it's him what's on duty when you're finished." Having delivered the lecture he believed appropriate, Mr. Overby discovered he had a problem. No one was to be allowed anywhere in the building without supervision. Both Lord Lonsdale and Mr. Fleming had been quite firm on that point. But he couldn't oversee the movements of both Mr. Cochrane and Mrs. Hudson unless he first took the two of them upstairs to the dormitory, and then came back downstairs with Mrs. Hudson. With the speed the woman traveled, he'd be all day going back and forth for no good reason he could see. Mr. Fleming wouldn't be arriving at the Club for at least two hours and would be none the wiser if he left the woman by herself. She was surely harmless.

"I'll just go back upstairs with you, Mr. Cochrane, and I'll leave you here to look for Mr. Holmes's pocket watch, Mrs. Hudson, but I'll ask you not to disturb things and not to leave the room until I get back, which I promise will be very soon." Having made clear to Mrs. Hudson the futility of attempting to make off with an Indian club or medicine ball, he nodded permission for Mr. Cochrane to proceed, then followed the coachman, liniment now in hand, down the corridor while Mrs. Hudson set about searching the room for the missing flask.

The room provided little opportunity for deception. The wardrobe stood open and bare. It was flush to the ground so there was no way to get anything beneath it, and close enough to the wall to make it almost as difficult to get anything behind it. Moreover, there were no marks along the floor to suggest the wardrobe had been moved. The two long tables were equally bare, and would stay that way until the next time fighters used them to sit on, lie on, or be lain upon. That left the shelves holding the gloves and clothing the fighters would need to enter the ring, and the healing agents and restoratives they would need upon their return.

Mrs. Hudson patted down the folded and stacked boxing tights and found nothing; the collection of gloves and rolled up towels offered promise, but it was a promise that went similarly unfulfilled. She ignored the rolled up stockings that were too small and too well spaced to permit a flask to be hidden among them, as well as the shoes that weren't broad enough to allow a flask to be hidden inside them. She looked past the bottles, the collection of powders, syrups, pills and plasters, among which nothing as large as a flask could disappear, then turned to the laundry pile pressed into the corner of a shelf, and attacked the mound of clothing with a vigor borne of awareness that her mistrustful guide would be returning soon.

The prize lay within a pair of tights stuffed inside a second pair in the apparent hope of hiding its bulge. The flask was silver-colored, without ornamentation, and typical of those appearing increasingly in shop windows. The only writing on it were the initials SIM just below its lid. She slipped the flask into her reticule and drew the purse strings to hide it from view. She was bent low inspecting the floor of the wardrobe when Mr. Overby returned to give her his undivided attention. She shook her head and offered the porter her best hangdog expression as she voiced frustration at not finding Mr. Holmes's pocket watch. He screwed his face into an imitation of sympathy, held it for the shortest time he felt obliged to show compassion, and then reported his need to get the Club ready for Mr. Fleming. Mrs. Hudson nodded her understanding of the porter's responsibilities, and allowed him to show her the way to the Club's front door.

It was late afternoon before Mrs. Hudson had retraced her steps and arrived back at Baker Street. She decreed it time for tea and joined the men in their sitting room. She reported the events of her day, emphasizing the unexpected appearance of Mr. Cochrane in the changing room, and her success in locating the flask which she removed from her reticule with a flourish worthy of a music hall magician. She handed the flask to Watson who held it gingerly as if this, their only clue, might come apart in his hands if not handled with great care.

"I'm wonderin' if we can call on one of your medical colleagues to tell us what's inside of this. I'd ask you to use your chemistry know-'ow, Mr. 'Olmes, but I'm thinkin' it would be best for you to travel to Yorkshire just as soon as possible. You can express your sympathies to Mrs. Mackenzie, and find out what's been goin' on at Mr. Trent's estate. I know you're not wantin' to be much in public until you're back to your old self, so I'm thinkin' you might make do with one of those dress-up affairs you do so well—at least until you're out of London. After you get to Yorkshire you'll be seein' more sheep than people, besides which Mr. Trent's staff will all 'ave 'eard about your fight and expect to see you marked up some."

Holmes made no reply. The prospect of leaving London in disguise made Mrs. Hudson's plan nearly palatable, but he was not yet prepared to appear accommodating.

Uncertain about his friend's thinking, Watson hurried to fill the silence. "I'm sure my old friend, Spooner, at the Medical College, will be intrigued by the task of analyzing the flask's contents. You've heard me speak of him, Holmes. He heads their toxicology lab and is quite well thought of." Watson had gotten as far as unscrewing the lid to peer into the flask's depths. Although he held it nearly erect, some of the liquid still ran over its neck and onto the sitting room floor. "Good, there's more than enough here for Spooner to analyze." Mrs. Hudson grunted acknowledgement of Watson's finding while she went to get a cloth from Holmes's worktable to clean up his discovery.

When her work was done, Mrs. Hudson seated herself again, holding on to the damp cloth she was certain her boarders would otherwise use to wipe glasses, plates and anything else that seemed in need of a quick substitute for cleaning. "We'll get the flask to your friend, Dr. Spooner, tomorrow, and see about gettin' to the people in town and in Yorkshire. It will be a busy day, but we've no other choice. For now, I'll fix us a nice dinner, after which you gentlemen will want a pipe, and I'll 'ave my tea and a bit of a sit-down with Professor Galton and 'is *Patterns in Thumb and Finger Marks* which I can tell you 'as got some very advanced ideas about investigation. Tomorrow, we'll 'ave an early breakfast and talk about what we'll doin' for the next few days. That way, we can at least 'ave one last quiet evening."

The quiet evening on which Mrs. Hudson planned lasted until nearly 3 a.m.

Chapter 5.
Lillie Langtry Needs Protection

From somewhere a bell was pealing its joyful announcement as a smiling young woman walked beneath a garland-entwined arch and into a sunlit world hand in hand with a proud and serious man wearing the helmet and uniform of the Metropolitan Police. They left a church without walls or pews or congregation, only a white-clothed table and the shadowy figure of a minister clutching his Bible, a cross hanging free in mid-air above him. The couple ran ahead on a manicured carpet of green sloping gently to a sea of perfect blue, where a clipper ship with billowing white sails waited them as its only passengers. A beaming captain waved greeting from the ship's rail as the couple raced toward him. But try as they might, the couple couldn't reach the smiling captain and the waiting ship. The young man ran ahead, the field of green giving way for him as it would not for the woman. Without words he promised to hold the ship for the two of them, but the captain could not wait, and the joyful pealing gave way to a steady tolling as the ship, the proud constable and the smiling captain became lost to sight. The woman kept running even as the sea itself began to disappear. And then the tolling of bells sounded as a chime, and the chime came finally to sound as the ringing of the bell at the front door of 221B Baker Street. Mrs. Hudson shook herself free of sleep; the young woman and her proud constable were now gone from view, and in another instant they slipped from memory.

Mrs. Hudson pulled the dressing gown from where it lay at the foot of her bed, wrapped it tight around her ruffled nightgown and crossed to the parlor window. With the aid of the street lamp, she could see the yellow carriage that yesterday had amused Holmes and embarrassed Watson. The coachman sat atop its box in stiff silhouette holding in check

65

chestnuts of exactly 15 hands, two inches, while a footman stood at attention beside its door; man and beast outfitted in a brilliant yellow, the spectacle wasted on empty streets.

Mrs. Hudson hurried to the door, stopping for just an instant to frown her acknowledgement of the older woman with gray hair hanging in unkempt strands framed in the parlor glass. She opened the door to admit Lord Lonsdale and whatever crisis had caused him to pay Mr. Holmes a visit at an hour when all of respectable London was home in bed. Mrs. Hudson looked to the grave countenance of the Earl of Lonsdale for only an instant as her attention was drawn, as the attention of many thousands before her had been drawn, to the woman leaning on his arm, the woman widely acclaimed the most beautiful in all of England. Although now 38, and no longer the frequent companion of the Prince of Wales, the violet-blue eyes, softly pouting mouth, creamy complexion, and the high-breasted, narrow-waisted figure, all told in a moment of Lillie Langtry's enduring capacity to entice even the most happily married of men, and to strike jealousy and fear into the hearts of even the most confident and attractive of wives. Mrs. Hudson stepped back to allow her guests entry into the parlor. Lord Lonsdale gave the housekeeper a curt nod while the Jersey Lily gave her a warm smile. Introductions were neither made nor requested. In fact, Lord Lonsdale wasn't certain of the housekeeper's name and had, in any event, come to see her lodgers, one in particular.

"I apologize for the hour, madam, but I must see Mr. Holmes. May I impose on you to tell him Lord Lonsdale and Mrs. Lillie Langtry wish to see him on a matter of great urgency. It would be desirable for Dr. Watson to join us as well. And might I trouble you for water or perhaps something stronger. Brandy would be excellent if you have it."

"I'll do what I can, Your Lordship. Might I ask you to take seats in the parlor while I see to Mr. 'Olmes and what we 'ave in the way of refreshments."

There was again a nod and a smile as the two accepted the housekeeper's invitation. Mrs. Hudson stayed long enough to help Lillie out of her jacket, to take the Earl's hat and stick, and to look the Jersey Lily to the couch and Lord Lonsdale to one of the three parlor chairs.

As it happened, it was unnecessary for Mrs. Hudson to climb the stairs to her lodgers' apartments. The opening and closing of doors had awakened Holmes, and he stood on the landing outside the sitting room he shared with Watson, the bottoms of a nightshirt visible beneath his dressing gown as he called to the housekeeper for an explanation. Lonsdale brushed past Mrs. Hudson, positioning himself in the entry hall where he would be visible to Holmes, and without explanation asked the bleary-eyed figure on the landing above to join him as quickly as he could, unnecessarily adding there was a problem needing his attention.

Holmes went in search of Watson while Mrs. Hudson went in search of the brandy she knew to be somewhere far to the back of a shelf in her pantry. She kept it available for medicinal purposes in a house in which illness was nearly unknown. She put up tea as well, certain that her lodgers would want a cup in view of the hour. Mrs. Hudson arrived with the well-aged liquor and four glasses at the same time as Holmes and Watson appeared in her parlor. Both men wore dressing gowns over their nightshirts, and sheepish looks they were unable to dispel as they were introduced to Mrs. Langtry. Their guest appeared to take no notice of their dress or its lack, but she stared a moment longer than was polite at Holmes's battered face. Although prepared for the sight by the Earl, the reality overwhelmed her imagining.

If Lonsdale took any note of their discomfort he did not show it. He poured a small glass of brandy for Lillie, and dangled the bottle toward Holmes and Watson, both of whom shook off his offer of Mrs. Hudson's liquor. He then poured himself a glass, gulped it down in a swallow, and began an explanation of his arrival at an hour he acknowledged to be unseemly.

"I apologize for this imposition, Holmes. I fully realize the extent of disruption I am creating for your entire household." Lonsdale looked grimly from Holmes to Watson, each of whom stared grimly back. "I feel certain you'll agree to its necessity when I describe the circumstances that have brought us here."

"Before Hugh begins, Mr. Holmes, Dr. Watson, I want to add my own apologies for this intrusion and thank you for your hospitality, whatever the evening's outcome." The voice was velvet in keeping with the two men's expectations and wishes.

"Yes, absolutely, thank you, Lillie." The Earl grunted his acknowledgement of the amenities he had ignored before returning to his theme. Mrs. Hudson had come to stand in the doorway between her kitchen and parlor, all the chairs in the parlor having been taken. She lingered for only a moment as Lillie Langtry patted a cushion on the couch and smiled an invitation to join her. Lonsdale took no notice, his attention fixed on the figure in the purple dressing gown whose lanky frame overhung the parlor chair he had chosen.

"As I was starting to explain, Holmes, Lillie—Mrs. Langtry—came to see me less than an hour ago to make certain she would be safe from … I'm sorry, Lillie … from that unspeakable bully and scoundrel, George Baird."

The unspeakable bully and scoundrel, George Baird, was well known to the three members of the Earl's audience, although none of them would have had the ill manners to describe him as such. Lillie Langtry had, for reasons known only to her, become the mistress of the brash Scotsman who liked to be addressed as Squire, and strived for recognition as one of London's leading sportsmen. His inheritance of ironworks in Glasgow, and of lands rich in coal in the south of England, had allowed him to achieve the former; his violently unpredictable nature had denied him the latter. Nonetheless, he continued to pursue his objective by maintaining stables of moderately successful racehorses and moderately accomplished boxers. His fighters provided him entertainment, as well as assistance in extricating himself from the difficulties that can befall a small but pugnacious man with a deep and abiding thirst. Unfortunately for Baird, his fighters were not always available, and given his disregard for rules of combat or the gender of his opponent, the Squire spent occasional evenings sobering up as the guest of London and provincial constabularies. His behavior had led to ostracism from polite society and the shunning of Lillie Langtry. Her status as someone's mistress was not objectionable, her status as George Baird's mistress was. Indeed, only two of her former companions excepted themselves from the rest of respectable society in this regard. Lord Lonsdale was one and the Prince of Wales was the other.

"The Squire has managed to get himself arrested for one of his altercations. He made the mistake of assaulting a … lady who was not aware of his identity and swore out a complaint before his goons had opportunity to threaten her, which has led to his confinement for at least the evening. This all happened after Mrs. Langtry locked the Squire out of her home on Cork Street because of his drinking and the threats he was making. We can be certain that when he is released from custody, he will seek revenge, which is why Mrs. Langtry came to me. Her maid was so frightened she ran off and I doubt will be heard from again. I would have happily provided the protection needed except it happens that Lady Lonsdale is in town for the week to do shopping. Lady Lonsdale is an extraordinarily gracious woman and a fine hostess, but of course I could not ask her to entertain Mrs. Langtry, and the hour does not permit me to arrange for her stay at one of my country homes. That's why I've come to you, Holmes. Baird won't think of looking for Lillie here, and even if he somehow did learn where she's staying, I know she'd be safe under your protection."

Mrs. Hudson eased herself from the couch, mumbled a request to be excused to get tea, and wondered if Dr. Watson would "lend some assistance with the crockery we'll be needin'." Only Lillie Langtry nodded recognition of the housekeeper's departure, and only Holmes took notice of her closing the pocket door between the parlor and kitchen.

When she and Dr. Watson returned with the promised tea as well as the few scones remaining from the afternoon, Lillie had just finished heaping praise on Lonsdale for his intercession, favoring the Earl with a warm smile that amply rewarded any sacrifice on his part. Mrs. Hudson poured tea for her lodgers and guests with the exception of Lonsdale who poured himself another brandy while belatedly waving off Lillie's tribute, and insisting his action was nothing more than anyone might have done. Holmes rejected the Earl's confidence in the courage of others, while separating himself from those pusillanimous others.

Having heard her situation described by the Earl, Lillie thought it time to speak for herself, with particular regard to her choice of companions. "Mr. Holmes, I hope you won't think poorly of me for the friends I've chosen. George can be a wonderfully generous and attentive man, but I'm afraid he does have a temper and can act emotionally as Hugh suggests. You may have read of my having once been the target of one of George's unfortunate outbursts." Indeed, all London had read of the Squire following Lillie Langtry to Paris, where he first savaged the young man who had accompanied her on a shopping expedition in that city, then turned his attention to Lillie and her accommodations, placing her in a Parisian hospital and destroying the hotel suite in which she had been staying.

"I had read something of that, yes."

"It's not something I expect to see repeated, but I agree

with Hugh it's just as well I stay away from George until he has had time to gather himself. If you can find it agreeable, I think it shouldn't be for more than a day or two." Again, the striking woman lavished her smile on all three of her hosts. "I am certain George will be himself by then."

No one expressed support for Lillie's optimism about the speed with which George would "be himself" or the desirability of that state, but it was left to the housekeeper to become the group's spokesperson. "You shouldn't concern yourself about the time, Mrs. Langtry. I'm sure we can accommodate you for as long as wanted."

Lillie Langtry beamed her gratitude and grasped Mrs. Hudson's hand where it lay in her lap, causing the housekeeper's cheeks to redden. It occurred to Lonsdale that the woman whose name he couldn't quite recall was not just the housekeeper who gave him entry and served him tea, but was in fact the landlady of the lodgings. "Ma'am, I thank you as well for that kindness. And I must insist on your allowing me to reimburse you for the inconvenience your kindness is bound to create."

Mrs. Hudson nodded her gratitude to the Earl before answering. "It's most kind of Your Lordship, but not at all necessary I assure you. There's no inconvenience to it. It will be a pleasure and an 'onor to 'ave an actress of Mrs. Langtry's quality stayin' under our roof." The housekeeper paused and adopted a look of concern she directed to Holmes. "I'm just afraid this will be upsettin' your plans to pay respects to Mrs. Mackenzie, Mr. 'Olmes."

Holmes looked to Mrs. Hudson with eyes widened. He recognized he was being led somewhere, but had no idea where. He knew, as well, that whatever the path he would be taking, it had been mapped out moments earlier since Mrs. Hudson had never before required assistance to carry dishes the 30 feet from her kitchen to the parlor. Watson took up the thread of Mrs. Hudson's concern and led Holmes a little further on his mysterious journey.

"There's one thing further I believe we need to consider. While I concur entirely with having Mrs. Langtry take sanctuary with us, I think we must examine just how secure our lodgings will actually be. As you have said, Lord Lonsdale, there aren't that many people of courage on whom to rely, and it is well known you are a loyal friend to Mrs. Langtry. With that in mind, we need to recognize that members of your staff are aware not only of Mrs. Langtry's visit to you tonight, but of your transporting her to these Baker Street lodgings. Moreover, those who are not already aware of the evening's events will surely become so in a very few hours. Without questioning the loyalty of your people, Lord Lonsdale, it is not beyond reason to think of Baird directing his stable of toughs to locate members of your staff on their day out, or when running an errand, or even at the servants' entrance to your home, and forcing one of them to reveal Mrs. Langtry's location. As Mrs. Langtry has reminded us, Baird's determined search for Mrs. Langtry would not be without precedent."

The Earl picked up, then set down the bottle of brandy he alone seemed intent on finishing. "It's a fair point, Doctor. It's true as well that Baird is like a spoiled child who'll do whatever he thinks it will take to get what he wants and, as you say, he has the goons at his disposal to do significant harm to any who get in his way. I'm sorry, Lillie, but it's well for us to be honest about what we're getting into." The hard lines around the Earl's mouth softened, but did not disappear as he fixed attention on his adopted charge before turning back to Watson. "I'm not clear what you're proposing, Doctor. "Are you saying the situation is simply too dangerous for you to get involved?" He looked from Watson to Holmes as he raised the question.

Watson waved away any such interpretation. "Quite the contrary, Lord Lonsdale. I know I speak for all of us in saying we are prepared to offer these lodgings and ourselves by way of protecting Mrs. Langtry now and for as long as necessary. That's not where the difficulty lies. The difficulty lies in locating a refuge for Mrs. Langtry that will give the greatest assurance of her continued safety."

Lonsdale grunted his acknowledgement of Watson's point, and turned to the one person in the room he felt capable of resolving the dilemma they faced. "What do you make of all this, Holmes?"

Holmes's furrowed brow and fierce squint appeared to Lonsdale and Lillie evidence the detective was considering every nuance of the discussion in preparation for leading them out of the wilderness of conflicting ideas. Watson and Mrs. Hudson knew the furrowed brow and fierce squint signaled that Holmes was deep into the wilderness and would need assistance finding his way out.

Holmes responded to the Earl with words carefully chosen to buy time until that assistance arrived. "Let me first echo the concern that has been spoken for Mrs. Langtry's safety." He favored the Jersey Lily with a look of appropriate compassion. "Be assured there is no one in this room who would not embrace the opportunity to offer protection without regard to the odds. The dilemma comes in knowing how best to go about guaranteeing the success of our actions." Holmes paused with the intent of allowing Watson opportunity to speak Mrs. Hudson's solution to that dilemma. While Watson considered the words needed to pose the housekeeper's proposal, an echo of their kitchen conversation sounded from an unexpected source.

"I agree, Mr. Holmes, and since I am responsible for that dilemma, I'd like to offer a suggestion." Lillie Langtry leaned forward from her position on the couch. The warm smile had been replaced by a look of earnest resolve. "While Mr. Trent is staying with you, Hugh, would you think it amiss to propose to him that I visit his estate in Oxley for a few days?

I know him to be a man of honor and if it is found agreeable, only Mr. Trent needs to know of our plans. His estate is so far from London and in such a remote place, I'm sure no one could possibly discover my whereabouts."

There were grave nods of assent from the members of Baker Street's consulting detective agency. Only Lonsdale seemed to hesitate a moment as if a stray thought had crossed his mind before he, too, joined the group's approval of Lillie's suggestion. It was left to Watson to express the additional concern that would pave the way for the full elaboration of Mrs. Hudson's plan.

"There is just one more thing, Mrs. Langtry. It's a small point, but you mentioned that your maid is no longer with you. I wonder if we shouldn't set about finding you a suitable replacement. It seems to me it would be good to have someone available to you if only for appearances—a lady such as yourself would be expected to be traveling with her maid. More importantly, a personal maid would provide you an ally should you need to send a message or have cause to seek assistance without drawing the Trents or any of their staff into the situation." Watson paused while the only person in the room capable of being transformed into a lady's maid sipped cold tea for effect rather than comfort.

"I recognize the magnitude of the request I'm about to make, and it's only the dire nature of the situation that leads me to raise it." Watson's face reflected the deep regret his words suggested. "Mrs. Hudson, I put it to you that you are in a unique position to be of assistance. I wonder if you could, for the short time needed, act as Mrs. Langtry's maid."

Mrs. Langtry looked warily to the housekeeper, waiting her reaction. All eyes followed Mrs. Langtry's to Mrs. Hudson who took another sip of cold tea before answering. "Well, of course, if all you gentlemen, and you, ma'am, believe it to be 'elpful, I'll be 'appy to do my part."

Lonsdale beamed his appreciation to Mrs. Hudson.

"Excellent! I will speak to Trent first thing in the morning about our plans. I'm certain he'll agree." With that, Lonsdale took a bite of the scone he had selected and his broad smile turned to wonder. "And are you also the author of these delicious scones?" His question elicited a blush and a nod from the housekeeper. "This is something I *won't* be speaking about to Trent. I told him the raisin scones he served at breakfast were the finest I'd ever had, but yours have them beat flat out. I give you fair warning, Holmes, when all this is done, I mean to be back here to steal your good woman if I possibly can." Holding his prize aloft as if to protect it from being snatched by others, Lonsdale went to tell his footman to fetch the chest Lillie had packed in the course of her hasty retreat from Cork Street.

It was quickly agreed that all needed their sleep, and the morning—mid-morning but no later—would give them sufficient time to put their plan into action. Lonsdale promised to send a boy around to confirm the expected agreement from Trent. He would have the boy pursue a circuitous route to Baker Street and return immediately. The note he would carry would say only "I look forward to seeing you" or, in the unlikely event things could not be worked out, "I regret I will be unable to see you." And with that, the Earl took his leave to return to Carlton Terrace, and the household at 221B Baker Street, augmented by one, prepared finally to settle itself for what little of the evening they could salvage.

Mrs. Hudson was to salvage very little of the evening. For the second time in six hours she left her bed while everyone else lay asleep in theirs. This time, however, it was her own choice and her bed was the couch in her parlor, having given up her bedroom to their guest after repeated protestations, and a final acquiescence based on Lillie's exhaustion and Mrs. Hudson's insistence on her ability to sleep anywhere. She opened the door a crack to check on

Lillie, and saw the curved still figure and cloud of auburn hair on the pillow that had earlier held Mrs. Hudson's gray coils. The housekeeper pulled the door shut, and made her way to the apartments upstairs.

After a quick search of the files she maintained on behalf of the consulting detective agency, she knocked on the doors of her two lodgers, ratcheting up the level and frequency of her tapping to meet the unbroken silence she encountered. She was rewarded finally with an irritated, "What is it?" from Holmes, and an only slightly more agreeable, "Is there a problem?" from Watson. Minutes later both men were gathered in their sitting room in the now familiar disarray of unplanned arousal while Mrs. Hudson outlined the tasks for the day.

"I'm sorry to wake you, but we need to work things out before Mrs. Langtry is up and about. Mr. 'Olmes, I know you're not wantin' to be out in public any more than you 'ave to, and with me now becomin' Mrs. Langtry's maid, there'll be no need for you to go to Yorkshire. I'll be able to talk to staff at Mr. Trent's estate, and 'ave a little look around without anybody bein' the wiser. You can go on over to the laboratory at the university, Mr. 'Olmes, and do your chemistry with Dr. Watson's friend."

"I'm afraid we'll 'ave you a bit on the run, Doctor. After you introduce Mr. 'Olmes to your chemist friend you'll need to get over to see Lord Lonsdale and Mr. Trent, and learn what you can about Mr. Mackenzie. You'll be actin' on behalf of Mr. 'Olmes who is feelin' awful about the way things turned out, and is wantin' to learn all 'e can about 'ow Mr. Mackenzie died and what was 'is part in the poor man's death. You'll need to ask about the goin's on at Mr. Trent's estate during the time Mr. Mackenzie was there, who 'e got along with and who 'e didn't—especially who 'e didn't. After that, you'll 'ave to nip over to the Sportin' Club to get a crack at the folk Inspector Lestrade is keepin' there for the day. You'll want to talk to the two managers of the fighters and the 'elper to Mr. Mackenzie's manager."

"Mackenzie's second," Holmes corrected in a low voice.

"Second, if that's what 'e's called. You'll be needin' to get from the files our list of 'Questions for friends and acquaintances of the deceased,' but you should also look at our 'Questions for witnesses to a crime.'"

Mrs. Hudson paused to look into the faces of her colleagues, fearing an absence of sleep might have robbed them of the concentration she felt essential. She found her fears groundless. Watson was, as expected, poised bulldog-like over his papers, and Holmes looked to her with eyes blazing and purpose certain.

"Very good, then we've only one problem to resolve. Mr. 'Olmes, I'll need you to telegraph me in Yorkshire so I can know what you find from your chemistry. The difficulty is you can't very well be sendin' a message to Mrs. Langtry's maid without gettin' everybody to scratchin' their 'eads as to what's goin' on, and you can't send it addressed to Mrs. Langtry without alertin' everyone to where she is. You'll want to send the telegram to Miss Emilie Le Breton care of Mrs. Trent. Emilie Le Breton is the maiden name of Mrs. Langtry according to what's in our files. I'm thinkin' if we word it around the worries she'll 'ave about 'er Mr. Baird she'll be bound to share it with me."

"A coded communication," Holmes sounded his approval. "I can arrange that every third word contains a message only you will understand, or maybe we should count words backwards from the end of the telegram."

"Those are fine ideas, Mr. 'Olmes, but likely I'll only 'ave a minute to see the message so it can't be anythin' too complicated. I'm thinkin' we just need to work with the first word of the telegram that's sent. If you find the flask 'as got somethin' more than whiskey in it, you can use Y for yes in the first word and say 'your friend is in the area,' or 'your friend is not in the area' dependin' on which is true of course. If you find there's nothing in the flask except whiskey, you can use N for no and say 'News is that your friend is in the area,' or 'is not in the area', whichever is right."

Holmes grunted reluctant agreement to the strategy suggested by his housekeeper. With the approaching dawn, his attention shifted to a new concern, and he expressed the hope Mrs. Hudson would have time to prepare breakfast before leaving with Mrs. Langtry. She assured Holmes she would provide a substantial start to both his and Watson's day.

When she arrived downstairs, she found Lillie Langtry awake and attending to her toilette. Mrs. Hudson wasn't certain whether Mrs. Langtry expected her to assume the duties of lady's maid immediately or whether the adoption of those duties might wait until they arrived in Yorkshire. She decided to do what she could to postpone their adoption.

"There's a cloth and a bar of carbolic soap for your use, Mrs. Langtry. For now, I was plannin' on startin' breakfast for you and the men."

Lillie smiled her appreciation before making a request. "Mrs. Hudson, I wonder do you have a glass I might use, and is there ice I might add to the basin. I like to wash with ice water whenever I can." Mrs. Hudson promised to bring her the mirror that hung in the parlor and to chip some ice off the block in the box in her kitchen. She backed her way from the room with a speed intended to be seemly while sufficient to avoid the possibility of additional requests. Her careful departure proved unnecessary as Lillie turned back to brushing out her hair without giving her new maid a second look.

Chapter 6.
Confessions to a Lady's Maid

Holmes and Watson agreed Mrs. Hudson had put out a fine breakfast, and Lillie Langtry expressed regret that her traveling companion could not play the role of both lady's maid and cook. In spite of her praise, Lillie provided little assistance to the men's efforts to reduce the mound of eggs, rashers of bacon, and generous slices of ham made available by the housekeeper. She removed several slices of toast and two spoonfuls of eggs with protestations of being too excited by the day's prospect to be able to eat any more. In fact, Lillie was making gallant effort to down a respectable serving in deference to Mrs. Hudson, her usual breakfast being two slices of toast and tea.

Her fellow diners had transformed themselves into models of sartorial elegance compared with their appearance hours earlier. Holmes again wore his purple dressing gown, but it now covered a white shirt and striped trousers, while Watson's outfit of frock coat, matching trousers, waistcoat, shirt and tie would have served as well for dinner as breakfast. Lillie Langtry, meanwhile, was resplendent in a rosy pink morning gown she had conjured up from the depths of the luggage that had been carried in the night before. When not complimenting their housekeeper, Holmes and Watson spoke of the sterling character of Lord Lonsdale; then urged Lillie to describe her impressions of America based on her theatrical tour, after which all three shared their views of the London stage with the Jersey Lilly recounting several amusing but respectful stories about her friend, Oscar Wilde. She encouraged each of them to attend his new play, *Lady Windermere's Fan*, without revealing she had refused his offer of its lead role. All in all, it was a conversation that filled the breakfast hour and would be forgotten by lunch.

After an hour of watching the men devour nearly the

whole of the feast the housekeeper had prepared, Lillie rose from her place, expressed her delight with their company, gave thanks yet again to Mrs. Hudson and, after indicating her need to prepare for the trip to the Trent estate, asked if she could impose on the housekeeper for assistance with dressing and packing.

By late morning, Lillie's traveling chest and Mrs. Hudson's carpetbag stood by the door. During her preparations Mrs. Hudson had been interrupted four times by reporters inquiring whether Mr. Holmes would be able to provide an interview. Each time Mrs. Hudson had informed the caller Mr. Holmes was not seeing anyone, and each time the reporter followed up her refusal with either a plaintive request for reconsideration, the whispered offer of a small reward, or a snarled threat of reprisal, often trying a second ploy after the first one failed. As Mrs. Hudson could tell from her kitchen window, none of those rebuffed moved farther than the opposite side of Baker Street where they huddled together, pointing and gesticulating in ways that made clear their frustration and its source.

The messenger Lonsdale had promised arrived between the third and fourth reporters, mercifully clad in colors that did not rival the sun overhead. After being admitted to the parlor from which Lillie had absented herself, he delivered his sealed message whose contents he swore were unknown to him. The message he brought contained the expected invitation for "appropriate parties" to visit the Trents' estate with the promise of a carriage to take them to McLellan Manor on their arrival at Oxley station. Watson provided the boy the munificent sum of three shillings for the combination of his courier duties, his promise "on his mother's eyes" to keep secret both the origin and destination of his journey, and to say nothing—"not even good day"—to the men standing outside. They watched him leave and he was as good as his word, although there was concern about what

80

might be happening when the youngster disappeared from sight with two reporters in hot pursuit. There was, however, no time to dwell on such; they were faced with the formidable task of getting Lillie and Mrs. Hudson to St. Pancras Station without informing all London of Lillie's travels.

In a voice calculated to convey careless heroism, Holmes announced his willingness to expose himself to "the voracious demands of an insatiable press" in the interest of providing a diversion that would allow Mrs. Langtry time to escape. He would lead the reporters away from Baker Street while Mrs. Langtry, disguised to look as ordinary a woman as could be managed, would leave for the station with Mrs. Hudson. Holmes noted that Mrs. Langtry was an accomplished actress who, he was certain, could carry off a number of roles, and that he, knowing a little something of playacting himself, might be of some assistance with a disguise.

True to his word, Holmes produced a series of items from the storehouse he kept in his bedroom. Her new identity began with a dark wig streaked with gray fitted over the net Mrs. Hudson helped her draw tightly around her auburn hair. Under Holmes's critical eye, Lillie etched charcoal lines into the corners by her eyes and around her mouth adding years to her age. She was certain she could convincingly portray an older woman, pointing out she'd played Lady Macbeth three years earlier to excellent reviews, although granting it was on the American stage. Disguising the exquisite figure posed greater problems. Padding was not possible as Lillie had only form-fitting clothing, and it was too warm to wear a coat for camouflage without attracting the attention she sought to avoid. She informed them she would wear a high-necked, ankle-length flounced gray dress with a matching gray jacket, and rely on makeup and her acting skills.

With cabs available outside the several elegant shops along Baker Street, it was time to put their plan into action.

Holmes pulled a huge floppy hat as low over his left eye as he could manage, took up a walking stick, and nodding to as appreciative an audience as any actor could wish, he allowed Mrs. Hudson to open the door to a world he had hoped to avoid.

The effect on the knot of reporters lounging across the roadway was as instantaneous as it was dramatic. Cigarettes were tossed and note pads clutched as they tore across the thoroughfare to join Holmes on his brisk walk to Marylebone Street. A pattern emerged such that a reporter would elbow his way past colleagues to pose a question, and while he stopped to record Holmes's response, his place was taken by another reporter who recapitulated the practice. The assembly of striding, sometimes jogging men, all with pads and pencils at the ready, and all of them surrounding a towering figure with a battered hat and features to match, excited the attention of passers-by and the curious stares of riders on the upper deck of a horse car that lumbered its way past them.

In response to their questions, Holmes reported he was fine physically, regretted terribly the accident the night before, felt that boxing remained an important and worthwhile sport in spite of its dangers, had no opinion as to whether the Marquis of Queensberry rules were preferable to London rules although he appreciated their importance in reducing injuries to a fighter's hands, and had no plans to engage in additional bouts. He arrived at the intersection of Marylebone and Gloucester Place, at which point he declared the interview to be at an end and, pointing his stick south as if he were claiming new lands, he turned onto Gloucester Place. The men of the press, content they had gotten as good as they would get—if considerably less than they had hoped—left Holmes to hail cabs for their return to Leeds Street where they would embroider stories whose bland accuracy would be unacceptable to their editors.

As the last of the small parade Holmes was leading

disappeared from sight, Watson took to the street, blowing his whistle once for a four-wheeler and informing the driver he would be taking two ladies to St. Pancras station. Watson carried a carpetbag with huge green evergreen leaves and red berries to the carriage; the coachman hefted a traveling chest while eyeing the carpetbag as if its inclusion risked contaminating his vehicle. He held the door for two older women whom he found strikingly different in appearance. Both walked slowly with the exaggerated care of middle age, but while one was small and shapeless in widow's weeds; the other led him to think fondly of his wife in ways he never thought of her during daylight hours, or in any event hadn't for years.

The women spoke little on the way to the railroad station. Lillie Langtry asked Mrs. Hudson about her husband and how long she had been widowed, how long she had lived at 221B Baker Street, how long she had known Holmes and Watson, and commented that marriage to a constable must have been good preparation for her two boarders.

Mrs. Hudson answered her questions, but felt unable to raise any of her own. There was no aspect of Mrs. Langtry's life that appeared appropriate for polite conversation. She might have inquired about her acting career except Mrs. Hudson had never attended a play and knew nothing of the theater. It had been Tobias Hudson's claim that "life is the genuine article and I can't see payin' good money to watch its imitation."

They arrived at St. Pancras station just as the clock in the bell tower of the mammoth Midland Grand Hotel was striking the half hour. The hotel and station stood alone on a tract of land, the huge Gothic structure looking more like it should be welcoming congregants hoping to assure their place in Heaven than travelers seeking to go only as far as Braxton and York. The two women hurried inside, in so far as real and pretended middle age allowed, intent on catching the 10:50

Midland Railway to Leeds to begin the first leg of their journey to McLellan Manor.

After settling themselves into their compartment, Lillie Langtry wedged herself into a corner by the window to get as much support as the thinly cushioned backing and wooden frame could provide. She took a book from her reticule whose title, *Leaves of Grass*, was embossed in gilt letters on a dark green cover. It had been sent to her from America in a packet that contained neither the sender's name nor address, but simply a note saying he (she was certain it was a he) was one of her fondest admirers (the word "fondest" was underlined). She opened the book to where a thin crimson ribbon held her place, and marveled again at the poet's celebration of life and unapologetic delight in the beauty of the human body.

Mrs. Hudson had purchased the *Morning Post*, *Standard* and *Times* from a news agent, and settled herself into the corner opposite Lillie to study the descriptions of Mr. Mackenzie's death by the morning press. She found the reports of events at the National Sporting Club highly similar across the different papers. Each used the term "unfortunate" to describe the events at the Club, one adding the word "accident," none supposing there to be anything suspicious, or finding cause to interview any of the Club officials. All three reported the National Sporting Club would be closed for 24 hours, one of them "citing respect for the family," although no family members were mentioned. Every paper also chose to feature the story on its back pages, perhaps because it had already been reported in the previous day's papers, perhaps for other reasons. No paper omitted Holmes's part in the evening's events, and all emphasized his amateur status as a fighter and professional standing as a consulting detective. All reported Holmes's regret about the fight's outcome, but continuing fierce support for the sport, in what each described as an exclusive interview.

Mrs. Hudson laid aside her papers, feeling guilty for having ignored her companion and determined to identify a subject that would permit an amiable conversation, only to find Lillie had fallen asleep clutching her book of poetry. The train had not yet left London. With a relief she had no reason to mask, Mrs. Hudson returned to the newspapers, looking first to the agony columns (an interest she had acquired from Holmes, a fact she kept to herself), and then to the crime reports, but she soon found the accounts of Londoners' foibles and misdeeds to be in unequal competition with the easy rocking of the Midlands Railway as it traveled the spine of England, and she soon joined Lillie Langtry in an effort to make up the sleep gone missing from the night before.

Their sleep was fitful at best. Each woke at nearly every station as the train jerked to a stop at towns that served as commercial centers for the miles of farms and dairies surrounding them, each marketing town bearing a striking resemblance to the last. There would be a brief view of shops set between rows of modest homes before the train lurched back to its steady pulse, and the small collection of buildings again gave way to fields of unidentifiable vegetation and meadows where cows or sheep meandered in search of the perfect clump of grass.

The women were barely aware of the towns at which the train stopped. When they awoke it was only long enough to cast a lazy glance to the world outside, sometimes smiling with polite indifference to each other before succumbing again to the train's gentle rhythm.

Arriving at the Methley station, Mrs. Hudson shook herself into a sitting position, smoothed down her dress and patted her hair into place. Consulting the railway schedule, Mrs. Hudson found there was only one more station before they would reach the train's last stop at Leeds. She glanced to her companion, who was slouched in sleep in the corner in which she had inserted herself, and saw reason to wake her.

Lillie's carefully fitted wig was now noticeably askew, and her age had become unevenly distributed across her face with some lines having been nearly obliterated, and others smudged in the course of her sleep. She spoke the woman's name softly, in little more than a whisper, and Lillie Langtry was instantly awake. She stretched and pushed herself upright, looked to Mrs. Hudson, then to the countryside speeding past the window and blearily questioned if they were nearing their station.

The housekeeper explained the circumstances and indicated the state into which her disguise had fallen. Lillie produced a small compact and mirror from her reticule, smoothed her wig back into place and, with the charcoal she had brought, reestablished her rapid aging. Again, the two women engaged in minimal conversation. Lillie Langtry asked if the look she referred to as "mature" was properly captured. Mrs. Hudson smiled her recognition of Lillie's delicacy and affirmed the success of her make-up. After the train had rocked its way in and out of the Hunslet station, they contacted a porter to assist them with their bags and fell into line behind the passengers who would be exiting onto Leeds's Wellington Station. For most, the Midlands hub would be their final destination; a few would, like the two of them, be traveling on to one of the small towns bordering the Yorkshire Dales and the moors beyond.

They had more than an hour between trains, and after arranging for their baggage, they set about finding a place to eat suitable for two unescorted women. They agreed with little more than a quick look to each other to reject the station pub, Mrs. Hudson believing and Lillie Langtry agreeing the Croydon Inn and Hotel across the street from the station would have a restaurant more likely to provide the decorous atmosphere they sought.

The builders of the Croydon Inn and Hotel appeared to have been given strict instruction to omit any evidence of frivolity in their creation. The result was a three story brick building that looked to be a warehouse mistakenly placed among the city center's bright shops. Several steps from the hotel entrance the single word "RESTAURANT" was printed discretely across the top of a leaded glass door.

Lillie Langtry pressed the door open and the two women stood inside the threshold waiting to be seated. It was apparent the dinner hour had ended. Only two tables were occupied, and on each a tea service alone remained from the diners' meals. Two men of widely differing ages sat at one. The younger of the two was in his mid-20s, dressed in a black frock coat and trousers, wearing a black cravat with black hat and gloves on the chair beside him. The other was in his middle years dressed in the gray colors of business with expression to match. He leaned into the words he spoke to his grimly attentive companion, indicating one or another of the several documents spread across their table. With each statement he made, he checked to make certain his words were understood. Each time the young man nodded, and appeared to shrink a little lower in his chair.

Recognizing that both men's clothing bore the rumpled look of travel, Mrs. Hudson concluded the young man wearing the black of mourning had come into a legacy of enough size to require advice from someone combining age and experience, and his plans were sufficiently secret to require meeting in a place where neither would be known. The young man had obtained the privacy he desired, but not the answers for which he hoped.

Several tables away another young man was engaged in an entirely different and apparently more promising undertaking. Wearing a dark frock coat, striped trousers and an engaging smile, he stared intently into the hazel eyes of the woman across from him, all the while maintaining a constant flow of words that met their objective of demure smiles, nods of embarrassed understanding, and the young woman's fierce interest in the hands she kept tightly clasped in her lap. Mrs. Hudson resisted the impulse to cross the room and speak to the young woman, whose cloak and gown again bore the signs of travel, although her companion's clothes showed no such wear. Mrs. Hudson feared the young woman could be headed for serious difficulty although she regarded as positive the absence of a carpetbag or other luggage, suggesting the selection of a point for rendezvous that gave the woman opportunity to return home later that same day.

The entrance of the two new customers interrupted the waiter's routine of glowering for several seconds at one couple, then transferring his glare to the other, while letting the teapots on both tables grow colder and colder. Seeing the restaurant's two new patrons, he silently cursed the unidentifiable fates that had chosen him for torment.

Striding stiffly across the room, he informed the intruders lunch was no longer being served by way of welcoming them to the Croydon Inn and Hotel Restaurant. Lillie ignored his greeting, and suggested that a collation of cold meats was all they required and, grasping Mrs. Hudson under her arm, thrust both of them a step farther into the restaurant to underscore her intent. The waiter took a step back and the field was won. He led them to a table of his choosing then backtracked to the table selected by Lillie to be as far from the two couples as she could calculate. The rationale for the woman's choice was beyond his understanding; the table selected was like all the others, covered with a white tablecloth and holding a small vase with a single sprig of heather. Lillie repeated the order for a plate of cold meats, and added a request for a pot of china tea before turning her attention from the waiter, effectively dismissing him to the kitchen, whose environs he had hoped to avoid until afternoon tea.

When the waiter was well out of earshot, Lillie expressed her hope the order was agreeable to Mrs. Hudson, who had, in fact, found both the order and its delivery to the officious waiter quite agreeable. Both women took a moment to acquaint themselves with their surroundings. The restaurant's interior faithfully maintained the austere, business-like spirit of the hotel's exterior. Dark wood and heavy burgundy drapes kept the room in a perpetual state of twilight. Only a series of line drawings, dispersed throughout the room at precisely equal heights, provided relief from the room's oppressive solemnity. The sketches depicted various railroad scenes, each one suggesting the exhilarating nature of train travel and, more particularly, of travel on the Midland Railway. There were pencil drawings of roaring locomotives, of happy passengers disembarking at Wellington station, baggage handlers pleased to be serving smilingly appreciative riders, dining car waiters equally pleased to be serving equally appreciative diners, and a family whose stylishly dressed parents nearly matched in enthusiasm the expressions of their son and daughter at the sight of some distant wonder to which the children were pointing.

The waiter returned with surprising speed and a more elaborate plate of meats than either woman had expected. He set down teacups, saucers, and a pot of what he proclaimed to be china tea in a voice suggesting he had traveled the distance necessary to assure its authenticity. He then returned to the kitchen door to resume his dispute with the fates. He had no sooner arrived at his self-selected post than his attention was unexpectedly, but agreeably drawn to the table with the two men. The older man was collecting his papers and, under the morose gaze of the younger, assembling them into a single neat bundle to be returned to the briefcase from which they had been drawn two and a half hours earlier. As the waiter knew would happen, with their business completed, both men searched anxiously for him and, upon finding him, waved for his prompt action.

Mrs. Hudson watched the small drama play itself out,

and then focused attention on her own table and the now familiar difficulty of finding a suitable topic for conversation. She remarked on the surprising variety of meats and Lillie Langtry declared herself pleased with the tea. Then Lillie set her cup back in its saucer, using a moment's delay to render the simple exercise an act of high drama, and with her other hand reached across the table to stay Mrs. Hudson from taking up the slice of venison she had pierced with her fork.

"Mrs. Hudson—I take it you prefer to be called Mrs. Hudson—I believe we need to have a word." Mrs. Hudson cocked her head to one side and waited to learn what word was needed.

"I believe we have two issues that bear discussion. One is fairly unremarkable and relates to how we should think of your responsibilities as my maid. In truth, I do not require a great deal of assistance, and I appreciate that service as a lady's maid is far removed from your usual duties so I will ask as little from you as possible. I will, however, require some help with dressing, and even in a country house there will be several changes a day." Lillie brushed aside any further discussion on the subject with a wave of her hand. "I'm certain we can work all that out.

"The second issue is more complex. I am a direct woman, Mrs. Hudson, so forgive my speech if it seems intemperate. We are different ages, come from different backgrounds and have had vastly different life experiences and, to put it at its simplest, I don't believe you like or approve of me. That doesn't matter a great deal, in fact it doesn't matter at all except that we are traveling together and you will be attending me at the manor, and we may not be able to find enough subjects for meaningless chatter to occupy the time." Lillie paused, and this time the ever-ready smile held within it the demand for response.

Mrs. Hudson surprised Lillie with her own enigmatic smile and prompt agreement. "It's a fair point, Mrs. Langtry, and it's one that's worried me as well. Only it's not a matter of like or dislike, and it's not for me to approve or disapprove. What we've got 'ere is simply difference." Mrs. Hudson was not above a bit of drama herself. She dabbed her clean mouth with her similarly unsullied napkin, and looked to either side of their table before speaking. "I'll try bein' as direct as you're bein'. I lived my whole life 'appy for there to be one man, my Tobias, as the only one I wanted or needed, and you've lived—as best I know—your whole life … different than that. I understand about marriages not workin' out and people goin' their separate ways, but you chose to go your separate way while you were still married."

A small smile stole across Lillie's face, then disappeared under her companion's earnest stare. "You do know I've been a divorcee for five years." Mrs. Hudson gave her a curt nod of acknowledgement. "But I know that's not what you're getting at." Lillie frowned her difficulty in finding the right words to bridge the gap in understanding that lay between them. "Let me put it this way. You've a lease on the Baker Street lodgings, and collect what I'd wager to be a handsome rent from your Mr. Holmes and Dr. Watson. It's the action you've taken to ensure a certain level of comfort now and to keep you from the workhouse tomorrow. Well, I too choose to live in comfort today and to assure my tomorrows. And I make no apology for the course I've taken. I looked at the world as it exists for a woman alone, looked at the assets I possess, and decided to make the best use of them I could."

Mrs. Hudson chose to ignore Lillie's assets which had, in any event, been well and often described elsewhere. She stayed with a course closer to her own experience. "And wasn't your Mr. Langtry up to bein' a 'elp with your todays and tomorrows?"

"You mean like your Tobias was. Well, to tell you the truth, Mrs. Hudson, I thought Edward would be. He was a fine figure of a man when we married, and appeared well-situated.

At least he appeared well-situated to the twenty year-old daughter of a clergyman whose whole life had been spent on the island of Jersey. Edward even owned a yacht, the *Red Gauntlet,* and I thought it the most wonderful thing in the world and surely a sign of the good life the two of us would have together. But it became clear very quickly that what seemed a fortune in Jersey would hardly let one get by in London. Edward had to sell our beautiful boat just to pay for the modest lodgings we took. That was not the first or the greatest disappointment in our marriage however." And, without so much as pausing for breath, Lillie plunged into a discussion that roused Mrs. Hudson's admiration for its candor, even as she felt her cheeks grow hot and redden at an unburdening whose like she had never heard.

"Edward had been married before—a sweet little woman who contracted tuberculosis. He would have been far better off remaining husband to her memory than choosing me for a second wife. Jane—that was her name—was his perfect wife, content to run his household and tend to her needlepoint. I never learned needlepoint and had no skills or experience in running a household. Moreover, I discovered that Edward was shy in his husbandly duties—very shy, Mrs. Hudson—and I found myself denied the comforts one expects in a marriage. Not that he was any happier with me than I was with him. He made no secret of that. On one occasion, I was standing near when Edward's friends complimented him on his marriage. He said nothing about me, but only told them they should have known the first girl he married."

"With all that, perhaps you can understand how I felt when an artist the stature of John Millais asked me to sit for him, and famous men I never expected to know sought out my company. And I learned the attention I was getting could lead to my having comforts I would otherwise be denied. I won't hide from you I had to do some playacting from time to time, but doesn't every woman sometimes pretend her companion is as witty or as able as he wants to believe he is, or even pretend at times to be something she is not. I'll wager there have been times when even Mrs. Hudson has done some playacting in her life." Lillie did not wait for a response, nor was one forthcoming.

"And I'll tell you another thing. It may sound a convenient justification, Mrs. Hudson, but I find men enjoy giving me gifts very nearly as much as I enjoy receiving them. I'm also well aware that neither the gifts nor the attention will last, and I mean to enjoy both while I can attract them and to store up memories and treasure for when I can't." Lillie paused, concerned that even though she had done all the talking, Mrs. Hudson might need to catch her breath. "I sincerely hope none of what I've said shocks or alarms you, but regardless I hope we can reach an understanding for however many days we will be together."

Having spoken the piece she felt obliged to share, Lillie took up a fork in preparation for an assault on the meats remaining on the serving plate when a sudden thought led her to delay that action. "I suppose there's one thing more. Undoubtedly, you're wondering how my friendship with George Baird fits into that picture." Mrs. Hudson's expression left no question she was wondering about it now if she hadn't been earlier. "I'll not deny I find him an exciting companion in a number of ways. He isn't afraid to say what he thinks or do what he pleases, and I find that delightfully refreshing. We share a variety of interests, most particularly racing, and he has always been very generous to me. If I would leave London, which I won't, he would establish me as the mistress—or if you'd rather the matron—of his family mansion in Glasgow, which he assures me is luxurious beyond imagination. He will even convert its conservatory to a private theater, provide me with a chef of my own choosing, and already possesses a wine cellar so complete I could have a different wine for each course sent up from his cellar by the dumbwaiter he had installed. I have told him I could only accept his offer if he would move the mansion from Glasgow to London, but it's a mark of how considerate George can be in spite of the stories I'm certain you've been hearing." Lillie studied Mrs. Hudson's face a moment in search of some reaction, found none, and concluded it was simply beyond her understanding. With nothing more to say, Lillie completed the task of making selection from the plate of cold meats.

Mrs. Hudson had been considering how to respond to Lillie's revelations, and now undertook that task. "I appreciate your 'elpin' me to understand your thinkin', Mrs. Langtry. I can understand the things you say about makin' your way in the world, and to tell you the truth I'm thinkin' a woman alone maybe 'as got to be a little sharper or a little luckier than some others. And I know what you mean about playactin'; there can be pretendin' even for a woman doin' nothin' more interestin' than lookin' after 'er lodgers. Besides which, I know I've been a fortunate woman what with my 'avin' the best of men for twenty-nine years, and now 'avin' the lodgings on Baker Street to see to my future." Mrs. Hudson pushed a slice of turkey from one side of her plate to the other. "I will say, Mrs. Langtry, your life is too exciting by 'alf for me, but I can see 'ow it suits you, and 'ow it lets a body get the things it needs to be content." Mrs. Hudson had no wish to dwell on the needs of Lillie's body for contentment, but felt that something should be said in deference to the woman's frank discussion. She was rewarded with a warm smile, concluded they had reached something of the accommodation Lillie had sought, and moved the conversation to a topic she felt certain to provoke less controversy and avoid any further self-revelation.

"I wondered if you know Mr. Trent or 'ad occasion to visit 'is Yorkshire estate."

Lillie grinned. "I have known Arthur Trent, although not in the Biblical sense." After allowing Mrs. Hudson time to partly disappear and fully reappear from behind her napkin, she described attending a dinner party with the Trents, although having only minimal contact with each of them. She went on to tell what she knew about Arthur Trent, prefacing her narration with the observation that he was a very private man unlike most of the men of her acquaintance.

"Not that he's ever less than straightforward with everyone. Indeed, pretension is unknown to the man. He puts on no airs, and talks frankly of his own and his wife's modest backgrounds. Perhaps it's because of that he's become a great favorite in the City whenever he chooses to visit. Men adore him and women are delighted with him. I suppose one might want it the other way round, but there it is. Regardless, he chooses to remain a virtual hermit tucked away on the moors without even a house in London—although I suppose you can't very well call a man a hermit when he lives with his family. But I should start at the beginning, or as much of a beginning as anyone seems to know. He lived as a boy in Scotland—you can hear a trace of it in his speech, they never quite lose the burr—before running off to Africa to seek his fortune. The details are a bit sketchy. It's said he went to a seaport—I've heard Zanzibar—where he became involved in trade of some kind. It gets a little clearer after that. He traveled to South Africa where he tried his hand at cotton farming before, as Trent puts it, 'stumbling onto a diamond field.' It made his fortune; that part at least is clear. And later he sold his holdings to DeBeer, which some say doubled his fortune.

"Afterward, he came back to England, met the widow Bascombe and married her within the year. That was 15 years ago. He purchased McLellan Manor for reasons no one could fathom, and moved his new wife, and the two children from her first marriage, to the Yorkshire moors about as far as one can get from London and still be called an Englishman. Nonetheless, as best as anyone can judge, they appear to thrive in their isolation. It's everyone to his own porridge as my mother used to say. I know they get to the City from time to time for the theater, and of course Mr. Trent is a member of the National Sporting Club. I believe their son is in school in London, and I suppose they come to the City to see him, but I really wouldn't know."

Lillie pursed her lips and squeezed her eyes shut as if trying to coax some last treasure from her memory. Finding none, she relaxed into the familiar smile, "That's as much as I know about the Trents, and this will be my first visit to McLellan Manor so I know nothing whatever about it."

It struck Lillie that the housekeeper had been listening with surprising attentiveness to her report of the dry facts of the Trents' life. She attributed it to the poor woman's dull existence. It was true she lived downstairs from the foremost detective in London, but likely had no more to do with him than admitting his visitors, cleaning and straightening his living quarters, and preparing some of the meals for Holmes and his doctor friend, almost certainly specializing in quantity rather than inventiveness judging by the breakfast. Now, the woman was chewing overlong on a slice of venison and seemed abstracted in thought. When she finally swallowed, she asked a question that struck Lillie as both odd and inconsequential.

"I'm wonderin' if you've any notion as to whether Mr. Trent brought anythin' back from 'is time in Africa. I'm thinkin' like flowers or plants or maybe insects. I've 'eard there's some that take an interest in such things when they're in foreign places." With that, Mrs. Hudson washed down the last of her meal with the last of her tea.

"I have no idea, Mrs. Hudson. Why in the world do you ask?"

"Oh, I just wouldn't want to get one of those jungle diseases, like that sleepin' sickness thing I've read about. I've trouble enough now gatherin' the strength to get my work done."

Lillie covered her mouth with her napkin, but it failed to stifle her laughter. This naivete was in keeping with what she expected from the woman. At times the housekeeper had seemed almost too quick for her background.

"I'm sure you'll be perfectly safe, Mrs. Hudson. I suspect even Yorkshire has exerted some civilizing effect on Mr. Trent. I did hear he came back from Africa with a black youth who has become his valet, but I have it on good authority he's been expressly forbidden to eat any of the guests without Mr. Trent's permission."

"I know you're 'avin' your little joke, Mrs. Langtry. All the same, I'll 'ave a look around when we get to the Manor to see things for myself. You can't be too careful where these foreign types are concerned."

"Have it your way, Mrs. Hudson, for now it might be well to ask for our bill and get back to the station."

Their waiter was only too pleased to provide them with their bill, thanking them profusely for their coming without encouraging their return. He turned back to his one remaining table to glare at the couple who remained unconcerned about his presence or the presence of anyone else.

Chapter 7.
Acquaintances Old and New

Watson placed the flask Mrs. Hudson had secured at the National Sporting Club in a small carpetbag, and together with Holmes went by hansom to the Medical College of the University of London. Holmes had argued briefly to return to the laboratory where he had been working at the time they first took lodgings at Baker Street, but was won over by Watson's argument that "old Spooner," who ran the Medical College laboratory, would provide him not only his full cooperation, but would give Holmes his own workbench and access to the latest in laboratory equipment.

Spooner proved every bit as gracious and helpful as Watson had promised. He was a tall, spare man, who was balding rather sooner than he expected and countered that deficiency by developing a dark beard extending some distance down his laboratory coat. He greeted Watson warmly and Holmes with something approaching homage. Having been prepared by Watson for Holmes's appearance, he showed no reaction to his visitor's marked and swollen face. The same could not be said for others in the laboratory, but Holmes's focus was elsewhere.

Once more the investigator scientist, he studied the work bench readied for him. He looked to the Bunsen burner and retort, beakers, pipettes, rows of test tubes, and neatly arranged spoons of varying size, nodding to each as though greeting old friends. Spooner directed Holmes's attention to a selection of reagents and litmus papers on a shelf attached to his bench, and promised his assistance in adding to the equipment anything his guest needed. Holmes pronounced his satisfaction with the arrangements, and Watson stated his gratitude for the careful attention on Spooner's part. He removed the flask gingerly from the carpetbag, commanding the attention of two other chemists and a laboratory assistant, all of them guessing—accurately and happily—they were witnessing the latest criminal investigation by the great consulting detective. Watson expressed the conviction that Holmes was in good hands, took one of those hands in his, shook it vigorously, nodded good-byes to the others at work in the laboratory, and went to locate a cab to take him to Carlton House Terrace and the first of his own several tasks.

The train to Skipton, with an intermediate stop at Oxley, left only minutes later than scheduled and arrived at the Oxley station on time at 3:35. It carried few passengers, and with the distance from London and a nearly empty coach, Lillie felt it safe to restore her identity, although she kept a wide brimmed hat low over her forehead and her face buried in her poetry. They were the only people to exit the train at Oxley and. in spite of the conductor's search up and down the platform and a spirited call for passengers, no one boarded.

The train's porter deposited their bags on the station platform, and the two women turned to find the carriage that would take them to McLellan Manor. They did not have to look far. A single carriage stood just beyond the platform and a beaming coachman was coming their way. He was in his late thirties, squarely built, hatless with straight black hair flattened against his head in two equal halves from its center part. He took obvious pride in a flowing moustache made all the more prominent by his otherwise clean-shaven face. His uniform was dark blue with pale blue piping at the cuffs and collar, but was tight in places that would have fit comfortably some time before. Mrs. Hudson suspected the coachman's one time aspirations to be the Lothario of the Manor's staff had gradually given way to appetites more easily served. After introducing himself as Doyle, he set Lillie's trunk on one shoulder, leaving a hand free to carry Mrs. Hudson's carpetbag and, without losing his broad smile of greeting, he led the way to the coach.

Only one other person was evident on the Oxley platform. As the three bound for McLellan Manor passed him, Mrs. Hudson studied the man and his small portmanteau, and came away concerned. He would be waiting for the train to Leeds, and judging by his flamboyant dress, London was his ultimate destination. He wore a large-checked brown coat and trousers, and a soft homburg slightly tilted toward his left ear from either side of which carrot-red hair spilled out in liberal quantities. She knew him to be a boxer. The bone beneath one eye appeared crushed, his nose held a valley between two small hills, and a thick white scar carried from his lower lip to a point just above his jaw. The man's attention was focused on Lillie, but his look reflected study rather than the admiration Mrs. Hudson had come to expect. Lillie ignored him, as she ignored all who looked her way whether they stood and gawked or stole a surreptitious glance. Mrs. Hudson did not ignore him.

It was too much to expect there to be two boxers in Oxley by sheer coincidence. The man on the platform would have planned to see Mackenzie with some sort of proposition and, having learned of the fighter's death, was now returning to London. Had he come as a friend he would have been to the Manor to offer condolences to Mackenzie's widow, but Doyle evidenced no knowledge of the man, indicating he had never been to McLellan Manor. Mrs. Hudson could not know what people the fighter might be seeing when he returned to London and that, combined with his study of Lillie Langtry, was cause for concern. What had been left out of her planning was a strategy for contacting Holmes and Watson if there was a problem in Oxley. And now she feared there was a problem.

The coachman, meanwhile, kept his attention focused on his two guests or, more accurately, on one of them. He opened the coach door with a well-practiced flourish and still grinning, he saw them into the coach expressing his hope "the weather will hold." After climbing aboard the box, he called a series of "hi-yups" and "ho-yahs" to his horse, received a series of small whinnies in return, and set out down the Skipton Road. Lillie looked to the sky for any sign of rain, and shrugged her confusion at Doyle's concern. Mrs. Hudson caught a last glimpse of the fighter as the carriage went through a half revolution to get onto the road. She was not surprised to find his eyes fixed on the coach as he lounged against the wall of the station waiting on the eastbound train.

The town of Oxley gave way first to farmland and forest, then to the ragged course of the moor out one side of the carriage, purple heather and coarse bracken competing for space across otherwise barren ground. Out the coach's other window there seemed only empty land interrupted now and again by a line of sheep moving with neither purpose nor speed parallel to the distant Wharfe River. The women shared astonishment at the forbidding nature of the land, and expressed wonder for the people who lived with the silent moor as their constant companion. Neither spoke of the Trents, but it was the Trents about whom they wondered.

And even as they marveled at the harsh tranquility of the countryside, a wind rose up from somewhere beyond their knowing, rushing thick gray clouds toward them, and dragging rain behind. It started as a steady, inoffensive drizzle, but as they drove farther the rain became pelting sheets and the wind came in frequent gusts, seemingly determined to whip horse and carriage from the narrow strip of road. Their driver wrapped himself in oilskins to meet the storm he had feared would overtake them. He called quiet assurance to his little horse as it struggled against wind and rain to comply with his urging, harboring hopes of a dry stall and a ration of feed at the end of its journey.

The 20 minutes it normally took to get from Oxley Station to McLellan Manor passed without the Manor coming into view. The two women spoke little as they were rocked together and apart, their silences no longer reflecting a failure to find safe topics, but each woman's effort to hold firm to her position in light of the coach's unsteady progress through the storm. Their windows gave them only a blurry vision of the countryside, and whenever they came upon irregular rectangles of light and dark greens signaling cultivated land, each woman harbored the hope McLellan Manor would appear after the next field or thicket. But their ride continued without sign of a house or barn, and fully 40 minutes passed before Mrs. Hudson got her first rain-streaked view of the Manor. She called to Lillie and pointed, and the two of them stared through the downpour at the mansion of russet-colored fieldstone on the distant hill.

As if anticipating their interest, the rain began to slacken, and the building's reddish stone came to glisten as the sun slowly emerged to challenge what had become a gentle shower. The Manor consisted of a center section with four multi-paned windows on each of its three levels, anchored on each side by rounded towers jutting forward from the larger body and extending several feet above it to gabled roofs, giving the whole the appearance of a fortress it would be unwise to assail.

Without benefit of direction from Doyle, the horse chose the semi-circular path up the small rise leading to the manor house, coming to a stop before a massive wooden door from which a young footman emerged, umbrella in hand, in time to reach the door of the coach directly as it drew to a stop. Without looking directly to the two women, or relinquishing an expression of haughty unconcern, he helped each from the carriage, one with "m' lady," and the other with "ma'am." He set the umbrella over them so that only he was exposed to the last remnant of the earlier storm. He showed the women into the front parlor, stealing one glance then another at Lillie, all the while retaining a pose of disinterest. Lillie Langtry took as little note of the footman as she had of the enigmatic figure on the station platform. She seated herself on the couch spreading her skirts across the cushion's intricate design of green tendrils coiling around and over each other in unending repetition. Mrs. Hudson settled herself in a chair near Lillie's right hand to study the room for what she might learn about its mistress.

Much of the room fit Mrs. Hudson's expectations. The clutter of antimacassars over the arms and backs of mahogany and walnut chairs caused the room to appear appropriate to an English lady's parlor a little behind time. Each of three tables held Chinese vases containing flowers of different size and colors. Two of the tables also held pictures of the children of the house, a boy of perhaps ten and girl of eight in one photograph, and the same two children six or seven years older in another. Seascapes hung on two of the walls and a sampler containing the Lord's Prayer on a third. All was as it should be until one looked to the room's far wall. The paintings on that wall, one of the moor and the second of McLellan Manor, were the product of a far less certain hand.

Mrs. Hudson concluded that Mrs. Trent chose to neither hide nor flaunt her interests and accomplishments. Instead, she set them at a discrete, but manageable distance from the traditional world she felt it her duty to maintain. It occurred to Mrs. Hudson that life in Oxley likely permitted greater expression of the modestly unconventional than would life in London, and might explain some part of the Trents' choice for a home. Her curiosity roused, Mrs. Hudson waited the appearance of their hostess with keen interest. She wondered whether she would see the artistic woman of independent expression or the decorous lady of the manor.

The woman who joined them was neither. She leaned heavily on a thick cane, her leg heavily bandaged, recalling to Mrs. Hudson Watson's account of her having been thrown from her horse. She was in her early fifties, tall, raw-boned, and seemingly out of place indoors. Her brunette hair was swept into a roll at the back of her neck, unselfconsciously emphasizing her long, thin-cheeked face and its rich tan—far too dark a tan even on a country estate.

Having expressed the pleasure she took in having Lillie as her guest, she explained her appearance, reprising the story of her morning ride with Lord Lonsdale and its unfortunate outcome. Her doctor, who she reported as being quite severe, had only allowed her out of bed if she promised to stay off her feet as much as possible and remain on the Manor's ground level for at least a week. Under duress, she had promised obedience, but now was being driven to distraction by her confinement and was delighted to have a visitor to her home, especially as accomplished a visitor as Mrs. Langtry. Mrs. Trent turned her attention finally to Lillie's maid, suggesting Mrs. Hudson might enjoy having a cup of tea in the servants' hall. Without waiting for a response, she rang for the parlor maid. As Mrs. Hudson left with the young woman who appeared, Mrs. Trent was stating her belief that she and Mrs. Langtry would soon be great friends.

Satisfied he had performed all the preliminary tests appropriate to the investigation of the flask's contents, and leaving it to Spooner to conduct the additional work they agreed would be useful, Holmes took it upon himself to initiate an action that had not been agreed to, or even discussed with his colleagues. Upon leaving the laboratory, he took a waiting hansom to the shop of Augustus Stinchcombe, Printer. It would be their first meeting; Watson had interviewed Stinchcombe and several other printers before securing Wiggins's apprenticeship.

The printer's name was whitewashed in two great arcs of Roman print across the shop's window. Holmes's entry triggered the tinkling of the shop's bell above the door, which triggered in turn the adoption of a genial smile by the short, plump man who came forward wiping his hands on a blue apron and announcing himself to be Augustus Stinchcombe.

He winced momentarily on seeing the somewhat misshapen face of his visitor, but was sufficiently accustomed to serving a diverse clientele to transition quickly to the pose of affable merchant.

"Good afternoon, sir. How may I help you?"

"I believe you employ a young man named Michael Wiggins."

The printer's broad smile fought with his sudden confusion, but ultimately won out in a somewhat muted form. "I do. May I ask what business you have with him?"

"My name is Sherlock Holmes. As you may know, I am a consulting detective and formerly had Master Wiggins in my employ. He was most helpful to me in one or two investigations and I have come today to request the use of his services for a brief period. I recognize he is learning a valuable trade and is no doubt already making contribution to your business. I assure you I would not be here or make this request if the situation was not dire. It's a situation I'm not at liberty to discuss; I can only tell you a woman's life is at stake." Holmes paused before sharing a second confidence in the event a woman's life proved insufficient to get the printer's cooperation. "You may also wish to know Scotland Yard will greatly appreciate your assistance in all of this." Holmes gave the printer a knowing look, then waited the positive response he was confident would be forthcoming.

Augustus Stinchcombe stared at Holmes with eyes wide and mouth open, but could contribute nothing beyond his obvious astonishment. A contribution came instead from the person on whom a woman's life depended, sounding entirely too cheerful for one charged with such awesome responsibility.

"Mr. Holmes, it's a great pleasure to see you again, and how may I ask is Dr. Watson and Mrs. Hudson?" A look of boyish innocence, most recently familiar to the residents of 221B Baker Street, and before that to innumerable shopkeepers, costermongers, and members of the London constabulary, was only partly obscured by the grime from his new job.

"We are all well, Master Wiggins, thank you." Holmes smiled acknowledgement of his former page. "Mr. Stinchcombe and I were just discussing your availability for some very important investigative work."

At the mention of his name, the printer once again found his voice. "It is certainly my wish to do all I can to support the work of Scotland Yard, and I am of course well aware of the many accomplishments of Mr. Sherlock Holmes. Indeed, sir, it is an honor to have you in this establishment. If you can share your thinking, Mr. Holmes, might I know what you plan for our Master Wiggins who, let me assure you—and I'd appreciate your sharing this with Dr. Watson—is making great strides in the printer's trade. Great strides."

Holmes pursed his lips in a look of deep disappointment. "I'm afraid the details of the mission, like the situation itself, must remain something of a secret. If the activities I have planned for Master Wiggins became known it could jeopardize everything we've worked for. I am certain of your own reliability, Mr. Stinchcombe, but in the unlikely event word were to reach our adversary it would be best for you to be able to claim ignorance. We will, of course, take every precaution to see that Master Wiggins is in no danger throughout this effort," Holmes gave the hint of a shudder before continuing, "and we're almost always successful in that regard."

Augustus Stinchcombe simultaneously swallowed and blinked as he edged toward his decision. "For how long would Master Wiggins's services be required, if that's something you feel you can share."

"I can tell you with some confidence that I—and the Yard—will require Master Wiggins's services for just two days, three at most. I promise he'll be back with you as soon as it can be managed without endangering lives."

"Lives? I thought you said it was one woman you were needing to protect?"

"And so it is … for now. We simply can't presume where this might lead." Having already employed a near shudder, Holmes now shook his head while looking as grave as the desperateness of the situation demanded.

The subject of the tug of war over his services followed the discussion with barely disguised eagerness. He had no idea what Holmes expected of him, but it was certain to involve greater challenge than mixing inks, gathering type, stacking supplies, and sweeping out the shop. He understood the need to learn a trade as Dr. Watson had explained it to him, but reasoned that a short delay in his education wouldn't hurt anything and might even allow him to return to his duties with greater dedication. He remained silent as he knew Mr. Stinchcombe believed he wanted nothing more than to become a master printer like himself, and Wiggins thought it useful for Mr. Stinchcombe to hold to that belief. He waited for the printer to declare finally the decision he, like Holmes, felt the man certain to reach.

"I can't very well stand in the way of Scotland Yard, or of you, Mr. Holmes." He turned from Holmes to Wiggins and his expression turned from resignation to undisputed authority over an underling. "Mr. Wiggins, I'll expect you to show Mr. Holmes the same courtesy you show me, and to conduct yourself with a dedication that will reflect favorably on our shop." With Wiggins's promise to bring glory to the enterprise of Augustus Stinchcombe, responsibility for the supervision of Michael Wiggins passed temporarily from the printer to Sherlock Holmes.

His first assignment was to clean up and make himself presentable. After passing Holmes's inspection, Wiggins and his former employer removed themselves to the alcove in back that served as Wiggins's bedchamber and was beyond the hearing of his current employer. Holmes first emphasized the delicacy of his mission, then described what would be expected of Wiggins. He was to take up a post that would allow him to keep watch on the front door of the home of George Baird. The Squire would be at home, having spent the prior evening and likely much of the day in a London jail. If Baird left the house, Wiggins was to shadow the Squire wherever he went. If Baird went to the train station, Wiggins was to learn his destination and relay that information instantly to Holmes. He could leave his post after dark, but was to return by seven the following morning. In exchange, Holmes provided him four shillings for transportation, and three shillings daily for wages with a half crown bonus to be paid when his assignment had been completed.

Wiggins listened attentively, asking only for a description of Squire Baird and an increase in his wages. Holmes had come prepared with the Squire's address and a picture of Baird from an *Illustrated News* article about the absentee owner of Glasgow United Ironworks, both of which he had removed from Mrs. Hudson's files. He made them available to Wiggins, while ignoring the request for an increase in wages. Satisfied with the arrangements, Holmes thanked Augustus Stinchcombe for his cooperation, and promised to share with Scotland Yard a report of his civic mindedness as he smiled his way out to the London street.

Chapter 8.
Discovering Sailor Mackenzie

Fourteen Carlton House Terrace had been created through the combining of two adjoining mansions, each of which would have comfortably housed a large family and extensive serving staff which, in their earlier histories, each of them had. It was a three-storied house, indistinguishable except by size from the 16 other white stucco homes that ran in a line along its street.

Watson walked between fluted columns to the recessed entryway and rang the bell, eschewing the ringed knocker in the mouth of a gilded ram's head, its angry stare discouraging the animal's disturbance. Within seconds of his ring, a footman, in the fiery livery that no longer surprised Watson, opened the door wide and asked to know his business, adding, "please, sir," to assure his demand was being made with the proper respect. Watson produced his card and indicated that his business involved Lord Lonsdale and Mr. Arthur Trent. He was admitted with a bow of well-practiced respect and led to a guest parlor, while a second footman was dispatched to transmit Watson's card and message. The footman who had acted as Watson's guide returned to his seat by the entrance, guaranteeing the next visitor would be admitted with no more delay than that suffered by Watson.

Lord Lonsdale entered the parlor not long after Watson had settled himself in an armless chair that would provide minimal interference with the note taking he planned. The Earl wore his trademark white gardenia pinned to the lapel of his coat, and greeted his guest with a look of genial bemusement.

"Dr. Watson, I'm delighted to see you again of course, but I must ask whether your being here indicates a difficulty for Lillie. Did she get away alright this morning?"

"Let me set your mind at ease on that score. Mrs.

Langtry got away without difficulty." Watson described Holmes's diversionary tactics much to Lonsdale's amusement. Before the good feeling could dissipate, Watson outlined the purpose of his visit. "Let me say at the outset I'm here on behalf of Holmes. There are some questions I would like to put to Trent, or rather that Holmes would like to, but he's not seeing people just yet as I'm sure you can understand." Watson paused long enough to elicit a grunted acknowledgement from the Earl.

"As I'm sure was clear to you last night, Holmes remains troubled about his part in the death of Sailor Mackenzie. He's asked me to follow up on his behalf with some questions about events leading up to the fight and the character of this man, Mackenzie." Watson had no idea whether Holmes's concerns were visible to the Earl, or to what extent they even existed, but he was certain Lonsdale would not deny sensitivity to the feelings he attributed to Holmes.

"I appreciate Holmes's concerns. It speaks to the character of our friend, but he must know he has no reason to reproach himself—absolutely none. We're all aware of the dangers involved in our sport, and Lord knows Mackenzie knew the dangers well enough after all his years in the ring. I'm sorry it happened of course, and I'm terribly sorry about Holmes's involvement, but it's certainly no fault of his. If I may say so, Dr. Watson, as a medical man, you would have a particular understanding of the dangers and might help Holmes to put all this behind him."

"We've talked, and I suspect at some level Holmes recognizes he cannot be held responsible, but there it is regardless. It's my strong belief, speaking as a medical man and friend, that a greater knowledge of the events leading up to the evening's tragedy will speed the process of Holmes putting it all behind him. It's in that spirit, I'd like to ask Trent a few questions about Mackenzie, and get his report of events at McLellan Manor the day before the fight."

Lonsdale shrugged his response. "Certainly, if it will help. I'll ask Trent to join us in the drawing room where we can be more comfortable." The Earl found a draw cord beside the stone fireplace and a footman appeared with a speed suggesting clairvoyance rather than reliance on bell pulls alone. Lonsdale requested that Mr. Trent be asked to join Dr. Watson and himself in the drawing room. After setting the footman on his mission, the Earl led his guest across the hall to the drawing room.

It was clear to Watson that the room had been furnished by someone other than Lord and Lady Lonsdale. It was all gilt and gingerbread, and thoroughly at odds with the sportsman image important to them both. Indeed, the room contained the furnishings of the second Earl of Lonsdale, Hugh Lowther's great uncle, William, who had been a collector of ornate furniture from France, and female opera singers from all nations. Lonsdale waved a hand toward one of three clusters of chairs, settees and couches. Watson considered the intricately carved chairs, judged them too delicate for their intended use and chose the couch instead, settling himself against the tufted cushion at its center and avoiding the swirls of mahogany carving on its either side.

"Dr. Watson, it's good to see you again." Trent had exchanged his black tie formal dress of the prior evening for a gray frock coat and striped trousers. He came forward to give Watson a vigorous handshake and wary smile.

"And I'm delighted to see you again, Trent. Let me first communicate Mrs. Langtry's gratitude for yours and Mrs. Trent's hospitality under these difficult circumstances. She's now on her way to Yorkshire and, as I was telling Lord Lonsdale, I'm here on a separate mission at the behest of my friend and colleague, Sherlock Holmes, who is not yet sufficiently recovered to be making calls on his own behalf. In a word, Holmes remains disturbed about his part in Mr. Mackenzie's death, and has asked me to pose some questions

111

to help clarify that situation."

Lord Lonsdale, hearing his name injected into the conversation, found it appropriate to reprise his earlier comments. "I've told Dr. Watson that Holmes should have no concern regarding his activities last night. He conducted himself entirely properly. I need hardly point out that Sailor Mackenzie was doing all he could to savage Holmes, and would, I am certain, show no comparable remorse if the outcome had been tragically different."

"I quite agree that Mackenzie was trying to inflict as much damage as he could without concern for his opponent, but I'm afraid that's not providing much comfort to Holmes." Watson looked to Trent as he posed his first question. "What can you tell me about the character and background of Mackenzie?" Watson withdrew from his waistcoat the accounts book he used for recording and an Eagle pencil, one of two he'd sharpened that morning. "He was with you at your estate for a while. I'd be grateful if you'd share any observations that might be helpful in knowing the man."

Trent scratched his thatch of gray hair and pursed his lips as he considered his response. "I'm not sure what I can tell you, Dr. Watson. He and Mrs. Mackenzie had their own cottage and rarely joined in the activities at the manor house. I should perhaps explain that the last owner of McLellan Manor had three small cottages built to house the workmen he would bring in from Leeds from time to time, and to accommodate staff of the guests they invited for weekend hunts and parties. We've also found them useful, and on this occasion we put the Mackenzies in one cottage, and Mackenzie's manager, Mr. Capelhorn, in a second. That arrangement permitted very little socializing.

I suppose you might expect there would be some getting together at mealtimes. In truth, there was virtually none. Capelhorn and the Mackenzies were to take their dinners in servants' hall, but Capelhorn often took his dinners in town, and the Mackenzies routinely had theirs brought to the cottage. Breakfast and mid-day they were free to share in the dishes set out on the sideboard, but I'd have to say they were all somewhat uncomfortable about eating with Mrs. Trent and me, and would typically eat and run with little effort at socializing. Indeed, Mackenzie might come for lunch, but regularly had his breakfast of scones and coffee sent over to him at eight each morning. I'm afraid what little observing of Mackenzie I did was during his sparring sessions and there was, of course, no communication at those times."

"I see. Can you tell me then, Mr. Trent, how was Mackenzie chosen for this fight?"

"Since I was the one who suggested the fight," Lonsdale said, "I might provide some of that background. I didn't know the man myself, but it was a Mackenzie kind of fighter I wanted—a journeyman who might give young Cochrane a good fight, or would at least make for an interesting one. I told Fleming what was needed, and left it to him to work things out. He knew Mr. Capelhorn had some fighters that might fill the bill and made the necessary arrangements." The Earl interrupted himself long enough to offer cigars. He held three aloft with eyebrows raised to match, but found himself the only taker. After lighting up and inspecting the lit end to make certain of its even burning, he rang for the butler and directed him to bring brandy and three glasses, this time without risking rejection by soliciting his guests' wishes.

Watson fidgeted while cigars were offered and brandy ordered, inserting a question as soon as that process was done. "How long was Mackenzie at your estate, Mr. Trent?"

"He was with us for twenty-four days if we count yesterday."

"That sounds a long period."

Trent took a moment to consider the observation he knew to be a question. "It might be a little long, but it's not much at odds with other members' experience."

"Ah, the brandy." Lonsdale rose to attend to the tray of Napoleon brandy the butler had taken from beneath the sideboard and set down on a table before edging his way noiselessly from the room. The Earl poured and they drank the Queen's health and, after a respectful examination of the empty glasses and comment on the excellence of the brandy, Watson tried to pick up the thread of his questioning.

"You've said you had opportunity to observe Mackenzie's preparations for the fight. Would you say he was well prepared?"

"Not very well, I'm afraid. He'd stick with his exercises for a few days at a time, but then he'd disappear for a day, sometimes more than that. There's no secret he had a liking for the bottle, and he'd often wander off somewhere to do his drinking. Of course there wasn't far for him to go, and Caplehorn or Simon would find him in a pub in Oxley or Wheatley, or in the stables behind a pub, and once in a ditch between towns. They'd pick him up, dry him out, and get him back on a training regimen until he went off for another round of drinking. I'm afraid it went on like that the whole time he was with us."

Watson reacted to the unfamiliar name. "Simon?"

"Simon is the man you saw working as Mackenzie's second. Simon is also my butler and valet. He knows a good deal about boxing, and so was valuable as a sparring partner and second to Mackenzie."

"Wherever did you find this Simon?"

"You mean wherever did I find a black man for my service?"

Watson showed an embarrassed smile. "I suppose I do, but not just that. Most valets are not also skilled sparring partners."

Trent grinned and waved off any need for Watson to explain himself further. "You're not the first to have question about Simon. In any event, his presence here is easily explained. As you may have heard, I made my fortune in Africa. Quite by accident really. I stumbled onto a diamond mine and became a rich prospector one day after spending years being a poor cotton farmer. It was while I was still a cotton farmer that I found Simon. He was an orphan, twelve or thirteen years old, and caught in a war between two tribes. His parents had been killed, and he would have been as well if the tribe that killed them caught up with him. I took him in and he's been with me ever since. Everyone except Simon thinks I've been taking care of him; Simon is convinced he's been taking care of me. He may well be the one who has it right. In any event, when I was ready to leave Africa I was told my new status demanded my having a man servant and butler. Simon had been working with me in a capacity not too far removed from that so it was an easy transition for both of us."

"And his knowledge of boxing?"

Trent ran his index finger around the rim of the empty glass still in his hand. "I suppose I'm responsible for that. I thought it might help Simon if ever we got separated and he had to defend himself from attack. Africa was a dangerous place in those days, Dr. Watson. A look at my face will give you some idea of what a man had to do to protect himself and his little bit of property." Trent fingered the white scar splitting his left eyebrow that Watson had noted when they were introduced. "And it could be terrifying for a lad without the protection of elders. Anyway, he took to fighting quite well and, after he filled out, even had a few amateur bouts with some of the Yorkshire laddies."

Lonsdale flicked ash from his thick cigar as he joined the conversation. "I've tried to convince Trent to part with Simon or at least lend him to the Club. We're always on the look-out for men with boxing know-how to act as seconds on fight nights. However, Trent is reluctant to give up Simon and, as I understand it, Simon is reluctant to leave Yorkshire and Trent."

Watson finished the last of his writing, nodded his appreciation for Lonsdale's addition, which he did not record, and turned back to Trent. "How did Mackenzie get along with Simon and the other people at the Manor?"

Arthur Trent shifted position in his chair before making reply. "The truth, Dr. Watson, is that he didn't get along with people. He simply didn't try to."

"How do you mean?"

"I mentioned that Mackenzie stayed to his own cottage most meals and didn't mix with others. It was probably just as well. I don't like to speak ill of any who can't speak for themselves, but the plain fact is he was a difficult man. He was accustomed to getting his own way and he could be quite unpleasant if he didn't. And, of course, it was worse when he was drinking. Since he was never without his flask, he was a handful a good bit of the time. Simon was probably the one person at the Manor Mackenzie seemed genuinely to fear. And for good reason. As I said, Simon was his frequent sparring partner, and there were times I thought Mackenzie risked far greater punishment in Oxley than he was likely to suffer in London."

"What of Mrs. Mackenzie? Where was she in all this?"

"I'm afraid she had the most difficult time of anyone. It's my understanding Mackenzie thought nothing of being verbally abusive, and I suspect he was abusive in other, more hurtful ways." Trent paused to swallow some of the brandy with which Lonsdale had refilled his glass before biting off a final comment to Watson. "Frankly, Doctor, I'm afraid Mackenzie won't be missed by any at the Manor, perhaps not even by Mrs. Mackenzie."

Lonsdale filled the silence that followed Trent's comment. "You do understand, Doctor, we're not dealing with graduates of Eton and Harrow in our sport—at least not yet. The men we have are bound to be a bit rough around the edges. And there are some, like Mackenzie, who seem to be all edges. Trent did us a great favor housing him, and we at the Club owe him and Mrs. Trent a considerable debt." There was another flick of ash and a warmer tone. "Might I offer anyone more brandy?"

Watson declined, expressing his appreciation for the offer. He indicated he had taken up enough of Trent's time and Lonsdale's hospitality, and should continue to his next stop, which was the National Sporting Club to meet with Capelhorn, Simon, and the senior Cochrane. He explained again his only objective was to provide Holmes with the fullest possible picture of the events leading up to Mackenzie's death. He asked Lonsdale if he'd be good enough to alert the Club's porter to his need for an office to conduct interviews. Trent's eyes grew wide and Lonsdale opened his mouth to offer a thought, but elected instead to wish Watson well and express the hope of seeing him with Holmes soon and under better circumstances. He promised to call and alert the doorkeeper to Watson's needs. As a seeming afterthought, he promised he would make certain the men understood their responsibility to work with the Doctor. He then called on one of the ever ready footmen at 14 Carlton House Terrace to hail a carriage for Watson.

Elizabeth, the parlor maid, and Mrs. Hudson's appointed guide, reported with something akin to pride of ownership that they would be going to the east tower "which the staff had to itself." She explained the servants' hall and kitchen were on the ground floor, the rocky ground making it impossible to create any lower level. Staff had their sleeping quarters on the two floors above the work area. With a noticeable lack of enthusiasm, Elizabeth informed Mrs. Hudson she would be sharing the parlor maid's room.

In the servants' hall, Elizabeth introduced Mrs.

Hudson to Mrs. Groover, the Trents' cook and Rachel, the scullery maid. She nodded toward a young man blacking and polishing boots on a bench against the side wall, informing Mrs. Hudson he was Charles, the second footman. She put a particular emphasis on the word "second." Charles waved a greeting before going back to his work, interrupting his labors from time to time to steal a glance to Rachel's shapely back, and to the small hill of scones on the dining table, both offering sweet promise, and both well beyond his reach. Elizabeth stayed only a moment before turning back with the explanation that Mrs. Charters would be looking for her, an explanation that drew nods of sympathetic understanding from the cook and the footman.

Mrs. Groover adopted the role of hostess. "You've come a dreadful long way, Mrs. Hudson. Can I get you a cuppa and maybe a scone and some raspberry jam?"

"Thank you, Mrs. Groover. That would be lovely. I'm afraid I'm gettin' to an age where these long days do take a toll on a body, and a cup of tea would be much appreciated. And I'd be most pleased to try one of your delicious lookin' scones." Mrs. Hudson narrowed her gaze in the direction of the plate of baked goods, arching an eyebrow as she critically assessed the brown of their crust when Mrs. Groover turned back to her stove.

While Mrs. Groover attended to tea, Mrs. Hudson turned her attention to the small domestic scene unfolding before her. Rachel avoided eye contact with Charles with such care it was apparent his interest was not unappreciated, and Mrs. Groover was looking to each of them too frequently, with too evident an air of disapproval, for it not to be clear that the relationship between her scullery maid and the young man was an ongoing issue.

"You are being careful to keep the blacking on the shoes and not on my furniture?"

"I am indeed, Mrs. Groover, I'm being *ever* so

careful." Rachel giggled at the footman's exaggerated show of deference, but kept her focus on the pots she was scrubbing. Mrs. Groover grunted her response, and Charles raised one boot to study it critically for any small imperfection before resuming its brushing with uncommon diligence.

Mrs. Hudson thought it wise to take the conversation in a new direction. "'Ow long is it you've been with the Trents, Mrs. Groover?"

"I joined the family going on ten, no eleven years ago. I was with a family in Skipton until the squire there passed. He was a handful, the old squire, but we got on alright and I couldn't think to stay after he was gone. I can tell you, Mrs. Hudson, the Good Lord was looking out for me on that day. Not a week before, the Trents' cook up and left to get married without so much as stopping to give notice. Well, of course, they was looking high and low for a cook, and I was looking high and low for a situation, and we sort of found each other. And I'll tell the world I've never regretted coming here, not for one second. I couldn't have come to a better family and that's the God's own truth."

"Amen to that, Mrs. Groover," Charles added.

Mrs. Groover shot Charles a look that lacked any trace of piety before setting the promised scone and raspberry jam at her guest's place.

"And yourself, Mrs. Hudson, have you been with Mrs. Langtry long? I'll not ask for stories now. When the staff is together will be time enough to hear about your lady, her being a famous actress and all."

Mrs. Hudson had not considered the interest she would generate in being lady's maid to a famous and slightly notorious person. She decided an honest reporting of the situation would be a prudent strategy. "I've only been with Mrs. Langtry a short time, Mrs. Groover. 'Er own maid left suddenly and I've sort of stepped in for a while. I'm afraid there's not much I can tell beyond all that people probably know."

"Is she really as beautiful as they say?" Charles had stopped brushing the boots and looked to Mrs. Hudson with an open, eager expression.

"Really, Charles, is that all you can think to ask?" Mrs. Groover was back to squinting her disdain for the footman.

"Well, there's more I'd like to know, but there's a lady present." He grinned across to Rachel who had turned from the sinkful of pots to watch the exchange, and now started giggling again before returning to her pots.

"There's three ladies present, and from all I can see there's not a single gentleman. If you've a mind to stay in my kitchen, Charles Davis, you'll keep a respectful tongue in your head."

Charles returned to the meticulous brushing of every inch of the boot he held, stopping to eye his work approvingly from time to time, without relinquishing the smile he lavished on Rachel's back.

"Of course, as my lady's personal maid I couldn't discuss any of 'er personal affa ... which is to say any of 'er business. But as to 'er bein' a beauty, I can tell you we can't go anywhere she don't get looks from every man we go by, yes and woman too, come to that."

"Cor, I'd like to see that." It was Rachel who spoke at last, drawing everyone's surprised attention to the figure, who having made her comment, turned back to running water over the pot she had been scrubbing.

"I'm sure we all would, Rachel, but for now we need to make certain we have everything ready for Mrs. Langtry." The speaker had entered the room without anyone's awareness. Mrs. Hudson knew from the command in her voice she was Mrs. Charters, the housekeeper. She was younger than Mrs. Hudson expected, not much more than 40, slight, with regular features and a ruddy complexion. She wore her once dark, now grey-streaked hair swept up in a tight knot adding little to her modest stature and greatly to her age. She might have been described as handsome, even attractive, if her features didn't seem frozen in permanent disapproval of the world with which she was forced to contend.

She held the hand of a girl of about 15 with straggly dark hair and the housekeeper's straight features, but lacking the scowl of her protector. The youngster wore a shapeless white outfit that seemed more shift than dress, but still failed to hide her budding figure. She looked all around the room without seeming to focus on anything before turning her attention finally to the people in it, giving to each an unchanging, open-mouthed smile that became a throaty giggle when she got to Mrs. Hudson. The older woman gently squeezed her hand, the giggling stopped, and the girl again looked with smiling incomprehension to each of the people in the kitchen. Except for Mrs. Hudson, who acknowledged her smile with one of her own, no one paid the girl any attention even as she spoke their names in sing-song fashion, carefully enunciating each syllable as she did so. "Char-lie and Ra-chel. Charl-ie and Ra-chel."

"I'm Mrs. Charters; I'm the housekeeper, and this is my daughter, Christine. I must apologize for not being here when you arrived, Mrs. Hudson. We were busy making things ready for your mistress." Having made clear the disturbance her "mistress" had created, the housekeeper became nearly cordial. "I see Mrs. Groover has gotten you some refreshments." She nodded approvingly in the direction of the table setting in front of Mrs. Hudson. Again, there came a rhythmic undercurrent as the housekeeper's words triggered an association for her daughter. "Mrs. Groover, good cook, Mrs. Groover, good cook."

"I've been well taken care of indeed, Mrs. Charters. I'm that thankful for the tea and scones. Everything is delicious, Mrs. Groover." Mrs. Hudson doubted the cook needed her support—a cook only answered to the lady of the house—but it would hurt nothing to retain Mrs. Groover as an ally, and later it might prove useful. With a smile and a long stare, Mrs. Hudson made a study of Mrs. Charters and her daughter.

She concluded Mrs. Charters had found it necessary to return to domestic service after becoming widowed or being deserted. The absence of a wedding ring suggested desertion. Only amputation could have caused Mrs. Hudson to cease wearing her wedding ring and she believed it would be the same with any happily married woman who had lost her husband. Moreover, the severity of Mrs. Charters's dress and demeanor indicated a calculated effort to avoid attention to the housekeeper's womanly qualities. In a woman her age, that effort suggested a wish to avoid renewing the disappointment experienced in an earlier relationship.

It was certain, as well, that Mrs. Charters had been in service before, and more particularly in service to Mrs. Trent. The two women shared an accent different from that of the Yorkshire staff. More significantly, as the mistress of McLellan Manor, Mrs. Trent was responsible for hiring its housekeeper, and while she might be expected to have sympathy for Mrs. Charters's situation, she could hardly be expected to hire her unless she had prior and positive experience with the woman. Given Christine's age, that experience would have occurred during Mrs. Trent's first marriage.

"Charles, I suspect those boots have as good a shine as they're likely to get. Please return them to the boot rack and see to brushing out Mr. Trent's brown tweeds. The master may want to go for a tramp on the moor after he gets back from the City." Mrs. Charters watched while Charles made a last critical assessment of his work. With that, he rose, gave a long look to the tray of scones, and accompanied by Christine's, "Charles gives a good shine, Charles gives a good shine," he strode to the corridor unaware of Rachel's effort to show in a glance the affection she felt for the footman.

The housekeeper's face relaxed more than smiled as she turned her attention to their guest. "I'll leave you to finish your tea, Mrs. Hudson, and look forward to seeing you at dinner. I'll have Elizabeth show you where you'll be staying and inform you where we've put your lady. I expect you'll want to get yourself settled as soon as you can to be ready to help Mrs. Langtry." Mrs. Charters held her gaze an extra moment as if trying to move her out of Mrs. Groover's kitchen through the power of suggestion. However, Mrs. Hudson had additional questions for the cook and proved every bit as stubborn as Mrs. Charters. She remained in place until the Manor's housekeeper could no longer delay her duties. The woman squeezed her daughter's hand and smiled to her with a softness that startled Mrs. Hudson, but which the child found unsurprising. "We have to go now, Christine. You'll see Mrs. Groover and everyone later." Once more fixing a determined scowl on her face, Mrs. Charters took herself and her daughter out of the room.

Mrs. Hudson sipped her tea and said nothing, waiting for the explanation she felt certain would be forthcoming. She was not disappointed.

"You mustn't mind Mrs. Charters. She's really a good soul. Just now she's got her hands full what with Mr. Simon— he's our butler—gone off to London with the master to help with the fighting and likely all that happened after. I'm just thankful they'll be here tomorrow so things can get back to normal."

Mrs. Groover poured herself a cup of tea, selected the largest scone on the plate and, after scooting her chair closer to Mrs. Hudson and leaning in as if to share a confidence, she continued in a voice that still filled the kitchen. "I'm sure you'll be wondering about Christine. You could see the poor girl is simple, always has been as far as anybody knows. There's nobody knows the whole story about her except Mrs.

Trent and the master of course. And there's the blessing of it. I mean the two of them have done for Mrs. Charters and the child without saying a word, all the time acting as if it's the most natural thing in the world.

"That was thirteen years ago and before my time, but what I've been told is that Mrs. Charters come to the Manor looking for a job and holding Christine's hand just like she was today, except Christine would have been just a little one of course. Mrs. Charters knew the mistress from the time of her first marriage when she was Mrs. Bascombe. It's not exactly clear what she done for the mistress, just that she was some kind of maid. And we don't know what Mrs. Charters's name was before she become Mrs. Charters. They say she married a soldier and he went off stringing wire all over half the Empire—or said he was. Anyway, he never come back, and left Mrs. Charters to take care of a little one all on her own. You might pay attention to this, Rachel." She shot a glance to the scullery maid who looked around red-faced to protest, "Oh, Mrs. Groover."

"Don't Mrs. Groover me. You just be careful, Rachel. You'll find yourself getting a lot of sweet talk just to get you under a blanket, and then they'll be off stringing wires in places you never heard of, or that's what they'll tell you. Maybe you found it different, Mrs. Hudson, I hope you have, but that's how come Mrs. Charters was back with the mistress, only this time with a child that's got simple ways. And from all what I heard, the mistress never blinked an eye, but agreed right off to make Mrs. Charters a housemaid and let her keep Christine with her. I'm here to tell you God don't make better souls than the mistress."

"And, Mrs. Groover, don't be forgetting what she done for Tyra, an important lady like her worrying about a poor old cat." Rachel had finished cleaning and drying the pots, and stood as close to the scones as she could manage, hoping to sneak one for Charles if Mrs. Groover would only turn the other way.

"Oh phoo for the cat, Rachel. Tyra very nearly lost you your position. Would you believe, Mrs. Hudson, this girl goes sneaking into Mr. Simon's pantry while he's taking care of dinner for our guests so she can get the fool cat's basket. I don't think I've ever seen Mr. Simon get so mad. And him the most patient man you could want to know."

"Well, she hadn't been sleeping right, Mrs. Groover, and I didn't think …"

"That's exactly right, Rachel. You didn't think."

Mrs. Groover rose to stir the pot on her stove with somewhat greater vigor than the task appeared to require. Rachel looked properly forlorn until Mrs. Groover had turned away, at which point the scullery maid snatched a scone. With a wink to Mrs. Hudson, she stuffed it under her apron and moved away from the diminished and suddenly incriminating pile.

Mrs. Hudson had concerns of her own—or at least made it appear so. "Can you tell me, Mrs. Groover, where this cat is stayin' and whether you're expectin' to 'ave it back in your kitchen any time soon. I'm terribly allergic to the animals and I'll feel a lot better if there's no plan for it to be back 'ere any time soon."

"There's no worry there, Mrs. Hudson." Mrs. Groover reclaimed her seat, squinting her displeasure at the stack of scones as she did so. "Tyra will be staying with Rachel for a while. He's a sweet old thing, but he's old and fat, and not a proper mouser any longer. He really should be put down, but nobody has the heart to do it."

"She, Mrs. Groover. Tyra's a she."

"Well, I know that. I'm just saying *she's* a nice enough animal, but not worth losing your situation over. Anyway, Mrs. Hudson, what Rachel is getting at is that we have to lay in the rat poison every now and again, and the mistress wouldn't have the men put it down until we make certain to get Tyra out of there which is how she has now got Rachel for company. Except that this time, what with the excitement there's been first with visitors and then with what happened to Mr. Mackenzie, there never was time to buy the poison." Mrs. Groover's voice took on a harsher tone as she looked to her scullery maid. "And Rachel girl, if you wanted a scone all you had to do was ask. As it is, you'll have crumbs all over and a trail of ants to follow."

"I'll clean up any crumbs, Mrs. Groover, I promise I will."

"Like the way you cleaned up my kitchen just the other night. Didn't I come downstairs to find ashes in my oven the very morning I'm having to make breakfast for the master and his guests before they leave for the City. I don't mean to be picking on you, Rachel. I'm just saying for your own good the places where you've got to improve."

"I'm sorry about that, Mrs. Groover. I thought sure I had done, but I was that tired from all the cleaning up after dinner I must of forgot. It won't happen again."

"Which is what you always say. You've a grand heart, Rachel girl, but you're just a little behind in your ways."

Mrs. Hudson was about to raise a question or two for Mrs. Groover "just out of curiosity" when Elizabeth arrived to announce she was ready to take Mrs. Hudson to her room which, she again reminded Mrs. Hudson, they would be sharing.

Once outside servants' hall, Elizabeth asked Mrs. Hudson how long she would be staying. Mrs. Hudson's response that she wasn't certain, possibly several nights, elicited a groan from the parlor maid. Mrs. Hudson judged there would be little difficulty discovering her roommate's feelings about things.

Elizabeth's room was little more than half the size of Mrs. Hudson's bedroom in Baker Street. Its furnishings were spartan at best, consisting of a well-used dresser and chair, small round table, wardrobe and two rope beds, one of which had been carefully made up while the other, on which Elizabeth laid her cap, had been only superficially straightened. Apart from a brush and the few other toiletries laid on the dresser, two personal items were visible. A photograph on the round table showed three strapping young men, two wearing the uniform of the Oxley constabulary, all of them standing with grim self-consciousness behind and on either side of the grinning parlor maid. Above the dresser, there was a black and white print of a Gothic-style church distinctive for a steeple that had at its center an open bell tower before tapering to a peak on which a cross seemed delicately balanced. The print improved the character of the room, but did little to relieve its overall dreariness.

"It's a fine picture you've got there. Did you bring that from 'ome?"

"Goodness no, where would I get such a thing? It's what the mistress give to me nearly three weeks ago. It used to be in the dining room which is where Mrs. Mackenzie spotted it the first time she come to breakfast. James was on his day out so Charles was at the sideboard. Mrs. Mackenzie tells him it's the very same church where she and Mr. Mackenzie got married, and with her being more like one of us than a real guest, Charles tells her it's the church where Mr. Trent got baptized. Which all of us know, just like all of us are supposed to know what's the master's own business. Anyway, it's after that the mistress said I can keep it for a while because I one time told her I admired it, but I was to leave it where it is. I think it does dress up the room some."

"I quite agree." Mrs . Hudson screwed her face into an expression of sudden concern. "Speakin' of Mrs. Mackenzie, I'm thinkin' we come at a bad time, given what's 'appened to poor Mr. Mackenzie. I couldn't 'elp but wonder 'ow Mrs. Mackenzie is gettin' on?"

Elizabeth surprised Mrs. Hudson with a crooked

smile. "I'll say nothing bad about them what's gone, but you'll not hear many as will put 'poor' next to the name 'Mr. Mackenzie'. He wasn't one to make friends; he was mostly good at the opposite. Mrs. Mackenzie is something else though. She's got her rough ways. She'd have to, living with the likes of him, but she's got a good heart as everyone here will tell you. Anyway, she's not been away from her cottage since she first got the news. The mistress wanted to visit with her, but the doctor wouldn't hear of her walking that distance what with her accident. We even had to fix up a bed for the mistress on the first floor so she wouldn't have to go up and down stairs. Anyway, Clara, the housemaid who's been bringing Mrs. Mackenzie her food, told me she looks to be herself. Of course, Clara's only just started bringing Mrs. Mackenzie her food after Mr. Mackenzie died, even though it was her job all along. She was that afraid of Mr. Mackenzie. They all were. It was Mrs. Charters took him his breakfast and me that collected his tray after, and the same at night except the other way around with me bringing over supper and Mrs. Charters collecting the trays in the morning.

"Mrs. Charters don't scare easy, not with all what she's been through. And the first time Mr. Mackenzie tried anything with me I told him I got three brothers, two of them constables which makes them half the Oxley police, and the other one's a mason, and bigger than his two brothers, with none of them impressed about him being a fighter, and all of them ready to take him on if he once tries anything with their sister.

"Well, I said I'd say nothing against the dead so I'll stop there and get myself ready to help downstairs. I eat at five with James and Charles—they're the footmen—and have to be ready to serve the family what eats at six. You can get your supper with the rest of the staff after eight when the family's done if you've a mind to." For the first time Elizabeth smiled, revealing dimples in her round cheeks and a warmth that had been previously well hidden.

While her roommate splashed water on her face from the bowl on the dresser and primped before the room's small mirror, Mrs. Hudson looked from Elizabeth's window to the lands at the back of the estate. Sheep straggled across a distant pasture near to where grounds and moor became indistinguishable. Nearer, there were stables and the coach house. Nearer still, were three small cottages arrayed in an uneven line parallel to the manor house. Two were sealed shut while the one farthest to her left showed two open windows identifying it as the temporary home of the newly widowed Mrs. Mackenzie.

Two other structures caught Mrs. Hudson's eye. A short distance from the stables a small square of well-trod ground had been marked off by four wooden posts. The posts would have established the limits of the makeshift boxing ring in which Mr. Mackenzie prepared for his scheduled fight with Rochester Cochrane, and his unscheduled one with Sherlock Holmes. The second structure was unlike any Mrs. Hudson had ever seen before. A short distance from the Mackenzie cottage there stood a long, single-story flat-roofed building made entirely of glass.

"Before you go, Elizabeth, I wonder can you tell me what is that glass 'ouse and what would it 'ave on its inside?"

Elizabeth had no need to go to the window to see what had captured Mrs. Hudson's attention. "That's the master's special toy. Anyway, that's what Mr. Henderson calls it except not in front of Mister Simon or Mrs. Charters. Mr. Trent's got all these plants in there from where he's lived that he likes to visit and to show off to everyone who comes to the Manor. There's even one that's poison." She looked to Mrs. Hudson with her head cocked and an eyebrow raised to make certain her visitor had absorbed the revelation. Mrs. Hudson had.

"I been inside of it once. Mr. Simon took me through

when I first come to work at the Manor like he does with everybody when they first come, and I can tell you there ain't nothing all that pretty growing inside of it. Nothing to compare to the wildflowers or even the heather you can see all over Oxley. But Mr. Trent goes walking through it regular to see how everything's getting along, and Mr. Simon is the only one he'll trust to take care of all that's growing in there. It makes Mr. Henderson powerful mad. He's the gardener for all the rest of the Manor grounds. Of course, he got a little of his own back yesterday when Mr. Simon lost his key to the greenhouse. He was asking everybody if they'd seen it. You see, it's only Mr. Simon and the master that are supposed to have keys. Mr. Henderson don't have a key even though he's told the master more than once he thinks if he's the gardener he should have a key to wherever there's plants growing. Anyway, that's what Mr. Henderson told us he said, and knowing Mr. Henderson, I'm sure it's true."

"When did Mr. Simon lose his key, Elizabeth?"

"Well, I don't know exactly. Mr. Henderson found it yesterday morning in the grass near the greenhouse door. It was too late to give it back to Mr. Simon though on account of he'd already gone with the others for the train. But I don't know when Mr. Simon first knew it had gone missing. I do know Mr. Simon took Mr. Capelhorn and Mr. Cochrane around the Manor and showed them the insides of the greenhouse Sunday afternoon. It was all part of the get-together his Lordship planned for the day before going to London. I suppose Mr. Simon must of dropped it after that. Mr. Henderson told Mrs. Charters that since he was the one to find the key, he should be the one to give it back to Mr. Simon." Elizabeth broke out into a broad grin. "I know Mr. Henderson is looking forward to that." She shook her head before setting her cap and going to the door. "The fuss that's made about a raggedy bunch of plants. Still and all, I guess a good man like the master is entitled to have his pa'ticular toys the rest of us don't exactly understand. Anyway, I suppose it's all harmless enough." She looked back as she opened the door to leave. "I'll say good day for now, Mrs. Hudson."

Left alone in the maid's bedroom, Mrs. Hudson set about removing her few belongings from the carpet bag. She would need to learn who was at the get-together Lord Lonsdale scheduled the day before Sailor Mackenzie died, and she would need a plan for getting inside the glass building she was certain housed toys that were anything but harmless.

Chapter 9.
Speaking Ill of the Dead

Watson received an only slightly warmer reception from the porter at the National Sporting Club than had Mrs. Hudson.

"You'd be Dr. Watson, I take it."

"That's correct."

"My name is Overby. I was told you'd be coming and I was to take care of you. I'm to put you in Lord Lonsdale's office." Overby made it sound as if Watson would be receiving an honor he couldn't possibly deserve.

He ignored the porter's judgment. "That's fine. I'll need to speak to several of the men who've been here overnight. I'll want to see them individually."

Overby sniffed his understanding and led the way to Lord Lonsdale's office. The room reflected the taste and life of the Earl of Lonsdale. It was dominated by a massive and bare mahogany desk whose rounded legs ended in the arched paws of an animal every visitor took to be a lion. Three matching chairs, whose arms and legs ended with the same clawed threat, were set at precisely equal distances from each other and from the desk they faced. A low bookcase stood along one wall with no more purpose than to hold a decanter of brownish liquid that might have been Scotch or rye whiskey, and was bounded on its sides by four glasses. Above the bookcase the wall was covered with a neatly arranged collection of photographs. Watson recognized one of the Earl astride one of his chestnuts, another he took to be Lady Lonsdale riding a hunter, two were from the Earl's Arctic expedition, one with dogs at temporary rest beside the sleds they had been pulling, and the second showing a group of men dressed in heavy parkas and leggings, waiting uncomfortably for the cameraman to record them for the posterity they hoped to achieve. There was as well an assortment of unrecognizable

132

fighters, most of them standing beside a smiling Lord Lonsdale, all of them glaring at the camera with the ferocity expected of members of their profession. Above a couch on the wall opposite the photographs, there was a painting of a horse, a powerful chestnut that appeared to have paused long enough to allow the artist to capture it at contented rest.

Watson pronounced himself satisfied with the arrangement and asked Overby to summon the senior Mr. Cochrane, Lord Lonsdale's coachman, he added by way of unnecessary clarification. Overby, who did not regard summoning guests a part of his duties, bristled momentarily before deciding the use of a disparaging tone would allow him to register his protest without jeopardizing his situation. "If that's your wish, sir." He decided to avoid additional requests for messenger services through the simple expedient of never again appearing in Watson's presence.

The coachman stood just outside the office, brushed back straight sandy hair that was already in place, and looked to the man behind the desk for direction.

"Please, Mr. Cochrane, come in and have a seat."

"Thank you, sir." Cochrane hesitated a moment, studying the three chairs as if only one would support him and he had to determine which. Catching sight of the portrait of the chestnut, he gave it a quick nod of recognition and took the chair nearest the painting. "Mr. Overby said you wanted to see me." His voice was as much incredulous as wary.

"That's quite right, Mr. Cochrane. My name is Dr. John Watson. I was at the boxing match last night. Let me say first you should be very proud of how well your son fought. Last night he was a little overmatched, but he has great style and heart, and I'm sure will be a fine fighter if he chooses to stay with the sport."

"Thank you for that, Doctor. My son has skills, but he is young. I'd have to agree that he wasn't ready to take on a fighter like Mackenzie. Not yet anyway." Cochrane's face creased its way into a worried frown before sharing the confession he'd been holding back. "I should tell you, sir, I'd left the boxing theater with my son after his fight, but I know who you are. You were with Mr. Holmes at the Club last night and in his corner during the fight with Mackenzie. You know they got Mr. Capelhorn and Mr. Simon upstairs together with me and Rochester. And the two of them are full of talk about Mr. Holmes and how he come off the floor to take Mackenzie out, and how Mackenzie died right after. Begging your pardon, Doctor, I just didn't want you to think I was pretending not to know who you are."

Watson waved away any suggestion of concern. "And what is it they're saying about the fight?"

Parker Cochrane moved his considerable bulk to one side of his chair, then back to its center before responding. "Nothing more than you might expect, sir. They was surprised by it was all. They thought your friend knew what he was about alright, but was still surprised to see Mackenzie go down like he did. But you should talk to them about it. I didn't see what happened. I was busy with my boy."

Watson laid aside his pencil and digressed from the course of questioning to attend to the coachman's obvious concern. "And how is your son?"

"He's coming along just fine now, thank you, sir. Doctor Lang says the punishment he took just made him a little silly for a while, but he'll be himself in a day or two and he looks to me like he's already near back to his old self."

"That's good to hear." Watson smiled his relief to the coachman. "How did the match between your son and Sailor Mackenzie come about?"

"It was Lord Lonsdale asked me did I think it would be alright to give Rochester a go against someone with a little more experience than the youngsters from the nearby towns he'd been fighting up to then. His Lordship seen him using this way of fighting I taught him where he stays on the move, hitting and running. I started him fighting that way because he's not yet got the punch to mix it up with some of the bigger men. It's worked real well with the local blokes, which is why His Lordship tells me he believes he's ready to take the next step. 'Take the next step' is just how he put it to me. Well, with him being His Lordship, and knowing as much about the sport as he does, of course I said yes." Cochrane shrugged his way to the rest of his response. "His Lordship got in touch with Mr. Fleming, who got in touch with Mr. Capelhorn, and the next thing I know we got us a match. As soon as everything is set, Lord Lonsdale went and brought in Jem Mace—he's the old champ, you know. He brought him to Lowther Castle to work with my boy and he done wonders. He showed Rochester things I never could have."

"What did you know about Sailor Mackenzie before the fight?"

The coachman's face was now a frown of confusion. "Begging your pardon, Doctor, but may I know why you're asking these questions? Why are you so concerned about the fight last night?"

Watson smiled his way to a more conciliatory tone. "It's not for myself I have these questions, Mr. Cochrane. My good friend, Mr. Holmes, is very concerned about Mackenzie's death and his part in causing it, and wishes to understand exactly what happened. It's for him I'll be making some notes as you and I talk."

"Well, with respect, sir, I would tell your Mr. Holmes he shouldn't be feeling responsible. These things happen. Especially when a fighter don't take care of himself."

"How do you mean he didn't take care of himself?"

"Mackenzie changed. There was a time Ian took the fight game seriously. It's no secret you get old and slow together, and when there's a love for the bottle thrown in, it can make for a bad end like it did here."

"I see. You called him Ian, and you say he's changed, does that mean you knew Sailor Mackenzie from an earlier time?"

Parker Cochrane again shifted position in his chair. "I did, sort of. I used to do a little fighting myself when I was a young man. Not any place like the Sporting Club, but I held my own in clubs in Liverpool and Manchester and the like. Mackenzie—he wasn't Sailor then, that came later—anyway, he was getting a little bit of a reputation for being a comer around the same time I was getting a little too old for the fight game. He'd come to Liverpool and we was supposed to have a fight—I thought it was all worked out—but the deal fell through. I quit for good after that, and I never come back into it until Rochester started fighting. And I only done it then because the boy asked me."

"And the son had the fight his father never did?" Watson remembered the boy's words to his father: 'I'm sorry, dad. I didn't get it done.'

"I guess you could say that." And with that the coachman gave up the struggle to find a comfortable position in his chair. He bolted straight up, pushing the chair from its careful arrangement, and without so much as a glance back, turned to walk away. Watson feared he was about to lose Cochrane and wondered whether a strategy of apology—he wasn't sure for what—or of demanding his cooperation would be the more likely to keep him in the room. But Watson's fears proved groundless. The coachman got only as far as the picture of the chestnut, and the man and the horse stared at each other for several seconds. Then, as abruptly as he had turned away from Watson, he pivoted back, acting as though his sudden interest in the room's artwork was the most natural thing imaginable.

"He's Merlin you know, His Lordship's favorite. A fine animal he is too." Cochrane came nearer, finally grasping the back of the chair that moments earlier had proven unequal to the task of holding him. In his large muscled hands it appeared as though the solid mahogany could be at risk. "There's more to tell about me leaving the fight game. It's nothing I'm proud of, but you'll hear it from others and you might just as well hear it from me. I quit fighting when my wife died. I had no stomach for the game after that—no, and not for anything else. She was my woman. It was up to me to take care of her and I couldn't raise the money for her doctoring. Not that I didn't try, I couldn't get a fight or land a job no matter who I asked or what I done, and it was only weeks after that she was gone. That's when I just give up. I put the boy with my sister and I started to drink, and I didn't stop until her husband come and half carried me to McLellan Manor, where my sister had got me the promise of a job with Mr. Trent. She had an in with Mrs. Trent from when she worked for her father before she got married and left service. Right off, with no questions asked, they made me a groom though I was more like a stable boy at the start, which was alright with me because even though I took to the horses right off, I knew I had a lot to learn. And they even let me bring Rochester to keep with me.

"I stopped drinking the day I arrived at the Manor. It was part because Mr. Trent told me he'd sack me the first time he saw me with a bottle in my hand, but mostly it was because I had my boy back with me. Anyways, I ain't touched a drop the whole time since and that's the God's honest truth. Later on, after Mr. Trent saw I had a way with horses, and that I had a hold of myself, he told me His Lordship was wanting a coachman, and it was time for me to better myself. He said he was recommending me for the position and I had better take it if I knew what was good for me. Of course, I took it on his say so, and I been with His Lordship out to Lowther Castle ever since." His confession complete, Cochrane pulled the chair back and sank his body into it. "And now you know the worst of it, though like I say there's none of it ain't known to some."

"I thank you for that, and I congratulate you on what you've done with your life and with your boy's life." There was a low grunt from Cochrane and an embarrassed nod. "I'm obliged to you, sir, for those good words." Watson seized on the happy turn in mood to resume the interview he had prepared. "I should like to get back to Mackenzie and his fight with your son. When I saw you last night I couldn't help but think you had some feelings about the man?"

"I don't like him if that's what you mean, or I guess I should say I didn't like him. I'm telling you that flat out. He was fighting against my son and he was a mean, dirty fighter and there's none would tell you different. No, I didn't like him, and I'll not say I did because he's now lying dead. And it's not just me. There's plenty will tell you Ian Mackenzie would as soon light a candle for the devil as wish a body good day."

"Would Mr. Capelhorn say that?"

Parker Cochrane licked dry lips and swallowed before responding. "There's stories I could tell about Sidney Capelhorn and Sailor Mackenzie, but it's not my place. I'll only say this. Sidney Capelhorn would be better off if he never laid eyes on Sailor Mackenzie, and he'll tell you so his own self."

"And Mrs. Mackenzie?"

"I've said my piece, sir. I'll say no more. I should get back to my son now. He's not yet over his hurting and the boy needs me." Cochrane pushed down on the clawed arms of his chair, but this time he waited for Watson to release him.

"I'll only keep you a little longer, Mr. Cochrane. I need to know what happened at the Manor the day before the fight? As I understand it, all of you were together at the Manor that day. Isn't that a somewhat unusual arrangement?"

Watson filled his pipe with tobacco and lit it, and found the simple act a matter of intense interest to the coachman. Cochrane watched the fire catch and a ribbon of smoke snake its way to the ceiling before speaking. "It's damned unusual if you'll pardon me for saying so, sir. His Lordship asked me to come to the Manor so of course I done so. Me and Rochester and my stable boy, who was to make like he was my second though I didn't want him to do any more than just carry the bucket and towel. His Lordship said I'd get a chance to see the Manor again after all my years away, and that we could all go back to the Club together, but I'd just as soon we went separate and I didn't see Mackenzie until the fight."

"And what of your day at the Manor?" Watson asked.

"Yes sir, I was about to tell you about that. We got there late Sunday morning. They put me and Rochester and the boy in one cottage, Mr. Capelhorn was by himself in another, and Mackenzie and his wife were in a third. Of course, Mr. Simon, being Mr. Trent's butler and valet, had his own room in the house. I can tell you I saw to it my boy stayed in the cottage most of the day and the whole time of the party they give that night.

"Anyway, in the afternoon while Mackenzie was off doing whatever he was doing, Mr. Simon walked Capelhorn and me all over the Manor. Of course, I seen it all before what with me having been a groom there years ago. The only thing I was really interested in was the stables and the horses out in the pasture. Mr. Trent has got himself a couple of fine hunters I did want to get a look at. And Mrs. Trent's bay was something beautiful to see. A mare she is, frisky as you like, and with as pretty a stride as you could hope for when she took it in her mind to take off for a run."

Cochrane's face relaxed into a near smile at the memory before hardening again as he continued. "We finally got to the greenhouse, which was the last thing Mr. Simon wanted us to see. I told him he already showed it to me when I first come to work at the Manor, which is something he does for everybody when they come to the Manor, but Mr. Simon said the master wanted me to see it again. Both of them—the master and Mr. Simon—are that proud of those plants. I guess because so many of them come from where they lived in Africa. And of course they always want you to see the plant that's got poison in it, and talk about how to handle it without the poison getting on you or your losing any of it. By the time he was done, I was glad to get back to the cabin on account of Rochester, and of me needing my rest.

"We all got together at supper except I still kept Rochester out of it. They did lay on a fine meal in the servants' hall with me being treated practically like gentry even though I was a groom with many of them. Even Mackenzie behaved himself for a while, drinking the beer Mr. Simon poured for us and not looking for more, but then Mr. Simon got called away for something by Mrs. Trent, and pretty soon Mackenzie was back to being Mackenzie. I never saw a man could get drunk so quick. His wife tried to get him to slow down, and what does he do but jump all over the poor woman in front of everybody."

"What do you mean 'jump all over' her"?

"He told her to shut her fool mouth or he'd shut it for her, except he was pretty soon so far gone he couldn't have shut anybody's mouth. That's when me and Mr. Capelhorn and Mr. Simon, who was back by then, all got together to carry him back to his cottage and put him to bed. They said it wasn't the first time they'd had to half carry him off after a drunk, and this time was better than most because he was pretty much passed out. Even so, we wasn't taking any chances. They said he could wake up as mean as before he went to sleep so Mrs. Charters, the housekeeper, told Mrs. Mackenzie she'd find a place for her in the staff's quarters. Mrs. Mackenzie said she'd just wait until Mackenzie was asleep so she could get the things she'd need before coming to the Manor. She said that after he got to sleep, a train could run through the room without him waking up. Mr. Simon said he'd go by the cottage later on just to be sure everything was alright."

"And was that the end of it?"

"Things went back to being pretty much the way they was if that's what you mean, except it was like somebody pulled a blanket over the whole crowd and they got to mumbling to each other instead of really talking or having a good time. I left not long after to get back to Rochester who'd had his food sent over on a tray for both him and Peter—that's the name of my stable boy. Peter is too shy to go to supper with a whole bunch of people he don't know, besides which he's a good boy and wanted to keep Rochester company."

Cochrane again pushed back hair he alone found unruly. "I guess you could say there was one other thing happened. I had trouble sleeping. I always do before a fight, my own or my boy's—prob'ly worse with my boy's. Anyway, I stayed out for a while, not wanting to wake Rochester or Peter, and it seemed like Mr. Simon wasn't the only one who was checking that things were alright or maybe like me they just needed a walk. There was two people I counted going by the Mackenzie's cottage that night. And don't ask me who they was. I kept my distance from both of them, on top of which there was no moon to speak of what with it being on the edge of rain all day and night, so I can only say there was two people and nothing about who they was, not even if they was men or women—though I can't see what a woman would be doing out at that hour."

Cochrane was again in search of a more comfortable position in his chair, and Watson spoke to the reason for his unease. "Mr. Cochrane, I know you want to get back upstairs so let me just ask about the next day, the day of the fight. When did you first see Mackenzie that morning?"

"I never did see him until the train. I grabbed some breakfast at the house and took some food over to Rochester and Peter. From what Mr. Capelhorn told me, Mackenzie had his breakfast at his cottage. Anyway, when we got to the train,

Mr. Caplehorn, Mr. Simon and Mackenzie were in one compartment and we were in another, all of it paid for by His Lordship, and I made sure me and my boy had nothing to do with them from the time we left the Manor up until the fight."

"Nothing at all?"

"Nothing except for the one time on the train where Mr. Caplehorn and Mr. Simon asked me to watch Mackenzie while they went to get something to eat. They promised me he was asleep, and that between him getting over the night before and all the nips he'd got out of his flask before they finally wrestled it away from him, they was sure he'd stay asleep. They give me the flask to hide anyway just in case he did come to. But it was like they said, he stayed asleep the whole time."

Cochrane's hands gripped the carved paws at the end of his chair's arms. "Now, sir, that's honestly all there is to tell, and with your permission, I really should be going."

Watson stood up from behind the desk, giving Cochrane license to stand as well. "That's fine, Mr. Cochrane. I appreciate your cooperation. Please give your boy my best, and tell him that both Mr. Holmes and I look forward to seeing him in the ring at some later time. For now, could you please ask Mr. Capelhorn to join me?"

"What can I do for you, Doctor?" The man who had been Sailor Mackenzie's manager until 24 hours earlier knocked on the open door and strode halfway into the room. He differed from his predecessor in appearance as well as demeanor. Whereas Cochrane was a large, burly man intent on making himself smaller, Caplehorn was short, wiry and unconcerned about his size. Watson judged him to be in his early 60s, but thought he might be misled by the fringe of gray hair half-circling his head, his baldness emphasized rather than relieved by the thick brush of moustache extending across his sunken cheeks.

Watson gestured for Caplehorn to sit. In response, the

manager moved a few steps forward from where he stood in the room's center, remaining several steps from the three chairs in front of him. "I understand from Cochrane you're asking questions about the fight on account of Mr. Holmes thinking there was something strange about it. I mean with Mackenzie dying and all. Is that about right?"

"That's correct."

Sidney Caplehorn grunted, and came forward to sink his weight onto the center chair. "So, what is it you want to know?"

"First, I'd like to know how long you and Sailor Mackenzie worked together, and how you came to take him on. It's my understanding he could be quite a handful."

Caplehorn gave a high-pitched laugh. "There's a polite way of saying it. I took him on three, no, closer to four years ago. Even then he was over the hill, but I thought he might still have a few good fights in him—as long as the competition wasn't too stiff and the referee wasn't too sharp—if you take my meaning. Then, too, there's always action somewhere for an older fighter going downhill if he's willing to be a stepping stone for a younger man going uphill. I got other bruisers like him, but to tell the truth you almost can't have too many. Bruisers his age are always either getting themselves hurt, or suddenly up and quitting the fight game. And them as stay half the time think they're still twenty years old and rate better fights—which means fights that will get them more money. Of course, there's nobody gonna get them the pay day they think they deserve, or more than likely their Judy thinks they deserve. When you get bruisers asking for more money than they've ever been worth, you know there's a Judy in there someplace egging them on. I don't know what's worse for the fight game, a woman or the bottle.

"Anyway, Mackenzie's Judy was alright, but he didn't listen to her anyway. His problem—which ended up being my problem—was the bottle. Not that he was easy to deal with

143

when he was sober. You got a taste of what he was like, but you only seen him at the end of the day. What you saw went on all day long. First, he complains we got him up too early so he's not gonna be at his best for the fight that night. Then, his breakfast scones have all of a sudden got sugar icing so he's gonna have trouble with his stomach all day. After that, there was something wrong with the train, I can't remember what. And he's really upset when he finds out he's sharing the changing room with Cochrane. Of course, I'm not sure I blame him on that one. And you saw him challenge everybody at the fight because he's insulted they threw a green fighter against him.

"With all of that, I'd be lying if I said he didn't have a plus side. If you could only get him to behave, he was money in the bank. He had that big punch, and he always put on a good show what with his being willing to go after whoever they threw up against him. And then there was always the story of him knocking down Charlie Mitchell. You can believe every promoter put the word out on that one as quick as he could."

Caplehorn shook his head over his loss, and Watson seized on his moment of despair to pose his question. "But as I hear it, the Club didn't ask for Mackenzie or any one fighter. You chose to give the fight to Mackenzie in spite of his being a problem. Why did you do that?"

Caplehorn interlocked the fingers of his two hands across his chest loudly cracking his knuckles before responding. "Well, there's a bit of a story there. When Mr. Fleming got in touch with me, he told me he was after one of my experienced fighters. Of course, I knew what that meant. Me and Mr. Fleming go back a way, back to before he come up in the world and gets with the likes of the National Sporting Club. From what he says I understand I'm to come up with somebody who could give a good fight, but maybe was past where he could give too good a fight—if you take my meaning. Don't get me wrong, I don't mean anything was worked out before the fight. Nothing like that. It was just he had a boy who was coming along, and maybe had a future in the game, and my bruiser was to have the style and reputation that could show off the boy's skills. And I had just the bruiser lined up for the job. A fighter needing a couple of solid pay days before he could get out of the business, but who could still entertain a crowd. He had the bottle under control, and a wife who was willing to stay out of his life, maybe a little too willing—if you take my meaning.

"Anyway, everything is set, except right about then Mackenzie gets wind of the fight and he comes to me and asks can he have it. And he makes such a fuss about the whole thing that I finally give it to him. I guess if he could have knowed your Mr. Holmes was going to be his second opponent that same night, he might of thought twice about asking for the fight."

Caplehorn looked around as if concerned someone had snuck into the room without his knowing. He leaned his way across the desk to speak to Watson. "All this talk is building up quite a thirst. Would there be anything a couple of men might share by way of being sociable?"

Watson looked to the bottle and glasses on the sideboard with Caplehorn closely following his glance. "By all means, Mr. Caplehorn, please pour yourself a drink. If you don't mind I won't join you just yet." Caplehorn had risen when Watson completed his first sentence, and showed no qualms about drinking alone in spite of his professed concern with sociability. After the manager was reseated and had drunk his benefactor's good health, Watson continued, now reading from the notes he had been making. "There are some things I'd like to ask you to explain, Mr. Caplehorn. I believe there's something more you can tell me about the fight arrangements. In particular, I'd like to know why you took the fight from the man you say had his drinking under control and gave it to Mackenzie who clearly did not. You don't strike me as a man who would do that just because Mackenzie asked you to."

Capelhorn pulled absently at a corner of his moustache while he considered his response. "I guess there's no harm in talking about it now. It's all ancient history anyway, and it might explain some of what happened." However, instead of providing the promised explanation, Capelhorn stood and started back to the tray of drinks, calling to Watson he thought he might have another short one first. Watson gave an indifferent wave as the permission Capelhorn hadn't sought. The manager poured what he liberally described as a short one, tossed it back and, stopping only to allow himself a small sigh of relief, returned to his chair and to Watson's question.

"I guess Cochrane didn't tell you any of this. Well, that's alright. It's bound to come out some time and now's as good a time as any. Partly, it's that Mackenzie and Cochrane go back a long ways. Not the young Cochrane of course; this goes back to when Parker was the age Mackenzie is now and Mackenzie was the age of young Rochester. There was a fight worked out between the two of them—I mean Mackenzie and Parker Cochrane. It was the same kind of set-up as was at the Club. You had a young fighter on his way up, which was Mackenzie, going against a bruiser on his way down, which was Parker Cochrane. Except the fight never comes off. What happens is Mackenzie decides he's being put in against a fighter he can't beat and he wants out. But he needs an excuse to get out, and it's got to be something that won't hurt his reputation. So he puts out the word that Cochrane has asked him to lie down, claiming if Mackenzie does that, he'll pay him off out of his winnings.

"Well, it's not like that kind of thing didn't happen in those days except it was supposed to be the promoter that did the fixing, and he was supposed to make sure the right people knew what was gonna happen before it happened. That's

146

major. If bruisers began making their own arrangements there'd be no way to keep things right for the bookmakers. That's why just the suspicion of a bruiser laying down on his own was enough to keep him from ever getting another fight. Which is exactly what happened to Cochrane.

"What I heard was that Mackenzie's story hit Cochrane at a bad time. His wife had some kind of sickness and he had a real need for the fight money. I don't know if that's true, there's always talk about the troubles people are having. Anyway, Cochrane done his best to put down Mackenzie's story, telling everybody who'd listen that he was a coward and a liar. Which I think a lot of people secretly believed, but nobody felt they could take a chance on Cochrane regardless. Besides which, nobody had to. Like I was telling you, there's always another over the hill bruiser ready to fill the bill. What I didn't know is that Mackenzie still has got it in for Cochrane all these years later for 'blackening his name' is the way he put it. So when he hears about this fight, he wants the action and badgers me into giving it to him."

"But I still don't understand, Mr. Capelhorn, even if Mackenzie wanted the fight, why did you feel it necessary to give it to him?"

"What I done I had my reasons for doing; I didn't break any laws and I don't see where it's anybody's business." To make his point, Capelhorn's mouth closed in a tight line giving every indication it might never open again.

Watson regarded him with the confidence of a card player holding a pat hand. "As I say, Mr. Capelhorn, my only interest is with understanding the events of Mackenzie's death in so far as they involve my friend, Mr. Holmes. However, if there appear to be things I can't explain, or that seem suspicious, I'm duty bound to bring those to the attention of Inspector Lestrade of Scotland Yard. I believe you saw the Inspector the night of Mackenzie's death. Of course, if I learn what I need to know and there's nothing that warrants going any further, that will be the end of it." Watson took up the pipe he had allowed to lose fire, relit it, and waited for Capelhorn to complete the argument he was having with himself.

"None of what I know has got anything to do with Mackenzie's death—none of it. But I can't afford to get involved with the bobbies. If I explain it to you, and you see where it's got nothing to do with Mackenzie's death, can I count on you to keep the whole thing just between us?"

"If it has nothing to do with the fighter's death, I'll say nothing to the police. You have my word on that."

Capelhorn stared a moment longer at Watson's impassive mask before deciding finally to risk sharing his story. "It was twenty or maybe nearer twenty-five years ago. I had a brother in those days. He's gone now so it don't matter what I say about him. Anyway, he was a cracksman and a good one. I was making a living with my fists, at least mostly that way, the same time he was getting into people's safes. We kept out of each other's way except he came to some of my fights when he wasn't working—if you take my meaning. But then there's this one time he comes to me with what he says is a problem. He's expecting the police to toss the place where he's staying and he's got a bunch of stuff he ain't been able to move yet. He's wanting to leave the swag with me because, he says, nobody would think to come to my place to look; plus, he says, he's got nobody else he can turn to and he promises it won't be for more than two days, probably just one.

"Well, what can I say? He's my brother and my baby brother at that. What he doesn't figure on is a blower from his own crowd going to the police and telling them all what he stole and where to find it, which is to say telling them where I live. They come to my place, and everything is sitting out because I don't take the time to hide anything with me only supposed to have it for a day or two. They take me down for having 'stolen articles' they call it, and they give me two ways to go. I can tell on my brother, who they know done the stealing, in which case I go scot-free, or I can keep my mouth shut and go inside. Which is what I done of course. I played like somebody left everything there while I was out—which was true enough—and I didn't know who had left it—which of course I did know. So I ended up doing fourteen months in Newgate for my brother." Capelhorn licked his lips, and glanced to the bottle on the side-table. Watson pretended not to follow his look; Capelhorn swallowed a phantom drink and continued.

"While I'm inside I catch the typhoid fever. I get over it okay, but I never get all my strength back, and between the typhoid and me getting a year older—more than a year actually—I find I ain't got it anymore to go back inside the ring. So I get back on the streets and I knock around for a while catching work anyplace I can find it, until it finally hits me that what I know best is boxing and maybe there are things I can do besides the fighting. Only I find out pretty quick that a history of being put away is going to keep me from getting work anyplace they know me. So I go up north to Liverpool where nobody knows me, and I catch on as a second working with a lot of different fighters in and around Liverpool. And gradually I start picking up my own bruisers who maybe got dropped by the managers they had, or didn't like the way they were being treated, and were ready for new management. You see, most all managers are on the lookout for a kid they can ride into the big money. Me, I'm happy to pick up the guys they leave behind. And pretty soon it's working out for me and I'm managing full time.

"By the time Mackenzie comes to see me I got a nice little business going. And I know all about Mackenzie so I know nobody wants to handle him, even with him being a draw, because his drinking has him not showing up, or showing up but not able to fight. I'm ready to give him the breeze like all the others done, when he tells me unless I take him on he's gonna put the word out about my having been in prison.

"It turns out that this one time he gets thrown in jail for breaking up a pub—which is something he was doing on a regular basis—he runs into somebody who knows me from when I did time in Newgate. That's how come Mackenzie comes looking for me, and that's how come I take him on, and it's why I gave him the fight with Cochrane's boy when he asks me to. At the time I had no idea he's still got it in for Cochrane. To tell you the truth, I thought the boy's style would be just the thing to put Mackenzie on his back and maybe get him out of my hair—what little I got—for good and all. Of course, I never figured it would be your Mr. Holmes that would get it done or that his leaving would be permanent.

"But like I been telling you, all this is from way in the past and is got nothing to do with your friend or what happened to Mackenzie. The way he was going this was bound to happen sooner or later. Anyway, it's also why I got out of the Club as fast as I could when Bettinson said he was calling the police, just in case you were wondering about that." Capelhorn looked evenly to Watson, holding his gaze while he waited a decision about his future. Watson did not keep him waiting long.

"I'll make no promises. I can't until I've finished my investigation, but as of the moment I see no reason for sharing anything you've told me with Scotland Yard."

Capelhorn nodded his understanding. "I'll take that as being as much as I can expect. Is there anything more you need from me?"

Watson asked Capelhorn what he knew of Mrs. Mackenzie, but like Cochrane he said nothing more than that he felt sympathy for the woman. Likewise, Capelhorn added little to Cochrane's report of the day's activity, dismissing Simon's tour as a bunch of things he was seeing for at least the second time, and claiming he joined the walk only to stretch his legs. He recounted the same story as Cochrane about Mackenzie getting drunk after Simon was called away, and having to be carried to his cottage after dinner the night before leaving for London, adding only they'd left the door unlocked at Simon's direction. Watson wondered if he could remember being out of his cottage that night and received Capelhorn's vigorous denial. He gave the same story as Cochrane about the train ride, elaborating only on the difficulty he and Simon had in wrestling Mackenzie's flask from him before he could drink himself out of the fight. After swearing he'd told all he knew, Watson told him he could go back upstairs, and asked him to send down Simon.

Simon waited entrance to Lord Lonsdale's office standing at an attention more perfect than any Watson had seen since leaving the Fusiliers. He was powerfully built, as Watson remembered from the National Sporting Club, although now he could also see a small paunch had begun to press against his white shirtfront. Long sideburns led to a closely trimmed small beard that framed a face dominated by narrow piercing eyes and a tight line of mouth. He was darker complected than the few blacks Watson had known, but Watson hadn't known any black men who had come to England directly from the African continent. Watson invited the man to be seated, and then found himself the object of the same intense study to which he subjected Simon. He concluded the Trent's valet had mastered the art of giving service without becoming servile.

Watson introduced himself and explained his purpose, although he was certain Simon was hearing the information for at least the second time. Adopting an affable tone, Watson again took up a pencil and began his questioning. "I know you are called Simon. Is that truly your only name?"

"I have another name. It is hard for European people

to say, so I am called Simon."

"I would be interested in learning your other name. May I have it for the records I am keeping?"

"I will tell you, but you will wish to call me Simon and I prefer that you do. I am of the Thembu tribe, a Xhosa speaking people. In Xhosa my name is Sipliwo Jadezwal. You will need me to spell that for your records."

Watson acknowledged the accuracy of the butler's judgment, and then found it necessary to request multiple spellings. "You're a long way from your home in Africa. I have heard from others that as a child you were orphaned in a war between tribes and came to be rescued by Mr. Trent. Can you tell me more about how you and Mr. Trent met and the years since?"

"I will, but you must first know my home is England. I have no home in Africa, and haven't had one since I first met Mr. Trent twenty-four years ago. There was, as you call it, a war, but it was not the kind of war there is in this part of the world. There were raids back and forth over many years, and it was in one of those raids my parents and my older brother and sister were killed. I hid in the fields far from our hut and was never found, but they burned the village and so I had no one and nothing to go back to. I was a boy, not yet a hunter or warrior, and besides I had no weapons even if I would have had the skills of a warrior. I walked for three or maybe four days eating grewia fruit until I decided there was no use going on and I crawled into a deep gully to say the death prayer. I lay down where Death could find me, but Mr. Trent found me first. He took me to his cabin where he fed me and cared for me until I was well again. I owe him my life so it is now my duty to protect his."

"Does Mr. Trent need protection in Yorkshire?"

Simon shrugged. "There can be dangers every place. It is my job to see that none of them get to Mr. Trent."

"Was Mackenzie a danger to Mr. Trent?"

A smile creased its way across Simon's face. "Mr. Mackenzie was a danger to himself."

Watson looked to the butler with raised eyebrows and waited. Simon met his gaze, but said nothing. Watson decided to take a new tack. "How did you come to be Mackenzie's second and what did that involve?"

The small trace of smile disappeared and was replaced by the butler's earlier look of bored indifference. "It was Mr. Trent's request. He asked me if I would be willing to work with Mr. Capelhorn and Mr. Mackenzie. I told him if he wanted me too, of course I would. I sparred with Mr. Mackenzie and did exercises with him, and other times I helped Mr. Capelhorn find him."

"Find him?"

"He liked his drink, and he had a way of disappearing to places where no one would bother him about it."

"It sounds as though he created quite a problem for you."

"He was not a problem for me." The butler's face was stone and his voice matched his expression.

"And staff? How did he get along with staff?"

Simon echoed his master's response to the same question. "He didn't get along, he never tried to."

"Does that mean there were bad feelings between Mackenzie and members of staff?"

"Staff kept their distance from Mr. Mackenzie, and most of the time Mr. Mackenzie had nothing to do with staff."

"Most of the time?"

"As I've said, Mr. Mackenzie was a man who drank too much. When he drank he could be ugly toward people, and disrespectful toward women."

"With what women was he disrespectful?"

"Women. Some at the Manor, some in town. It would not be right for me to share names. I can tell you he stopped bothering anyone at the Manor." Simon sniffed a grim satisfaction at the last.

"And in town?"

"Town was not my concern."

Watson looked to the butler's expressionless eyes and elected to change the topic. "Tell me about the activities at the Manor the weekend before the fight at the National Sporting Club."

"There's nothing much to tell. Lord Lonsdale arrived by himself, Mr. Bettinson and Mr. Fleming arrived with their wives a little past mid-day Saturday. Mr. Cochrane and his son arrived at the Manor Sunday morning. After they had lunch, I offered to take Mr. Cochrane and his son on a tour of the grounds as Mr. Trent had asked me to do. He said a walk might do them good after sitting for a while, and Mr. Cochrane might enjoy seeing the Manor again after all his years away. Mr. Cochrane joined me, but his son chose to stay behind. Mr. Capelhorn said he needed the exercise and also came with us. That evening there was a dinner for Mr. Cochrane in servants' hall which ended with Mr. Mackenzie drinking too much and having to be helped to his cottage, and Mrs. Mackenzie taking a bed at the Manor. The next morning we rose before the others, and together with Mr. Mackenzie, we traveled to London."

"I understand Mackenzie's door was left unlocked after you took him to his cottage. Was that your idea?"

"It was. Mrs. Mackenzie had to get into the cottage to get her things, and I wanted to be able to enter later without waking him. I thought I should make certain there was nothing wrong with Mr. Mackenzie since he had the fight the next day."

"And did you?"

"Yes, and Mr. Mackenzie was sleeping soundly."

"Did you see anyone else while you were out?"

"No one, but I wasn't looking for anyone."

"Did you see Mrs. Mackenzie return? Do you know

how long she was gone?'

"I saw no reason to track Mrs. Mackenzie's movements and know nothing of her activities."

Watson pressed on, feeling himself slogging through mud toward an unknown, but clearly distant destination. "I understand the greenhouse was part of your afternoon tour. What can you tell me about it?"

"It's got plants Mr. Trent collected from when he was in Africa and from different parts of England. The greenhouse is specially heated to keep them alive no matter what the weather is like outside."

"Are any of the plants poisonous?"

Simon shrugged. "There's one that is." He made it sound as though every home might have one.

"And you showed Mr. Capelhorn and Mr. Cochrane that plant?"

"It's what we show all guests and new staff."

"And what did you show them about the plant?"

There was again the small trace of a smile as Simon challenged Watson's impatient stare. "I showed them where the poison collects, and I told them how native South Africans get to it and use the poison in hunting. It's something I show all new staff. Mr. Trent had shown the same things to his guests the day before."

"And it's only you and Mr. Trent who have keys to the greenhouse?"

"That is correct."

"And you would never lend your key to anyone. They are always with you?"

For the first time the butler's face clouded over, and he turned his gaze away from Watson. "There was one instance in which my key went missing. It was Sunday afternoon or night before we left for London. I'm certain it will turn up."

"Then it's still missing?" Watson asked in mock

surprise.

"It is." Simon again sounded an observer at his own interrogation. "It will be found if it hasn't already."

"Perhaps. Tell me please, what is the name of the poisonous plant?"

"In English, Latin, or Xhosa?"

"English and Latin will do, thank you."

"The passionflower in English, Adenia digitata in Latin."

Watson studied his notes and was grateful to find he had no additional questions. "That will be all, Simon."

"Very good, sir."

Chapter 10.
Mrs. Hudson Pays Her Respects

Following Elizabeth's directions, Mrs. Hudson made her way to Lillie Langtry's bedroom. The room seemed designed especially for Lillie. A canopied bed trimmed with white ruffles stood between saffron curtained windows that looked out to the Wharfe River. A dressing table and stool, three easy chairs and round table were all rich curves and bowed legs while the room's wallpaper guaranteed the eternal blossoming of hundreds of tiny coral-colored flowers. Lillie sat with her pink lounging robe gathered in folds about her, the small book of Whitman's poems open on her lap. She turned at Mrs. Hudson's knock and smiled a greeting.

Mrs. Hudson's words reflected the confusion she felt about her role. "I expect you'll be needin' some 'elp with dressin' for dinner."

Lillie's smiled broadened. "I could use some assistance, Mrs. Hudson. I was planning on wearing the blue silk and I'll require some help with my hair as well."

For the next half hour Mrs. Hudson helped Lillie with her ablutions, then with fitting her into the gown she had selected. Elbow-length puffy sleeves exposed bare arms while the low scoop of neckline revealed a tempting expanse of Lillie's milky bosom. The dress was drawn tight at the waist before widening broadly to its hem. It showed modest pleating at its back where the now unfashionable bustle would have been. It was a newer and more daring fashion than would have made its way to Oxley, or might ever make its way. It was, however, exactly what would be expected of Lillie Langtry.

After dressing her hair in accord with Lillie's direction, Mrs. Hudson took the box of jewelry from the wardrobe shelf and held it for Lillie to make her selection. She chose a double string of small pearls that would show at the base of her neck. It was, Mrs. Hudson told her, "very becomin'." Lillie acknowledged her judgment, but looked to her glass before pronouncing herself satisfied. With Lillie's preparation complete, Mrs. Hudson felt it time to address her own plans for the evening.

"Mrs. Langtry, I'm wonderin' if I can ask a favor."

Lillie looked warily to her newly anointed maid. "What would that be?"

Mrs. Hudson abhorred lies, even small ones, but had come to accept that the work of investigation sometimes required lying, and the lies were not always small. Once having decided it was necessary to lie, she made a study of the elements essential to lying effectively and concluded there were only two. First, the lie had to be simple. Simplicity guaranteed it would be easy to remember and occasion few questions, ideally no questions at all. Questions risked the need to develop additional supporting lies, each one of which had to be consistent with every other lie in the chain, a nearly impossible feat. Second, the lie had to be untraceable. There had to be no way to check that it was, in fact, a lie. That was best accomplished by creating a lie based solely in one's own history and experience. A third element, desirable but not critical, was to attach emotion to the lie such that the person lied to would feel sympathy for the person telling the lie, and be less inclined to question the story that's been told.

"Elizabeth, the parlor maid, tells me that visitors and the Manor staff 'ave been to see the insides of the glass 'ouse out back. I was wantin' to see that myself. Tobias and I talked about startin' up our own garden someday. Of course it wouldn't be anythin' near so grand as what's in the glass 'ouse, but if I could just get a look at the flowers Mr. Trent 'as brought back from 'is wanderin's, it would give me some idea of what goes into a proper garden. If you've no objection, I was wonderin' if you might ask Mrs. Trent if I could see the insides of the glass 'ouse later today."

Lillie Langtry looked quizzically to Mrs. Hudson

before shrugging her indifference. "I can't see any harm to it, Mrs. Hudson. I'll speak to Mrs. Trent."

"Thank you, ma'am. I thought I might go while you're all at supper. It's my understandin' Mr. 'Enderson, the gardener, 'as got a key, and that way I can be back in time to 'elp with your gettin' ready for bed." Mrs. Hudson's eyes widened as if surprised by a sudden thought. "Oh, and if I see Mrs. Mackenzie in my travels, I'll give 'er your sympathies."

Lillie's confusion was evident as she struggled to recognize the name of the woman for whom she felt sympathy before groaning softly with the memory of the woman and her plight. "That would be very nice, Mrs. Hudson. Thank you for thinking of it. And I'll speak to Mrs. Trent about the greenhouse before dinner. I'll get word to you in the servants' hall. Now, if you would, please lay out my peignoir and nightgown."

Mrs. Hudson took her leave and made her way to the servants' hall to orchestrate the next step in her plans for the evening. As she expected, she found Mrs. Charters hand in hand with Christine overseeing the evening's preparations in the absence of Mr. Simon. She was doing her best to appear unflustered by her enlarged duties while being tugged by a child who had become suddenly hungry in the midst of a rich assortment of foods. The housekeeper interrupted supervision of the staff and her child to make perfunctory introduction of Mrs. Hudson to James, the Manor's first footman, whom Mrs. Hudson recognized as having met her coach. He paused in the process of shoveling a forkful of peas into his mouth long enough to nod acknowledgement of the lady's maid without hazarding to put his greeting into speech. James struck Mrs. Hudson as a taller, older and more sober version of Charles. Both men were already dressed in white tie and dress coat in consequence of their being in service later in the evening.

Mrs. Charters resumed explaining to James the duties

he would be expected to fulfill in tJameshe absence of Mr. Simon. Those duties seemed to consist largely of supervising Charles, although he would also have to coordinate the several wines with the different courses, and carve the roast when the table was ready for its serving. James nodded dutifully at appropriate intervals, all the while focusing attention on the broad back of Mrs. Groover and the happy prospect of her turning to him with a slice of seed-cake in hand. Charles was focused on Rachel's more shapely back, and the equally happy prospect of her turning around to catch a glimpse of the smile he held in readiness for her. Mrs. Hudson took note of both men's stares and hopes, but her larger interest was with the tray of food on a warming table to one side of the oven.

"Mrs. Charters, I know I'm a guest in Mrs. Groover's kitchen, but I'm wonderin' if there isn't somethin' I can do to 'elp since you're short-'anded. I'd be pleased to make myself useful if I could."

"Mrs. Hudson, it's kind of you I'm sure, but Mrs. Trent doesn't make use of a lady's maid. She believes it to be more of a city fashion." From her tone it was apparent Mrs. Charters was in full agreement with her mistress. "If there's need for assistance, Elizabeth can provide it." With that, Mrs. Charters returned to a review of seating arrangements for dinner while James warmly greeted his slice of seed-cake, and Charles looked in vain to be rewarded for his own earnest concentration.

"Mrs. Charters, I wondered if I might suggest somethin' else to be of assistance to you." The housekeeper turned from James to squint her skepticism at Mrs. Hudson while her daughter showed her now familiar blank smile. "I was noticin' you've set out Mrs. Mackenzie's dinner on the tray as it would seem she'll not be joinin' us. I know you're too busy yourself to take it, and with Elizabeth upstairs with Mrs. Trent, and James and Charles havin' their own jobs to do, I thought I could take the tray for you. To tell the truth,

Mrs. Charters, you'd be doin' Mrs. Langtry a good turn if you'd allow me to do so. I know she's wantin' to express 'er condolences to Mrs. Mackenzie. If I could take dinner, it would give me a chance to chat for a bit, and tell Mrs. Mackenzie of Mrs. Langtry's sympathies for 'er condition." Mrs. Hudson affected what she hoped was a warm smile to complement her second effort in less than an hour to incorporate all elements necessary to lying effectively.

"That is most generous, Mrs. Hudson, and very thoughtful of Mrs. Langtry." There was murmured approval from Mrs. Groover and an echo of her approval from Christine. Whether won over by Mrs. Hudson's argument, Mrs. Groover's concurrence, or a wish to rid the kitchen of all personnel she deemed nonessential to the evening's labors, Mrs. Charters was ready to admit her guest to service. "It's usually Clara's job, Mrs. Hudson, but I'd be delighted to have your assistance, and give you opportunity, as you say, to pay Mrs. Langtry's respects. Do you know the cottage in which Mrs. Mackenzie is staying?"

"Thank you, Mrs. Charters, I believe I do."

When Watson returned to Baker Street, he found Holmes in his dressing gown, his briar well lit, leafing through the afternoon *Standard*. "Watson, you're back. Excellent! I've decided you were right about our taking advantage of the City's attractions, at least in terms of dinner. There's a very favorable report in the paper about this Escoffier chap who's the new chef at the Savoy's River Restaurant, and it's been too good a day to allow the marks of honorable battle detain me any further."

Watson was mindful of the notes he would need to prepare for Mrs. Hudson, and the risk of sacrificing accurate reporting to the influence of rich food and fine wine. "Holmes, the River Restaurant is a fine idea. It would be a pleasant change from the food we've been reduced to in Mrs. Hudson's absence, but I'd like to take just a moment to jot down what you and Spooner were able to get done."

Holmes smiled a concession to Watson's concern. "I think we made a good start," Holmes reported. "I removed the alcohol and water from the whiskey in Mackenzie's flask, and was left with a residue indicating that something had indeed been added to the whiskey. I injected a sample of the residue into a mouse and have left it for Spooner to observe what happens to the animal, and follow up with an autopsy if, as we expect, the mouse does not survive. There's nothing more to be done for the moment.

"Oh, and one more thing, Watson," Holmes spoke in as off-hand a manner as he could manage. "I made arrangements for our friend Wiggins to keep watch on George Baird for the next two days. I thought it wise to keep an eye out just in case Baird learns of Lillie's whereabouts in spite of our efforts. I'm thinking a hansom driver or one of the Earl's staff could still undo our plans."

Watson opened his mouth to comment, thought better of it, and replacing the accounts book in his waistcoat, pronounced himself finished with his note-taking.

"Fine," said Holmes, "then let us dress for dinner and determine for ourselves if this Escoffier is truly the chef people say he is."

While Holmes and Watson dined on *supremes de volailles Jeanette*, not very many streets away Wiggins devoured the fish pie he'd bought at the pie shop near to the printer. For an additional penny he'd bought a cherry pie, knowing that cherries were in season and the pie would be fresh. He had removed all evidence of fish pie with a careful swipe of his forearm when a four-wheeler stopped beneath the street light fronting the entrance to Squire Baird's terraced house. The man who stepped from the coach wore a brown-checked frock coat and trousers, and had carrot-red hair that poked its way from under a soft homburg. There was a brief and unhappy exchange between the driver and his fare, ending with the passenger slapping coins into the coachman's hand and turning to enter the Baird home.

Twenty minutes later, the same man exited the Baird home, looked around for a cab and, seeing none, walked in the direction of Piccadilly where he would be certain to find one. The man had more spring to his step leaving than he had had coming, and a sly smile had replaced his earlier look of arrogant resolve. In Wiggins's world that could only mean one thing, the man had profited handsomely from his visit to George Baird. Wiggins munched on his cherry pie, and waited to see if the red-headed man's visit triggered any activity from inside the house. He stayed at his post even after the newly installed electric street lamps blinked on, creating pools of light beneath them and eerie shadows beyond. All the while, no one else entered or left Squire Baird's house. Only after the lights on the lower floors were extinguished, did Wiggins decide it was time to return to his room in the back of Augustus Stinchcombe's shop, but something told him it would be well for him to be in front of the Baird home by sun-up the next morning.

Except for the lamp that could be seen flickering through the open window, Mrs. Mackenzie's cottage was indistinguishable from the other two Mrs. Hudson passed as she picked her way over the stone path leading to its door. The three cottages, like the Manor, were constructed of fieldstone, but unlike the Manor's striking russet stonework, the cottages were built of brown and gray stone, and faded easily into the estate's drab background. Mrs. Hudson balanced the tray in one hand and rapped three times with her free hand. She was greeted by a seemingly disembodied head that angled itself to one side of the barely opened door. The head gave a single word of greeting, "Yes?"

"Good evenin', ma'am. I'm Mrs. 'Udson. I'm the maid to Mrs. Lillie Langtry who you may know is stayin' at the Manor. I've brought your dinner by way of 'elpin' out Mrs. Charters."

The head studied her a moment longer before opening the door to reveal the whole woman and allow Mrs. Hudson to bring her meal inside. Mrs. Mackenzie gave her a wan smile by way of meeting the essentials of sociability before pointing to a table on which Mrs. Hudson could place her tray. Her voice sounded remote, but not unfriendly. It was the voice of a woman whose experiences had taught her to be wary of the unknown, even a maid bringing her dinner.

"It's good o' ye to do this ... Mrs. Hudson, is it?" She got a confirming nod. "I'm not yet comfortable being with people; I'm sure ye can understand."

What Mrs. Hudson understood was that the woman was recovering from her recent loss with remarkable speed— if she had experienced any loss. There was no evidence of puffiness or redness beneath her eyes. There was, however, a trace of purpling above her left eye reminiscent of the injury sustained by Holmes, and almost certainly having the same source.

She seated herself in front of the fried sole and peas and potatoes, and was prepared to pay proper tribute to Mrs. Groover's cooking when either her curiosity or a sudden concern with propriety caused a delay in attacking her meal, and led her to give Mrs. Hudson her divided attention. "Were ye saying that ye're here with Mrs. Lillie Langtry?"

"I am indeed. We 'ave reason to be out of London and the Trents 'ave been good enough to welcome Mrs. Langtry as their guest. Indeed, Mrs. Langtry wanted me to extend 'er sympathy to you on Mr. Mackenzie's passin'. It must 'ave come as an awful shock."

The widow's small bow of a mouth came open as she turned her head slowly from side to side upon being reminded of her loss. "It's still that hard for me to believe he's gone. In the prime o' life as it were."

Mrs. Mackenzie made a second wan smile and waited on her server to excuse herself. Mrs. Hudson did not budge. "I'm a widow myself, Mrs. Mackenzie, and know what that's like. I still miss my Tobias every day." Mrs. Hudson seemed to have just become aware the woman had her dinner in front of her. "But I don't mean to keep you from your meal."

Since her server was making no move to leave, it appeared to Mrs. Mackenzie that if she was to have her food while it was warm—and perhaps if she was to have it at all— she would need to pretend a welcome.

"Won't ye have a seat, Mrs. Hudson—if ye don't mind sitting with me while I have myself a wee bite? Can I get ye a cup o' tea? I've the kettle on and it's no trouble." She half rose from her chair before Mrs. Hudson shooed her back down.

"You just go ahead and eat. You've 'ad quite enough to deal with. I'll get the tea for us both."

Mrs. Hudson went to the stove and returned with two cups of tea and, after a second trip for the sugar and lemon Mrs. Mackenzie said she took, she seated herself opposite her reluctant hostess. She took a sip of tea and closed her eyes as though overcome by a moment of utter contentment. "There's nothin' in the world to bring comfort like a cup of tea." Her voice took on a casual air. "I take it you'll be goin' on 'ome now. I couldn't 'elp noticin' you've got a fine Scottish lilt to your voice. Is your 'ome a long way from 'ere?"

Mrs. Mackenzie paused in gathering peas onto her fork. "I canna say there's anywhere I can rightly call home, Mrs. Hudson. Me and Ian—Ian's my man's right name—we moved around so much it would be hard to say where home might be. Mrs. Trent is saying I can stay as long as I need, but I know I'll have to move on sometime. I guess I'll likely go back to Glasgow, I've kin there—a sister, a brother, too, I think."

"Did Mr. Mackenzie 'ave family as well?"

"A brother, but the two o' them ain't spoke in years. I only know him 'cause his wife kept in touch with me for a while. She was a great one for family and the two of us got on even if our men never did. They're living in Glasgow's North End where her husband's got a little stationery store."

Mrs. Hudson nodded sympathetically and sipped her tea. "Is Glasgow where you're from?"

"It's where I was born and where I met Ian. He was so big and strong even when he weren't much more than a lad that the landlords would hire him to keep order in their pubs. It was a big joke that he wasn't old enough to drink, but he was big enough to tend to those who did. That's how Mr. Garfoyle found him and took him on to be one o' his bruisers."

"This Mr. Garfoyle was 'is manager?"

"More like the father he never had. And, if ye was fighting in Glasgow ye had to know Mr. Garfoyle or ye wasn't fighting in Glasgow. At least that's what Ian said and I never heard anyone say different." Having made short work of the fish and vegetables on the tray, Mrs. Mackenzie looked longingly to the seed-cake Mrs. Groover had provided, then to her guest. "I'm sorry to be going on like this, eating in front of ye with nothing to offer." She held a spoon in readiness of Mrs. Hudson's denial of concern, and her optimism was quickly rewarded.

"Oh, please think nothin' of it. I'll be gettin' my own supper shortly, and the tea and a chance to sit for a while is a blessin'. Please, you go right ahead." To prove her point, Mrs. Hudson took a long swallow of tea before continuing. "Were you and Mr. Mackenzie plannin' to go back to Glasgow?"

The woman delayed cutting into her seed-cake to respond to Mrs. Hudson's question.

"I'll tell ye the truth, ma'am, I can't say. It would have been up to Ian, and he was saying he was right comfortable here at the Manor. I'd no idea what he was thinking; we was

166

always on the move up to then. When one fight was over we'd go wherever Mr. Capelhorn had arranged for us to go for the next one. But Ian said we wouldn't be needing Mr. Capelhorn anymore. He said he'd had a wee talk with Mr. Trent not long after we got here, and it was agreed we could stay for just as long as we liked, which I thought couldn't be right, but Ian said that's how it was. I didn't know what it was all about, but it was true there was nobody telling us to pack up and go. Still and all, like I say, I'm thinking that I'll soon have to find a place for myself."

Mrs. Mackenzie seemed in danger of lapsing into a melancholy the death of her husband hadn't been able to rouse, and Mrs. Hudson moved to another subject.

"I see your little cottage is right close to Mr. Trent's glass 'ouse. I was goin' to get a little look at the buildin' myself later on. 'Ave you 'ad a chance to see its insides? Is there anythin' special I should see?"

Mrs. Mackenzie looked up from her plate with the corner of her mouth curled in an expression of distaste. "Mr. Simon took Ian and me for a visit not long after we got here. Truth to tell, I think it's a bit of a waste. There's not a plant in there can match what's growing outside your own door. And the one what's got poison in it just gives me the willies. Anyway, that's my feeling and I can tell ye I'm not alone." Mrs. Mackenzie laid her fork across an empty dish and gave a brave smile to Mrs. Hudson. "I'm most grateful to ye for bringing dinner, and I appreciate the talk and yer own lady's thinking of me which is really most kind, but now I'm feeling awful tired and I'd really like to rest."

"Yes, of course, Mrs. Mackenzie, and I thank you for the tea. I can wash up our cups if you like." The two women had gotten up from the table, and Mrs. Mackenzie was edging as quickly as politeness permitted in the direction of the door.

"Thank ye kindly, but that won't be necessary. There's just the two cups and I can easy do those."

167

"Then I'll just gather up the tray and say good evenin' to you. Remember, if there's anythin' further I can do, just call for Mrs. 'Udson."

Mrs. Mackenzie looked her out the door with a fixed smile that made clear to Mrs. Hudson she should not expect a call.

Chapter 11.
The Greenhouse at McLellan Manor

Within the hour, Mrs. Hudson was retracing her steps toward Mrs. Mackenzie's cottage, then passing it as she made her way to the greenhouse just beyond. Henderson trailed close behind, outside her line of sight, but well within grumbling distance. Henderson was unhappy with Mrs. Hudson, unhappy with his assignment, very likely unhappy with much of his life, and unconcerned who knew it. After first complaining to Mrs. Hudson about being put upon mercilessly and continuously, and receiving no response; he took to complaining to himself on the same subject with no loss in volume, but with the sure knowledge of finding a sympathetic audience. He caught up to Mrs. Hudson to unlock the door to the greenhouse, stood by it until she was inside, then closed it quickly behind her, speaking his first full sentence since they had begun their trek across the grounds. "They're very partic'lar about the temperature of the place."

Mrs. Hudson grunted acknowledgement, and started down the rows of plants in broad boxes and deep earthen pots. The plants were carefully labeled with their English and Latin names, and areas of origin.

"I'm told your husband had an interest in gardening." Henderson's inflection indicated he was raising a question, not stating a fact.

"I'm not sure I'd put it that way exactly. Where did you 'ear it?"

"It's what Mrs. Charters said when she asked me to show you the greenhouse. Ain't that the truth of it?" Henderson raised his voice as he grimaced his query. He still hadn't moved from the front door after closing it behind Mrs. Hudson.

Mrs. Hudson continued her leisurely walk past an area of ferns some with large fine-toothed leaves, others with small broad leaves, all of them subject to Mrs. Hudson's exaggerated study. "It's true in a way. 'E liked the idea of gardenin' and 'e was lookin' forward to spendin' time at it, but died before either of us got the chance. It's not somethin' I like to talk about." Mrs. Hudson's felt it wise to change the subject. "'Ave you been with the Trents long, Mr. 'Enderson?"

"You might ask how long I been with the Manor. It's longer than my being with the Trents. You could say I come with the place." Mrs. Hudson had the sense that he had said just that many times earlier. "I worked for the two families that come before, and my father for the family that come before them."

"And was the glass 'ouse 'ere then?"

Henderson spit out his response. "It was not. The plants was all outside the way God intended. Now, there's all these strange things growing inside. It ain't natural, but if you got the money, I guess you don't have to be natural, or respect God's own laws come to that. Here now, don't go touching anything. You don't know what it could be." The gardener had become alarmed as Mrs. Hudson bent to inspect a flowering plant more closely. "You've got to watch yourself, ma'am. You want to keep your distance from these plants. There's just the one that's marked poison, and that's only if you was to swallow the sap what's inside, but there's others I'm sure could have you scratching for days or breaking out in some kind of rash, and those ones ain't marked."

Mrs. Hudson backed obediently away, and resumed walking down the row. At set intervals small work tables were placed between the plants. Some were bare, but most held some combination of watering cans, racks of pipettes, and three-toothed rakes. Here and there a table also held a young plant growing from the seed of plants located nearby. In answer to her question, Henderson explained the tables were used for repotting, and the pipettes for feeding some of the plants requiring that kind of care. He added that he'd of thought anyone who'd been around plants would know that. Mrs. Hudson took no offense, and noted she'd never been around plants as fine and delicate as these. Henderson sniffed acknowledgement, disapproval or disbelief. Mrs. Hudson didn't turn to discover which. She had found what she was looking for. On one small table was a watering can, a rake, and a rack for three pipettes, one of which was in the rack, another lay on the table, and the third was missing. Looking at the cards identifying the nearby plants, she found one containing the single word she was searching for. The card identified the broad-leafed potted plant as passionflower, Adenia digitata, and beneath its Latin name was the word **"POISON**."

"Mr. 'Enderson, I do thank you for showin' me your glass 'ouse. It's truly a wonder, but I'm glad my Tobias never got into such things. I'd be that worried every time 'e went into the place that 'e might not come out. It's a wonder anybody wants to care for such dangerous things."

Henderson sniffed again. This time there was no mistaking his disapproval. "There's a woman for you. There's dangers enough in every corner of life. Living in the city like you do, you can catch your death from any of a dozen diseases from all what I hear, and if you don't catch one of them, you can get run down by some fool carriage driver carrying gentry faster than anybody needs to go. When all is said and done, handling plants that's got poison in them is prob'ly a lot safer than living in London."

Henderson's gruff speech turned suddenly wistful. "Anyways, if you're all through ma'am, we might be starting back. I ain't had a bite to eat since morning what with getting things ready for your lady, and I could do with whatever fixings Mrs. Groover has put together."

"Thank you, Mr. 'Enderson, I think I've seen everythin' I wanted to see."

On their return to the servants' hall, Henderson's optimism about the feast awaiting them was instantly confirmed. Rachel was in the process of setting on the table platters of the fried sole, potatoes, and peas Mrs. Hudson had delivered in comparative miniature to Mrs. Mackenzie. There were, in addition, pitchers of beer and lemonade that had been lacking from the widow's serving. It was already past eight. Mrs. Hudson knew she had only a short time to eat and work her questions into the dinner conversation before attending to Lillie. At Mrs. Charters's invitation, she took a seat beside the housekeeper's place at the foot of the table. Christine sat on Mrs. Charters's other side, eating the food as much with her hands as with her spoon and fork, and looking up every now and again to smile her way around the table in her unfocused way.

Mrs. Hudson was reacquainted with Mrs. Groover and Doyle, the coachman. She smiled to Elizabeth who nodded stiffly in return, and was introduced to Clara, the under-housemaid, and Lucas, the groom. James and Charles were still serving table in the dining room. As she expected, Mrs. Hudson found herself being coaxed into revealing what she would about Lillie Langtry. Elizabeth had been elected to pose the first question on the assumption she had come the closest to establishing a relationship with Mrs. Hudson. There was the additional consideration that Elizabeth would, as Henderson put it, "ask the Devil how he got his horns." Elizabeth set about fulfilling the group's expectations. Without preamble, she raised the question she found most compelling. "Is Mrs. Langtry still seeing the Prince of Wales?"

Mrs. Hudson adopted an appropriately sanctimonious expression and addressed her response to the group rather than to Elizabeth alone. "I can understand your interest, all of London wonders about such things, but I know you can understand why I can't talk to you about Mrs. Langtry's private activities. I'm sure you'd feel the same about your own mistress."

Mrs. Charters alone smiled approval. Among the rest there was muttered agreement combined with palpable disappointment—so much so that Mrs. Hudson relented a little.

"I'll tell you one thing about Mrs. Langtry you wouldn't know because there's no one knows." The eyes of all staff were on Mrs. Hudson, no one raised a fork from where it lay on their plates, and those with forks in hand held them in place as if any further movement might discourage Mrs. Hudson from sharing her revelation. Only Christine continued eating, pausing to say "no one knows, no one knows" in her sing-song way, before taking another mouthful of meat after first pushing it onto her fork with her free hand.

"Of course, everyone says what a beautiful woman my mistress is. And what a fine actress. You may know she 'ad quite the tour of America not so very long ago. But what you won't know is Mrs. Langtry isn't just a beauty, but is also a very smart businesswoman who plans most carefully for 'er future—I'll say no more about that—but I will tell you this. She's got a literary side to her no one knows about; she is right now readin' a book of poetry by one of America's most important writers. It was sent to 'er by one of 'er secret admirers from across the ocean. 'E didn't even sign 'is name, just sent it to 'er out of 'is admiration." Mrs. Hudson paused to look the table up and down. "And that's somethin' you won't be readin' in the dailies, or even in the smartest magazines comin' out of London." Mrs. Hudson picked up her fork to a chorus of subdued sighs of appreciation followed by the silence of frustrated expectation.

Doyle broke the silence. "Well, what I'm hearing is that Mrs. Langtry is a woman of many parts and I do thank you for sharing that, Mrs. Hudson, but it's still her being a rare beauty that I'll remember after she's gone from the Manor."

173

The coachman's choice for remembrance drew a mix of murmured approvals and groans in association with the gender of the respondent.

"Well, I'll tell you what I admire about Mrs. Langtry," Henderson pushed back from the table to give himself room to share his contribution. Eyebrows raised and mouths opened as Henderson's audience warily awaited what the gardener might find admirable about their house guest. "Whatever you want to say about the way she done it, she come from nowheres to make a name for herself." Finding his comment more circumspect than they had anticipated, the scraping of plates resumed although it slowed again as the gardener continued on his unpredictable course. "She come from Jersey, and as I heard it she's the daughter of a preacher, and we all know they're every one of them half broke living on the bits and pieces of what they get from their congregation. So when she comes of age, it's only natural for a beautiful woman like her …"

"That's all as may be, Mr. Henderson." Concerned about what might be considered only natural to Henderson, Mrs. Charters interrupted his speech. "And it's wonderful what Mrs. Langtry has made of herself, being a well-known stage actress which I'll not say anything against, Mrs. Hudson. I'm certain there's many in that work who are quite respectable. All I'm saying, Mr. Henderson, is you don't have to go to London to find those as have made something of themselves. Didn't our own Mr. Trent go all the way to Africa and come back with a fortune? And him no more than a boy of eighteen when he went according to Mr. Simon. Why, anyone with eyes can still see the marks on his face from the battles he went through just to survive in that heathen place. And can't you say exactly the same about the mistress? Don't I know better than anyone how she wasn't no more than the daughter of a baker, a master baker as the mistress says, but still not a rich man. And how, after she marries, and is maybe just getting up in the world, her Mr. Bascombe dies and she has to go back to living with her folks all over again, only this time with two little ones. As I say, Mrs. Hudson, it's nothing against your Mrs. Langtry, but you don't have to go outside this house to find some as have made their mark with things lined up against them." After framing a smile for Mrs. Hudson to make clear she intended no ill feeling, Mrs. Charters glowered at Henderson to make clear she did.

Mrs. Hudson waited for the polite murmurs of approval she expected to follow the housekeeper's remarks, but the approval was not murmured. The voices were distinct, full-throated and, save for Mr. Henderson, uniform around the table. Christine, as usual, had the last words. "Mrs. Charters has got it right; Mrs. Charters has got it right."

Hoping to reduce the discord for which she felt partly responsible, Mrs. Hudson raised a new and more agreeable topic. "Mrs. Groover, this is as fine a meal as I've 'ad since I don't know when." Mrs. Groover beamed in appreciation. "I can't begin to imagine the dinner my lady and the family are 'avin'." A sudden thought seemed to strike Mrs. Hudson. "Speakin' of the family, I suppose tomorrow will be a big day what with Mr. Trent and Mr. Simon gettin' back, and I believe you mentioned there are two children as well, Mrs. Charters."

"That's correct, Mrs. Hudson. There's Mister Byron and Miss Esther. As you say, the master and Mr. Simon will be returning tomorrow, but the children returned from London today. They were on the early train."

"How wonderful for them, I mean to be able to visit London."

"I guess you could say that. Miss Esther was on a sort of visit seeing as how she was staying with friends; Mister Byron is taking his studies at Oxford and was meeting with his professors." Mrs. Charters's words were for Mrs. Hudson, but her glare to Henderson was to urge him to hold his tongue. She failed as she knew she would.

175

"And now that Mackenzie won't be here no more, Miss Esther won't be needing to see her London friends for a while." Henderson gave a knowing smile and wink to those around the table who squirmed their understanding of his comment. Once again, Mrs. Charters regretted the absence of the Trents' butler who could silence Henderson with a glance.

Mrs. Hudson saw no need to pursue the connection between Mackenzie's death and Esther's return. It was of a piece with Christine's formless dress and Elizabeth's boast of her own invulnerability. "Well now, there's a point to consider. What with Mrs. Mackenzie bein' 'ere, are there some kind of plans for what's to be done with the remains of Mr. Mackenzie. I mean is there to be a funeral or burial service? I don't mean to pry, I'm only askin' for Mrs. Langtry in terms of the clothes she's brought."

It was again the seemingly incorrigible gardener who responded. "I suppose we can bury Mackenzie in the sheep pens. That's if the sheep don't mind." This time Henderson's comment elicited neither censure or embarrassed silence. This time, what began as snickering sputtered to a crescendo of hilarity enjoyed by all around the table. Doyle went so far as to raise his glass to Henderson, who acknowledged the unaccustomed tribute with a broad grin. Christine joined the laughter late and continued as the laughter of others subsided to head shakes and broad smiles.

On the heels of Henderson's comment, the mood turned permanently light. There was a good-natured discussion of the relative merits of living in London and living in the country, the country being the clear favorite of all but Mrs. Hudson, who was forgiven her obvious bias. The conversation turned again to Mrs. Langtry, with Doyle wondering if she wasn't the most famous person ever to visit McLellan Manor. There turned out to be some confusion as to whether one of the Henrys had visited the lands on which the Manor stood and whether, if he did, that counted as a visit to the Manor. The consensus seemed to favor Mrs. Langtry, after which Mrs. Hudson said the discussion reminded her she had to attend to her mistress. She thanked Mrs. Groover again for a splendid meal and left to meet with Lillie, and to become the next topic of conversation in servants' hall.

Lillie was just entering her room when Mrs. Hudson arrived at the top of the stair. Following Lillie into the room, she shut the door behind them, turned down the bed, and after first putting away her jewelry, began to help Lillie out of her evening dress and into her nightgown.

"And 'ow was your evenin', ma'am?"

"Oh, pleasant enough under the circumstances. One has to be mindful that it was very gracious of Mrs. Trent to accommodate us, and especially to accommodate us on such short notice. I believe we both tried our best at polite conversation, but we have so little in common. I was prepared to talk of life in London, of concerts and the theater, and she was prepared to talk of life in Yorkshire and an upcoming church fete. We compromised on a discussion of horses and riding. It appears riding is the only interest she and Trent *don't* share, and she looks forward to having guests that have her same passion for horses. She spoke at length of her accident and how helpful Lord Lonsdale was in getting her back to the Manor. That was by far the most exciting part of our dinner conversation. I fear Master Byron has much in common with the Sphinx although that may not be entirely fair to the Sphinx. Thank goodness for Esther. She had endless questions about the theater, although I couldn't believe she spent two weeks in London and never went to see a play. Did you know she and Byron got back just before us? Ouch." Lillie pulled away from Mrs. Hudson who was undoing hooks at her back. "Do please be careful, Mrs. Hudson."

"I'm sorry, ma'am."

"And your evening, Mrs. Hudson? Was it wretched?"

177

Mrs. Hudson was still at Lillie's back working the last of the hooks and so the actress did not see the emphatic shake of her head. "No, not at all. I gave your sympathies to Mrs. Mackenzie—I took supper to 'er—and I did get to see the glass 'ouse out back which is full of what they call exotic plants. Besides that, I 'ad some nice talks with staff and a good dinner."

"And what did they ask you about Lillie Langtry—and what did you tell them?"

Mrs. Hudson reddened before stumbling her way to an answer. "They did want to know somethin' about you and the Prince of Wales, but they learned right off they wouldn't 'ear nothin' from me, not that there's anythin' I know or care to know, and we went on to other things."

Lillie threw up her hands in an exaggerated display of pique. "It's always the same. 'Is it true what they say about Lillie Langtry and the Prince of Wales?' Except it's never clear who 'they' are, or just exactly what it is they say." She adopted a sad smile as she let the nightgown descend over the figure that had sparked the interest of the royal in question. "I suppose I should simply be grateful that word of Squire Baird hasn't yet traveled to the hinterlands or they would be asking 'Is it true what they say about Lillie Langtry and George Baird?'

"In any event, Mrs. Hudson, if you're as tired as I am—and you have every reason to be—you'll want your rest as much as I want mine. I'll get an early night and I suggest you do the same. I'll send for you in the morning when I'm ready. And I thank you for all the assistance you provided today."

Lillie was pulling a sheet up to her shoulders as Mrs. Hudson closed the door behind her.

The next morning, well before Mrs. Hudson was to attend to Lillie, Michael Wiggins was at his post in front of

178

Squire Baird's terraced house. What he would learn would lead George Baird's name to become well known in one corner of Yorkshire's hinterlands, and cause Lillie to have one less thing for which to be grateful.

Late that morning, Lillie Langtry summoned Mrs. Hudson to her room. Having left Lillie in good spirits after dressing her for breakfast, it required little of her investigative skills to recognize a problem had newly arisen. Lillie was staring at the fog that hid from view all that lay outside the window, her back to the open door on which Mrs. Hudson rapped softly, then more loudly to announce her presence. She knew in an instant what was troubling Lillie.

"Is Squire Baird already on his way to Oxley?"

Lillie turned with her own question. "How in the world did you know?"

Mrs. Hudson brushed past an explanation. "There's a bunched up telegram sittin' on top of your book of Mr. Whitman's poetry. It would 'ave come from Mr. 'Olmes who was to let you know Mr. Baird's whereabouts. With you starin' out the window and there bein' nothin' to see, and then not 'earin' me at the door just now, it would be clear to anyone you've gotten some bad news, and bad news could only be somethin' about Mr. Baird knowin' where you are."

"When you put it that way perhaps it is obvious to anyone, or perhaps a little of Mr. Holmes has rubbed off on you. In any event, I did receive a telegram and the Squire is coming here. You may wish to read Mr. Holmes's rather cryptic message for yourself."

Mrs. Hudson smoothed the telegram and read the message Holmes had sent in code in spite of Mrs. Hudson's urging. As she grasped the detail it contained, she forgave him his subterfuge.

"Unknown how B found you. Am certain the man is a real threat. B traveling now Oxley for investigating with you

179

nature as well strength your feelings. Watson and I traveling to McLellan Manor behind B and two fighters with him."

Mrs. Hudson recognized the telegram held three messages. There was first, of course, that Squire Baird had somehow learned Lillie's location, and was on his way to McLellan Manor unpacified and accompanied by two professional fighters with Holmes and Watson close behind.

There was also Holmes's use of "U" for "Unknown" rather than the "Y" or "N" they had agreed on. He did not yet know what was in the flask, but did know there was something additional to whiskey in it. He used every third word after the first to report the state of his chemical analysis:

"Unknown … found. Certain … is … threat. Now … investigating … nature … strength."

Lillie interrupted her thinking, having again become the calm, deliberate woman familiar to Mrs. Hudson. "It appears we can expect a visit from George shortly. I'm not so much concerned for my own safety as I am with keeping the Trents, and your Mr. Holmes and Dr. Watson from getting any further caught up in my troubles."

"Are you sayin' you mean to be goin' back with Mr. Baird?" Mrs. Hudson was aware she was overstepping the bounds of her role, but the answer was vital to her planning.

"You really need to develop skills in forbearance if you are ever to be an effective lady's maid." She gave Mrs. Hudson the beginning of a smile, then turned quickly serious to match her maid's earnest expression. "I've told you how I choose to live my life and my reasons for doing so. Yes, I'll very likely be going back with him. With him and to my own house, and my own stables, and the stage career I've established. But I do want to be certain George has become manageable. It's a bad sign that he's brought his fighters with him. They'll get each other liquored up and goad each other, and by the time they get off the train they'll be ready to burn the Manor to the ground if George asks it."

"Well then, we need to keep them from gettin' to the Manor at least until the men get back."

"And how do you propose we do that?"

"I'd suggest you ask Mrs. Trent to 'ave a talk with Elizabeth, 'er parlor maid. I believe we'll be wantin' Elizabeth to get in touch with 'er brothers."

At the Oxley station, two large, burly men, and one considerably smaller, somewhat unsteadily confronted three middle-sized burly men, two of them wearing uniforms of the local constabulary, and all of them standing very steadily in their path. The policemen paused only long enough to tip their helmets and nod good-days to men they identified as Your Honor and Mr. Simon before gathering up the three men between them, and urging the travelers to choose between a night as guests of the Inn of the Moors or of the Oxley jail. The non-uniformed member of the group indicated the greater comfort and better food available at the Inn. He informed them as well that the Inn's clerk was to contact the two uniformed members of the group if the men sought transportation out of town, and that Oxley's seven carriage drivers had been similarly instructed. The three men glared acknowledgement of the terms presented by their implacable reception committee before accepting an offer of transportation to the Inn of the Moors.

Chapter 12.
Mrs. Hudson Has a Plan

Arthur Trent and Simon proceeded behind Doyle and Charles to the waiting coach unaware of the small drama being conducted on their behalf. The two men were, in fact, preoccupied with their own difficulty. Arthur Trent had volunteered to take responsibility for the body of Sailor Mackenzie, but had neglected to alert the Manor regarding its unanticipated, if undemanding guest. Trent watched while Doyle and Charles loaded onto the coach three portmanteaus and a carpetbag, then dispatched them to fetch Old Taggett and his cart on which they were to load the wooden box containing the last earthly remains of Sailor Mackenzie. Old Taggett was little more than 40, but required a sobriquet capable of distinguishing him from his son with whom he shared the first name, Absalom, as had the first sons of every Taggett for more generations than anyone knew. Senior and junior seemed out of place for the men of the Taggett family, and since Oxley had never had opportunity to boast of three contemporaneous Absalom Taggets, Old Taggett and Young Taggett served quite well. A half crown drew the eager attention and immediate assistance of Old Taggett and, in a short time, he and his silent passenger were following the coach carrying Arthur Trent and Simon to McLellan Manor.

Mrs. Hudson arranged to be at a window when the odd procession arrived and watched the warm greeting given Trent by Mrs. Trent, who, cane in hand, had limped her way onto the veranda to await her husband in company with their two children. She watched as he pointed to the cart turned hearse and gave what seemed an elaborate explanation of its presence. Simon gave whispered instruction to James who, together with Charles, had materialized on the front porch and, after taking Trent's baggage to his room, the two footmen transported Sailor Mackenzie to his penultimate resting place, which turned out to be the tack room adjoining the stable. Doyle, contemplating nights spent one level above a dead man, watched the proceedings with undisguised distress.

The Trent family saw neither the removal of Sailor Mackenzie or their coachman's displeasure. Arthur Trent and Mrs. Trent linked arms, and followed by a beaming Byron and Esther, entered the manor house after stopping to speak to a short, balding man who gave an embarrassed smile as he tilted his considerable weight from one leg to the other, and pressed in place eyeglasses that made continuous effort to slide the length of his small nose. The medical bag he carried marked him as Oxley's local physician who had come to check on the condition of his most prominent patient. Bestowing a last smile on each of the Trents, he shifted his weight forward and took his leave, promising to return soon. The Trents joined Lillie Langtry who had lingered in the center hall waiting completion of the family reunion and the medical consultation.

While the master of the house was being welcomed home, Simon supervised the careful insertion of Mackenzie's coffin among saddles, bridles and halters. He then made his way to the servants' hall where Mrs. Hudson had gone to introduce herself to the butler whose return triggered a wave of relief across the staff, and occasioned a smile to break through Mrs. Charters's seemingly impenetrable scowl, complementing her daughter's giggling welcome.

After brief discussions with his wife and Mrs. Mackenzie, it was agreed Arthur Trent would use his influence with the vicar to locate a gravesite in the churchyard that would grant Mr. Mackenzie a sanctity he could not have claimed in life. After learning his train carried Squire Baird and two of his fighters, Trent alerted Simon, then assured Lillie that his staff, together with the Oxley constabulary, would be more than a match for Squire Baird. When told that

Holmes and Watson were on their way to McLellan Manor, he pursed his lips in a small pout and declared their presence wholly unnecessary. Lillie smiled acknowledgement of Trent's judgment, but said nothing.

Doyle was sent to meet the afternoon train and collect the two men described to him by Simon. As it turned out there were not two, but three additional guests to be transported to McLellan Manor. Lord Lonsdale, on learning the plans for Lillie's protection had come undone, insisted to Holmes he shared responsibility for making things come right and traveled the same trains as Holmes and Watson, although keeping to his own compartment. All three were greeted warmly by the Trents, with the broadest smiles and most vigorous handshakes clearly reserved for Lonsdale. With welcoming to McLellan Manor concluded, James came forward to give Holmes a telegram that had arrived earlier in the day. He kept his eyes averted from Holmes's face, taking literally his instructions to ignore the guest's swollen features.

While Mrs. Trent and Lillie retired to the morning room for tea, the men gathered in the drawing room to discuss strategy over brandy and each man's choice of tobacco. With brandies well sampled and the room taking on the pungent odor of the men's deliberations, Lonsdale wondered aloud how Lillie might have been found out and queried Arthur Trent about the trustworthiness of his staff. Trent vigorously defended his household without making the observation, obvious to all but the Earl, that the leak was far more likely to have come from Carlton House Terrace than from McLellan Manor. Holmes relieved both men of any need to expose their staffs to inquisition as he recounted Wiggins's earlier report to him, and the actions of the red-headed man in a brown-checked suit. Neither the Earl or Trent could identify him, but Lonsdale declared he sounded exactly "the sort of sorry lot who would be in Baird's employ." They agreed, as Trent had

184

concluded earlier in the day, that any threat could be effectively countered by themselves, the Manor staff and, as necessary, the police.

With the major issue facing them resolved, Holmes described himself as feeling some particular concern about Mrs. Hudson. He reminded them that the woman was really his housekeeper, was getting on in years, and had been asked to take on responsibilities for which she was woefully unprepared. He went on to describe the strain of the trip to Yorkshire, and the element of danger that would no doubt trouble her deeply, accustomed as she was to the quiet routine he and Watson tried to create for her. When he had exhausted his litany of the woman's frailties, Holmes declared the need for Watson and himself to meet with "the dear old soul" to allow her to share what he was certain were her many concerns and allay her understandable fears. His proposal met a chorus of praise capped by Lonsdale's statement that it spoke eloquently to Holmes's unfailing thoughtfulness. Trent committed uninterrupted use of the library for as long as needed, promising tea and refreshments after they got settled.

The library was designed to be a retreat for quiet contemplation. Two well separated clusters of furniture held within them dark-wooded easy chairs, a straight-backed desk chair, and a writing table having no more ornamentation than an inkpot and indentation for a pen. Along the walls on either side of the door, shelves of books stood behind leaded glass doors that seemed to encourage the appreciation of literature from a distance. Massive windows faced out to the front of the Manor, and might have relieved the room's overbearing solemnity were they not half hidden behind floor to ceiling curtains.

Mrs. Hudson selected a chair that gave her an unobstructed view of the door and adopted an expression consistent with the tenor of the room. Holmes, taking a somewhat more relaxed view of the situation, spread himself generously across a second chair within the cluster Mrs. Hudson had selected. Watson sat at the writing table, withdrawing the ever ready pencil from his waistcoat together with the accounts book that held the notes from his interviews at 14 Carlton House Terrace and the National Sporting Club. Without waiting to be asked, he began a report of those interviews, indicating he would restrict himself to the highlights in view of the limited time available. In fact, Watson was too meticulous a reporter to restrict himself to highlights and shared at length the considerable detail contained in his notes. He paused only once, when Elizabeth brought in tea and refreshments, and the conversation turned to an appreciation of their hostess' hospitality.

With Elizabeth's exit, he completed his portrayal of Mackenzie as abusive toward his wife, unpleasant at best toward Manor staff and, if not a drunkard, the next thing to it. Watson went on to tell how both Capelhorn and the senior Cochrane had long-standing personal grievances against Mackenzie, while Simon appeared to harbor a more recent antipathy, implying the fighter had taken liberties with the Trents' daughter—among other women. Watson told of the lost—or stolen—key to the greenhouse and of the instruction all at the Manor had received for handling the poisonous Adenia digitata. He spoke of Mackenzie's very sound, drunken sleep alone in his cottage, and shared Cochrane's report of seeing two people in the area of Mackenzie's cottage, one of whom was likely Simon. He noted that Arthur Trent was absent from McLellan Manor throughout the night. He went on to detail the accounts he had been given of the train trip to London as well as the separate, but highly comparable descriptions of Mackenzie's character by the people he had interviewed.

Watson drew back and waited the questions he thought inevitable, but there was only one. Mrs. Hudson asked him to repeat Capelhorn's litany of complaints about Mackenzie's behavior the day of the fight. When that was done, Mrs. Hudson turned her attention to Holmes and his report of the chemical analysis. He took a last draw of his pipe, and watched the smoke as it trailed under and around the beams of the room's timbered ceiling before speaking.

"As I told Watson earlier, to learn whether a poison could have been added to Mackenzie's flask, I first separated out the water and alcohol from the liquid in Mackenzie's flask and found there was indeed an adulterant. I injected some of that adulterant in a laboratory mouse, and left it for Spooner to observe the animal and send word to Oxley of his findings. And Spooner has done just that." Holmes waved the telegram James had given him and his eyes shown with the excitement of discovery. "The mouse is dead! It's proof that poison was added to Mackenzie's flask. But there's more.

"Knowing from the conversation at the National Sporting Club that Trent keeps a collection of plants, I asked Spooner to conduct Stillmark's procedure with the animal. It's the technique he developed in his work isolating the plant toxin he named ricin. Spooner got the same clumping of red blood cells with our mouse as Stillmark reported finding in his test animals. In short, it makes it clear we need to look to the plants Trent collects in that greenhouse of his, especially knowing one of them—this Adenia--contains poison."

"That's good work, Mr. 'Olmes. It confirms everythin' we thought," Mrs. Hudson smiled her appreciation to a somewhat crestfallen Holmes. "Mr. Mackenzie was poisoned with that African plant and between Mr. Simon losin' 'is key, and all the comin's and goin's that night, we don't lack for people with opportunity to use it. Besides which, when I went through the green'ouse I found there was what I believe is called a pipette missin' from the table nearest the plant. I find that most interestin'."

Mrs. Hudson took a long drink of tea before settling

her cup emphatically on its saucer. "But there's still another problem that needs solvin'. Two problems really. There's first that we made a promise to Mrs. Langtry she'd be protected and now we've got Mr. Baird showin' up with 'is two fighters. It's likely the Oxley constabulary can keep them in town only so long, and if they come to the Manor there's bound to be a row. I know a way to get Mr. Baird and 'is fighters out of Oxley. It means a trip to Glasgow for the two of you, but I'm thinkin' it's a trip worth makin' on a couple of counts."

"Glasgow, Mrs. Hudson?" Watson made no effort to hide his surprise.

"Glasgow, Dr. Watson. Squire Baird 'as got a 'ouse in Glasgow and I believe I've a way to get 'im to want to go there. If we can work that out, it will keep Mr. Baird away from the Manor, and give us a chance to find out what 'appened in Glasgow thirty-five years ago."

Holmes looked to Mrs. Hudson as if she had finally achieved the senility he had long anticipated. "Why would events from thirty-five years ago in Glasgow be any concern of ours?"

Mrs. Hudson smiled patiently. "Just see 'ow everythin' centers around Glasgow, Mr. 'Olmes. It's where both the Mackenzies and Mr. Trent come from." Mrs. Hudson looked to the two faces of mirrored confusion and explained, "It's got to do with the picture of a church Mrs. Mackenzie recognized as the one where she and Mr. Mackenzie got married, and which she was told was the church where Mr. Trent got baptized. Mrs. Trent 'ad it moved to the maid's room so that no other guest would see it—she bein' too much of an artist 'erself not to put it somewhere it could still be enjoyed by someone. Anyway, Mr. Mackenzie would 'ave learned about it from 'is wife, and it's right after that 'e's talkin' about stayin' at the Manor for as long as 'e likes. Whatever it is that gave Mr. Mackenzie a grip on Mr. Trent 'appened in Glasgow thirty-five years ago. It 'ad to be serious enough to cause Mr.

Trent to light out for Africa then, and to be willin' to pay Mr. Mackenzie blackmail now, which is why I'm guessin' it's somethin' that put 'im wrong side of the law."

Both men fidgeted their way to the backs of their chairs as they considered Mrs. Hudson's analysis. It was left to Watson to voice the unthinkable.

"You're surely not suggesting Trent poisoned Mackenzie to avoid being blackmailed by him. It's true, of course, he had knowledge of this plant and its poisonous properties, but as we've said so did practically everyone else at the Manor. And even if he had reason for wanting to be rid of Mackenzie and the ability to get it done, there's still the fact that he was with the vicar the night the poison would have had to be put in Mackenzie's flask to be sure of its action the following day. I hardly think the church would conspire to protect Trent whatever his standing in Oxley."

Watson warmed to the argument on behalf of his host and hostess. "And I must rule out Mrs. Trent in light of her injury. I judge from the care being provided by her physician and Lonsdale's description of the accident that Mrs. Trent likely suffered a deep bone bruise and severe sprain. I'm sure her physician would prefer she be on bed rest, but she's simply too active a woman for that. Still, with those injuries it would be a struggle at best for her to cross the grounds during the day, and virtually impossible for her to travel from the Manor to the greenhouse, to Mackenzie's cottage, and back again on a night described as overcast."

"I'm not accusin' or rulin' anybody out just yet, Doctor. We need to know a good deal more before we start on that. For now, there's a loose thread that needs tyin' up or tearin' out. To get that done we're goin' to need the both of you to investigate things in Glasgow, and to do that we'll be wantin' the assistance of Inspector Lestrade and Squire Baird."

This time both men spoke at once. "Squire Baird?"

"Squire Baird 'as got connections to Glasgow and to boxin', and I'm thinkin' both of those will be useful before all this is done."

"And Lestrade?" Watson asked.

"That 'as to do with our findin' out from the Glasgow police what they 'ave as unsolved crimes from thirty-five years ago."

"Mr. 'Olmes, it's all goin' to make for a busy morning. You'll need to go to the post office in town to send a telegram to the Inspector askin' 'im to make contact with the police in Glasgow, and then you'll be 'avin' a get-together with Squire Baird which I believe will be right up your street." She swallowed the last of her biscuit, poured enough tea to warm the little still in her cup, and took a sip as if to fortify herself for the campaign ahead.

"Now, let me tell you what I'm thinkin', and then you need to get back to the others before they start wonderin' what's goin' on in 'ere. You'll be tellin' them you've got a way of gettin' Squire Baird out of Oxley which you'll be doin' tomorrow, and it's better they don't know the 'ow of it."

"Were you aware of Mr. Holmes's plans to get Squire Baird to go to Glasgow?" Lillie's question came with Mrs. Hudson at her back unfastening the dress she had worn to dinner.

"Yes, ma'am. I 'eard somethin' of that." Over dinner in the servants' hall, she had, in fact, heard a good deal about Holmes's plans after Mr. Simon and the two footmen joined them at table, although no one seemed to know how Holmes meant to remove Squire Baird from Oxley.

"He was really quite mysterious you know. I suppose that's his way. Your Dr. Watson was equally close-mouthed." Lillie let the statement hang in the air long enough for it to become a question.

Mrs. Hudson took her meaning, but not her bait.

"That's just like the two of them. Very mysterious about their ways."

"Well, I hope he does get George to go to Glasgow. I'm afraid he needs more time to settle down. Are you certain you know nothing of Mr. Holmes's plans? You were with them a good long time in the library earlier today." Having been helped to change from her dinner dress to her night dress, Lillie took up a brush and began running it through her hair while Mrs. Hudson put away the day's clothing.

"You're surely not thinkin' Mr. 'Olmes would share 'is plans with the likes of me." Mrs. Hudson stammered her disbelief. "We did have a nice little talk, it's true. I was that worried about things in Baker Street. You can't imagine how untidy my men are, and then there's the butcher who would 'ave sent 'is boy around and will be wonderin' where I am, and the iceman, and all the things that aren't gettin' done and will 'ave to be gotten done. I 'ad to share it all with Mr. 'Olmes and Dr.Watson, who tried to make me feel better, but it's still a worry for me."

Lillie turned to the diminutive woman in black who looked every bit as miserable as she sounded. Lillie had been prepared with follow-up questions, but they seemed pointless after hearing Mrs. Hudson's response.

"That will be all, Mrs. Hudson. Have a pleasant evening."

Chapter 13.
The Death of Josiah Krebs

The morning found Holmes looking every bit the country gentleman in tweeds, calf-length boots, deerstalker hat, and walking stick pointed in the direction of town. Fortified by a substantial breakfast and the good wishes of Watson, he started down the path that ran along the edge of the moor to Oxley. Holmes had learned from Trent that the chemist's shop, which also housed the Oxley post office and the Oxley telegraph office, opened for business at half eight, and he hoped to complete his business without having to endure the curiosity of the chemist's other customers.

He arrived at the shop of Aldous Bauer, Chemist, to find its proprietor setting in place the syrups and powders of his profession, and the practiced smile of shopkeepers everywhere. When he learned Holmes had no need of his services and wished only to see the postmistress, the smile on his round, florid face dimmed substantially. He pointed to the young woman sitting behind a desk in the small corner of the shop allotted to Oxley's contact with the outside world. The woman's flushed full cheeks made clear all commercial activities being conducted on the site of Aldous Bauer, Chemist, were being conducted by members of the Bauer family.

Holmes handed her the message and address to which it was to be sent. The look of earnest concentration she had adopted as appropriate to her position gave way to open-mouthed astonishment as she read the sender's name and the contents of his message. It was the same name she had seen twice the day before. Sherlock Holmes was the author of the confusing telegram sent from London to an Emilie Le Breton staying at McLellan Manor, and the recipient only hours later of a telegram from London about a mouse dying. Now, here he was, standing in front of her and sending yet another telegram, this one to an inspector in Scotland Yard asking about a crime occurring years before she was born. She would have liked to ask him what these telegrams were all about except there was nothing in the man's somewhat swollen face inviting inquiry. Instead, she assumed his same air of businesslike efficiency and turned to tap out the telegram.

His message sent, Holmes gave the woman a curt nod, paid the two shillings, six pence she demanded, and made arrangements for Lestrade's reply to come to him at McLellan Manor as soon as it was received. She promised the boy would bring the telegram to the Manor immediately it came to her, and Holmes guessed he was destined to meet yet another member of the Bauer family. He left as a stout, middle-aged woman with a tall-feathered hat and a preoccupied look brushed past him to engage the services of Mr. Bauer, and to become shortly thereafter the first link in a chain that would carry news of an extraordinary stranger and his mysterious message throughout much of Oxley.

Unaware of the excitement he had created, Holmes proceeded down Church Street to the Tudor styled Inn of the Moors. The clerk on duty peered over his half glasses at the man who entered the hotel's foyer, and found himself momentarily lost before spotting the reception desk right-angled to the entryway. The moment of confusion made clear the man was not a guest; the absence of baggage made clear he would not be checking in. Indeed, a glance at the man's battered features made it unclear whether the man even belonged in the lobby of the Inn of the Moors. Accordingly, the clerk's greeting was civil without any hint of the warmth he reserved for guests of the Inn.

"Good morning. May I help you in some way?"

Holmes matched the clerk's indifference with his own breezy detachment. "I believe you have a George Baird staying with you. Please tell him that Sherlock Holmes is here to see him."

At the sound of the visitor's name, the clerk dropped all evidence of disinterest and stared at Holmes with unaffected wonder. "Is that Mr. Sherlock Holmes, the consulting detective?"

Holmes nodded without change in expression. "It is."

The clerk's jaw dropped and he took an involuntary step back as if finding himself standing too close to a fire. "Mr. Holmes, this is a rare moment, sir. The wife and me have been following your achievements in the papers for just about as long as I can remember." He looked around the lobby area, hoping to find someone who might be a witness to his extraordinary fortune. Finding no one, he turned back to Holmes, having now become the very soul of accommodation. "I'll send the boy for Mr. Baird. May I be of any further service?"

"Do you have a writing room?"

"We do, sir. If you go back into the foyer and make a right, the second door you come to will be the writing room."

"Thank you. Please ask Mr. Baird to meet me there. And I will need you to arrange for us not to be disturbed for a period of approximately twenty minutes."

The now beaming clerk held in readiness the bell he'd removed from the counter while he apologized for a delay in meeting Holmes's request. "The boy's just taken the day's paper to a guest. I'll have him down here and attending to this immediately, Mr. Holmes."

Holmes rewarded the man with a small smile, and the clerk responded by ringing his bell with a fervor that would have made Quasimodo proud.

In spite of its name, the writing room offered little support to a guest's efforts at literary achievement. A single desk and straight-backed chair stood in a corner of the room, while a couch and several deep cushioned chairs were distributed around the room. All were leather covered and set well enough apart to afford guests the option of casual conversation, or comfortably ignoring the person sitting nearest them. Holmes took no note of the room's décor as he strode to the window to look out on the street. The town was just beginning to stir to its mercantile obligations. Across the road the Bank of Leeds had opened its doors to the citizens of Oxley, although the adjoining bicycle shop and jewelers remained tightly shuttered. Holmes's attention centered on a solid appearing man in a short gray coat and knickerbockers, possessing a neatly clipped moustache, somber expression, and inordinate interest in the Church Street shops. Every now and again his attention seemed to wander from the windows of the area merchants and come to focus on the windows of the Inn of the Moors. As planned, Watson, after a brief conversation with Lillie Langtry, had taken the same path as Holmes to town and now stood where he had a clear view of the inn, and where those inside would have a clear view of him. Holmes moved the curtain to and fro until Watson raised his walking stick in acknowledgement of the agreed-upon signal.

"Sherlock Holmes, is it? Well, what business do you have with me?"

Holmes turned to face the speaker and found himself confronting three men. The group's spokesperson was nonetheless easily identified. The same person who had questioned the authority of the Oxley constabulary one day earlier now questioned that of Holmes. Squire George Baird wore an open-necked silk shirt and dark pants exposing a compact muscular form. He was, however, dwarfed by his companions, both of whom were dressed with similar informality. Holmes recognized the small-mouthed man with the slowly receding hairline as the one-time English champion, Charlie Mitchell. He didn't recognize the dark-haired man with the boyish face, but it was obvious he shared Mitchell's profession.

"I have a good deal of business with you. I'd suggest you … and your friends be seated so we can get on with it."

The three men stood in the room's center, pointedly ignoring the several chairs and couch, and Holmes's invitation to make use of them. Holmes shrugged and continued. "As you like, I am only concerned for your comfort. We can remain standing to discuss your future with Lillie Langtry—if you are to have one."

The Squire bristled, and Holmes readied himself for something more demanding than a verbal exchange, but Baird elected only to glare his contempt and, after a lengthy pause in which neither man could claim advantage, he waved the fighters to seats on the couch and took an easy chair for himself.

"What have you to tell me about Lillie?"

"I can tell you that you can't storm the Manor where she's staying even with these gentlemen." Holmes waved in the direction of the fighters and smiled to each of them. He saw little point to antagonizing people considerably larger than himself who might, at any moment, be asked to reestablish and add to the injuries he had recently sustained. "And I can tell you Mrs. Langtry is not disposed to leave the Manor—at least not yet. In short, Squire Baird, we have something of a stand-off."

"What makes you think I have any intention to what you call 'storm the Manor'? It is true I may wish to present myself at McLellan Manor by way of introducing myself to Mr. Trent as one gentleman to another. You are aware we share an interest in boxing. He may wish to meet my colleagues in accord with that interest. And, of course, I could then offer to escort Mrs. Langtry back to London."

"You can call it what you like, and attempt to bring whom you like," Holmes nodded to Baird's beefy companions, "but I can tell you the whole of the Oxley constabulary, some of whom you met yesterday, as well as the several men of Mr. Trent's staff, and my colleague, Dr. Watson, and myself are prepared to honor Mrs. Langtry's wish for privacy."

"And what if I choose to remove one of the obstacles to my seeing Lillie right here and now?"

"In that event, I'm afraid you'd find yourself spending the day in less attractive accommodations. If you look outside the window you'll see a man in gray coat and knickerbockers lounging about the shops across the road. He is tracking my movements, and if I'm not outside in what is now," Holmes paused to consult a pocket watch, "fourteen minutes, he is to proceed to the police station on the assumption I have met with foul play. So you see we haven't any time to waste, and I have a proposition to put to you which I believe can be mutually beneficial."

Hearing their patron addressed as they had never heard him addressed before, the two fighters hunched forward, looking to the Squire for instruction while Baird searched Holmes's face, eager to exploit the fear he found in most men. This time he found none.

"What is it you propose, Mr. Holmes?" He spoke the name as if it was a curse.

"I propose that you and Mr. Mitchell accompany Dr. Watson and myself to Glasgow. I want you to contact Mr. Garfoyle before we leave and arrange a fight between one of his boxers and Mr. Mitchell. Today being Friday, the fight should be scheduled for next Thursday. That will give time for the fighters to prepare and for Mr. Garfoyle to get word out about the contest. I assume Mr. Mitchell is in condition." Holmes glanced to the man he had volunteered to do battle who gave an affirmative grunt before thinking to look to Baird for instruction. "If you do these things, Mr. Baird, and are cooperative throughout our time in Glasgow, I will promise to act on your behalf to encourage Mrs. Langtry to meet with you. Whether you are able to convince her of your better intentions will be up to you. I will only promise to make it possible for you to do so." Holmes paused as if to allow his message to sink in. In fact, he was about to go beyond the plan developed by Mrs. Hudson.

"There is one more thing which you must also understand. If Mrs. Langtry chooses to reestablish a relationship with you, I would take it very badly if I were ever to hear that she was later subjected to abuse by you or any of your confederates. Am I clear?"

Squire Baird drew his face into a tight scowl, his expression, but not his words, making clear his awareness of Holmes's threat. "Why do you want Charlie to fight in Glasgow? What in the world has that got to do with anything?"

Holmes studied his pocket watch before responding. "That will become clear in time. For now, time is slipping away and I need you to tell me your intention. "Are we to travel to Glasgow, or do you sit in Oxley until you tire of its rustic charm?"

Squire Baird stood, working his jaw as if he had bitten into something distasteful and now had to decide whether to swallow or spit it out. He decided to swallow. "I'll go with you to Glasgow, but I'll give you something to understand as well, Mr. Holmes. If you go back on your word or try to play me for a fool, I'll come for you, and I'll find you, and I'll make certain you'll think more than twice before doing any such foolishness again."

"Be ready to travel tomorrow morning. There's a train to Leeds at ten forty-two, and we can get from there to Glasgow by three fifteen. It's my understanding your home in Glasgow is unoccupied. I should like for Dr. Watson and myself to stay there for the time we're in the city."

"Is there anything else you require, Mr. Holmes? Perhaps you'd like to dictate the menus for the time you'll be staying with me."

"I leave the food preparation to you, but I do have an additional question, Squire. I know Mr. Mitchell of course. I'm afraid I'm not acquainted with this other gentleman whom I assume will be joining us as well."

The subject of Holmes's query answered in a surprisingly soft voice, "Jem Hall."

The quick flight of Holmes's eyebrows revealed his recognition of the fighter's name. "I am well aware of your career and accomplishments, Mr. Hall, and pleased to make your acquaintance." The fighter gave Holmes a deep nod, softening, but not wholly relinquishing the glare he had assumed at the outset of their meeting.

Baird rose and the two fighters quickly followed his example. "Tomorrow at ten forty-two."

"And don't forget to get in touch with Mr. Garfoyle to schedule the fight. That is critical."

The three men turned away from Holmes and left without making response.

In response to Arthur Trent's request, the vicar agreed to allot a far corner of the churchyard for the boxer's earthly remains and promised to officiate at a graveside ceremony. The service was scheduled for late afternoon and prompted an immediate concern with the selection of dress appropriate to the occasion. Of the visitors to McLellan Manor, Mrs. Hudson alone had brought clothes appropriate to a funeral, if only because her everyday clothing was appropriate to a funeral. Lillie decided on a brown dress and matching jacket as properly subdued, choosing to ignore the hint of red that made it a match for her auburn hair. Holmes and Watson were absolved of making difficult choices from their limited wardrobe after Holmes suggested their presence could prove disturbing to Mrs. Mackenzie. With a knowing look to Lonsdale and Arthur Trent, he reasoned it might also be well for them to remain at the Manor just in case Squire Baird and his associates eluded the Oxley constabulary. Neither man needed to be reminded of the Squire's belligerent history, and both agreed with the soundness of Holmes's suggestion.

Mrs. Hudson reported to Lillie Langtry her intention to remain at the Manor as well "if she wouldn't be missed," indicating she would be uncomfortable, given her relationship to Mr. Holmes, attending the funeral of the man who died while fighting him. Lillie rolled her eyes at the thought anyone would take note of Mrs. Hudson's presence or absence at the ceremony, and indeed her absence later in the day drew no comment other than surprise at learning of her association with Holmes.

In the end, the turnout for Mackenzie's funeral was far greater than would have been predicted by any who had known Mackenzie in life. Besides Holmes, Watson and Mrs. Hudson, only Esther Trent, Charles and Clara did not make the trip to the churchyard. No one questioned Esther's decision. Her choice, coupled with that of Holmes and Watson, triggered Trent's request that Charles and Clara remain behind to attend to Esther and their guests as needed.

At the funeral, the vicar did his best to provide a respectful service, although handicapped by having only the most general information about the deceased. He had been informed by Trent that the man was married and was a fighter who had died in the ring. Everyone in the village had that information, but the vicar smiled and nodded, pretending it was new to him. His sermon was, for the most part, received with appropriate sobriety. It was only when he described Mackenzie as a beloved husband that there began a good deal of coughing and shuffling of feet. When the vicar later characterized him as a man dedicated to his craft, the spirit of quiet reflection was broken for a second and last time. The vicar guessed correctly he was venturing into hazardous territory, and eliminated discussion of the deceased's many friends and loss to the community. He moved to a recitation of the 23rd Psalm, having been assured by his widow it was the dead man's favorite. It would have been a safe choice in any event. The 23rd Psalm was everyone's favorite, most people not knowing any other. When he had finished, the vicar came to Mrs. Mackenzie to reprise his condolences which the widow tearlessly accepted.

While the vicar officiated at Mackenzie's funeral, Esther spent her time reading the latest issue of *Girl's Own Paper*; Charles, on Mr. Simon's instruction, polished silver; Clara, at Mrs. Charters's direction, straightened and cleaned Mrs. Mackenzie's cottage. Charles's work was interrupted just once when he was called upon to respond to an insistent front door bell. Fearing the worst, he was comforted to find Holmes and Watson already waiting when he arrived in the center hall. The two men nodded a grim-faced welcome to the footman, who selected the thickest walking stick he could find in the stand by the door. With Holmes and Watson on his either side, and the weapon held aloft in one hand, he pulled the door open to find himself looking down into the saucer-sized eyes of Isaiah Bauer, the 14 year-old delivery boy for Aldous Bauer, Chemist. The youngster looked to the footman brandishing a walking stick, and the two strangers who appeared equally intent on his destruction for reasons he felt it unwise to explore. He pressed the envelope he carried into Charles's free hand, backed his way from the porch with strides that would have been impressive in someone a foot taller, and called out, "Telegram for Mr. Sherlock Holmes," at the same time mounting the bicycle he had left lying against the bottom step. In another moment he was pedaling as fast as he could manage back to his father's shop where he would justify his failure to collect a delivery fee on the need to escape with his life from the three crazed people who had taken control of the Manor.

Charles, after first calling the boy's name repeatedly

and to no effect, replaced the walking stick in the stand from which it had been snatched, and assumed the look of studied indifference he had seen Mr. Simon adopt many times, and had himself practiced at length in front of his glass. He spoke a single word, "sir," to Holmes, before providing him the telegram the youngest Bauer had delivered. Charles then turned on his heel to return to the kitchen to resume polishing the silver, and searching for treats in the absence of anyone to deny him that pleasure.

Holmes tore open the envelope to read Lestrade's response to his earlier telegram.

"It's what we expected, Watson." Watson wondered about the "we" in this case, but elected to remain silent until he could learn what it was they expected. Mrs. Hudson joined them, her curiosity roused by the doorbell. After learning of Lestrade's telegram, they went again to the library to consider what Lestrade had to tell them, and to review the plan for their time in Glasgow.

"What does the Inspector 'ave to say, Mr. 'Olmes?"

"It's just as we expected." Like Watson, Mrs. Hudson wondered at the reference to "we;" like Watson, she elected to stay silent as Holmes read the telegram's contents.

"Murder in 1858. Murderer never apprehended. Identity known to be Calvin Jamison, boxer. Victim, Josiah Krebs, gambler. Believed to have lost large wager on outcome of fight. Argued with Jamison in fighter's room. Stabbed. Three witnesses, all same story. Only one of three available. Flinty McMahon, fight manager, dead. John Garfoyle, Sr., fight promoter, in second childhood. Alfred Campbell, Jamison's second, left boxing after murder, works at Glasgow United. Jamison believed in Africa. Not clear what any of this to do with Mackenzie. Will wait to learn. Lestrade"

Holmes put the telegram aside and added his analysis. "It seems clear we are now in a position to assist the Glasgow police in apprehending the murderer of Josiah Krebs. Indeed,

I would say we now know the identity of the murderer of both Josiah Krebs and Sailor Mackenzie." Holmes looked to each of his colleagues for a sign of dissent, found none and continued. "There seems little question that Trent—which is to say Calvin Jamison—is our man. Mackenzie discovered Trent's connection to Jamison through that church picture, and threatened to expose him, leaving Trent—which is to say Jamison—no alternative but to do away with him. We just need to understand how he engineered Mackenzie's killing."

Mrs. Hudson fell back against the cushion of her easy chair. "You're right, Mr. 'Olmes, Mr. Trent and Calvin Jamison are the same man. And the murder of Mr. Krebs explains 'is trip to Africa. As you say, Mr. Mackenzie must 'ave made the connection between Mr. Trent and the murder. 'E would 'ave 'eard about the killin' from fighters in Glasgow. Those stories never go away, but just get bigger over time. Still and all, there's a good deal more for us to know before we go to namin' our murderer or, come to that, the murderer of the unfortunate Mr. Krebs."

Holmes's voice was nearly plaintive in objection. "But surely, Mrs. Hudson, with eye witnesses to Krebs's murder we can be assured of Trent's guilt for that crime at least."

"Maybe so, Mr. 'Olmes, maybe so. But 'ow many times 'ave I 'eard you talk about the sad state of boxin', and the way the criminal element 'as got itself deep into what could be a grand sport. I'm thinkin' the criminal element was likely a good deal deeper into your grand sport years ago when Calvin Jamison was fightin' and there was even less people keepin' watch on things. And then look at the killin'. Why does a young man fit enough to be a boxer choose to use a knife against a bookmaker 'e's only been arguin' with? Why don't any of the three men standin' there do somethin' to stop 'im? I'd say there's a good deal more to be learned about the death of Josiah Krebs before we go to accusin' anyone, and before we can understand the way it fits into the death of Ian

Mackenzie—which is why you and Dr. Watson need to be rubbin' elbows as it were with some in the Glasgow fight game."

Mrs. Hudson pursed her lips and became pensive. "It's the 'ow we go about it I've been goin' over in my mind, and I'm thinkin' there's a way that'll depend on your doin' some of your playactin', Mr. 'Olmes. Am I correct you brought some of the things you use to make yourself into somebody else?" She got a deep nod from Holmes. "Good. We're going to need you to become another person while you're in Glasgow. And we're goin' to need Inspector Lestrade to join us the day before the fight you were arrangin'. You'll be sendin' another telegram to the Inspector, Mr. 'Olmes, askin' 'im to come to Glasgow this Tuesday. The Inspector will need to bring Wiggins to Glasgow as well. He can tell Mr. Stinchcombe it's critical to the investigation you got Wiggins involved in earlier. We'll need Alfred Campbell as well, but we'll get Mr. Baird to take care of that." Mrs. Hudson tapped two fingers against her pursed lips. "Very good. Then all we've got left to do is go over what you know about conductin' a séance."

At ten the following morning, Holmes and Watson took leave of their host in the center hall where they had been welcomed two days earlier. Arthur Trent expressed his trust in Holmes's judgment and skills, and wished success for his efforts. His words expressed a greater confidence than his voice conveyed. For his part, Holmes promised to be back in a week with a much chastened Squire Baird. His words and voice were perfectly in sync.

Once arrived at the station, Holmes left Watson to await the Squire and his entourage while he walked the two streets to Aldous Bauer, Chemist, to send a telegram to Lestrade that would again raise the eyebrows of Miss Bauer, and whet the curiosity of as many citizens of Oxley as she could reach the rest of the day.

Holmes returned from the Bauers just as his newly acquired companions were coming three abreast down the street toward the station. The girth of the two fighters, and the arrogance of their manager, guaranteed that passage would have been denied to any trying to get by them had there been anyone besides Holmes on the street. As it was, he came together with the three, and all four entered the station appearing to be together, although they were, in fact, far apart. It seemed a harbinger of events for the week ahead.

After purchasing tickets, the Squire took a seat on one of the two benches at the Oxley station together with his two burly colleagues. Holmes stopped beside him only long enough to ask Baird if he'd made arrangements with Garfoyle for the bout.

"Said I would. It's set for Thursday night with the details to be worked out. But Garfoyle's already doing publicity." The Squire set his jaw and squinted up to the hawk-like figure hovering above him. "Understand, I'm not cutting you in for so much as a ha'penny. Our share will be split between Charlie, Jem and me." Baird looked as defiant as he could manage from two feet below his adversary.

Holmes thought about demanding a share of the earnings be given Mrs. Mackenzie, but decided that could require considerable discussion, and perhaps an appeal to the Squire's better nature, whose existence he doubted.

"That's no problem. I've no interest in the money Mr. Mitchell and Mr. Hall earn. However, there is one thing I will ask you to do. I want you to bring on Alfred Campbell as Mr. Mitchell's second."

Emboldened by his success in demanding the profits from the boxing match, Baird was ready to challenge Holmes on a second point. "And who in the bloody hell is Alfred Campbell, and why do I want him for a second?"

Holmes straightened to his greater than six feet in

height, bending his head the slightest bit to look down his aquiline nose at the smaller man. "Alfred Campbell is your employee at Glasgow United, a foundry you own." Holmes was uncertain Baird would be aware of his own holdings. "At one time he worked as a second, although that was some years ago. And you'll want him for a second because I want him for a second. I told you our agreement depends on your being cooperative throughout the time we're in Glasgow. That will be less than a week, and some of my requests will require a good deal more effort on your part than this simple one."

The Squire began to rumble his response to Holmes, but was drowned out by the on-time arrival of the 10:42 to Leeds.

Chapter 14.
Introducing Makepeace Godwin

Relations between the two camps were unlikely to thaw on the short ride to Leeds or the longer one to Glasgow. To preserve their fragile truce, on each leg of the journey the second group to board the train selected a passenger car other than the one chosen by the first group. At the Glasgow station they were met by the Squire's coach and driver, and Holmes and Watson feared for a moment they might be expected to find a separate carriage. Jem Hall removed that concern by holding the door open for the two of them after climbing aboard. They sat without speaking or catching each other's eye for the 20 minute ride to the outskirts of Glasgow and Baird Castle.

The Castle was a baronial three story estate set on the crest of a small hill and consuming the whole of it. The estate seemed well-suited to its owner. Great blocks of grey stone cut from the family's own quarry had been joined to create a structure displaying neither subtlety nor imagination, instead overwhelming the visitor with its size and drab solidity. Bay windows, overhung by undecorated cornices, jutted from the first and second levels, and were themselves framed by tall, narrow windows at which it appeared archers might show themselves at any moment.

A tall slender man in his early 50s with watery blue expressionless eyes, wearing the clothes and authority of the Castle's long-time butler, emerged with two younger and more agile footmen who proceeded without instruction to gather the baggage of the five arrivals. The butler alone waited the direction that was not long in coming.

"These two gentlemen will be staying with us." Baird gestured in the direction of Holmes and Watson. "I'll want them settled in the east wing; I and my guests will be in our usual places in the west wing." Baird's intonation set both men to wondering if the east wing wasn't the site of the Castle's dungeon. The butler responded with a, "Very good sir," spoken in the automatic style of one accustomed to unquestioning obedience whatever the demand. Secure in his own home, Baird emptied himself of the feelings he had been at pains to hold in check.

"You are now my guests. I'll do all that I promised and expect you to do the same. But I see no reason to pretend we enjoy each other's company. I will see you both at dinner, assuming none of us have made other plans, and I have no intention, and certainly no wish to see either of you at any other times. Breakfast and midday meals will be provided in the dining room or you may prefer to eat in your rooms. You can dress for dinner or not as you like. I believe that covers everything, and that we now have a satisfactory understanding." The Squire turned to go, in as much as he at least could claim a satisfactory understanding.

Holmes's booming reply, "I think not," temporarily halted the retreat of Baird and the two fighters from the Castle's center hall. The butler and footmen, having grasped as much of the luggage as they were able, proceeded up the curved center stairway, but appeared to move without either the speed appropriate to their task or the disinterest appropriate to their station. "There are tasks scheduled for next week about which you will be informed. But first let me assure you that Dr. Watson and I seek no greater association with you than you do with us." Holmes stared down his red-faced host while the two fighters watched with eyes and mouths open wide, and the servants' slow progress up the stairs improbably slackened further.

Holmes, having taken careful notice of all in his audience, now pretended to be unaware of any of them. "I will remind you that you are expected to obtain the services of Alfred Campbell as the second to Mr. Mitchell. That is critical, and without that being done we have no arrangement and I am simply your unwelcome guest. Second, on Tuesday and Wednesday next, this house will play host to two of my friends. At that time I will require your assistance, and the participation of Mr. Mitchell and Mr. Hall in a small theatrical. I will not divulge the nature of that activity at this time, but I can tell you it will require some considerable preparation and *all* of us should be prepared to play our parts. Tonight, at dinner, we can talk about the issues involved in obtaining the services of Mr. Campbell. I will await word from you as to the time dinner is served. And now, Mr. Baird, would you ask your man to show Dr. Watson and myself to our rooms. I believe we have now reached a satisfactory understanding."

Whatever the shortcomings in the Squire's welcome, they were not reflected in the quality of his table. Duck, venison and turbot followed a pheasant soup, oysters and sweetbreads, and were themselves followed by charlotte russe and a variety of fresh fruits. Three bottles of wine were consumed—primarily by Squire Baird and Charlie Mitchell, although not without generous assistance from Jem Hall. Holmes and Watson drank sparingly and alone commented on the quality of the claret and the two white burgundies they shared.

Holmes had hoped to hold off discussing the business of the evening until a modicum of amiability had been achieved. However, he discovered his companions regarded amiability as nothing more than a way station on the road to the hilarity still to be achieved through the consumption of a large quantity of wine over a short period of time. He would have to raise his issues sooner rather than later if there was to be any hope for their coherent discussion.

"There are some things we need to review before meeting with Mr. Garfoyle. In particular, I spoke of the need to recruit Alfred Campbell to be Mr. Mitchell's second."

Charlie Mitchell looked up from scooping two oysters into his mouth with a single swipe, and Baird held his glass aloft for a moment before gulping a generous portion of the Montrachet that had just been added to it. Jem Hall alone looked to Holmes with neither fork nor glass in hand, but only amused wonder on his face.

"Alfred Campbell has not acted as a boxer's second in many years and Mr. Garfoyle may be expected to question your interest in his services, Mr. Mitchell. It will be up to you to insist that you know of Mr. Campbell from his work years ago. You can say you have no patience with the youngsters today who lack a proper appreciation for the history of the sport or of boxing as it should be practiced. I will need both you and Mr. Baird to be especially persuasive. I'm telling you again it is essential we have Mr. Campbell in Mr. Mitchell's corner."

The intended recipients of his comments were at that moment negotiating through a series of hand gestures which was to get the last of the Montrachet before moving on to the claret. Charlie Mitchell held up four fingers to indicate the number of glasses consumed by his host, and the Squire extended his thumb and index figure in close proximity to each other to indicate how small his last glass had been. The watery-eyed butler waited patiently to be told how to apportion the wine remaining; he had a long history of awaiting the outcome of such conflicts. At last, it was decided to divide the wine equally, and both men watched intently as the butler performed the Solomon-like feat demanded. When it was done, Baird responded to Holmes.

"I understand perfectly well what is required. As you've said, Holmes, the man works for me. I can order him to act as Charlie's second and Charlie won't have to do any playacting. Charlie's a bruiser, he's not Beerbohm Tree and I don't see why he should try to be."

"I have my reasons for doing it this way, Squire." The

testiness in Holmes's voice belied his pretense to congeniality. "We want as little suspicion raised about our selection of Mr. Campbell as possible. The two of you will need to carry that off. I will be attending the meeting with you, but as of tomorrow I will be Makepeace Godwin, Mr. Mitchell's spiritual advisor, concerned only with the battle for his soul."

Holmes's announcement left all but Watson staring at him open-mouthed. Holmes paused long enough to take a sip of the wine still in his glass, which he complimented again to an audience still trying to absorb his earlier statement.

"Great bloody hell" was the only response from the man who moments earlier had been provided a spiritual advisor.

Assured now of the attention of his audience, Holmes continued, directing special attention to his newly anointed disciple. "Beginning tomorrow you will refer to me as Makepeace Godwin. I assure you, when you see me tomorrow I will be Makepeace Godwin. I provide you access to the spirit world, and I alone can banish the negative forces that will otherwise sap your powers when you are in the ring."

"And just wot spirits have you got in mind, if you don't mind my asking? I don't fancy meeting no ghosts if that's what you got in mind, Mr. Holmes."

"Ghosts are exactly what I have in mind, Mr. Mitchell, but you won't be meeting them until later in the week." Holmes accepted a generous slice of venison from the butler who appeared for the moment in danger of tipping his tray into the detective's lap.

It wasn't long before any further sober consideration of Holmes's ideas, or of any ideas more profound than the proper allotment of food and wine was no longer possible. When at last the fighters and their patron had consumed as much of both as they were able, Squire Baird pronounced himself ready for brandy and cigars, and set off in the direction of the drawing room listing from side to side like a small boat buffeted by heavy winds. His two companions joined him without waiting to be invited, Charlie Mitchell seemingly caught in the same rough seas, while Jem Hall managed a somewhat steadier course. Holmes and Watson excused themselves to no one in particular indicating a need for sleep. Before they left, Jem Hall turned back from the support he was providing Charlie Mitchell and winked to Holmes. Speaking in his incongruously soft voice, he assured Holmes all would be well the next day and wished both men a good night.

Holmes and Watson rose early the next morning and dined alone as they anticipated was likely given their host's promise of sociability, and the group's undoubted need for a period of recovery from the excesses of the past evening. The appointment with Garfoyle was scheduled for two so there was little initial concern about the absence of the Squire. Watson jotted a few notes to capture the conversation of the earlier evening, and then began a study of the two recent issues of *Lancet* he had packed for the trip, in one of which Professor Murri's hydrophobia cure was still waiting discovery.

Holmes, meanwhile, transformed himself into Makepeace Godwin. He thought Charlie Mitchell's spiritual advisor should be an older man with a somewhat wild look about him. To that end, in addition to the lines he added to his face and the hollowing he made of his cheeks, he fitted a wig of gray curly hair that appeared to have been kept consistently and purposely unkempt throughout Makepeace Godwin's lifetime. He added a thick moustache and a beard that fell nearly to his chest, both of which showed a similar unfamiliarity with either comb or brush. He was pleased to see his new persona neatly covered what discoloration and swelling still marked the appearance of Sherlock Holmes. A slightly frayed frock coat, and dark pants that appeared to have been slept in completed the appearance of an intense older man more concerned with the spiritual than the material world.

He strode the room, practicing a hunched walk and a piercing glare. When he had perfected both, he tried several speech patterns, initially affecting a Scottish accent, but rejecting that in as much as Garfoyle was Scottish and would be aware of any misstep. He next tried a dialect drawn from the London streets, but found himself falling into a Cockney accent and rejected that, fearing it conveyed an inferior intelligence. He settled finally on the precise and somewhat pedantic speech he remembered as typical of some of the dons of his acquaintance at Cambridge, at the same time lowering his voice a half octave and adding the rhythmic lilt of a preacher he had heard at a revival meeting.

Through his several incarnations, Watson, who had seen the process unfold many times before, remained absorbed with his scientific journals, turning his attention to Holmes only when his critical opinion was requested. At noon, they decided that whatever the Squire's wishes about their having as little to do with each other as possible, the session scheduled with Garfoyle that afternoon demanded some preliminary discussion. Watson rang for the butler who abandoned his blasé demeanor on catching sight of Makepeace Godwin, then quickly reestablished it.

"May I be of some service, sir?"

Watson answered for both men, while Holmes practiced a beneficent smile. "We wanted to know if you've heard from Mr. Baird or his other guests. More particularly, we wondered if you could tell us their whereabouts."

"Yes, sir. Misters Mitchell and Hall are in the gymnasium where they are engaged in some sort of play fighting and the Squire left some time ago to go riding."

"Can you tell me … what is your name please?"

"Sanderson, sir."

"Sanderson, then, can you tell me when the Squire is scheduled to return?"

"I neglected to ask, sir."

Watson searched for a break in the butler's solid facade, but found none. "Thank you, Sanderson, we will be down to eat shortly. Please inform us when Mr. Baird returns."

"Very good, sir."

By the time Holmes and Watson arrived in the dining room, the two fighters had finished a session with medicine balls, Indian clubs and shadow boxing in a gymnasium fashioned from the Castle's conservatory, and were now pursuing their favorite activity at Baird Castle, that of devouring large quantities of the Squire's store of meat, fish, and drink. They were as taken aback by Holmes's appearance as had been Sanderson, but failed to show the butler's swift recovery. They stopped in their efforts to determine how much their platters could hold of the chicken, ham, woodcock and rabbit each was displacing from the trays set out on the sideboard, and pointed their forks at Holmes as they gaped and shook their heads at the improbable vision they shared. Charlie Mitchell was the first to find his voice. "Mr. Holmes, if it is Mr. Holmes what's hiding under all that hair, what is it you mean to be doing? Why are you looking like someone who's come to us fresh from Bedlam?"

Watson answered for his friend. "Mr. Mitchell, let me introduce you to Makepeace Godwin who, you will recall from our discussion last night, is your spiritual advisor. You have come to rely on him and his ability to dispel the evil forces that might otherwise rob you of your strength and fighting ability. Indeed, Mr. Godwin has become so critical to your fighting career you keep him constantly by your side."

As Watson completed his introduction of Makepeace Godwin a broad grin swept across Charlie Mitchell's face. He gave an exaggerated bow to the man he had just learned to be critical to his fighting ability. "I am delighted to make your acquaintance, sir. I am Charlie Mitchell, the English heavyweight champion or at least I used to be, and with your spir'chal help that's what I mean to be again."

Makepeace Godwin returned the boxer's good-natured grin with a fierce stare. "And so you shall if you'll but follow my instruction." The voice was low-pitched, melodious and authoritative.

Charlie Mitchell stopped smiling, and looked to Makepeace Godwin open-mouthed as he searched in vain for the Sherlock Holmes whose body was now possessed by this odd and unexpectedly intimidating stranger.

It was left to Jem Hall to clarify the situation for his friend. "We've seen the last of Mr. Holmes for a while, Charlie. From now on it's gonna be Mr. Godwin, and Mr. Godwin has some things he'll want doing. Is that about it, Mr. Godwin?"

"Thank you, Mr. Hall; that's it exactly." The voice sounded as a decree from on high. "Let me remind you one of those things involves your coming to appreciate the dedication and skill that existed among handlers in the fight game when you were young. You've heard that Alfred Campbell was one of those men, and you want him in your corner for the fight and during the week of preparation. Indeed, you insist on having him as a condition of the match."

Between the sepulchral tones of Makepeace Godwin and the good-natured support of Jem Hall, Charlie Mitchell began to understand what would be expected of him and warmed to the prospect of playing his part in the drama being created. "I thank you, Mr. Godwin, for you being there for me and I do mean to keep you close on that account. It was a rare day and a fine one that the fates brought you into my life. And as for Alfred Campbell, it's long been my understanding he's one of the finest men ever to work a corner, and I mean to have him for my fight or there'll be no fight."

"What's all this then? Who's deciding whether you

fight or don't fight?" George Baird, still in riding coat and boots, had caught Mitchell's last statement and now suspected the worst. A look to Holmes, or the man he took to be Holmes, added to his suspicion that, in his own house, a conspiracy was being organized around him, if not against him. "And who in the bloody creation are you supposed to be?"

"This here is my very own spir'chal advisor, Mr. Makepeace Godwin. It's him what keeps the evil forces from me and lets me stay strong."

"We will—*all of us*—have parts to play in the coming week, Squire, and we are just now exploring them." Holmes spoke to Baird in his own voice, thereby sounding strangely inappropriate to everyone but the Squire.

George Baird looked to his two boxers, both with broad grins and eyes blazing at the prospect of playing out their new parts, and he saw his authority over the men he'd housed, fed, and extensively wined now slipping away. He bowed to the inevitable, but not without first making clear the disgust he felt for all that was happening.

"And what part would you have me play, Mr. Holmes? Perhaps I can go as one of Charlie's evil forces. Maybe I could be the left uppercut he's not seeing very well lately."

For the moment Holmes continued speaking as Holmes. He spoke slowly, patiently, as if he were addressing a child bent on being disagreeable—which was not far from his view of George Baird. "It will be up to you, Squire, to support Mr. Mitchell's reliance on Makepeace Godwin, and to make clear your concern with acquiring the services of Alfred Campbell. Beyond that, you may, of course, make whatever business arrangements you choose." And now the voice descended a half octave and sounded again as though from the Heavens. "Makepeace Godwin's concerns are on a loftier plane."

Charlie Mitchell clapped his hands, and Jem Hall roared at the change in character. Squire Baird grunted, and

216

did his best to appear satisfied with the arrangement.

Chapter 15.

A Boxing Match Is Arranged

While Watson went off on his own assignment, Makepeace Godwin set out with his three associates to meet with John Garfoyle at the Pugilism Society of Glasgow. There was no confusing the Society with the National Sporting Club. It was miles from the city's theaters and music halls, and its building was distinctive from its neighbors only by virtue of being more oppressively drab. It had been the MacPherson Warehouse one life earlier and still bore its name overhead. Professional boxing was illegal in Scotland as it was everywhere in the British Isles, but the Pugilism Society, unlike the National Sporting Club, did not have a membership capable of forcing the issue.

Squire Baird pressed the button beside the Society's unlettered door and was rewarded with a sound that called to mind a swarm of bees—a large and angry swarm. When his call was not answered instantly, Baird again stirred the hive and supplemented that with a loud knocking.

"Who's thair?" The voice from the door's other side was a baritone so deep and powerful, it competed successfully with the din created by the Squire.

"George Baird, open the door."

There was a long moment's pause before the door opened to reveal a guardian who might well have been the brother of Charlie Mitchell and Jem Hall—their big brother. He was in his mid to late 40s, his silver gray hair making him appear still older. His frame filled the doorway and he made no effort to remove it. Small scars were visible in many parts of his hairless face making clear his profession prior to being employed as doorman at the Pugilism Society. He looked over the four men as if deciding which of them was capable of causing him the greatest difficulty. He gave Baird a quick glance of dismissal, which did not escape the Squire's attention or endear him to the behemoth blocking his entry. The behemoth settled his attention on the two fighters and spoke only to them, "This way," and turned to lead the entourage down the corridor that extended from the small lobby.

They passed one door, and their guide knocked twice at the second with a restraint out of keeping with his appearance. The response from within was immediate and friendly. "Enter, please." The guide admitted the four men, then waited at the door he closed behind them.

John Garfoyle stood behind the round conference table that served as his desk. He was of the same approximate weight as the man standing guard for him, but his weight was distributed in a far more horizontal direction. He might have been five foot five standing on his toes, but he appeared unlikely to engage in such strenuous activity. He wore no coat and his white shirt seemed on the verge of overlapping the trousers into which it was only barely tucked. His round face was pallid suggesting a limited acquaintance with sunlight, and his several chins shook as he nodded his pleasure at meeting his eminent visitors. He extended a hand to George Baird, unlike his doorman quickly identifying the group's leader, and vigorously shook the hand the Squire reluctantly offered.

"John Garfoyle here, John Garfoyle, Junior, and it's an honor, sir, a pure honor, to have such a great sportsman as yourself visit our modest establishment. And this, of course, is the British heavyweight champion, the renowned Charlie Mitchell. A great honor, sir." And with that he pumped a second hand. For just a moment he looked quizzically at the second fighter in the room. "And you must be ... why you could only be the remarkable Jem Hall. Yes, of course you are. Well, this is a day." And a third hand was pumped. When he turned finally to Holmes, his eyes took on a fierce squint and furrows struggled to make an indentation in his forehead as he tried to recall who he might be. "I'm afraid I don't know this gentleman."

Employing a somber tone and shooting a hand in the direction of Holmes, Charlie Mitchell responded on his behalf. "This here is my very own spir'chal advisor. I have the pleasure to interduce Mr. Makepeace Godwin, what is the only man that can remove the evil forces from my path and allow me to keep my strength." Charlie Mitchell set his jaw and smiled his satisfaction at having incorporated all aspects of the story he had been given. Jem Hall, however, was not to be denied an opportunity to command his own moment on the stage.

"He can't go nowhere without Mr. Godwin. He's that kind of a miracle worker—meaning no disrespect to any man's religion."

John Garfoyle waved away any thought he might be offended and grinned even more broadly to Makepeace Godwin, dismissing him as a charlatan who had somehow worked his way into the inner circle of these supposed big city sophisticates. It was no concern of his as long as Makepeace Godwin did not threaten the profits he intended to reap from the presence of Charlie Mitchell in his club. "None taken, Mr. Hall, none taken. I've been around the fight game long enough to know there are many ways of preparing for a fight, but I'm forgetting my manners." He pointed to the chairs circling the table and for a moment the grin disappeared. "I see we're one chair short. Please, Wilfred, would you be so good as to obtain one more chair for us." All four men looked with wonder to Wilfred, but no one thought it wise to make comment.

"May I offer you gentlemen some refreshments?" Garfoyle received three enthusiastic acceptances of his offer, only Makepeace Godwin declining "the kind offer of spirits."

"Ye're in Glasgow, gentlemen, and so ye have access to our wonderful Scotch whiskeys. I'm going to suggest a fine single malt I only make available on special occasions for special people." Garfoyle turned again to his oversized doorkeeper who had returned with the requested chair. "Wilfred, if ye would, we'll each have a glass of the Glenkinchie except for Mr. Godwin. And please pour yerself a glass as well."

The visitors took seats around the table, toasted their host's good health, tossed back their drinks and pronounced the whiskey excellent. They waited the offer of a second drink, but none was forthcoming.

"Perhaps now is the time for us to finalize our business arrangement. I don't know what things are like in London, but here the standard arrangement is forty percent of the purse to the winner, twenty percent to the loser, and forty percent to the promoter which is, of course, me." He dropped his voice at the last to make clear his displeasure at having to accept any reward for facilitating the upcoming match, then brightened with a sudden thought. "However, I want to be fair. We all know Charlie Mitchell will be the draw. Not that the bruiser we have lined up to go against him isn't a good lad. He won't be a pushover, Charlie, but he nae may be in your class just yet." He gave the boxer a knowing wink which Charlie returned with a tentative smile. "I'll give up an additional five percent of my share if you'll agree to make Charlie's sparring sessions public and we share equally in the take from their attendance." Garfoyle settled back in his chair, smiling his good fellowship to George Baird. The action was wasted on its target.

"Garfoyle, I'm not one of your country bumpkins. I'll take twenty percent of the purse over and above our share of the fight, and I'll take sixty-five percent of the take to watch the sparring sessions, which I'll remind you will be between my two fighters."

The smile never left the boxing promoter's face as he listened to the expected counter-offer while Baird's face hardened into lines of barely contained fury. The mountain fidgeted at his position by the door, and Garfoyle made a fluttering motion with his hand urging him to relax. The promoter was on familiar ground, the Squire was in unfamiliar territory. Baird knew only to command and bully, and those qualities would be useless in this negotiation.

The two boxers settled back to observe a process that routinely took place well out of their sight, while Makepeace Godwin gazed skyward, doing his best to appear above the petty concerns of finance. In the end, an agreement was reached with the forty percent to the winner and twenty percent to the loser affirmed, Garfoyle splitting equally with Baird the promoter's fee, and Baird getting sixty percent of the take from admissions to the sparring sessions. Garfoyle clapped his hands and reprised his offer of single malt Scotch whiskey. A fuming Squire Baird, feeling himself cheated in some way he couldn't identify, spurned the offer much to the consternation of his two fighters who believed the drinks their just reward for sitting through the contest of wills.

Baird motioned to his fighters he was ready to leave when Makepeace Godwin cleared his throat and, in a soft but compelling tone, wondered if there wasn't need for some additional discussion about the choice of a second for Mr. Mitchell.

Charlie Mitchell, recognizing his cue to action, again stepped before the footlights. "Mr. Godwin is got it exactly right. It's me partic'lar wish to have …" And at that point the boxer realized he had forgotten the name of the second whose presence was essential for the fight just negotiated. Jem Hall came instantly to the rescue. He leaned close to his colleague and spoke to him in a hoarse whisper heard by everyone in the room. "You was in need of the experience and know-how of Alfred Campbell. You was desperate for him."

Garfoyle looked to Jem Hall then to Charlie Mitchell and finally to George Baird, eyes wide with surprise before shaking several chins in disbelief at what he was hearing.

"Alfie Campbell? Why, the man hasn't participated in a match since I was a boy. Are ye sure it's Alfie you want?"

Now possessed of the name of the man he couldn't do without, Charlie Mitchell was prepared to make the most of the second chance he'd been given. "It's Alfie. It's definitely Alfie. I'll have nothing to do with these kids they're throwing at you nowadays. I only want to work with them as know their business and have a care what they do. I heard about your Alfie from the bruisers what have been around a while. It's him and Jem I'll have in my corner or there'll be no fight at all."

"Well, of course ye can have whoever ye like, but I warn ye, while Alfie comes to the fights often enough, I doubt he'll want to get back in the ring after all these years. Meanwhile, if it's agreeable, Mr. Baird, I'll draw up the papers of our agreement and we can sign them when we get together for the first sparring session."

There was a grunt from Baird that Garfoyle took to be an affirmation and he pressed down hard on the table by way of getting to his feet. He kept both hands on the table leaning a short distance across as each man rose to take his leave. "Gentlemen, I look forward to our working together to put on a fine match that I'm certain will be greatly to our mutual advantage." He nodded good-byes to each of them and then eased himself back into his chair. "Wilfred can show ye out." Garfoyle was no longer smiling.

When Alfie Campbell was summoned to report to the executive offices, he expected the worst. Nobody was ever taken off the floor and told to report upstairs unless there was a problem—a big problem. But he had no idea what that problem could be. He worked as a finisher now, knocking the excess metal off molds for parts that were then loaded for transport to ship builders on the River Clyde. It was a cushy job. He'd be the first to admit that, but it came to him after 35 years of his doing every other foundry job there was, the whole time keeping his hands busy and his mouth shut. His conversation with the bosses was confined to, "Yes sir," and his exchanges with the men on the floor rarely got beyond, "Good morning," and, "Good evening." He had, in fact, become known to two generations of workers as "the quiet man." He made no enemies, but neither did he make friends or appear to feel their absence. No one of his fellow workers had ever visited the two-room flat that had long been his home or knew anyone who had. As he mounted the open staircase to the "boss's floor," he excited more interest from the men below than at any time any of them would have been able to recall.

The clerk, who had come to get him, pointed to the door he was to enter, and then left to get back to the office he shared with three other clerks. Alfie smoothed the fringes of gray hair back under his ears, knocked softly on the door and was rewarded with an impatient cry of, "Come in, come in," from a voice unfamiliar to him.

Four men sat in comfortable chairs around a low table, their leisurely posture contrasting dramatically with the clanging, hissing and frenzied activity on the floor below. He recognized two of the men, and his thoughts turned from the possibility of being declared redundant to confusion as to why two of his country's greatest boxers were sitting in the executive offices of the Glasgow United Ironworks. He said nothing, waiting for the men to state their intentions.

"I'm glad to make your acquaintance, Alfie, if it's alright for me to call you that. I'm Charlie Mitchell and this here is Jem Hall, and our manager, Squire George Baird, and the other man," here there was a broad sweep of his arm, "is Mr. Makepeace Godwin who's my spir'chal advisor, and the four of us have got a proposition for you what's gonna be just your cup of tea."

In spite of the fighter's hearty welcome, Alfie

Campbell had not been invited to sit. He looked to the smiling Charlie Mitchell and Jem Hall, the two men he recognized, and then to the other two. Of course, he knew all about George Baird. He was the owner of the ironworks nobody ever saw. More significant to Alfie, who tracked everything that happened in boxing, he was the fight manager who'd been thrown out of the Pelican Club after protesting the outcome of a match first with his fists and then with a knife.

"I know who ye ahr, Mr. Mitchell and Mr. Hall. I foller the fights as best I can." He ignored Squire Baird, not certain if it was appropriate for him to admit knowing the foundry's owner. "I'm wondering what the likes of you could possibly want with me."

"Do you follow boxing then, Mr. Campbell?"

Alfie turned to the man with unruly hair and beard who had raised the question. "I foller the sport well enough. I don't see the harm to that."

"Nor do I, Mr. Campbell. Indeed, I'm glad of it. Perhaps Mr. Mitchell can explain what he means when he says he has a proposition for you."

But it wasn't Charlie Mitchell who responded. Squire Baird had taken as much as he could of jousting with one of his own employees. "We want you to act as a second to Charlie Mitchell in a fight he's got scheduled for Thursday next. We'll also expect you to be at the two sessions where he'll be sparring with Jem. It's all to take place at Garfoyle's club. I believe you know it."

Alfie gave a hesitant nod.

"That's it then. There's ten pounds to be paid to you when the fight's over."

"We believe you can make a real contribution to Mr. Mitchell's fight, which is why we have come to ask you to work with us." The voice was a melodic baritone that seemed to wash gently over Alfie. He met the eyes of the spiritual advisor for a moment, then turned away.

"What're ye wanting me for? I ain't worked a corner for … I couldn't even tell ye how many years."

Charlie Mitchell embraced the task of convincing Alfie of the need for his assistance. "Alfie, I know—all of us do—that you was once a fine handler. I need somebody like you in my corner who knows to do things the right way. I don't want none of these young pups that got no sense of the way things ought to be done. It's you what Jem and I need, and what we want."

"And there's something more," Jem Hall's eyes were bright with the sudden epiphany he was certain would carry the day. "Alfie, you know the situation in Glasgow and me and Charlie don't. You follow the fights so I'm betting you know all about the local referees in these parts. You'll know who does long counts and who does short, who sees the punches that go below the waistband and who looks the other way, who might be influenced by there being a local boy and who don't care where a fighter comes from. Of course, we're planning on Charlie taking his man out, but we got to be prepared for anything. And it's you who would know all about the local scene and the things that can turn a fight."

Charlie Mitchell nodded his agreement, muttering as much to himself as to anyone at the table, "That's true, that's very true," while Makepeace Goodwin's eyes widened as if trying to place the heavyset stranger who had unexpectedly joined the group. Even George Baird nodded his admiration for the fighter's unanticipated contribution.

Alfie Campbell too was impressed with Jem Hall's reasoning. He was impressed as well with the 10 quid he could receive for very little effort on his behalf. But he was impressed most of all by the opportunity to work the corner of the former British heavyweight champion, and to work it in company with a leading contender for the same title. It was a once in a lifetime opportunity and Alfie Campbell was running out of lifetime.

"I guess, when ye put it like that, there's ways I could help. If it's all right with the bosses, I'd be willing to do what I can for the week." At the last he glanced to George Baird then quickly away.

"I'll arrange that. You be at Garfoyle's club tomorrow at one o'clock sharp. The sparring session is set for two and you'll be needed to get Charlie and Jem ready."

The voice from the wild man was again softly melodic, and wholly in control of all that was happening in a way Alfie sensed, but could not understand. "We're delighted to have you with us, Mr. Campbell."

There was a last grunt from Squire Baird, smiles from the two fighters, and a nod from the spiritual advisor. Alfie returned to the floor below, his every step taken under the scrutiny of the men he was once again joining. The quiet man looked to none of them, but took his place behind the rack of molds needing to be trimmed.

Chapter 16.
Holmes and Watson Compare Notes

Holmes, still in the guise of Makepeace Goodwin, breezed his way into Watson's room, greeted the Doctor with his accustomed voice and an unaccustomed grin, and collapsed into the nearest chair. Bowing to the inevitable, Watson laid aside the papers with which he was recording notes from his own afternoon travels and took up fresh sheets of foolscap.

"I take it things went well, Holmes."

"In truth, Watson, things could not have gone better. We got off to a difficult start with Garfoyle, but arrived finally at a mutually satisfactory understanding. And we secured Alfred Campbell's services with relatively little difficulty. You'll be meeting him tomorrow at the sparring session scheduled for the Pugilism Society. I think we can safely say we are well prepared for our gathering Wednesday night." Holmes went on to detail the activity of Charlie Mitchell, the surprising contribution of Jem Hall, the reticence of Squire Baird, the hard bargaining of John Garfoyle, and the cautious participation of Alfie Campbell. When he was satisfied he had shared everything of importance and Watson had finished the last of his jottings, he asked about his friend's adventures.

"Things went well for me also, Holmes. I've just been recording some notes from my visit to the Glasgow Herald. I explained I was studying unsolved crimes and wished to see their files on the murder of Josiah Krebs, and they couldn't have been more obliging. They assumed I was a writer and I'm afraid I did nothing to disabuse them of that belief. I may even have given the impression some of their names would appear in whatever materialized from my research."

"Well it's no lie you're a writer, Watson. And should you wish to insert their names in one of your little stories you will have been perfectly straightforward with them. But tell me, what were you able to learn?"

"Nothing that changes our thinking about the killing, but some things that may help Makepeace Godwin's performance."

Holmes's raised eyebrows urged Watson to go on.

"I'm putting it all together now and will have it for you shortly." Holmes's eyebrows rose a fraction higher and Watson relented. "There are some things I can share. The knife used to commit the murder was highly unusual. It had a haft made of white shell and the blade was serrated along one edge. It belonged to Calvin Jamison—or Arthur Trent, if you prefer. He never denied it was his, he just said he didn't use it to kill Krebs; he claimed he never met Josiah Krebs and didn't know anybody by that name. He also claimed he wasn't in his room at the time the murder took place. He reported he went from the fight to the nearest surgery to get his cuts and bruises treated, but there was no record of his having been at the surgery and nobody reported taking him there. The newspaper accounts detail the same three eye witnesses reported by Lestrade. I must say it's easy to understand why he ran off. There was no one to speak for him and a whole array of people to speak against him. I doubt he would have had any chance in court." Holmes waved away any further recitation by Watson.

"I am at a complete loss to understand Mrs. Hudson's interest in this line of inquiry. It's clear enough that Trent killed this Josiah Krebs. Mackenzie knew about it and had to be killed. I admit I don't yet know how Trent managed it, but it seems obvious he masterminded the murder." Holmes shrugged a final thought. "We can inform Lestrade of our findings when he arrives. It's not as if Trent will be going anywhere."

"There's more, Holmes, a good deal more although I doubt it will cause you to think any differently. It seems that, in the course of his statement to the Chief Constable, Calvin

229

Jamison blurted out that the fight preceding the killing had been pre-arranged. Jamison said he had been instructed to fall down and stay down for the count, but only after the fight had gone long enough to appear genuine. What he said he didn't figure on was the brittleness of his opponent's jaw and the weakness of his defense. As Jamison told it, the fighter practically ran into his left hand, went down and was counted out before he had a chance to take a fall. The newspaper report went on to say that fights were well known to be arranged, but since boxing itself was against the law there was no way for the police to regulate any of its activities. And indeed, Josiah Krebs is described as ... Watson searched his notes. "Here it is, Krebs is described as 'a punter believed to have wagered a considerable sum'.

"It was shortly thereafter Calvin Jamison went missing. He escaped from custody, apparently while being transported to the surgery, but it gets quite vague on that point. After that, the story slowly disappears from the paper. There was an initial search of areas in Glasgow to which it was thought he might have gone, but those efforts were abandoned after it was concluded he'd left the country. It was believed, from word he left with a young lady, that he was bound for Cape Town."

Holmes gave the fireplace a long stare before continuing. "And what of your other task, Watson? Were you able to locate our stationery shop proprietor?"

"I did. Forrest Mackenzie and his wife have a nice little shop in the North End near the canal just as Mrs. Hudson learned from Mrs. Mackenzie. As it turned out, my concern about breaking the news of his brother's death was completely unwarranted. He said he'd been expecting to hear of his death for years given the way he lived. His wife was a different story. She asked after Mrs. Mackenzie, and said I was to tell her she was welcome to stay with them until she's back on her feet. I can't say Mr. Mackenzie looked too pleased with that, but he said nothing. In any event, he had no objection to signing the paper I gave him. He said he didn't see how it could do any harm, but he made it very clear he had no intention of closing up his business and traveling to London, or anywhere else on his brother's account. He said the two of them came to a parting of the ways a long time back and there was no point to pretending otherwise now."

Holmes shrugged his unconcern about Forrest Mackenzie's travel plans, and sought the comfort of his briar and the shag he took from a pocket.

Watson watched him fill his pipe before raising the issue he felt the need to air.

"Holmes, we both know the way Mrs. Hudson thinks. She wouldn't have us going to all the bother that's planned for this week if she didn't feel there's a good deal more to be learned about what happened in Glasgow thirty-five years ago." Watson paused to watch a curl of smoke from Holmes's pipe wind a serpentine path toward the ceiling. "And she would want us to keep an open mind as we examine the situation."

Holmes struggled with his position in the chair before speaking. "If we are to suppose Jamison is not our guilty party, everyone else quite simply has to be lying. But why would that be? What does anyone stand to gain by lying about Krebs's killing?" Holmes paused, shook his head once, then again before pursing his lips and staring intently first to the pipe he now held, then back to Watson. "I will say this. There is one thing I find curious. It's to do with Alfie Godwin quitting his work as a second shortly after giving his eye witness testimony about Jamison killing Krebs. I'll grant that raises a question, but the answer could be as simple as being offered a better paying, more dependable job, or just having his fill of hanging around changing rooms and picking up after fighters. We still have Jamison's knife as the murder weapon, and we have the murder taking place in his room in front of three witnesses when he says he was at a surgery, which has no record of his being there. Men have gone to the gallows with far less against them."

"I have to agree, Holmes, although you make an interesting point about Campbell and his sudden retirement. In any event, we'll know a good deal more about everything after Wednesday night."

Holmes grumbled his response. "I suppose. Speaking of which, Watson, I'm of a mind we should review our procedures for the evening not too long after Lestrade and Wiggins get here."

"I quite agree, Holmes, I suggest Wednesday morning since no sparring is set for that day. I think the less time Baird and his fighters have to think about things the better."

The two men reached quick agreement as they usually did. Afterward, they shared a pipe and their opinions about Baird—a mutual revulsion, Baird and Lillie—disappointment joined with confusion, and Charlie Mitchell and Jem Hall—amused regard for both and some genuine admiration for Hall.

Life at Baird Castle settled into a nearly unvaried pattern. Holmes and Watson took breakfast by themselves with little to engage their attention at the table or for the rest of the morning. After lunch, they traveled to the Pugilism Society to observe a sparring session in which the fighters seemed at pains to leave each other unmarked, their caution doing little to dampen the spirits of the faithful who had paid anywhere from one to three shillings for the privilege of telling and retelling the time they saw two of Britain's greatest fighters in the ring together. Dinners were somewhat better with Charlie Mitchell and Jem Hall attempting to outdo each other with stories of past accomplishments and of the other's ineptitude in the ring earlier that day.

Two things occurred over the course of the week that surprised the detectives. While the Squire's intake of alcohol showed no change over time, both Mitchell and Hall began limiting their drinking beginning the first night after sparring, each of them approaching moderation as the night of the match neared. And Alfie Campbell, not knowing the reason for which he had been chosen as Mitchell's second, insisted on making real contribution to the former champion's preparation for the fight. He had seen Mitchell's opponent in action, and described him as typical of the inexperienced youngsters who fought at the Pugilism Society.

"He's a head-hunter is what he is, and the lad is only knowing one way to fight. The laddies around here fight mostly four-rounders, and they're always looking for the quick knockout. He'll be expecting ye to do the same, especially being as ye're Charlie Mitchell. Except this here is an eight-rounder, and there can be more pace to it, something that's outside the lad's experience. What ye don't want to do is to play his game. The lad's got a punch—there should be no mistaking that. Ye'll be able to see his right coming, he's got a way o' lunging into it so he'll hunch forward before he throws it. Stay away from that and wear him down with short punches to the body which he'll leave unprotected. That way ye can easy take him down later if ye don't see an opening early on."

It wasn't just Holmes and Watson who were impressed with the second's knowledge, Alfie Campbell received the avid attention of both boxers. The two detectives found themselves suffering small pangs of guilt about what they knew to be in store for the small man who had become nearly garrulous since being drafted as Charlie Mitchell's second. It made them all the more anxious to get past Wednesday meeting and the Thursday fight, and back to the comfort of their Baker Street apartments.

Chapter 17.
Alfie Campbell Hears Voices

When Lestrade and Wiggins arrived at McLellan Manor late Tuesday afternoon, Holmes and Watson formed their reception committee, and both wondered about the travels together of the Inspector and the printer's devil. A quick glance to each decided them against raising the subject. Wiggins was all wide-eyed wonder, and seemed barely able to keep himself from dancing into every corner to explore the new world he had entered. Lestrade regarded his companion and Baird Castle with a policeman's cold indifference. He nodded greetings to Holmes and Watson, and looked to the same corners that attracted Wiggins's attention, but his eyes seemed to be searching for faults in the Castle's construction.

Holmes and Watson had left the sparring session early, advising Baird of their need to welcome the company expected, and receiving a dismissive growl by way of acknowledgement. Holmes appeared as Holmes, feeling the introduction of Makepeace Goodwin might be more than the visitors could handle after their long journey. Sanderson joined them long enough to assign Lestrade and Wiggins rooms near those of Holmes and Watson. The new guests were given time to get settled before the four men met together in Holmes's room to bring Lestrade and Wiggins up to date about their host, his two fighters, Calvin Jamison, and their findings about the murder of Josiah Krebs. Holmes prepared them for later introduction to Makepeace Godwin, and indicated the need to lay plans for the meeting to be held the following night.

Before dinner, Watson sought out Wiggins to speak with him about his behavior at the evening meal. He was unconcerned about Wiggins's table manners, which had, in any event, undergone substantial improvement under Mrs. Hudson's unstinting direction. Watson wanted to make certain

Wiggins would show some control over his typically unrestrained admiration for Holmes. There was no need for any comparable discussion with Lestrade.

As it turned out, the evening's dinner conversation was again dominated by the two fighters who had enjoyed an almost spirited sparring session, and were eager to share their exploits with the expanded audience. Each man proceeded to describe his own near superhuman feats before detailing his opponent's pitifully inadequate efforts. There followed a back and forth of empty threats and unanswered challenges. Lestrade chuckled his way through the exchange between the two men in spite of his feelings about their sport. Even Baird relaxed his mask of disapproval long enough to shake his head in feigned amazement at his fighters' verbal sparring.

When a brief silence descended on the table, Wiggins stepped in to share experiences from his work as printer's devil. He told of the lady who ordered notices tastefully bordered in black announcing the death and burial service for her parrot. When that contribution drew the desired response of bewildered amusement, he followed it up with the story of the man who wanted 5000 handbills printed announcing 1900 would see the end of the world, and urging people to repent while there was time. Wiggins reported Mr. Stinchcombe was willing to print notice of a parrot's funeral, but not the end of the world. There was general support for Mr. Stinchcombe's position, and Baird went so far as to propose a toast in his honor which was joined with good-natured enthusiasm by his guests. A genial conversation proceeded from vermicelli soup to lamb cutlets and chicken patties, and held sway up to saddle of mutton and roast duck. It was then Jem Hall asked Lestrade his occupation which Holmes and Watson had been hoping might not emerge until a more suitable time or, better still, never.

Lestrade was not a man to tolerate deception in others or himself. "I'm an inspector with Scotland Yard."

After first establishing he was not pulling their leg, then reestablishing he was not pulling their leg, conversation began to flag before disappearing altogether lest any of those associated with the illegal activity of boxing say anything that could prove more incriminating than everything they'd already said. Wiggins made a gallant effort with yet another story about a man running for Parliament in a by-election who requested handbills describing his opponent as a man given to drink. The opponent, Wiggins reported, gathered up armloads of the handbills and distributed them throughout the area pubs, stopping only long enough at each to stand drinks for all those present. He proceeded to soundly thrash his abstinent adversary in the election. Wiggins's report drew only polite smiles.

They ate their desserts in silence except for Holmes's admonition that it would be necessary to meet after breakfast the next day to prepare for the events scheduled for that evening. Holmes suggested 10 a.m., but allowed himself to be talked into 11. The evening ended without suggestion they share after-dinner pipes and cigars. The omission elicited no protest and each man sought out his own amusement or simply his own bed.

At 11, everyone had assembled in the Castle's drawing room except the Castle's owner. The two fighters had entered the room together well before the prescribed time for meeting, and taken seats on a couch angled to face the center door through which all others would enter. Charlie Mitchell beamed a greeting to each new arrival while Jem Hall adopted a muted reflection of his colleague's good humor. Wiggins came next and grinned a response to the fighters before dropping down in an easy chair separated from them by a round table holding a statue of a horse and rider joined in fierce determination to hurdle an unseen object. Lestrade entered the room moments before the hall clock could be heard striking the hour, selecting an easy chair at the outer edge of the clutch of furniture in which the others had seated themselves. More accustomed than the others to the theatrics about to be sprung on them, he lit his pipe and waited impassively for the performance to begin. Watson and Holmes entered moments later, Watson seating himself across from Lestrade, notebook and pencil in hand should anything arise that merited recording. Holmes took note of the seating arrangement and set himself in a corner down from the door where, in the character of Makepeace Godwin, he was certain to have the group's attention.

The two fighters greeted him as an old friend returned at last. Seeing him for the first time, Wiggins slapped a knee and roared a mix of surprise and delight; Lestrade took his briar in hand to permit himself the ability to chuckle quietly. Holmes waited for Baird to make his entrance, confident his antipathy toward the proceedings would delay his joining them, and his curiosity would prevent that delay being prolonged. When the Squire sauntered into the room a few minutes after 11, he looked to neither Holmes nor his guests, and found a chair as far from the others as he could manage without giving up all pretense of participation in the events to follow. Holmes was now ready to begin.

"All of you now know me as Makepeace Godwin," he began in the low register sing-song voice he had given his character. "I will ask you to use only that name for the remainder of the time we are together. As already arranged, Mr. Mitchell and Mr. Hall will be having a light workout here at the Castle in final preparation for tomorrow's fight. That will be at half two this afternoon. They will be joined by Alfred Campbell, Mr. Mitchell's second. I will ask Inspector Lestrade and Mr. Wiggins to absent themselves from those proceedings. Mr. Wiggins, you will inspect the dumbwaiter and find the most comfortable position to fit yourself into it. Watson and I have studied it at length and we don't believe it will be a problem." Wiggins nodded several times, each time with deep solemnity. He knew better than to question Holmes about the need to explore positions for stuffing himself in a dumbwaiter. He was certain, in due time, he would come to see it as making perfect sense.

"Mr. Wiggins, I'm afraid you'll need to be out of sight throughout the day and evening. There'll be tea and dinner for you in servants' hall.

"Inspector, you will join us for tea and for dinner. However, if it's agreeable to you, you will be known for the rest of the day and evening as Mr. Lestrade. I'm afraid introducing an inspector from Scotland Yard to Mr. Campbell could prove disastrous to our plans for the evening.

"Dinner will be served in the small dining room and our meeting after dinner will take place in the main dining room. Mr. Hall will excuse himself claiming to be feeling poorly. I suggest you say something you ate disagreed with you. You will join Mr. Wiggins, and we will rely on your obvious strength to assist our effort. Mr. Campbell believes himself to be coming for a meeting in which we will expel the evil forces that would otherwise steal Mr. Mitchell's power. He doesn't know the nature of our meeting beyond that. I will describe that meeting to you and what will be expected of you tonight. It will be essential for each of you to play your part exactly as I describe it." He turned his attention to Baird who met his stare and held it fast before finally nodding his head the slightest bit and looking away.

With that, Makepeace Godwin detailed his instructions as they had been detailed to Sherlock Holmes earlier in the week. His words were greeted with respectful silence, interrupted periodically by sharp intakes of breath and snickering, followed by an, "Oh my God," or, "The Devil you say," depending on the supernatural force with which the speaker was more familiar. In the end, they achieved an understanding of the roles each was to play although enthusiasm for the evening's performance varied among its participants.

The dinner conversation was, as usual, carried by the two fighters. Both Charlie Mitchell and Jem Hall were satisfied with the final workout and with Charlie's preparation for the fight. They solicited the judgment of their second and Alfie mumbled his agreement. He knew what he was about as long there was a ring and two men mixing it up. Taking his dinner with the owner of the foundry, and having somebody in fancy dress putting food in front of him over one shoulder and taking it away over the other was near torture. He struggled through the evening looking to the fighters he knew and ignoring, as best he could, everyone else.

When the last of the custard pudding was gone, Makepeace Godwin rose slowly from his place, gripped the table with both his large hands and stared reverently at his empty dish. All those at the table followed his example and so finally did Alfie, unclear whether he should be giving thanks or asking for a blessing as he stared at his well scraped dish. Makepeace Godwin muttered something that sounded vaguely pious, pronounced himself well satisfied, and asked Squire Baird to escort the party into the room set aside for their meeting. Baird replied with words that were equally indistinct, but sounded a good deal less spiritual. Everyone followed the Squire except for Jem Hall, who put a hand over his stomach and complained that something he ate must have disagreed with him, and he wouldn't be able to join them. Watson, asserting his medical authority, diagnosed it as too much rich food combined with physical exertion, and Hall was excused from further participation. The remaining group proceeded to the dining room where heavy crimson curtains had been drawn to shut out the last rays of the summer day, the room's only illumination coming from a gas lamp set in a sconce in a far corner of the room. Mackenzie Godwin urged the men to find places around the long, cloth-covered table.

The dining room table was less than ideal for Holmes's purposes. A round table would have allowed all to join hands and made Makepeace Godwin more easily the focus of everyone's attention. Instead, from his position at head of the rectangular table, Makepeace Godwin took Watson's hand on his right and Charlie Mitchell's hand on his left, and directed the men on each side of the table to take each other's hands. Down one side, Watson, Lestrade and Baird clasped hands; across from them Charlie Mitchell gripped Alfie Campbell's hand with a vigor that made the small man wince. Nearly 15 feet behind the fighter and his second was the dumbwaiter Wiggins had explored that afternoon. In a well-lit room the closed lift would have been difficult to spot, the thin crimson lines against background gold of the wallpaper flowing seamlessly from above the dumbwaiter to the wall beneath it. In the darkened room, the dumbwaiter was invisible.

Godwin hunched forward, staring down to the table as if waiting for it to reveal secrets he alone knew it to possess. All others around the table followed his example with only the beginning of a grumble from Baird that stopped suddenly when he found his hand grasped with unexpected force by the Scotland Yard inspector to his right. Alfie Campbell raised his eyes to gauge the reactions of those around him, but caught Charlie Mitchell's disapproving glance and he too sought wisdom from the cloth before him.

Makepeace Godwin interrupted the group's silent meditation. "Beloved spirit who protects our Charlie Mitchell, we seek to commune with you." Godwin waited to a count of five during the expected silence. "Beloved spirit, can you hear me? If you will favor us with your presence, please signal with a single knock from whatever portal you have chosen to enter."

The room again became silent. Then, about the time Watson had decided Wiggins's flair for the dramatic excessive, there came a single rap from the area of the well-hidden dumbwaiter. Alfie came bolt upright, released Mitchell's hand and looked to each of the men around the table in turn. No one stirred or removed his eyes from the table. Charlie Mitchell quickly grabbed Alfie's hand as if the action was necessary to hold Alfie in place.

Makepeace Godwin was well into the world of his own creation and appeared unaware of anything unusual occurring. "Are you the spirit who has come to protect Charlie Mitchell from harm? Rap once if you are that spirit, rap twice if you are another spirit." This time two raps came in quick succession.

"Dear spirit, can you speak?"

There came a single knock.

Makepeace Godwin's voice now came in a hoarse whisper. "Tell us then, good spirit, if you cannot give protection, can you be a friend?" A small tremor in Godwin's left hand was transmitted to Mitchell and from him to Alfie Campbell while a low groan came from Watson across the table. He expected to be joined in an expression of foreboding by Lestrade and Baird, but if the two men shared nothing else, they shared a dislike for pretending to feelings they didn't own and were united for the moment, if only in silence.

A clattering sound now replaced the earlier rapping. Wiggins's understanding of spirits was drawn heavily from his reading of *A Christmas Carol*, which was one of several books Mrs. Hudson had insisted he read to improve himself while a page at 221B Baker Street. Inspired by his reading, he did his best to simulate the links of chain dragged by Marley's Ghost through the rattling of a spoon around a large pot. When he quieted his chains, he spoke in a quavering falsetto to sound as ethereal as he thought a proper ghost should sound, and added his impression of a Scottish accent to further his claim on authenticity.

"I canna be a friend to any at this table. Not while ye

sit with a bloke what goes by the name of Alfred Campbell."

Now all eyes turned to Alfie, and he looked fearfully back to all those eyes and then away from them. Mitchell held his hand more tightly, only loosening his grip when Alfie gave a sharp cry of pain.

Makepeace Godwin spoke again to the spirit of the dumbwaiter. "Please, kind and generous spirit, tell us who you are and explain to us your grievance with Alfred Campbell."

There came again the sound of a spoon rattling its way around a pot. "I be the ghost of Josiah Krebs." The name triggered an audible gasp from Alfie Campbell. "I must walk the earth until my killer is found."

"Just a second there ... Mister Spirit, or Mister Krebs, if that's okay with you, I heard about your murder. It's true they ain't been able to catch the bloke what done it, but it's well known it's somebody what goes by the name Jamison." Charlie Mitchell delivered his lines with an authority born of long and careful practice.

The rattling noise returned, sounding more intense before stopping suddenly, only to be followed by an adlibbed shriek that echoed through the small cavern from which it came, taking all at the table by surprise and rousing alarm in Alfie. "There is one sitting with ye what knows the truth of my murder. Let him say if it was Calvin Jamison what done me in."

"Of whom do you speak, dear spirit?"

Another rattle; another shriek. "It's Alfred Campbell what knows the truth. It's him can set my spirit free."

"I'm feeling my power getting drained away, Mr. Godwin. The spirits are grabbing a hold of me. I need you to help me, Alfie. You got to say something." Charlie Mitchell spoke the remaining lines of dialogue allotted him with a fervor he believed worthy of the London stage.

Across the table came Watson's cry, "Speak." Then Lestrade's, "Speak," and finally, in response to a glare from

Makepeace Godwin and the grip of the Inspector, Baird called out as well.

Makepeace Godwin released the hands of Watson and Mitchell, tore at his hair, and ran his open hands up and down his cheeks, finally ending his torment by crossing his arms over his chest and swaying back and forth as though struggling to hold his own spirit in check. All the while he let sound a piteous cry less shrill than the one that had come from the dumbwaiter, but sounding no less distressing to Alfie Campbell. And then the cries came again from Mitchell and Watson, "Speak! Speak! Speak!"—their shouts sounding against the rattle that might be chains, and the wail that might be the spirit of Josiah Krebs.

The bedlam seemed as though it would never let up even as Makepeace Godwin now roared above the din, "Help us, Brother Campbell. Help this unhappy spirit. Tell us what you know of the terrible night of Josiah Krebs's death." And with that, the rattling and voices grew even louder until they were finally interrupted by a scream and a cry of, "Stop! Please stop!" And then the same voice desperate and near to tears.

"I know what the spirit is saying. I know the truth of Josiah Krebs's murder. Forgive me, Mr. Krebs, please forgive me. I had nae choice in all what happened. I swear I had nae choice."

Makepeace Godwin spoke. "Tell us all and tell it now. You may yet save yourself and give the spirit of Josiah Krebs rest."

"And leave me to win my fight by getting rid of the spirits what would try to take it from me." Charlie Mitchell made his play for an additional moment of glory.

"Yes, all of that." Makepeace Godwin murmured, and then sharply and insistently, "Speak, Mr. Campbell, speak now before it is too late." The rattling and the wail echoed encouragement from their dumbwaiter origins.

"I'll tell. I promise, I'll tell it all. But first, ye got to believe me," Alfie looked from one man to the next, all the while pleading for understanding from the spirit he couldn't see. "I'm sorry, Mr. Krebs. I didn't mean for nothing to hurt ye. I promise I'll make it up to ye and help get ye rest. But ye got to believe me when I say I had to do what I did. They'd of killed me for sure if I didn't."

With that, Alfie Campbell's thin shoulders heaved; he covered his eyes with his free hand and he began to weep. It was a reaction for which no one at the table was prepared and they watched him in silence, his soft whimpering the only sound in the room. Only Wiggins, who could not see or hear Alfie, wondered at the halt in the man's confession. In his experience a break in the statement of an accused signaled a hesitancy to reveal anything further about his crime. He added some further banging of his pot and a final ghastly shriek as Charlie Mitchell squeezed Alfie's hand in a display of mock horror.

"I'll tell ye. I'll tell ye all. Just leave me be and I'll tell ye." Alfie raised his head, wiped a tear-stained face with the back of his hand and looked to Makepeace Godwin, but spoke again to the spirit of Josiah Krebs.

"It was all old man Garfoyle's idea. The whole of it. I just got dragged in. I didn't even know what was going on. It was all arranged by Garfoyle. I swear it, Mr. Krebs. Calvin Jamison was to go down and take a ten count, but only after he got a signal from Mr. Garfoyle. There was big money in it for Mr. Garfoyle and some of his friends because all the sucker bets were on Jamison winning, begging your pardon, Mr. Krebs, but that's how it was.

"Well, ye know what happened. This other fighter walks into a right hand, and he hits the deck like a tree fell on him, when it's all the time a right hand that wouldn't o' hurt your sister. Right away, Mr. Garfoyle stands to lose his shirt, what with him having to pay out to everybody who bet on

244

Jamison, not knowing he was set up to lose. And you come up the biggest winner of all, Mr. Krebs—or at least ye should have done."

Alfie paused, having now come to the most difficult part of his confession. The silence led Wiggins to conclude Alfie was again in need of encouragement to continue. A screeching now joined the familiar clattering and continued until Alfie cried out.

"Mr. Krebs, Mr. Krebs, sir, please let me tell. He couldn't pay ye is why he told ye to meet him in his room. Except the room he gave ye wasn't his, but was Jamison's. I swear to ye I had no idea o' what was coming next. But after, I could see Mr. Garfoyle must o' had it planned the whole time to kill two birds with one stone so to speak, and begging your pardon for putting it that way, Mr. Krebs, but it must o' been his thinking. See, Jamison was meantimes being taken to the surgery 'cause he had to take a lot o' punches to make things look good, and he got a 'specially bad cut over his one eye. I'm ready to go home myself and just forget the whole thing, and I know Flinty, Jamison's manager, feels the same, except Garfoyle says he wants the two of us in his room, which ain't his room, and to be with him before ye get there, Mr. Krebs. That's where I started getting a bad feeling about what's coming next. And it gets still worse when he asks me do I know where Jamison keeps his knife."

Alfie paused again, this time in the hope of gaining a show of sympathy from his audience. The dumbwaiter was uncompromising. Again near tears, he fairly screamed his pleading.

"Forgive me, Mr. Krebs. Please forgive me. I swear I didn't know. I thought he meant to scare you was all. I'd never …. Please forgive me." And then he was no longer near to tears, he was consumed by them.

The spirit persisted, "Go on Alfred Campbell. Tell me all. If you'd save your soul, tell me all."

Alfie did his best to obey. Between sobs he completed his story. "Ye … ye know most of the rest, Mr. Krebs." Alfie wiped his eyes with a sleeve and swallowed hard. "Ye got there and asked for yer money, which was the right thing for ye to do, Mr. Krebs. And Mr. Garfoyle had no right to accuse ye o' fixing the match for yerself. O' course he was just trying to start a fight, but I didn't know it then. Well, that's when everything got crazy. Ye come at him just like he wanted ye to, only he grabs Jamison's knife which, God forgive me, I had found for him. And the next thing I know yer life is bleeding out o' you, Mr. Krebs." Alfie swallowed down tears, determined to get through his story once and for all.

"And then Mr. Garfoyle tells us—I mean me and Flinty—that we got to say the killing was done by Jamison or we'll get just the same as you got, Mr. Krebs. Which we both knew he could do, what with the friends he's got, and we both of us—God forgive me—said we'd do it. Which we done when the bobbies come to question us. Meantimes, Mr. Garfoyle gets one o' his bruisers, whose wife works at the surgery, to steal the records from Jamison's visit there, while he pays the cabman to say he never took Jamison to the surgery. So all of a sudden Jamison's got no alibi, and has only got witnesses lined up against him. Which is when he does the only sensible thing he could do and takes a runner, after which nobody hears anything from him ever again.

"It's why I quit the fight game, Mr. Krebs. I quit it then and there. And even with that, Mr. Krebs, I ain't had a peaceful day since I seen ye killed. And I'm sorry for what I done to ye and to Calvin Jamison, although ye got to know they would o' killed me if I'd of done anything different. Anyway, it's now all o' it been said and I'm glad that's done. Really I am. I know I'll spend my eternity in Hell, but maybe now yer spirit can get its rest, Mr. Krebs." And with the story complete, Alfie put his head in his arms, his right hand having been freed by Charlie Mitchell, and sobbed without letup into a handkerchief that came to him from Makepeace Godwin.

It was left to the spirit of the dumbwaiter to render final judgment. Based on his encounters with earthly judges, Wiggins took to the role of celestial arbiter with uncommon ease, although lapsing in the process from his Scottish persona. "You done a good thing today, Mr. Krebs. It is now for you to make something positive of the rest of your life. My spirit is now been freed, and as long as you don't bollix things up in the future I won't be having you before me ever again. That is my final word."

And as Jem Hall manned the pulleys from his station below, the spirit of Josiah Krebs was lowered to the depths of the wine cellar with Alfie calling after it, pledging his intention to do right.

Makepeace Godwin waited a respectful few moments for the spirit to descend and Alfie's sobs to subside before drawing the session to a close. "We thank you, dear spirit, for being with us today. We join Mr. Campbell in wishing that you find rest. We are grateful that our brother, Charlie Mitchell, has had a negative force removed and will have his strength for the upcoming struggle. Let us share a moment of silence as each of us offers thanks for this moment."

Each man bowed his head a respectful few seconds, the silence broken only by the sniffling to which Alfie's sobbing had given way. Afterward, Alfie was helped to find a four-wheeler to take him home, and Lestrade gathered Mitchell, Watson, and Baird in the newly illuminated dining room, where he had each of them write out and sign a statement of what he had learned about the murder of Josiah Krebs.

Chapter 18.
A Problem Resolved, a Second Created

"Will you now be arresting the senior Mr. Garfoyle, Inspector?" Watson raised the question to Lestrade in the library where the three men and Wiggins sat reviewing the evening's activities. All but Wiggins were enjoying a last pipe of the day while they considered what had been accomplished.

Lestrade covered a cough that sounded a great deal as if it had begun as a laugh. "I think not, Dr. Watson. From your report, the senior Mr. Garfoyle is well into his second childhood and wouldn't be capable of standing trial. And besides, if I were to ask for his arrest based on information obtained by Makepeace Godwin at a séance in which the spirit of a dead man was contained in a dumbwaiter, I'm afraid they might believe I was in my second childhood as well. The same can be said for Mr. Campbell. While Alfie Campbell could stand trial, I'd not want to reveal our strategy for obtaining his confession." Lestrade took a long draw on his briar before continuing.

"No, Dr. Watson, I mean to wrap this up with as little attention drawn to it as possible. I have sworn statements from you, Mr. Mitchell, and Mr. Baird, which is to say statements from everyone who wasn't pretending to be someone they weren't, providing evidence that Calvin Jamison was not the murderer of Josiah Krebs. I'll turn that over to the Glasgow police and enter it into the Yard's records. Then, if Calvin Jamison does turn up any place, he won't have to worry about being arrested." He turned to the figure still disguised as Charlie Mitchell's spiritual advisor. "I would think that might take a considerable burden from the man and from any family he may have acquired along the way."

"I feel certain you're right, Lestrade, and rest assured it will be attended to."

"I leave that to you, Mr. Holmes. All in all, this was

most enjoyable and I'm glad I was able to join you. And Mr. Wiggins, you gave a rare performance. It was better than being at the music hall."

Wiggins puffed with pride. "It was a rare treat to be a help to you, Mr. Lestrade."

"I dare say it provided a pleasing change of pace," Lestrade observed drily. "I expect that Mr. Wiggins and I will be leaving for London after breakfast tomorrow. What are your plans, Mr. Holmes?"

"Watson and I still have a fight to attend, Inspector. Makepeace Godwin must be present one last time to act as Mr. Mitchell's spiritual advisor, and then, after a stop at McLellan Manor to complete our business there, we will join you in London to sort things out."

At the last Lestrade's face clouded. "Well, that's a subject for another time. For now, Mr. Holmes, Dr. Watson, I believe I'll prepare for bed and plan on an early start in the morning." Lestrade looked to Wiggins who said nothing, reluctant to relinquish his hold on the evening's triumph or his association with men he revered. To emphasize his intent, Lestrade rose and bent over the ashtray into which he tapped out the still lit tobacco in his pipe's bowl. As he did so, Wiggins found his voice and dared a question.

"Inspector Lestrade, sir, do you think there might ever be a place for the likes of me at Scotland Yard?"

Wiggins looked to the Inspector, eyes wide and pleading. Lestrade took account of the boy's expression as well as his question. "Truly, you did a fine job today. One that any man at the Yard would be proud of. But I can see where there might be a problem. May I ask how tall you are, Mr. Wiggins?"

Wiggins sat bolt upright in his chair. "Well, you know I'm still growing, Mr. Lestrade." The Inspector gave a solemn nod. "I'm five foot six and plan on getting bigger."

Lestrade guessed Wiggins was five foot four and

hoping to get bigger, but any answer would have served his purpose. "There's the problem, Mr. Wiggins, a member of the constabulary has got to be five foot ten. I know it sounds a foolish rule, but there it is and we have to obey it. I'm suggesting, at least for now, you stick with Mr. Stinchcombe and learn the printer's trade. And just as soon as you get to be five foot ten, you come and see me about a job at the Yard."

Lestrade pocketed his empty pipe, walked to where Wiggins sat, and extended a hand to formalize their agreement. Wiggins stood, stretched to as much height as he could muster, and placed his hand in Lestrade's with all the gravity the act demanded. The bargain concluded, the two left the room together and without further word. Holmes and Watson stayed a while longer exchanging little in conversation, but sharing a very satisfying last pipe of the day.

Lestrade and Wiggins left after a pre-dawn conversation between the Inspector and Holmes, and the full breakfast for which Wiggins begged. They were seen off by Watson, Sanderson, and a newly troubled Holmes. Their absence drew no comment from the late rising fighters or their manager.

As planned, Alfie Campbell joined them in the late morning for a last round of exercises in the Castle's gymnasium. His thin face was even more drawn than usual and his eyes seemed at times to lose focus. No mention was made of the events of the preceding evening that was nonetheless at the center of everyone's thinking. The two fighters' limited conversation dealt with the upcoming fight and tributes to their laconic second. Jem Hall congratulated Alfie on "all what he'd done to get Charlie ready." Charlie Mitchell told him he was the best second he'd ever had, then repeated himself, "the absolute best ever."

They were exaggerating only slightly their genuine feelings. Both fighters appreciated Alfie's contribution to

Charlie's preparation, and both were familiar with Alfie's dilemma. They had had their own share of experiences with arranged fights and gamblers who felt themselves ill-used, and neither man blamed Alfie for his indiscretion. One time or another each had made peace with his own moral lapse in a way Alfie had never been able to.

At lunch, he spoke only when spoken to and then responded minimally. Watson joined the fighters' praise for Alfie's contribution to Charlie's preparation and reminded him of the forgiving nature of Josiah Krebs's spirit. He vigorously asserted his own belief in every man's right to protect himself against certain harm, to which Makepeace Godwin nodded his agreement but said nothing, his mind plainly elsewhere. Alfie shared with the two of them the same fragment of a smile he'd earlier shown Charlie Mitchell and Jem Hall.

Squire Baird did not join them for lunch. He had gone to the Pugilism Society where he engaged John Garfoyle, Junior, in a new round of negotiation over the division of revenue, liberally injecting the name, Josiah Krebs, into the discussion. When he returned to the Castle later that afternoon, the Squire was in an uncharacteristically expansive mood.

The fight took place in the same high-ceilinged theater that had been the site for the sparring sessions earlier in the week. Now, as then, the only chairs in evidence were those the fighters would use between rounds. Chairs would have represented lost revenue in terms of both their cost to install and the space they would have taken. Instead, connoisseurs of the sport paid from two to four shillings to stand at varying distances from ringside. John Garfoyle leaned his great bulk against a far wall of the arena. Wilfred scowled his surveillance of the crowd from a position to Garfoyle's left, while a second man, considerably less than half Wilfred's size, stood to Garfoyle's right holding firmly to a pad, pencil, and look of intense concentration as he recorded the wagers his employer was accepting—almost entirely involving the round in which Charlie would dispatch his opponent. No bets were accepted on Charlie's victory, that being a foregone conclusion.

The fight followed the course predicted by Alfie Campbell. The raw youngster Charlie Mitchell faced was anxious to prove his mettle against the former champion and went for blows to the head that delighted his audience, although none of his punches hit their mark with authority. Meanwhile, Charlie peppered him with short jabs to the stomach and below the heart, and by the sixth round the fighter was badly winded and barely able to defend himself. Charlie started going to the head as he was counseled by Alfie, and as he knew to be the appropriate strategy. In the seventh round he knocked the young man down twice, each time with a right cross. When he went down a third time from an uppercut, his corner urged him to stay down and he complied with advice he found hugely welcome.

After a respectful pause allowing the victor and the vanquished to congratulate each other, and the crowd to salute them both, the Squire went to collect his share of the evening's earnings from Garfoyle. Charlie, Jem, and Alfie were escorted to the bar conveniently adjoining the boxing theater, where they were toasted repeatedly. The fight completed, the two boxers reverted to the drinking pattern Holmes and Watson had observed earlier in the week—Jem drinking enough to become pleasantly wobbly, Charlie requiring assistance to stumble his way to a waiting hansom. Makepeace Godwin and Watson left the Club under their own power and without anyone taking notice. Alfie remained behind, waiting to get his 10 pounds from Baird, and enduring, as best he could, accolades from the many in the crowd who had heretofore been only dimly aware of his existence.

Back at the Castle, the triumphant fighters, joined a short time later by their ebullient manager, decided to prolong the evening, until finally a dry Riesling achieved what the young fighter had been unable to, and Charlie Mitchell lay unconscious straddling the cushions of a couch in the drawing room. Jem Hall, meanwhile, chose a roomy easy chair for his slumbers, while Squire Baird settled for the floor. Sanderson discreetly closed the door to the drawing room, and made his way to his own bed and well deserved rest.

While their companions celebrated victory, Holmes and Watson shared a last pipe, and Holmes revealed the cause for his daylong moodiness.

"Watson, I need to tell you about my conversation with Lestrade early this morning. I'm afraid it greatly complicates our ability to bring Mackenzie's killer to justice."

Holmes pursed his lips before continuing and his voice sounded the distaste he felt for the message he proceeded to deliver. "Lestrade told me he was given instruction to regard the investigation into Mackenzie's death as closed. The official ruling of death by accident has been accepted by the Home Office, and Scotland Yard has been directed to act accordingly. Naturally, I told him we would do whatever we felt appropriate regardless of the Yard's action. He warned me there would be no one to act on whatever findings we produced. You should understand, Watson, Lestrade was quite upset by what he had to tell me. He explained that if he did otherwise than what the Yard demanded he would be jeopardizing his career, if not his job. I thanked him for letting me know the situation and for his assistance to this point. Truthfully, Watson, I was embarrassed for him. He couldn't get out of my room fast enough after giving me his news. Of course, *we* have no choice other than to go forward with the investigation regardless."

Watson's response was immediate and emphatic. "I agree entirely, Holmes. We must finish the job we started and hope to shame the authorities into acting responsibly."

Both men lapsed into silence as each considered Lestrade's report of the Yard's inaction and dealt with the disappointment it created. They would present the situation to Mrs. Hudson on their return to McLellan Manor, but stood in unspoken agreement she would be as outraged as they were at the prospect of justice going undone.

The mood was as solemn for those at McLellan Manor waiting the return of Holmes and Watson as it was for the two men returning. All professed a wish to see Holmes and Watson again, and all kept their enthusiasm for the upcoming reunion firmly in check. Lillie shared with Mrs. Hudson that Lord Lonsdale had reported receiving word from his London contacts of an Inspector Lestrade of Scotland Yard joining Holmes and Watson in Glasgow. The reason given for the Inspector's visit—that of tying up a few loose ends surrounding Mackenzie's death—was quickly discounted, and speculation as to the real cause for Lestrade's visit began over drinks before dinner, continued from soup through entrees and dessert, and had not yet achieved resolution by the time of tea for the ladies, and brandy and cigars for the men. Lillie reported to Mrs. Hudson there was a general suspicion Holmes had discovered something in Glasgow sufficient to occasion a visit from Scotland Yard. That something had to be serious because, as Lord Lonsdale put it, "Nobody traveled to Glasgow for pleasure."

Servants' hall was on edge as well. All knew of Squire Baird and the two bruisers he had brought with him. Charles and Henderson vowed to defend the honor and safety of the Manor and its guests, the one with a tender look to the scullery maid and the other with a fierce look to everyone else. The remaining staff expressed support publicly, but wondered privately about the danger they might face. Only Simon and Elizabeth seemed unperturbed, the former confident in his own resources, the latter confident in the strength of family.

Mrs. Hudson alone looked forward to the return of Holmes and Watson with enthusiasm undimmed by worries of vengeful assault on the inhabitants of McLellan Manor. She felt certain that time, the diversion of the fight in Glasgow, and the wish to win back Lillie would have reduced Squire Baird to a semblance of tranquility. Unaware of Lestrade's conversation with Holmes, she was anxious to undertake the final steps in revealing Ian Mackenzie's slayer.

While Holmes and Watson felt the burden of the information they would be bringing to Oxley, Squire Baird was concerned about the information he was lacking as he prepared to return to Oxley. On the morning of their scheduled travel, Baird summoned Holmes to his study to rectify that situation. Gesturing to a straight-backed chair opposite the chair he had chosen for himself, he creased his face into a harsh grimace in anticipation of the quarrel he expected.

"It's my belief I've held up my part of the bargain over the week, and now I'm wanting to know if you'll be holding up yours."

Holmes was determined to be as cordial as the Squire's combativeness permitted. "I agree, Baird, you've done what was asked. I plan to tell Mrs. Langtry you now regret your earlier actions." Holmes raised his voice at the end making clear the need for a response, and paused long enough to coax a grunt from the Squire. "And you wish to reconcile." A second grunt. Holmes had found the first acceptable, the second tore at the veneer of amiability he was struggling to maintain.

"I need to know if I am correctly stating your position."

The Squire grunted a third time, but on this occasion it was a preamble to speech, even as the words seemed to be pried from his body. "What you say is right. I want Lillie back and I'm sorry for all that happened. I'll say that much, but don't go expecting some big flowery speech, and I can tell you Lillie won't expect it either."

Holmes believed Baird was probably right about Lillie, and judged the Squire had expressed as much remorse as he was capable of sharing. Holmes nonetheless reminded him of his promise of retribution if Baird reverted to his earlier behaviors toward Lillie. Holmes then directed him to appear at McLellan Manor mid-morning the following day alone and sober, and prepared to accept whatever message Lillie sent him through Holmes. There was no handshake between the men although Baird's jaw relaxed and his brow unfurrowed as he pressed an envelope into Holmes's hands for delivery to Lillie when he next spoke to her. The men parted on terms that were correct, if not cordial.

With Holmes's assurance of support for his efforts with Lillie, his having gotten much the better of Garfoyle in the division of spoils, and Charlie Mitchell's victory in the ring, Baird was of a mind to make the return to Oxley far more agreeable than had been the trip leaving it. The Squire and his two fighters chose to shoehorn themselves into a single compartment with Holmes and Watson for the trip to Leeds. Settling themselves with pipes and cigarettes to each man's preference, there followed a good-natured exchange about the events of the last two evenings, substantially aided by liberal helpings from the bottle of Scotch whiskey Baird had secreted on board. Baird revealed he had extracted nearly 60 additional pounds from Garfoyle—he didn't explain how, and no one felt the need to ask—and he now proposed to share his new found largesse with both fighters and, forgetting his earlier declaration, with Holmes whom he viewed as having made the increased sum possible. Holmes rejected the offer and suggested he might instead reward Alfie for his work with Charlie Mitchell.

Baird surprised everyone with the revelation he had already made arrangements to provide Alfie with a substantial bonus for his work during the preceding week, and a modest increase in wages for his future work with Glasgow United. With that, he returned to the bottle he was intent on draining, pouring the brown malt into his own glass and the waiting glasses of his two fighters, who paused long enough to toast their manager's beneficent nature before downing their drinks. Holmes and Watson acknowledged that same nature with sips from the glasses that had been filled earlier.

The two men took advantage of the ongoing celebration of the Squire's benevolence to excuse themselves to take tea and a snack in the dining car. Holmes shared with Watson his morning conversation with Baird and his intention to put the Squire's case to Lillie. Watson groaned his apprehension about Lillie's decision while Holmes shrugged at what he regarded as inevitable.

When they returned to the compartment, they found their fellow travelers bemoaning there being a single bottle for refreshment, that bottle having been emptied of its contents. The three exited the train at Leeds with assistance from Holmes and Watson, and boarded the train to Oxley with assistance from Holmes, Watson and two conductors. For the short trip remaining, Holmes and Watson again took a separate compartment, leaving their companions to sleep off the effects of a night and morning of celebration, while the two friends shared their views on the murder of Sailor Mackenzie.

They agreed there was a surfeit of suspects with motive and opportunity. Holmes was all the more certain that Trent, or Calvin Jamison as they now knew him to be, was the most likely of those suspects. Watson focused on the small stocky figure they'd seen leaving the changing room of the National Sporting Club and wondered how that person figured into the murder. They were both of the opinion they would need more information—a good deal more information—before they could identify Mackenzie's killer. What they did not know was that the third member of their team felt certain as to the killer's identity and was waiting only their return to make her findings known.

Chapter 19.
Preparing the Net

Mrs. Hudson needed time alone with her colleagues to confirm her beliefs about Josiah Krebs's murderer, and to lay the groundwork for revealing Ian Mackenzie's murderer. But getting time alone at the Manor would be difficult. Lillie would want to meet with them to learn the state in which they left Squire Baird. The Trents and Lord Lonsdale would want to know what Holmes and Watson could tell them about the visit by Inspector Lestrade. And even if time came unexpectedly available, Mrs. Hudson had no reason to be anyplace other than servants' hall unless summoned for service by Lillie. The situation called for extreme measures and Mrs. Hudson had an extreme solution.

She was called to Lillie's room a little past eight to help Lillie with her morning toilette. Lillie selected a high-necked yellow silk with sky blue piping for the morning and Mrs. Hudson laid it in readiness across a settee. After brushing out her hair in front and fluffing it in back, Mrs. Hudson slipped the dress over her head and fastened its hooks in back. From its position on the wardrobe shelf, she took the tortoise shell compact containing the Japanese rice powder that was Lillie's only makeup.

When Lilly had finished applying the powder, she handed the compact to Mrs. Hudson who turned to replace it on the wardrobe shelf. As she did so, she appeared to catch her shoe in the carpet, causing her to pitch forward and lose her grip on the compact as she grabbed the arm of a nearby chair to keep from falling. Lillie stared unbelieving as her remaining rice powder spilled over furniture, the carpet, and Mrs. Hudson. She now faced the prospect of being without her special makeup at dinner that night, as well as the next day when she expected to be reunited with George and return to London. She could be certain neither Mrs. Trent nor Esther would have any face powder, much less Japanese rice powder. The use of makeup was acceptable for women on the stage, but not for women in more reputable walks of life.

"I am so sorry, Mrs. Langtry, I don't know 'ow I could 'ave done such a thing. I just got my shoe caught in the carpet." Mrs. Hudson hung her head and made effort to look as contrite as she professed to feel. "You must let me go to the chemist in town. There's bound to be powders there you can use, ma'am. Mr. 'Olmes says 'e's very well equipped." Mr. Holmes had said only that the chemist was well equipped for sending telegrams, but having contrived to destroy Lillie's supply of face powder, Mrs. Hudson felt her extravagant interpretation of Mr. Holmes's comment a small indiscretion.

"I rather doubt the Oxley chemist will have the powder I use, Mrs. Hudson." Lillie curled her lip at the ridiculous suggestion. "Nevertheless, if you have the morning free I suppose there's no harm done in your visiting him." Lillie looked back to the glass, critically assessing what she found until finally the image nodded its satisfaction to her, and she gave her attention again to Mrs. Hudson.

"I can finish up here. If you'd just clean up the powder that's been spilled and put away my night clothes, you may go on to town and see what the chemist has available."

"Yes, ma'am, I'll go on to Oxley right away. I can see about gettin' a ride back with Mr. Doyle when he comes to collect Mr. 'Olmes and Dr. Watson."

To her great surprise, Aldous Bauer, Chemist, did stock Japanese rice powder, although after making study of his customer, Bauer informed her he had other powders, considerably less dear, guaranteed to hide blemishes and birthmarks just as well. Mrs. Hudson, who was without either blemish or birthmark, announced the preparation was for Mrs. Lillie Langtry, who was staying at McLellan Manor. The chemist sucked in a deep and noisy breath before spluttering as much to himself as to Mrs. Hudson, "Well, well, well. Lillie Langtry, right here in Oxley." And then, feeling the need for additional comment, but having nothing additional to say, he reversed the sequence of his earlier observation. "Right here in Oxley, Lillie Langtry. Well, well, well."

Mrs. Hudson enjoyed the effect of her revelation on the chemist. Exposing her location no longer posed a threat to Lillie and forced the shop owner to view Mrs. Hudson in a new light, even if that light was a reflected one. Indeed, Aldous Bauer's round face creased its way to the broad smile he normally reserved for only his most loyal customers before he turned to fill her request.

The exchange between the chemist and Mrs. Hudson was overheard by his daughter and a large matronly woman who had requested a single stamp, and was receiving her purchase together with an account of "the real story" behind the butcher's oldest son running off to Leeds. The customer, who had already heard two other versions of the real story behind the butcher's son running off to Leeds—both of them more lurid than the postmistress's version—was now anxious to conclude her purchase and carry this latest revelation to as many venues as time permitted.

With his grin still in place, Aldous Bauer returned from behind the curtain separating customers from the mysteries of his art, holding a small vial of white powder triumphantly aloft. With near apology he exchanged the powder for the coins Mrs. Hudson offered, and joined his daughter and her customer in marking every step of Mrs. Hudson's exit from the shop.

She proceeded to the Oxley station, and was within half a street of her destination when the rain began to fall. The approaching storm was as unexpected as had been the rain and wind that greeted Lillie and Mrs. Hudson on their arrival in Oxley. The sky had held only puffy white clouds with no apparent purpose other than to provide contrast to its otherwise perfect blue. Now that sky was being invaded by an unseemly bank of gray clouds intent on sweeping aside everything in its path to make way for the rain behind. Having seen all this before, Mrs. Hudson was not fooled by the initial harmless drizzle and made her way quickly to the train station, followed closely by the pelting sheets she anticipated.

Inside the small waiting room, she took note of the stationmaster, visible from the waist up in the closet-like alcove from which he dispensed passage to the world beyond Oxley. Ignoring his hopeful stare, Mrs. Hudson took a seat on one of the two long benches facing each other from opposite walls. At the far end of the station, a porter watched the rain through the room's single soot streaked window. Mrs. Hudson's only other company was a family of three, a mother and two sons she judged to be six, four, and demonic.

The two boys, having been thrust into a world they found unrelentingly dreary, left seats beside their mother and began a game of running across the space between benches to come as close to Mrs. Hudson as they dared, emitting high pitched squeals at each approach, reflecting their joy at having found suitable entertainment in attempting to terrify Mrs. Hudson. The woman nominally in charge of the two boys never spoke to Mrs. Hudson, but glanced to her frequently, and always with an apologetic smile. She looked to her children with more confusion than determination as she called on each to "please stop" and to "please leave the nice lady alone." Certain from past experience that no punishment was in the offing, the children continued the game they had invented. Mrs. Hudson smiled a tolerance she did not feel toward the two horrors masquerading as playful children, and a forgiveness she did not feel toward the woman unable to control either her children or her life.

She judged the woman to be no more than 30, almost certainly a good deal less, but her ashen appearance and slack-jaw made her look older, her eyes were puffy with no effort to hide the redness beneath them. The portmanteau and two carpet bags at her feet, simple traveling outfit, and absent husband, all made clear the woman's fate. Her husband had deserted her, and now she was taking the children home to her parents. Had she been recently widowed, she would have been in black with family to support her. She was the kind of woman one could only pity. Mrs. Hudson hoped her life would turn around, doubted it would, and welcomed the sound of the train's whistle, and her freedom from the marauding children and their sad mother.

There had been no let-up in the rain, and the stationmaster had left his sanctum to carry a broad umbrella designed to shield the woman and the children who now hung on her either side. The porter preceded them, managing somehow to carry the woman's three bags as well as the steps he would set down to allow the family to board the train. Watching them, Mrs. Hudson guessed the two men likely would brave far greater difficulties than rain to restore tranquility to their waiting room. While the troubled family boarded the train, five men disembarked and lumbered their way across the platform. Although the distance was a short one, three of the men were experiencing significant difficulty with the journey. It was left to Holmes and Watson to steady their gently weaving companions and help them sway their way onto the step of the four-wheeler that had materialized in anticipation of its need. There followed a brief period of leave-taking with frequent expressions of gratitude offered by the men being wedged into the carriage to the two men doing the wedging. At the last, Squire Baird took a small box from his pocket and fumbled his way to a pocket in Holmes's coat to insert his package, at the same time mumbling a request it be given to Lillie together with the envelope he had handed Holmes earlier.

With the safe return to the Inn of the Moors assured for the Squire and his two bruisers, Holmes and Watson turned to search for Doyle and the coach that would take them back to McLellan Manor, but found instead their housekeeper. Stopping only a moment to register their surprise, all three agreed on the need to seek the protection of the waiting room. The rain had given Mrs. Hudson a fresh thought which she shared with the two men and which they accepted with a speed and air of relief she found troublesome. As a result of their brief exchange, Holmes suggested to the newly arrived Doyle they delay returning to the Manor until the worst of the storm had passed. He asked the coachman if there wasn't a place he could stable the horse for a short period and get himself dried out. Doyle knew of such a place. In fact he knew of two such places, both of them conveniently adjoining Oxley pubs. He thanked Holmes for his consideration, and they agreed to meet back at the station an hour later in the hope the rain would have eased by then. The three members of Baker Street's consulting detective agency allowed Doyle to drop them at the Royal Oxley Hotel to make use of the hotel's dining room.

The Royal Oxley Hotel reflected its owners' lofty objectives. Not content with having the most elegant hotel in Oxley, they sought recognition for being "the destination of choice for the sophisticated traveler to Yorkshire." The owners felt certain, as they continuously assured each other, that the Rombalds Moor and the hydropathic treatment in nearby Wheatley would one day attract travelers from London and even the Continent, and with just a trace of desperation each insisted that day was near. Of the three guests at the hotel's registration desk, two were clearly the kind of travelers the owners had in mind. A husband and wife stood together in matching traveling coats, a bellhop watched over their matching luggage, while they tolerated with matching indifference the obsequious pleasantries of the Royal Oxley registration clerk. The third guest had a single carpetbag and the weary no-nonsense air of a business traveler who planned as little time in Oxley as possible, and would leave unaware of its moor or nearby healing waters. The three members of Baker Street's consulting detective agency passed under the shimmering crystal chandelier imported from Stockholm that had been visited at one time or another by nearly every one of Oxley's residents, and strode across the reception area's genuine Persian carpet to enter the Parisian Room as the hotel's dining room had been christened.

The room was painted a pale yellow, far too muted to suit Lord Lonsdale, but which, in combination with pleated white curtains over the windows, gave the room a bright airy look. The drawn curtains served the further purpose of shutting out the town of Oxley and allowing the Parisian Room to become its own world. The illusion of relocation was encouraged by a profusion of posters largely concerned with publicizing the opening of a new Paris night club, the Moulin Rouge, as celebrated by the artist Toulouse Lautrec. The maitre d'hotel led them past pictures of female dancers with skirts raised well above their knees, of men in formal dress sipping cognac in the company of languorous women, and of waiters in full aprons holding trays of wine and glasses on outstretched fingers above the heads of men and women engaged in high revelry. Holmes and Watson expressed their approval of the artist's extraordinary way with his subject matter while Mrs. Hudson sniffed her bare tolerance of the surroundings. They were taken to a white clothed table in a corner of the room where they planned a private conversation. They rejected the offer of an aperitif, opting for tea—chamomile for Mrs. Hudson, Darjeeling for the men.

With the maitre d'hotel dispatched for tea and their waiter not yet in evidence, Mrs. Hudson called for a review of their time in Glasgow. Thereafter, between placing their orders and receiving the crepes and salade nicoise requested, Mrs. Hudson was told the events of the séance and the revelations of Alfie Campbell. Wiggins's accomplishments were recounted with every bit as much relish as those of

Makepeace Godwin, and both resulted in Mrs. Hudson burying her face in her napkin several times during the reporting the two men shared.

The mood changed dramatically when Holmes revealed the details of his conversation with Lestrade. Mrs. Hudson bit her lower lip, and stared at her plate without evidencing any inclination to resume eating. "That complicates things," was all she said before raising her eyes to meet Watson's. "Were you able to locate Mr. Mackenzie's brother?"

"I did, Mrs. Hudson, and he signed the paper I offered."

Mrs. Hudson pushed away her plate although a healthy portion of lamb and mushroom still lay beside the remains of the crepe that had contained them. "Then this is what we must do no matter what the Yard chooses to do."

The two men listened in a silence that once might have shielded disbelief in the intricate tale of intrigue and murder their housekeeper reported. But ten years and innumerable investigations had made them believers in the improbable and tolerant of the impossible. When she was done, and they had asked their few questions about the next day's procedure, it was time to rejoin Doyle at the station.

As they had hoped, the rain had slowed to the harmless drizzle with which it had begun, and the once tempestuous wind could manage only the occasional gust as a reminder of its former strength. Standing at the coach's open door, Doyle swept off his hat by way of greeting, saw each of his passengers seated, and mounted his box, pulling the oilskins loosely around him, and urging his horse forward with the mixture of hi-yups and ho-yahs Mrs. Hudson found as incomprehensible now as she had a week earlier. As Watson commented, Doyle's good cheer appeared in large part artificially induced, but was welcome nonetheless.

Once settled in the carriage and out of the coachman's

hearing, Holmes began a description of his exchange with Squire Baird and the nature of his plans to make amends to Lillie. When he had finished, each member of London's premier consulting detective agency rode the rest of the way consumed by private thought, Holmes staring out to the moor, but thinking only about the performance he would be giving the next day, Watson still fuming over Lillie's return to the Squire, and Mrs. Hudson drawn once more to the writings of Sir Edmund Du Cane and the complex task of administering justice.

Chapter 20.
Holmes Reveals All

When it was apparent the inspector from Scotland Yard was not accompanying them, Holmes and Watson were greeted by the Trents and Lonsdale with both relief and good feeling. Indeed, relief spilled over into good feeling and increased its quantity. Lillie came onto the porch behind the others and joined in the celebration of the two men's return. She extended her hand to each of them and accompanied its grasp with a warm smile. The question her eyes held would wait to be answered at a later time.

The travelers were excused to refresh themselves before dinner and, in short order, all had made their apologies and gone to their rooms to ready themselves for dinner, and the revelations they hoped to wring from Holmes and Watson. Mrs. Hudson joined Lillie Langtry to help her dress for the evening, and was immediately set upon to learn what details she might know of Holmes's visit with the Squire. She pleaded ignorance, which she felt reasonable depending on one's definition of "details." In spite of her maid's unhelpfulness, Lillie did not have long to wait to learn those details. As she was making certain her gown fell properly about her, Elizabeth knocked and entered with a note from Holmes requesting a meeting in the downstairs parlor. Lillie broke off any further preparation, even omitting to apply the rice powder Mrs. Hudson had been at pains to procure.

She arrived first in the parlor, and took a seat on the same green cushioned couch she had occupied when she and Mrs. Hudson first arrived at McLellan Manor. Holmes entered shortly after, seated himself in an easy chair opposite Lillie, and set about giving as unbiased a presentation of the Squire's case as he was able.

"Mr. Baird has asked me to convey his regrets for the concern his behavior has caused you. He wants me to assure you that his affection for you is undimmed. Finally, he wishes you to return with him to London and the house in Cork Street." Holmes withdrew the envelope Baird had passed to him. "He also asked me to give you this."

Lillie removed a single sheet of paper from the envelope and, in spite of her effort to maintain a show of reserve, her eyebrows rose well into her forehead, and she uttered a very audible sigh combining pleasure and surprise in equal parts. After giving her the moment she needed to recover, Holmes handed her the second package he had been given to deliver to Lillie. "He wanted me to tell you, and these are the Squire's own words, he 'hopes this might grace your lovely neck.'"

Lillie opened the box to reveal a double strand of pearls which she appeared to appraise more than admire. There was no sigh and her eyebrows stayed in place, leading Holmes to wonder what could possibly be on the piece of paper.

"Tell me, Mr. Holmes, in what state did you leave George? Do you believe he is now in control of his emotions?" She stared hard at Holmes, suggesting his answer would be treated with a weight commensurate with whatever was written on the page that lay on Lillie's lap.

"I believe he is for now. Whether he can remain so is something you can judge better than I, Mrs. Langtry. I can only tell you I believe he'd sincerely like to, and I have reason to believe he's been given additional incentive to keep himself in line." Lillie's brow furrowed as she worked to digest the last, and Holmes went quickly on before she could phrase the question his comment wakened.

"I've told him to come to the Manor mid-morning tomorrow, and to come alone. At that time you can choose to meet with him or not. If you do not choose to see him, he knows there are those at the Manor committed to enforcing your decision." Holmes drew back in his chair and looked to

Lillie, his steely expression making clear one of those protectors was sitting before her.

Lillie acknowledged his concern with a return of the soft smile Holmes hadn't seen since Baker Street. "I'll see George, Mr. Holmes. I appreciate all you've done, and all that Dr. Watson and Mrs. Hudson have done. I know you find it hard to understand my actions and I'd like you to understand them even if you don't agree." Lillie absently fingered the pearls she had set on top of the paper in her lap. "George is a generous man and I don't deny that is important to me, but I wouldn't want you to think that's all there is to our relationship. I don't know if you've ever been in love, Mr. Holmes. The truth is I don't know that I am. I know I'm infatuated with George, and that may be better and safer than love with a man like George." She paused, and Holmes thought her smile grew sad. "I appreciate your not asking for explanation, Mr. Holmes. You have been my undemanding knight errant, and I am more indebted to you for that than you can ever know. Now, perhaps we should get back to the others. As you are undoubtedly aware, they have a great many questions for you."

Holmes nodded his grave assent and followed Lillie to the drawing room where they arrived just as Simon was announcing dinner was served.

In light of the expectation she had of her host and the debt she owed Holmes, Lillie moved to capture the dinner conversation and forestall Holmes's inquisition. She explained she had had a most pleasant discussion with Mr. Holmes, and he had assured her that his efforts to mollify George Baird had been successful. She made no mention of the single sheet of paper the Squire had sent or the double-strand pearl necklace, but spoke instead of the debt she owed the Trents, Lord Lonsdale and her "dear friend," Mr. Holmes. She gave him a private smile; and then invited everyone present to visit her in

270

London, sweeping the table with her sad blue eyes, before coming finally to focus on Esther, holding her gaze a moment longer than any of the others.

Lillie indicated she would be meeting with the Squire the next morning as arranged by Mr. Holmes, and if all went as expected, she would be leaving a short time later. She acknowledged George could be excitable and sometimes difficult, although she viewed this latest incident as something of an aberration and was now certain of her own safety. Her optimism was greeted with silence from most, muted support from some, and vehement indignation from Lonsdale.

"I do wish I could share your positive view, Lillie. Really I do. But I can't help having concern for your safety. Baird has been a problem before and I fear he will be again—and you may not have friends nearby to come to your assistance the next time."

The room fell silent for the moment as everyone developed an intense interest in the dishes in front of them. Mrs. Trent, assuming a hostess' duties, sought to lessen the tension Lonsdale had created.

"I'm certain you know Mr. Baird better than anyone, Mrs. Langtry. We will be guided by your judgment, but I want to assure you that you are free to stay with us for as long as you like. Mr. Trent and I deem it a pleasure and a privilege to have you as our guest."

Nodding his vigorous assent, Trent seconded his wife's invitation. "That is absolutely the case, Mrs. Langtry. We—all of us—count ourselves honored to have you as a guest in our house."

Lillie looked to the Trents with a smile that seemed to hide tears. Watson wondered whether he was watching the woman or the actress and decided at such times the two were likely indistinguishable.

"I will always hold dear the time I have spent at your lovely home. I can't remember when I have been treated with greater kindness, but I assure you it's no longer necessary for me to impose on your hospitality. And besides, as you know, I have a career to think of. I dare not be away from the London stage for too long. There are entirely too many talented actresses available for me to risk the public remembering for long an absent Lillie Langtry."

After allowing protestations of Lillie's near immortality to sound and echo throughout the room, Trent felt it time to turn the group's attention to the topic that had consumed all but Lillie over the preceding several days.

"I trust your visit to Glasgow went well, Mr. Holmes, Dr. Watson?" It might have been taken as the polite inquiry one puts to a returning tourist, but everyone at the table knew better. Each of them picked at the stuffed oysters and pheasant pie Mrs. Groover had worried over earlier that day, and waited for a response from one of the men questioned.

"Quite well, I would say." And Holmes cut into a particularly plump oyster while his audience waited on the elaboration of his decidedly unsatisfactory response. Lillie Langtry was not, however, the only one at the table with stage presence. "And may I say these oysters are magnificent, and magnificently prepared." And the magnificently prepared oyster temporarily postponed all further speech. After swallowing and dabbing his mouth, both acts closely followed by all at the table, Holmes spoke of his visit to Glasgow, reporting carefully selected portions of that visit in accord with decisions reached in the Parisian Room of the Royal Oxley Hotel.

He described Baird Castle, giving greater weight to the Squire's efforts to be hospitable than he might have if Lillie had not been present. He talked about Charlie Mitchell and Jem Hall, reporting at length the byplay of their conversations and the size of their appetites. He spoke of the Pugilism Society of Glasgow, comparing it unfavorably to the National Sporting Club, and described the negotiations between Baird and John Garfoyle, pointedly raising the boxing promoter's name several times in the course of his account. Watson felt certain there was a stirring at the table when Garfoyle's name was mentioned, and that the reaction was not confined to Arthur Trent. At no time did Holmes make mention of Lestrade, Wiggins or Makepeace Godwin.

To growing unease around the table, he went on to describe the preparation for the Thursday fight, the sparring sessions at the Pugilism Society and the workouts at Baird Castle. He recounted the course and outcome of the fight itself, making no mention of Alfie Campbell. While his audience seethed its way through an unerring display of good manners, Holmes plodded on to a goal of brandy, cigars, and the sharing of wholly trivial information.

Lonsdale, however, had no intention of allowing dinner to end without learning more than the quality of Baird's hospitality and events of the fight at Glasgow's Pugilism Society.

"Thank you, Holmes. Thank you for your account of the visit to Glasgow and especially for your success in resolving difficulties with Squire Baird." Holmes nodded acknowledgement of the Earl's accolade with the grace of a medieval king accepting tribute from a vassal. "However, Holmes, it has come to our attention an Inspector Lestrade from Scotland Yard traveled to Glasgow at the same time you did. I believe him to be the same man who was called to the Club the evening of Mackenzie's death." Lonsdale looked to Holmes, whose own attention was fixed on the last of the fresh fruit dessert still on his plate. "I am told the Inspector believed it necessary to tie up some loose ends, or at least that's how it was described to me. I wasn't aware of any loose ends needing to be tied, and wondered if you'd seen this person while you were in Glasgow."

Holmes took a long sip of his Madeira before speaking. "I can perhaps shed some light on that area, Lord

Lonsdale. But the hour is late and I'm afraid the explanation is lengthy. Moreover, Watson and I have had a very long day only partly relieved by this delightful dinner and conversation." Holmes nodded appreciation to Mrs. Trent who reciprocated with a dim smile. "I must ask your indulgence and put off until tomorrow a full explanation of all you ask."

Dispensing with protocol, Holmes rose before any at the table could object. He was instantly joined in his breach of etiquette by Watson, who appeared to apologize and clear his throat simultaneously. "Shall we say shortly after lunch, two o'clock if that's agreeable. That will give Mrs. Langtry time to meet with Mr. Baird and make her plans. And now I must ask you to forgive Dr. Watson and myself if we make it an early evening." Giving a last nod of appreciation to Mrs. Trent, the two exited without a single person making comment in spite of the several left open-mouthed by their sudden departure.

It was not, however, an early evening for either Watson or Holmes. Holmes agreed with Watson that the performance they had scheduled for the next day required the substantial preparation Mrs. Hudson had encouraged. Working from the Doctor's notes, the two men toiled well into the night organizing and practicing their parts.

But it was not just Holmes and Watson who found sleep difficult to come by. Nearly all their dinner companions lay awake wondering what discoveries might be in store for them. Only Lillie Langtry slept well, perhaps dreaming of the yacht, *The White Lady*, whose bill of sale showing her as its owner was the single sheet of paper in the envelope given her by Holmes. Even Mrs. Hudson found herself listening to the soft gurgling of Elizabeth's sleep while she reviewed all she had shared with Holmes and Watson in search of anything she might have missed. There was, of course, nothing.

As he had promised, Squire Baird appeared at McLellan Manor mid-morning and alone. Simon admitted him to the library and waited on the room's threshold while Charles summoned Holmes. Neither Lillie nor the Trents came to greet Baird, and, with some difficulty, Lord Lonsdale was dissuaded from providing the welcome he believed appropriate. Determining the Squire to be sober and temperate, Holmes asked Charles to summon Mrs. Langtry, then waited with Simon for her arrival. They took positions on either side of the door behind which Lillie and Baird held their conference. The two men shared neither a word nor a look in spite of their joint mission.

Inside the library, the Squire offered Lillie a brusque apology, a diamond studded emerald bracelet he described as a family heirloom, and a bank draft that raised her eyebrows to unaccustomed heights for the second time in two days. Lillie accepted his gifts and his apology, and after making clear her expectations for his future behavior, agreed to return with him to London. Baird left to prepare himself and his two fighters for the trip. Upon his exit, the two sentries disappeared and others in the household gradually reappeared. Lillie called upon Mrs. Hudson for one last turn as lady's maid. She helped Lillie change into a tan velveteen jacket and skirt together with a ruffled white blouse, packed her remaining clothes and toiletries, and graciously refused the 50 pound note Lillie informed her she richly deserved. A little more than an hour later Lillie left for the station.

After seeing Lillie off, Holmes and Watson shared a light and solitary lunch before returning to their rooms for a last review of the parts they were to play that afternoon. Each took the further precaution of packing, in accord with a conviction their presence at McLellan Manor would no longer be wanted by the time their presentation was complete.

Mrs. Hudson was feeling a similar isolation even as she took her lunch in the company of Manor staff. They blamed Holmes and Watson for creating the tension they sensed, and assigned guilt by association to Mrs. Hudson, pointedly ignoring her while she sat with them at table. She left servants' hall without acknowledgement of her leaving, and returned to the room she shared with Elizabeth to put her few belongings in her carpetbag, holding to her colleagues' belief their welcome was wearing thin and would be threadbare by the afternoon's end.

At 2 o'clock, Holmes and Watson entered the drawing room to find everyone already assembled and waiting on them. Hushed conversations quieted altogether as all eyes turned to the two men. Holmes moved with studied ease to a place beside the fireplace that guaranteed his remaining the focus of everyone's attention. Watson seated himself in a place where he could jot notes without becoming an object of curiosity or concern.

Arthur and Mrs. Trent sat together on one settee. A round table holding a large Chinese vase separated them from Byron and Esther who had chosen a couch angled from their parents. Simon stood behind the Trents while Mrs. Charters, holding tight to her daughter's hand, stood behind the Trent children. It seemed to Watson the Manor staff and gentry had closed ranks and now sought to draw strength from each other. Lonsdale selected a Morris chair beside Byron and Esther. He lit a long thick cigar and nestled into the chair's cushions, unaware his effort to convey a relaxed pose was undone by the lines in his face, the aftereffects of a restless night. Christine, too, seemed to sense the tension. Holding to an enigmatic smile, she observed the code of silence that had come over the room.

Holmes stretched to his more than six feet and looked around to everyone as if taking attendance. "I thank you all for coming. There's a good deal to cover and I'd like to get right into it so as not to try your patience. Last evening, Lord Lonsdale raised question about the presence of Scotland Yard in Glasgow during the time Dr. Watson and I were there. To answer his question, it is true that Inspector Lestrade *was* there to tie up loose ends surrounding Mackenzie's death, and it is true as well that the Inspector and I were in contact.

"You see, I had another reason for going to Glasgow beyond getting George Baird and his two fighters away from Oxley. Glasgow was the site of a murder thirty-five years ago. The victim was a man named Josiah Krebs, a gambler of sorts, and his murderer was believed to be a fighter named Calvin Jamison. The case against Jamison seemed so strong the young fighter fled the country rather than risk going to trial, and he has remained a fugitive from justice to this day."

From the beginning of his report, no member of Holmes's audience had stirred, and now it appeared as though none dare breathe or risk display of any emotion. Holmes ignored the sea of stony faces, knowing the room would be his in another moment, just as it would be lost to him forever a short time later.

"In that regard, Inspector Lestrade's presence in Glasgow was most fortuitous. I had grave doubts about the guilt of Calvin Jamison and was able to provide the Inspector with an accurate account of events in the death of Josiah Krebs. I'll not say how it was done—it's of no importance in any event—but identification was made of Krebs's real killer, and witnesses to that unveiling have provided sworn statements which the Inspector will be sharing with Scotland Yard and the Glasgow constabulary—if he has not done so already. In a word, Calvin Jamison is absolved of any part in Josiah Krebs's murder, and need no longer consider himself a fugitive from justice."

Holmes paused, but still no one said a word even as the room's oxygen supply seemed suddenly replenished. Finally, Lonsdale came bolt upright in his chair, raising high his cigar. "That's splendid, Holmes. I am certain this Jamison chap will feel himself deeply in your debt. It is a great comfort to learn justice has been done, however belatedly. Of course, I don't expect we'll ever hear anything from Jamison, but it's to your credit nonetheless, Holmes. And, from what you say, it's a credit to this Inspector Lestrade as well. I'm certain a word in the right place won't do him any harm." The Earl cocked his head and raised his eyebrows to Holmes in a confidential gesture that was witnessed by everyone in the room.

"I'm certain it won't." Holmes paused again to allow others to comment. Only Christine, again sensing the mood of the room, now happily repeated "certain it won't, certain it won't" and giggled her way to silence. Holmes allowed the good feelings Christine reflected to wash over the room before turning to the subject that would put an end to them.

"We must still address the matter of Sailor Mackenzie's death. I had reservations from the first about Mackenzie's death being solely the result of his injuries in the ring." Watson winced on hearing Holmes's generous view of his farsightedness, but his position in the room allowed his startle to be seen only by Holmes who ignored it. "I had, first of all, to consider the punishment Mackenzie took from myself and young Cochrane and, on balance, I can't say it was severe enough to cause Mackenzie's death. I don't believe Cochrane landed a single blow and I can only remember landing two solidly, both of them to the body."

"Which can be enough with an older fighter who's clearly out of condition." Lonsdale jabbed the air with his cigar to punctuate his point.

"Perhaps, but there were other things I found disquieting. My friend and colleague, Dr. Watson, noted that Mackenzie did not look well from the time he entered the ring. Not only was he sweating profusely before the fight with Cochrane had even begun, but he seemed dizzy, staggering at times during the fight although, as I've said, he took few blows from either of us. He grabbed at his mid-section several times, and he went down finally with his legs pulled up to his stomach and throw-up around his mouth. All of that was consistent with a judgment that something additional to the punches thrown was involved in Mackenzie's death.

"An autopsy would have clarified things, but Dr. Lang saw no need for an autopsy and his opinion held sway." Holmes paused, tempted to voice the criticism he felt for Dr. Lang, but yielded finally to Mrs. Hudson's judgment that it would provide a less than useful digression to his presentation. "Inspector Lestrade did gather up for analysis all the things at ringside from which Mackenzie could have drunk, but nothing suspicious was found.

"However, when we were together at the National Sporting Club, Mr. Trent told us that Mackenzie carried a flask of Scotch whiskey wherever he went, and everyone agreed he made liberal use of its contents. The flask wasn't at ringside, so it was not among the items collected by the Inspector. It was therefore important for us to locate it. Indeed, it appeared critical to locate the flask in light of our seeing a stocky figure in a workman's jacket and cap hurrying from the changing room immediately after Mackenzie had been declared dead. We suspected the figure was there to recover the incriminating flask, and got frightened off before he—or she—had time to do so. And indeed, when I sent my housekeeper to the Club the following day she was able to locate the flask and bring it to us for analysis. Exactly as I expected, analysis of the flask's contents revealed that it contained a poison, a poison that is obtained from certain plants and causes death within a day of its administration. As all of you know, there is a plant, the Adenia digitata, in the Manor's greenhouse whose sap is lethal. I am certain an analysis of that sap would prove it identical to the distillate from Mackenzie's flask." Holmes studied the faces of his audience. As he expected, he found no evidence of the good feeling he had briefly generated.

"Knowing the Adenia to be the source of the poison, and the poison to be slow-acting, we could conclude the murderer is someone who was at the Manor within a day of the fight and had access to both the poison and Mackenzie's flask. That, however, ruled out no one.

"Consider the poison first. Mr. Trent took such pride in his exotic collection of plants that he routinely gave both guests and new staff tours of the greenhouse at which he or Simon demonstrated where poison can be found in the Adenia and discussed its safe collection. It is true access to the greenhouse was limited since only Mr. Trent and Simon have keys, but then we have the rather fortuitous incident of Simon's key having gone missing the night before the boxing match. Indeed, the key was only recovered after several of you had left for London.

"And if there was ready access to the poison, access to Mackenzie's flask may have been even more easily managed. The same night the key to the greenhouse went missing, Mackenzie became so drunk he had to be helped to his cottage and his bed, and Mrs. Mackenzie had to be housed in the Manor for her protection. Mackenzie was alone in his cottage with the door unlocked and, as stated by Mrs. Mackenzie, when her husband had drunk his fill, a railroad train could go through the room without his waking—as Cochrane reported her rather colorful words to Dr. Watson. Cochrane also told Watson he saw two people walking in the neighborhood of Mackenzie's cottage that same night, but claimed he was unable to identify them. We can guess that one was Simon since he had promised to look in on Mackenzie.

"The next day, on the train to London, Cochrane, Capelhorn and Simon all had access to Mackenzie's flask as they reported to Dr. Watson. Indeed, the only persons without access to either the Adenia plant or Mackenzie's flask during the period in question were the members of the Trent family. Mr. Trent had been spirited away to mediate a dispute between two of his tenants, and spent the night in the company of Oxley's Chief Constable and vicar, two gentlemen whose character is obviously above reproach. Mrs. Trent, having sustained a severe injury when her horse threw her, was forced to hobble around with the aid of a cane, and both Byron and Esther were in London during the whole of whatever events were taking place at McLellan Manor."

Holmes answered the question Mrs. Hudson had thought would be in the minds of some in his audience. "I have chosen not to ask Capelhorn or Cochrane to join us. While both men have their own well-earned grievances with Mackenzie, those grievances are old and appeared to me unlikely to stimulate sudden action. Moreover, even had they been moved to act it seems hardly likely they would make use of an exotic poison they would have had to extract from a plant in the dead of night, employing a procedure with which they had limited familiarity. Similarly, I've excluded Mrs. Mackenzie from consideration. The woman has spent her life tolerating her husband's abuse and, however justified her action might have appeared, it seemed to me unlikely she would have waited for this moment or used a means barely known to her to rid herself of him. I have, of course, also dismissed Bettinson and Fleming from consideration since they lack any apparent motivation to have murdered Mackenzie."

Lonsdale flicked cigar ash into the oversized glass tray on the table by his chair before posing a question in a voice with too hard an edge to convey the humor he intended. "So tell me Holmes, shall I confess now or should I wait for the end of your admittedly compelling story."

"I appreciate your gracious offer, Lord Lonsdale. I suggest you hold your confession to a more appropriate time."

The Earl closed his mouth firmly around the cigar he set back in place, squared his jaw beneath it, and decided against any further attempts at good fellowship.

Holmes continued as if there had been no interruption, but he now stood a little straighter, his brow was more furrowed, and his eyes more piercing. Watson had seen the change before. Indeed, he had seen it every time Holmes's reasoning or procedure was challenged; Watson had never thought it wise to inform his friend he was taking offense to attacks on the reasoning and procedures of his housekeeper.

"As I have said, everything pointed to the flask as the means by which poison from the Adenia plant was administered to Mackenzie." Holmes scanned his audience before settling his gaze on its two youngest members for a long moment. "Or at least almost everything. There was something I found disquieting about the flask we recovered. Capelhorn, Cochrane and Simon all reported to Dr. Watson that Mackenzie took several swallows from his flask before it could finally be wrestled away from him. Yet, the flask we found in the changing room was so full of liquid that some of it spilled onto the floor of our sitting room when its top was removed.

"And there was something else that was curious. My housekeeper reported to me that when she was given a tour of the greenhouse by the Manor's gardener she noticed there was one pipette missing from the rack of pipettes on the worktable nearest the Adenia plant. I must tell you the woman is a stickler for neatness, and is terribly impressed by such things. She saw it as evidence of poor housekeeping; I suspected it to be something more.

"And then we need to consider the person Watson and I saw fleeing the changing room. To now, we have assumed the figure was surprised by us and fled before he or she was able to remove the flask containing poison—the murder weapon as we have supposed. But what if the figure was there not to remove the poisoned flask, but rather to remove Mackenzie's innocuous flask and to replace it with a flask containing poison, knowing it would eventually be discovered. That is, what if the murderer wanted us to think the flask was the murder weapon and therefore substituted the poisoned flask for the one containing good Scotch whiskey. To get the poison into the second flask, the person responsible would have needed a receptacle for safely carrying the poison from the greenhouse, which explains the missing pipette that so appalled my housekeeper.

"Obtaining a copy of Mackenzie's flask would be simple enough. I observed it to be quite ordinary; its only distinguishing feature was Mackenzie's initials engraved below its neck. Such a flask could be purchased in London with the explanation that it was to be a gift for a family member or friend, and the engraving would then be considered unremarkable. Its purchaser would need only combine good Scotch whiskey with the poison from the pipette to prepare the new flask. During the excitement of the fight upstairs, someone could enter through the building's side entrance, exchange flasks and exit the way they entered. We know that person to be below middle height and we have thought him to be husky, but that was because of the bulky jacket the person wore. Such a jacket might hide the slender frame of a smaller person, perhaps someone not yet fully grown, and the effort at disguise would explain the wearing of a bulky jacket on a summer evening. Indeed, the workman's cap could even allow a young woman to pile her hair beneath it and be mistaken for a man."

Holmes again locked eyes, first with Byron, then with Esther Trent. Byron challenged his stare, but Esther divided her attention between Holmes and the hands she clasped tightly in her lap.

"I'm guessing that gallantry demanded Master Byron make the exchange." At the mention of his name, Byron glowered at Holmes, making clear if he was the murderer, he had a second victim in mind. He looked away finally only to have his father take up his glare and add to it an explosion of words.

"Mr. Holmes, this is a monstrous charge. I demand you put an end to these fantastic accusations and apologize to Byron at once. My son is no murderer—if Mackenzie was even murdered."

"I assure you, Mr. Trent, Mackenzie was murdered. However, I agree about your son. Byron carried the pipette filled with poison on his last trip to Oxford and contaminated the flask he purchased, but he is not our murderer. Someone else in this room is." Holmes's voice was as even as Trent's was passionate, and in Arthur Trent's own house carried the greater authority.

"Holmes, I can only conclude you have been so disturbed by your part in Mackenzie's death that your usually flawless reasoning has been severely and very negatively affected. You know Mackenzie's death has been ruled accidental by Scotland Yard and there the matter must finally end." Lonsdale spoke as though he considered himself the only rational person in the room. "But let us say you are right and the flask that was found contains poison, and was nonetheless *not* the lethal instrument. Why would anyone go to all the trouble of preparing a poison that was never to be used?"

"That was a question I had to ask myself in the course of this investigation." Watson looked quizzically to Holmes, and Holmes looked not at all to Watson. Holmes had indeed raised the question with much the same incredulity as was now being expressed by the Earl, and he proceeded to report the answer that had been provided by the person to whom his query had been addressed.

"The timing of a slow-acting poison, like that taken from the Adenia plant, is not wholly predictable. While the murderer could know the poison would take effect sometime within the day of administration, the exact timing could not be known. The intent was to have the poison take effect in association with the increased flow of blood to the heart and brain brought on by the activity of the fight, and thus the death would be seen as another unfortunate ring accident. When found, the flask in that instance would be seen as of no consequence since everyone knew Mackenzie carried and routinely hid a flask of whiskey.

"But things could go wrong—at least from our killer's standpoint. The poison might take effect some time before the fight. Mackenzie's exertions in his fight might be so limited that death would occur later outside the ring—as of course very nearly happened. In short, the appearance of a ring accident was the intent, but could not be assured. And if Mackenzie did not die as conveniently as planned, it was likely that foul play would be suspected—in which case tampering with the fighter's flask would provide a foolproof strategy for diverting attention from the real means of doing away with Mackenzie. The use of a second flask even provided the murderer with two additional suspects, each of them with access to the flask as well as possessing a longtime grievance against Mackenzie. Indeed, with the key to the greenhouse gone conveniently missing, and Mackenzie in his cottage dead to the world—so to speak—there would be no lack of suspects. And so, Lord Lonsdale, your question begs two further questions. Who would have devised such an intricate plot, and for what reason?" Holmes turned to face Lonsdale, and for a long moment made him the center of attention.

"But I believe you know considerably more about that than you are sharing with us. The plot was likely developed in the course of a morning ride with Mrs. Trent a little more than three weeks ago." Holmes released Lonsdale from scrutiny and let his gaze again sweep across his audience. "Lord Lonsdale has told us he visited the Manor to look over the competitor for his young protégé. It would have been then he learned of the difficulties Mackenzie was creating for his hosts.

"Growing up in Glasgow's boxing community, Mackenzie had no doubt heard the stories about Calvin Jamison and Josiah Krebs. He would know that Jamison was said to have fled to Africa and, as luck would have it, he finds himself at a manor whose master has made his fortune in Africa. He would see the scar splitting Mr. Trent's eyebrow and recognize it as more likely acquired in the boxing ring than in Africa as his host reports. His suspicions would be confirmed with his learning of the picture of a Glasgow church with which both he and Mr. Trent shared a close association. By happenstance, that picture is now in the room where my housekeeper is sleeping, and I can tell you she was quite taken with it. So much so that she asked Elizabeth about it, and, quite unwittingly, the maid related to her the picture's history and significance.

"All in all, Ian Mackenzie had found a home he need never leave. But, as agreeable as that prospect might have seemed to some, a man like Mackenzie was unlikely to be satisfied with just food and lodging for long, and there was no telling what further demands he would come to make. The situation was clearly untenable.

"To change that situation required a scheme that would not only protect those who would discharge it, but would protect as well the one person who could play no part in it. That's why you were spirited away, Mr. Trent, to intercede in a long-standing dispute between tenants. If we explored further, I'm sure we'd find that this latest flare-up was manufactured, and involved calling in impeccable witnesses on your behalf who believed themselves acting to keep the peace when they were unwittingly abetting a murder. When you were done establishing order, you found your key missing, a simple accomplishment for a trusted valet. Returning to the Manor without a key would make necessary your raising a great row alerting everyone to your having been gone most of the night. Your choosing to spend the night in the company of the vicar was a welcome addition as it made even clearer your lack of involvement with whatever was happening at the Manor.

"Mrs. Mackenzie had to be removed from the scene as well to advance the charade of a poisoned flask being prepared for the next day. That was not difficult. In the absence of Simon, and the presence of an unlimited quantity of alcohol, Mackenzie would again become a combative drunk, and Mrs. Mackenzie would again need to be put up in the staff's quarters for her own safety."

"Are you saying that some member of my staff poisoned Mackenzie? That's ridiculous, Holmes. Who would do such a thing—whatever the provocation—and how could they possibly get it done?"

"Your loyalty to your staff does you proud, Mr. Trent—and it complements the loyalty they feel for you." Holmes gave his host a small smile. "Let me answer your second question as to how this was done. Mackenzie regularly had scones for breakfast, a man of large appetites he could be expected to devour a large number of scones, and it was scones that provided the route for delivery of the poison that would kill Mackenzie."

"That's simply impossible! We all of us had scones for breakfast and we are all fine."

"But you did not all have the *same* scones for breakfast. You'll recall my housekeeper spent a great deal of time in servants' hall in her capacity as Mrs. Langtry's maid. As I've told you, she takes note of everything that looks to her untidy, and with no one else to talk to, she shares it all with Watson and me. That's how I heard of your cook's complaint about ashes in the oven and crumbs on the floor when she came into the kitchen to prepare breakfast. The ashes and the crumbs were, of course, the residue from the preparation of scones the night before. Indeed, Lord Lonsdale, we have your words confirming the scones were baked for Mackenzie alone. At Baker Street, you congratulated Mrs. Hudson on her raisin scones, which you described as even better than the raisin scones you had at breakfast at McLellan Manor. But Capelhorn reported to Dr. Watson that Mackenzie complained his scones that same morning were sugar iced and too sweet. Mackenzie's scones had to be iced to hide the taste of the poison and to cover the punctures made to insert the poison."

Again, it was left to Arthur Trent to offer exasperated protest to Holmes's charges. "Who then is your supposed killer—Mrs. Groover, Mrs. Charters, or perhaps Rachel our scullery maid?"

And again, Holmes's reply was calm without calming. "Neither Mrs. Groover nor your scullery maid could play any role in preparing the scones which is why the baking occurred in the middle of the night. Mrs. Charters did play a role and a very significant one. She carried the scones to Mackenzie the following morning. It was her accustomed task to take Mackenzie's breakfast trays to him and for Elizabeth to retrieve the empty tray. She had only to substitute the scones prepared by Mrs. Groover for the scones prepared earlier that morning and stored in either her own small office or the butler's pantry. I can't say which, but I can tell you the butler's pantry served as the place where the poison was stored until it could be added to the scones."

Holmes looked to each of the residents of McLellan Manor returning indifference for the fear and rage he found in nearly equal parts. "I find it's often the case that a seemingly trivial event can result in the most significant revelation. In this case my housekeeper's aversion to cats was responsible for shedding further light on the nature of Mackenzie's death. The poor woman is convinced she has a terrible allergy to cats, and was terrified to learn a cat was kept in the kitchen. She was comforted to hear it had been removed to the scullery maid's room, but was so concerned about its return she went on at length to me about the godforsaken animal. That's how I learned about Simon's uncharacteristic show of outrage when he found the scullery maid had gone into his pantry to retrieve the cat's basket. His concern, of course, was that the poison he had extracted from the Adenia could be discovered. The butler's pantry had seemed an ideal place to store it; the pantry is regularly locked and Simon has the only key. A rather transparent story about a need to put down rat poison was fabricated to get the cat out of there to be certain she didn't accidentally get to the toxin. It might have been a more credible tale if someone had thought to buy the rat poison."

Arthur Trent threw up his hands. "Well that's it then. Everyone is accounted for. Unless you believe Simon prepared the scones, there's no one left who could have committed the murder you alone insist as having occurred."

"There is one person left. The person whose family and home would be destroyed by the monster she could see no other way to remove. The woman who grew up in a bake shop. You'll recall your own words that the last time she suffered a sprain she still had to light the ovens for her father. And the woman who shares with you the loyalty of a staff determined to return the favors they've received, and protect you and your family from certain blackmail and likely persecution by a very vicious man."

The bluster was gone; Trent spoke as if caught in a sudden fog with only Holmes to lead him out. "But you know as well as I, Holmes, my wife can barely walk. How could she commit such a crime in her condition?"

"Mrs. Trent's 'condition', as you put it, was in fact critical to her ability to act. Because of her condition, Mrs. Trent could not climb stairs. She had to spend the night on the ground floor, the same floor as the kitchen, while guests and all staff not involved in the evening's activities slept on the floors above. And then there is the condition itself. Mrs. Trent would have complained of sharp pain and difficulty walking after her fall. Your doctor did what any good doctor would do. I rely here on the opinion of my colleague, Dr. Watson, who is an excellent doctor. He would have probed for broken bones and, finding none, he would have diagnosed Mrs. Trent's condition as a severe sprain, bandaged it as best he could, and prescribed rest, the customary treatment for a sprain. However, as Dr. Watson can attest, a sprain is one of the most difficult diagnoses to make. The physician's judgment rests entirely on the symptoms reported by the patient. In this case, to suggest any lesser diagnosis would have required the doctor to refute the complaints of the wife of the most powerful man in the village.

"And who would question the word of Lord Lonsdale—the sole witness to the event preceding Mrs. Trent's report of symptoms? But there we have the curious case of Mrs. Trent's bay. Although the horse was said to have stepped in a hole, Cochrane reported to Watson the animal he observed had a pretty little gallop and was quite frisky. My own father was a country squire. I've seen horses after they've stepped in holes deep enough to throw their riders. I can tell you it would be most unusual for the animal not to suffer a dislocation, or tendon damage, or some such injury. I wonder how that would accord with your experience, Lord Lonsdale?"

The object of his question crushed the last of his cigar in the ashtray and, glaring defiance at Holmes, posed his own question. "What is it you propose doing with this theory of yours, Holmes?" The voice was cold, determined and wholly without evidence of the fear one might have anticipated in response to a charge of complicity in murder.

"I should think my responsibility in all this is clear. I will make my findings available to Scotland Yard and leave it to them to take the action they see fit."

"And what do you think that will be?" Lonsdale's glare became a sly smile. "Scotland Yard, and more importantly the Home Office, is convinced Sailor Mackenzie died as a result of blows inflicted by Sherlock Holmes. I can say with confidence that is how the official records will read."

"There may be a wish on the part of some to put Mackenzie's death behind them with no further action, but a finding of poison in the dead man's body may impel action regardless of those persons' wishes."

"Such a discovery might, as you say 'impel action', but as you're aware Mackenzie's body is well below ground and already providing nourishment to creatures that were his brothers in life. Only his wife has the power to request Mackenzie be dug up and an autopsy conducted, and I can assure you Mrs. Mackenzie will have no wish to do so. I don't recommend you try to convince her otherwise, Holmes. The poor woman has suffered enough and need not have old wounds reopened. Moreover, I believe she will be given ample reason to reject any request to exhume Mackenzie's body, very ample reason."

"I appreciate the advice, Lord Lonsdale, and I have no intention of pressuring Mrs. Mackenzie. There is, in fact, no need for me to do so. You see it's not just Mrs. Mackenzie who can request an autopsy. Anyone in Mackenzie's immediate family who suspects foul play can make such request." Holmes stepped to a point nearer his audience as he prepared to deliver the final stroke. "Mackenzie has a brother, a quite respectable businessman in Glasgow that my colleague, Dr. Watson, went to visit. Please share the result of your meeting, Watson."

Eight heads turned to fix Watson in their sight. Christine, twice repeating his name in her robotic way, was ignored as always by everyone in the room. "As Holmes reports, I went to visit Mr. Forrest Mackenzie at his shop to inform him of his brother's death, advise him of the circumstances, and ask his interest in obtaining a greater understanding of the cause of death. In a word, Mr. Mackenzie has signed an order requesting that his brother's body be exhumed and investigation be made into cause of death. I suspect the Yard will call in Professor Franklin Spooner of the Medical College of the University of London, the pathologist who worked with Mr. Holmes to isolate and identify the toxic agent in the flask left at the National Sporting Club. I might add that Professor Spooner is frequently consulted by the Yard to examine murder victims."

"Quite right, Watson, I'm sure old Spooner would be the one called upon. Good man, I enjoyed working with him."

Holmes judged the success of his performance by the discomfort of his audience and found reason to be well satisfied. There was a good deal of heavy breathing, searching for more comfortable sitting positions, and a considerable variety of dance steps on display beneath the two sofas. Only Mrs. Trent and Lord Lonsdale sat motionless, the one eyeing Holmes with unbridled loathing; the other, having relinquished defiance as a strategy, eyeing Holmes with a mixture of admiration and contempt as he embarked on a new strategy.

"You realize, Holmes, the request for an autopsy doesn't mean the automatic granting of one—even if the requestor is the dead man's brother."

"That's true, but they will need to consider that request in association with the information I intend to provide regarding Calvin Jamison, the exotic African plants maintained in the Manor's greenhouse and the events as I know them leading up to Mackenzie's death. Even the Home Office might feel it necessary to make inquiries based on all that. Likely, they will choose to question the several people who played parts in those events. Each one of those questioned will need to provide testimony consistent with every other one if a single story is to be believed. Perhaps they all will, but none of them have had experience with Scotland Yard procedures and the expert questioning the Yard conducts."

Lonsdale grunted and clenched the arms of his chair, but said nothing. Holmes took the opportunity to make the offer Mrs. Hudson had insisted on, although no member of the consulting detective agency expected its acceptance.

"There is one course available to keep all of that from happening. The guilty party can step forward and accept responsibility for the murder, explaining the extenuating circumstances in whatever language she chooses."

Holmes's suggestion was successful in only one regard. It resulted in the group finding a common voice. The voice was incoherent in its specific content, but clear and united in its intent. Arthur Trent waited for the angriest voices to subside before speaking for them all. "You can keep that kind of suggestion to yourself, Mr. Holmes. Indeed, I see no reason for your continued presence in my home. I ask that you and Dr. Watson pack and be prepared to leave the Manor within the hour. Mrs. Charters will communicate that same request to your housekeeper. I'll have Doyle transport all of you to the station, and I'll be pleased never to see any one of you ever again." Arthur Trent rose and led his family and staff from the drawing room. Only Lonsdale lingered behind.

"I believe you've overplayed your hand, Holmes. That body will never be dug up and there'll be no investigation by Scotland Yard."

"Maybe not, but such inaction may itself demand explanation—perhaps by the press."

With that, Lord Lonsdale turned on his heel and stomped off to join the Trents.

Chapter 21.
The End of the Road

As promised, one hour from the time Arthur Trent announced Holmes had exhausted his host's goodwill, Doyle was at the Manor's front door ready to take the members of the Baker Street consulting detective agency to Oxley station. No one but the coachman and Charles were there to see them off, the one sitting silent on the coach's box, the other uttering only two well-spaced grunts as he loaded their bags. On the ride to the station, Holmes and Watson gave Mrs. Hudson a detailed account of their meeting. She responded with a series of nods, murmurs of approval for Holmes, and sniffs of disapproval for Lord Lonsdale and the Trents. By the time of their arrival at the station, she had granted that Holmes had handled things with "some real skill." Watson was considerably more forthcoming with praise that Holmes acknowledged with a small nod.

Although nearly alone in the passenger coach taking them to Leeds, they spoke little. Mrs. Hudson closed her eyes and waited hopefully for sleep that never came. Holmes tried to focus attention on the *Leeds Mercury* he had purchased from a news agent, but found himself re-reading paragraphs whose content he had failed to grasp in a first reading. Watson pulled out the later of the two *Lancets* he had inserted in a jacket pocket for just such a time, but found himself unable to concentrate on articles detailing medical practice and its study, and focused instead on the obituary of Mr. Thomas Cook of Leicester, who was credited with "having reduced the evils and discomforts of travel and having enormously contributed to the width of men's ideas of the world." When he had finished reading, he turned his eyes to the Yorkshire countryside, but found the width of his own ideas confined to the world of McLellan Manor.

He folded the journal back into his jacket pocket, filled

and lit his briar, then watched a thin stream of smoke spiral its way above his head, his eyes a fierce squint as if he believed the smoke to be taking the wrong path. The signs were familiar to Mrs. Hudson who had given up waiting for sleep to overtake her. The Doctor was wrestling with a dilemma and searching for the words that would allow him to share it with his companions. They came haltingly, but with the resolve to which she was accustomed.

"In a way, I can't help wondering if we're doing the right thing. I'm aware we're doing what the law demands, but I take no comfort in that. This Mackenzie was an incredibly evil man. He was abusive to his wife, abusive toward other women, and a bully toward whomever he believed weaker than himself. His lies about Cochrane almost certainly contributed to the death of that man's wife. He was essentially blackmailing Capelhorn to further what little career he still had as a fighter, and now he was planning to blackmail the Trents—or the Jamisons if you prefer—with what ugly schemes we can't even guess. His death grieved no one, not even his wife or brother, and removed a tyrant from a great many lives. And what will be gained by giving evidence to Lestrade and his colleagues at the Yard? Mrs. Trent will spend the rest of her days in Newgate, assuming of course she escapes the gallows. Her children, certainly Byron, will be charged as accessories as will Simon and Mrs. Charters, and perhaps even Lonsdale. If Mrs. Charters is convicted, her daughter will be placed in an institution. I can't see how the destruction of so many worthwhile lives on behalf of one wholly lacking in value can be viewed as justice." Watson kept his gaze fixedly apart from his companions as he puffed on his pipe more to exercise his strong feeling than to obtain pleasure. He waited to be challenged by Mrs. Hudson, but the next voice was that of Holmes.

"Bravo, Watson. I too feel no requirement whatsoever to make anything we learn available to the authorities. We're not Scotland Yard, and as helpful as we often try to be to them, we are our own agents. More particularly, I agree, Watson, it is pointless to ruin a large number of lives to avenge the death of one scoundrel."

His piece said, Holmes dug out his own briar and tobacco to join Watson in a pipe, and await Mrs. Hudson's opinion. It was not long in coming. The concerns Watson and Holmes expressed had formed the basis for the many debates Mrs. Hudson had been conducting with herself over the preceding several days.

"I'll say at the start I've no more sympathy for Mr. Mackenzie than either one of you. 'E's a right nasty piece of baggage and there's every reason to believe 'e fully intended to go on bein' just that to the end of 'is days. And there's no arguin' years on the treadmill, or turnin' the crank will do nothin' for the character of Master Byron or Miss Esther, or for Mr. Simon or Mrs. Charters come to that. Besides which, what you say about Christine is almost certainly true as well. If Mrs. Charters is put away, the girl will be sent to a place that cares for simple folk and she won't get near the attention she's gettin' now. And you could say all that we've seen amounts to nothin' more than a family tryin' to protect itself against a scoundrel the best and only way they knew 'ow." Holmes and Watson waited, knowing full well the brief period of accord was about to end.

"From my way of lookin' at it, there's still two things to consider. There's first of all 'ow far any of us 'ave a right to go in considerin' the character of the man—or the woman—that's been killed. To my mind it's a dangerous road we're travelin' if we let our ideas about justice depend on what we think of the person that's been killed. I'm sure I don't want to live in a place where people go around decidin' all on their own who's got a right to live and who to die. Pretty soon we'll 'ave a country where everyone's carryin' guns to get rid of the folk they think don't deserve to live, or to protect themselves from the folk who think *they* don't deserve to live. Before you know it, we'll be no better than America.

"And there's somethin' else to think about. There's fairness. The law's got to be the same for everyone. We know all about Mrs. Trent and Mr. Mackenzie, but what do we know or try to find out about the woman from Bethnal Green who poisons 'er 'usband's tea. Who asks 'ow often 'e beat 'er or their children, or whether 'e was a tosspot who spent the family's money on drink, or a rotter who spent it on another woman? But 'ere's Mrs. Trent, a lady of the manor, and one with connections clean up to the 'Ome Office, at least through 'er friend, Lord Lonsdale, and no doubt already gettin' special consideration on that account. She should be given 'er day in court like everyone else, but she doesn't rate a better day than anyone else. She's to be treated the same whether she's a grand lady or a char. Otherwise, there's no such thing as justice."

Mrs. Hudson smoothed down invisible wrinkles in her dress before continuing. "There's somethin' more I should tell you. None of what we say about Mrs. Trent and all the others bein' brought to justice is goin' to amount to anythin' anyway. By the time we get to Inspector Lestrade and 'e puts the matter to 'is superiors at Scotland Yard, the Trents will be someplace far away from McLellan Manor, and likely from the whole of England. I'm guessin' we'll never see any one of them ever again." With that, Mrs. Hudson wriggled her way as deeply as she could into the thin cushion at her back, mumbled something about how good it would be to get back to Baker Street, closed her eyes, and finally drifted off to sleep. Holmes and Watson looked to each other, then to the Midlands, the rolling green hills a backdrop to meadows and small farms separated one from another other by thickets of bushy aspens and hawthorn interspersed among towering poplars and oaks. All of it was bathed in the bright sun of a cloudless mid-summer day, and none of it was able to raise their mood or distract either man from his solitary consideration of the quality of English justice.

Within two days of their arrival in London, Holmes and Watson recounted to Lestrade all they had learned and all they suspected of Mackenzie's death. Lestrade received the news in virtual silence, his mouth a tight line, his gaze so intense he might have been trying to read their thoughts rather than just hear their words. He waved off Mrs. Hudson's offer of tea and the raisin-filled scones she knew to be his favorite. He left, mumbling something of his intention to see them again at some unspecified time. It was nearly a week before the members of London's premier consulting detective agency learned the reason for Lestrade's unusual behavior and the accuracy of Mrs. Hudson's earlier prediction. The dishes from Sunday's breakfast were still in her tub when Mrs. Hudson went to answer the front door bell. Inspector Lestrade had returned as promised, and now squeezed his way into the small vestibule as quickly as she opened the door to admit him.

"Good morning, ma'am. I apologize for arriving unannounced at this hour, but I need to see Mr. Holmes if he's available and Dr. Watson."

Mrs. Hudson asked Lestrade to wait in her parlor after first apologizing for its state, although it appeared immaculate to the Inspector. Mrs. Hudson went to advise her lodgers of their visitor. She found Holmes swirling a beaker of foul smelling liquid over a Bunsen burner. She dared not ask the beaker's contents, and assumed it posed no immediate danger to the flat in as much as Watson was paying Holmes no mind, and was bent over the *Standard* with the first pipe of the day clamped between his teeth. Both men brightened instantly on hearing of their visitor and Holmes extinguished the flame beneath the burner, giving up his research with unprecedented haste as he exchanged his stool at the worktable for his accustomed place on the settee. Watson put his newspaper aside and took up his accounts book and a newly sharpened Eagle pencil.

Lestrade climbed the steps to the two men's apartments while Mrs. Hudson went to put up tea and gather what scones she had available. She clucked her disappointment that she would be offering scones that were a day old and plain, and waited impatiently for the tea to brew, anxious to hear the decisions reached at Scotland Yard, and learn what had become of the Trents.

When she entered the sitting room, the Inspector was just finishing the first part of his report. "It all adds up to what I think the literary folk call an irony. Here's Mr. Trent, as they're still calling him, going from being a wanted man for thirty-five years to being free for less than a week before becoming a wanted man all over again. Of course, this time it's not just Trent who's gone missing, but Mrs. Trent, the two children and their butler and housekeeper. I'm told the housekeeper has got her daughter with her as well, a child they say has got simple ways."

So as not to interrupt the Inspector, Mrs. Hudson placed the cup of tea she had poured on the table next to his chair and set a scone beside his tea. Catching sight of his server, Lestrade's face relaxed into a broad smile. "Ah, thank you, Mrs. Hudson. Another of your delicious scones. Thank you very much."

"I'm afraid it's plain, Inspector, not the raisin-filled I know you fancy. And I'm sorry to say it's from yesterday's bakin'."

Lestrade waved away her concern. "If it's from your kitchen I know I'll find it delicious. But what's all this I hear from Dr. Watson about you being a lady's maid to Mrs. Lillie Langtry during her stay at McLellan Manor." Mrs. Hudson gave the Inspector an embarrassed smile by way of acknowledgement.

"Well then, it's only right you stay and hear all that's happened since you were there—that is, if you've no objection, Mr. Holmes."

Holmes appeared puzzled Lestrade could even raise the possibility of his objection and vigorously shook his head in wordless denial of any such notion.

"How thoughtful of you, Inspector. Of course I'd very much like to 'ear all that's 'appened at the Manor."

"I was just telling Mr. Holmes that the place is closed up, what with the Trents now gone."

"Tell me, Lestrade," Holmes asked, "when you learned the Trents had gone missing, did you make inquiry of the Oxley townspeople? It appeared to me the chemist's was a particularly promising site for gathering information."

"It's my understanding some people from the Yard made effort to interview the local people. Of course, as I was telling you, they've taken me off this investigation and everything I report is at least once removed. So I don't know if they went to the chemist's or exactly who they got to. Regardless, I'm told everybody they talked to—or tried to talk to—was close-mouthed, even the Oxley constabulary. Not a surprise really, a town can get awfully quiet when strangers come by asking questions about one of their own, even when the strangers are from Scotland Yard—maybe especially when the strangers are from Scotland Yard." The Inspector bit off a corner of the scone he had been holding tantalizingly close to his mouth throughout his report, then washed it down with a healthy swallow of tea and grinned his appreciation to Mrs. Hudson before continuing.

"Of course, you and I know there's one person who could tell us where the Trents have gone off to." He leaned his way confidentially toward Holmes. "You can bet Lord Lonsdale knows exactly where to find the Trents. But all we know about him is that he's someplace on the continent—nobody knows where, or is trying very hard to find out, come to that. The Home Office did send one of its own to question Lady Lonsdale, and she told him she had no idea where he's gone off to or when he'll be back. Anytime now I'm expecting to hear he's off on another one of his expeditions. Maybe this time to see the Fuzzy-Wuzzies, wherever they are."

"North Africa." Watson's voice was barely audible.

"What was that, Dr. Watson?"

"The Fuzzy-Wuzzies, Inspector. They're in North Africa. The Soudan."

Lestrade gave an appreciative nod for information he would very shortly forget.

"Lestrade, what of Mackenzie's remains?" Holmes asked. "Was his body dug up and an autopsy conducted?"

"There's been no analysis of Mackenzie's body, Mr. Holmes, for the very good reason that Mackenzie's body has never been found. Sometime during the whole back and forth between the Yard and the Home Office about whether or not to order an autopsy, Mackenzie's body was dug up and moved to someplace we don't yet know and probably never will. So Mackenzie is one more person we can't account for, although we figure him to stay put wherever his travels take him. Mackenzie's disappearance isn't widely known yet, but an open grave won't stay secret very long. And of course nobody in Oxley knows anything about that either. It's all a bit of a mess, and I can tell you it's not something the Yard is looking forward to reading about in the papers."

"And you've come to see us on a Sunday, your day free, to share things it might be difficult to share while you're on duty?" Watson gave the Inspector a small smile of understanding.

The Inspector's own smile was sheepish. "That's exactly right, Doctor. I did feel you had a right to hear about things—at least as much as I know about them. I have to tell you, Mr. Holmes, you may find yourself without too many friends at the Yard for the moment. They won't tell you so, but they sort of blame you for getting them in this predicament. There's some who figure if you hadn't insisted on investigating Mackenzie's death they wouldn't be in the fix they're in now."

Lestrade downed the rest of his scone, took a sip of tea, and recaptured his thought. "For a while you won't be hearing much from the Yard, Mr. Holmes. But you know it won't last. The Yard will be coming around to Baker Street when it finds it needs you." He looked from Holmes to Mrs. Hudson who had set her pot down, having refilled everyone's cup including her own. "There'll be another problem and I'll be coming around here for advice, and for tea and some more of these scones. Isn't that about right, Mrs. Hudson?"

The housekeeper looked modestly away at the mention of her name. "I'm sure I wouldn't be knowin' about such things, Inspector, but it does seem the way it's always been."

Lestrade stood, and raised his cup high as he looked to his hosts. "And may it always be that way."

Amid a muffled chorus of "Here, here" two bodies bolted from their chairs while a third rose with somewhat greater deliberation. All raised their cups in concert with the Inspector and drank a toast to the words he spoke, and to the good feeling that lay beneath them.

Epilogue

George Baird, the self-styled Squire Baird, continued to live life to excess, but did no further harm to Lillie Langtry. The same could not be said for all the business establishments he visited. In 1893, one year after the events described in this book, Baird decided America offered him possibilities that England denied him, if only because England knew him better. He sailed to New York with several of his fighters, intending to challenge Gentleman Jim Corbett to fight Charlie Mitchell. The Squire's efforts, already complicated by the brief detention of Mitchell as an ex-convict upon his arrival in America, were dealt a lethal blow when Gentleman Jim declined his offer in as much as he was making more money with less risk by appearing in the hit play, *Gentleman Jack.*

The Squire proceeded to New Orleans where he arranged a bout between Jem Hall and Bob Fitzsimmons in which Fitzsimmons dispatched Hall in the fourth round. Baird was intent on not allowing that setback to dampen his spirits. In the course of an all-night celebration he contracted pneumonia and died two days later at the age of 31. He left an estate worth nearly a million pounds with no part of it allotted to Lillie.

Charlie Mitchell did meet Jim Corbett in the National Sporting Club one year after the fight that never happened in America, and was knocked out in three rounds. He was 32, but the veteran of 100 bare knuckle fights and perhaps 30 bouts fought under Marquis of Queensberry rules. He retired from the ring a short time later, from all accounts to live a quiet life. He spent his last years in the seacoast town of Hove, where he passed away in 1918 at the age of 56.

Jem Hall fought successfully in England and then the Unites States following his loss to Fitzsimmons. However, alcohol increasingly took its toll on the Australian born fighter, and both fights and victories became less frequent. Ultimately, he contracted tuberculosis, for which he obtained treatment first in Chicago and later in Wisconsin where he died in 1913 at age 44. His grave went without a headstone for 93 years until the situation was rectified by a member of the boxing press.

Hugh Lowther, the fifth Earl of Lonsdale, continued the free-spending ways that allowed him to earn the title of "England's greatest sporting gentleman," and die nearly penniless in 1944 at age 87. Along the way he established stables of perhaps the finest thoroughbreds in England, while maintaining two castles, a London town house, and a comparatively modest 20-bedroom hunting lodge. Keeping up with the times, Lord Lonsdale also purchased a Mercedes, the first of a fleet of cars he maintained—all painted his signature brilliant yellow—and became the founder and first president of Britain's Automobile Association. Hunting, yachting, dog trials, racing and jumping were all interests of the Earl, but boxing remained his passion and achieving its respectability his legacy. He established the Lonsdale Belt to be awarded the British boxer who was champion of his weight class, and that award remains today a mark of boxing excellence, while the artifacts gathered on his Arctic expedition are maintained as a part of the British Museum's collection.

Having acquired a yacht, *The White Lady* (nicknamed *The Black Eye* by her detractors), as well as a bank draft for an estimated 50,000 pounds from George Baird by way of apology for his behavior, Lillie Langtry turned her attention again to acting, finally retiring from the stage in 1906 at 53, returning only to raise money for World War I relief efforts. In 1899 she married Hugo Gerald de Bathe, 19 years her junior and heir to a baronetcy, allowing Lillie to succeed to the title of Lady de Bathe on the occasion of her father-in-law's death six years after her marriage. In her later years, Lillie became owner and manager of London's Imperial Theatre, kept champion horses, wrote a novel, appeared in vaudeville, starred in a movie and, on one notable occasion, broke the bank in Monte Carlo—the first woman to do so. She said of herself: "In life I have had all that I really wanted very much—a yacht, a racing stable, a theatre of my own, lovely gardens." Lillie died in 1929 in her villa in Monaco overlooking the Mediterranean. She was buried in the churchyard of St. Saviour's Parish on the Isle of Jersey, her grave not far beyond the shadow of the rectory where she had been born 75 years earlier.

Sir Edmund du Cane died in 1903, outliving his reforms by eight years. In 1895 the Gladstone Report rejected a reliance on punishment and deterrence as the sole objectives of imprisonment. The crank and treadmill were abolished, the initial period of solitary confinement greatly reduced, and both educational opportunities and support for productive labor greatly increased.

For all others in this story the reader is invited to create his or her own final chapters—keeping in mind only that the principles of Baker Street's consulting detective agency appear destined to outlive all those who choose to chronicle their exploits.

Also from Barry S Brown

The Unpleasantness at Parkerton Manor
(Mrs Hudson of Baker Street Book 1)

Mrs. Hudson and the Irish Invincibles
(Mrs Hudson of Baker Street Book 2)

Mrs. Hudson In New York
(Mrs Hudson of Baker Street Book 4)

Mrs. Hudson's Olympic Triumph
(Mrs Hudson of Baker Street Book 5)

Also from MX Publishing

MX Publishing is the world's largest specialist Sherlock Holmes publisher, with over a hundred titles and fifty authors creating the latest in Sherlock Holmes fiction and non-fiction.

From traditional short stories and novels to travel guides and quiz books, MX Publishing cater for all Holmes fans.

The collection includes leading titles such as *Benedict Cumberbatch In Transition* and *The Norwood Author* which won the 2011 Howlett Award (Sherlock Holmes Book of the Year).

MX Publishing also has one of the largest communities of Holmes fans on Facebook with regular contributions from dozens of authors.

www.mxpublishing.com

Also from MX Publishing

 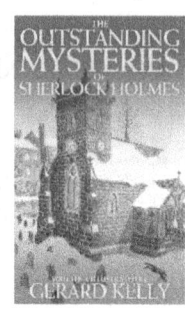 

Our bestselling books are our short story collections;

'Lost Stories of Sherlock Holmes's , 'The Outstanding Mysteries of Sherlock Holmes's, The Papers of Sherlock Holmes Volume 1 and 2, 'Untold Adventures of Sherlock Holmes's (and the sequel 'Studies in Legacy) and 'Sherlock Holmes in Pursuit', 'The Cotswold Werewolf and Other Stories of Sherlock Holmes's – and many more......

www.mxpublishing.com

Also from MX Publishing

"Phil Growick's, 'The Secret Journal of Dr Watson', is an adventure which takes place in the latter part of Holmes and Watson's lives. They are entrusted by HM Government (although not officially) and the King no less to undertake a rescue mission to save the Romanovs, Russia's Royal family from a grisly end at the hand of the Bolsheviks. There is a wealth of detail in the story but not so much as would detract us from the enjoyment of the story. Espionage, counter-espionage, the ace of spies himself, double-agents, double-crossers...all these flit across the pages in a realistic and exciting way. All the characters are extremely well-drawn and Mr Growick, most importantly, does not falter with a very good ear for Holmesian dialogue indeed. Highly recommended. A five-star effort."
The Baker Street Society

Also from MX Publishing

The Missing Authors Series

Sherlock Holmes and The Adventure of The Grinning Cat
Sherlock Holmes and The Nautilus Adventure
Sherlock Holmes and The Round Table Adventure

"Joseph Svec, III is brilliant in entwining two endearing and enduring classics of literature, blending the factual with the fantastical; the playful with the pensive; and the mischievous with the mysterious. We shall, all of us young and old, benefit with a cup of tea, a tranquil afternoon, and a copy of Sherlock Holmes, The Adventure of the Grinning Cat."
Amador County Holmes Hounds Sherlockian Society

Also from MX Publishing

The American Literati Series

The Final Page of Baker Street
The Baron of Brede Place
Seventeen Minutes To Baker Street

"The really amazing thing about this book is the author's ability to call up the 'essence' of both the Baker Street 'digs' of Holmes and Watson as well as that of the 'mean streets' of Marlowe's Los Angeles. Although none of the action takes place in either place, Holmes and Watson share a sense of camaraderie and self-confidence in facing threats and problems that also pervades many of the later tales in the Canon. Following their conversations and banter is a return to Edwardian England and its certainties and hope for the future. This is definitely the world before The Great War."
Philip K Jones

Also from MX Publishing

The Detective and The Woman Series

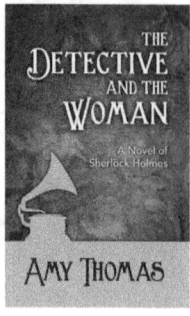  

The Detective and The Woman
The Detective, The Woman and The Winking Tree
The Detective, The Woman and The Silent Hive

"The book is entertaining, puzzling and a lot of fun. I believe the author has hit on the only type of long-term relationship possible for Sherlock Holmes and Irene Adler. The details of the narrative only add force to the romantic defects we expect in both of them and their growth and development are truly marvelous to watch. This is not a love story. Instead, it is a coming-of-age tale starring two of our favorite characters."
Philip K Jones

Also from MX Publishing

The Sherlock Holmes and Enoch Hale Series

The Amateur Executioner
The Poisoned Penman
The Egyptian Curse

"The Amateur Executioner: Enoch Hale Meets Sherlock Holmes", the first collaboration between Dan Andriacco and Kieran McMullen, concerns the possibility of a Fenian attack in London. Hale, a native Bostonian, is a reporter for London's Central News Syndicate - where, in 1920, Horace Harker is still a familiar figure, though far from revered. "The Amateur Executioner" takes us into an ambiguous and murky world where right and wrong aren't always distinguishable. I look forward to reading more about Enoch Hale."
Sherlock Holmes Society of London

Also from MX Publishing

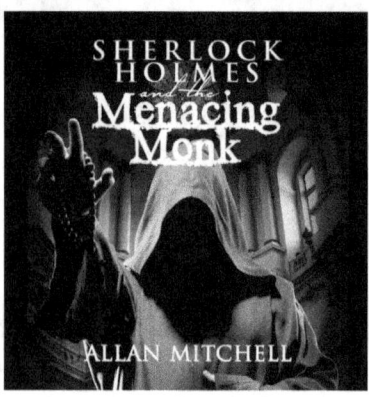

All four novellas have been released also in audio format with narration by Steve White

Sherlock Holmes and The Menacing Moors
Sherlock Holmes and The Menacing Metropolis
Sherlock Holmes and The Menacing Melbournian
Sherlock Holmes and The Menacing Monk

"The story is really good and the Herculean effort it must have been to write it all in verse—well, my hat is off to you, Mr. Allan Mitchell! I wouldn't dream of seeing such work get less than five plus stars from me..." **The Raven**

Also from MX Publishing

When the papal apartments are burgled in 1901, Sherlock Holmes is summoned to Rome by Pope Leo XII. After learning from the pontiff that several priceless cameos that could prove compromising to the church, and perhaps determine the future of the newly unified Italy, have been stolen, Holmes is asked to recover them. In a parallel story, Michelangelo, the toast of Rome in 1501 after the unveiling of his Pieta, is commissioned by Pope Alexander VI, the last of the Borgia pontiffs, with creating the cameos that will bedevil Holmes and the papacy four centuries later. For fans of Conan Doyle's immortal detective, the game is always afoot. However, the great detective has never encountered an adversary quite like the one with whom he crosses swords in "The Vatican Cameos.."

"An extravagantly imagined and beautifully written Holmes story"
(**Lee Child**, NY Times Bestselling author, Jack Reacher series)

Also from MX Publishing

The Conan Doyle Notes (The Hunt For Jack The Ripper)

"Holmesians have long speculated on the fact that the Ripper murders aren't mentioned in the canon, though the obvious reason is undoubtedly the correct one: even if Conan Doyle had suspected the killer's identity he'd never have considered mentioning it in the context of a fictional entertainment. Ms Madsen's novel equates his silence with that of the dog in the night-time, assuming that Conan Doyle did know who the Ripper was but chose not to say – which, of course, implies that good old stand-by, the government cover-up. It seems unlikely to me that the Ripper was anyone famous or distinguished, but fiction is not fact, and "The Conan Doyle Notes" is a gripping tale, with an intelligent, courageous and very likable protagonist in DD McGil."
The Sherlock Holmes Society of London

Also from MX Publishing

During the elaborate funeral for Queen Victoria, a group of Irish separatists breaks into Westminster Abbey and steals the Coronation Stone, on which every monarch of England has been crowned since the 14th century. After learning of the theft from Mycroft, Sherlock Holmes is tasked with recovering the stone and returning it to England. In pursuit of the many-named stone, which has a rich and colorful history, Holmes and Watson travel to Ireland in disguise as they try to infiltrate the Irish Republican Brotherhood, the group they believe responsible for the theft. The story features a number of historical characters, including a very young Michael Collins, who would go on to play a prominent role in Irish history; John Theodore Tussaud, the grandson of Madame Tussaud; and George Bradley, the dean of Westminster at the time of the theft. There are also references to a number of other Victorian luminaries, including Joseph Lister and Frederick Treves.

www.ingramcontent.com/pod-product-compliance
Lightning Source LLC
Chambersburg PA
CBHW051237260626
47162CB00002B/486